THE FIRES
OF HELL

THE JACKALS

THE FIRES OF HELL

WILLIAM W. JOHNSTONE

AND J.A. JOHNSTONE

PINNACLE BOOKS
Kensington Publishing Corp.
www.kensingtonbooks.com

PINNACLE BOOKS are published by

Kensington Publishing Corp.
119 West 40th Street
New York, NY 10018

PUBLISHER'S NOTE: Following the death of William W. Johnstone, the Johnstone family is working with a carefully selected writer to organize and complete Mr. Johnstone's outlines and many unfinished manuscripts to create additional novels in all of his series like The Last Gunfighter, Mountain Man, and Eagles, among others. This novel was inspired by Mr. Johnstone's superb storytelling.

Special book excerpts or customized printings can also be created to fit specific needs. For details, write or phone the office of the Kensington Sales Manager: Kensington Publishing Corp., 119 West 40th Street, New York, NY 10018. Attn. Sales Department. Phone: 1-800-221-2647.

PINNACLE BOOKS, the Pinnacle logo, and the WWJ steer head logo Reg. U.S. Pat. & TM Off.

First Printing: February 2023
ISBN-13: 978-0-7860-4959-2
ISBN-13: 978-0-7860-4960-8 (eBook)

10 9 8 7 6 5 4 3 2 1

Printed in the United States of America

PROLOGUE

To the Editor of The Emigrant City Weekly
Clarion & Light:

Dear Sir:

A copy of your newspaper from the 23rd inst.
came into my possession after it had been
discarded on a stagecoach in Purgatory City and
shown to me for amusement. At least, I am merely
guessing that was the fool's reason for bringing that
rag, wadded up and stained from the mud wagon's
floor and dust from its travels from your city far to
the north and east.

I was not amused, as the lad learned when he
left with, as I read in another one of your articles in
the edition of the 23rd inst., "his tail tucked
between his legs."

While I did enjoy looking at your advertisements
for cigar manufacturers, and the piano salesman,
and Mr. Bowman's Fine Art Gallery and
Photography, and the bookstore owned by Madam
Woodlawn, and the houses for sale, and your very
own architect and builder of the new steam
sawmill, and all those attorneys, the lots for sale,

the dental surgeon, and, gosh, Oswego Corn Starch For Puddings, Blanc Mange, Ice Cream, Etc., and so many tonic pills and clothiers and treatments for epilepsy or fits, cookstoves and the next meeting of the Agricultural and Mechanical Association—alas, I won't be able to attend the next fine session— and your timetables for your riverboats and railways, so many luxuries that we just don't seem to get out here, far removed from civilization that you most certainly have in Emigrant City.

What I did not enjoy, sir, was that article on Page 4. Your last page.

If you don't recall the article, it is the one butted up against the ad for the Fulton & Schneider General Store announcing the Staple and Fancy Dry Goods, Silks, Hosiery, Notions, Dress Trimmings, Ribbons, Kid Gloves, Ties, Parasols, Fans, Hair Braids, Corsets (French and American), Bleached Domestics, Gents' Furnishings, Carpets, Wall Paper, Straw, Fur, and Woolen Hats, Hardware and Crockery and "Showing Goods To You Is NEVER a Problem."

We had a store almost like that here in Purgatory City till Sean Keegan tore down half of it in a brawl last week, although I don't think Mr. Pendergrass stocked corsets, French or American.

The headline of the article was "Forth Jackal in Purgatory City! Fine Traders Butchered by West Texas Renegades. A Cry for Law and Order. Texas Rangers at Wit's End. Barbarous Butchers Call Honest Traders RENEGADES. But The TRUE Renegades are Revealed. And THEY are THE JACKALS. Once Three, Now FOUR! JUSTICE DEMANDED!"

My, oh, my. That sure looks like a lot of headline for a story that is but six paragraphs long. Please pardon my ignorance about English and spelling and such, being an uneducated rube from the far frontier and not of your civilized city of railroads, riverboats, and universities whilst you proudly point out being a newspaper editor for more than twenty-nine years, but should not Forth be Fourth?

Let me point out some glaring factual errors in this article you deemed worthy of publication.

In the first paragraph, you identify Purgatory City's "resident Jackals" being led by Captain Mike McCullock, a former Texas Ranger. Well, MATTHEW McCulloch is indeed a former Texas Ranger—driven out of that valiant organization by politics, not justice—but he never served as a captain. You call him a notorious horse thief. He catches wild mustangs, sir. Usually, he's only stealing them from the herd of wild mustangs. Horse thieves, as you have rightfully pointed out, are among the lowest dregs of humanity and they are often summarily executed. Very true. Out here, where a person's life might very well depend on his horse, we West Texans tend to regard horses as our best friends when the chips are down. So when a man steals a horse, he puts the horse's owner's life at risk. And I have seen at least one man who was hanging from a telegraph pole for stealing a horse. However, Matthew McCulloch, as far as I know— and I know him pretty well—has never once hanged a horse thief. Granted, he has beaten one or two to a pulp, and he said he shot Grover Blue in the thigh when that rapscallion tried to steal a fine stallion with some thoroughbred running in its blood, but

McCulloch knows the laws of Texas. And stealing a horse has never, ever, been a capital offense.

Likewise in your narrative, you missed your aim in your description of Sean Keegan, who I have previously mentioned in this letter. But at least you spelled his name right. However, Sean Keegan, who like many a good Irishman and many a Yankee soldier does enjoy a go at fisticuffs every now and then—quite possibly, he's brawling somewhere as I write these words, and quite probably he's knocking a tooth loose while you read my letter—but you call him a former Army Captain. Why, sir, such a libel as that would send Sean Keegan riding hell bent for leather from here to Emigrant City to challenge you to a fight for the sake of his County Cork honor. Sean Keegan would never have accepted an officer's commission. During his valiant service in the postwar Army, he was a sergeant—many times a sergeant, when he wasn't being stripped of a stripe and bumped down to corporal or rank trooper for defending his Irish honor or, more than likely, having one or twenty too many rounds of his beloved Irish whiskey.

And, lastly, there is your description of Jeb Breene. Jed. With a D. Not Jeb with a B. And Breen without an E at the end. You call Jed a bounty KILLER. The proper term, sir, is bounty HUNTER. Yes, Jed Breen has killed, but only when his life or someone else's life was at risk. While he has the reputation of bringing more men in dead than alive, if you took time to check with Texas Rangers, US marshals, judges, jailers, attorneys-at-law and county sheriffs, you will learn that most of the men Jed brings to justice are turned in standing, breathing, maybe bruised, but certainly alive—at least long enough to hang by the neck till they are dead, dead, dead. You also described Mr. Breen as the "silver-haired fox." His hair is pure white, sir, not silver. White as a summer cloud. White as a handkerchief freshly laundered.

Now about those "traders" you refer to as honest, law-abiding merchants. I suppose they are traders, although I don't think the law allows for what they have been trading. Recently, hundreds of thousands of Americans died to end the barbaric— yes, I say this as a Texan—practice of slavery. Traders might be one way to describe them. White slavers is another, although that is not entirely accurate, either, for these so-called traders you describe as "Fine" and "Honest" dealt Indians from Mexico and New Mexico Territory, and Mexicans from south of the Rio Grande and even some from the fine state of Texas, and, yes, whites too. White, Indian and Mexican women and children, especially young boys who could be sold to work as slaves in the mines down in Mexico. "Fine" and "Honest," Mr. Editor, are not adjectives I would ever use to describe a Comanchero.

They aren't even human beings. They are, instead, the "Barbarous Butchers" and "True Renegades"—and they are the foul, evil vermin who have the Texas Rangers and US Army and sheriffs and citizens of the westernmost reaches of our state at our wits' end. They sell guns and liquor and ammunition and women and children to the last Comanche holdouts—hence, their name, Comancheros—and lately, the Apaches who come up from south of the border or from New Mexico and/or Arizona territories, even Cheyennes and

Kiowas. Comancheros are dung. They should be wiped off the face of the earth.

Honest Traders? Ask your wife, your daughter, your mistress, your mother, your grandmother if they would rather do business with a Comanchero or your glorious and wonderful Fulton & Schneider General Store.

The candle is about to burn out, and my fingers are cramping from holding this pencil for so long, so I must close this letter but not before I point out your final error. That regards to the Fourth or Forth Jackal.

If Killing a Dozen traders (i.e., Comancheros) makes me a Jackal, I will gladly take that honor. In fact, when such a title was first handed to me, I felt pride almost boiling over. Sir, in West Texas, human beings, red, white, black, brown, kill other human beings, red, white, black, brown, to stay alive. To protect their loved ones. To survive another day when lightning, rain, smallpox or some other disease, not to mention childbirth, or a horse's hoof or a horse's stumble can kill you just as dead as a gunman's bullet or a Comanche arrow.

But, sir, I must protest your libelous claim that I, the Fourth—or Forth—Jackal killed a dozen honest traders. They were certainly not honest. I doubt if they ever heard the word. But only a dozen?

Why you low-down, lying fool. I am sure I cut down at least thirty. But no more than forty-five of those wretched, evil men. And I hope to double that if ever I run into more Comancheros.

> *Unsigned.*
> *A Perdition County Citizen*

P.S.: Pardon my West Texas ignorance again, but . . . what exactly is Blanc Mange?

CHAPTER 1

The bullet whined off the rock the moment Sean Keegan looked up. Gravel and dust kicked into his eyes and sent him sliding back behind the big chunk of granite for cover.

Cover? The chunk of lead that had briefly blinded Keegan whined past Keegan's right ear, slammed into the canyon wall a few feet behind him, and zinged back—the lead now cut in half. One chunk struck the rock about an inch or two from Keegan's right arm, the one holding his Springfield carbine. The other spit up sand in front of Keegan and thumped harmlessly against the former cavalry trooper's left boot.

"Confound it, Jed!" Keegan shouted to his partner. "I liked to have just been crippled on account of you."

Another gunshot rang out from the dugout down the hill. That bullet hit the canyon wall and zinged off into oblivion.

Sean Keegan cursed again. Cursed, while cringing like a yellow-bellied coward or some greenhorn trooper. A soldier might eventually get used to the sound of gunfire, but the noise of a ricocheting bullet put the fear of the Almighty into even the most hardened veteran.

"Stick your head over that stone again, Sean."

Keegan turned to give his meanest look at Jed Breen, but that was just a waste of effort.

The white-haired bounty hunter wasn't even looking in Keegan's direction. He crouched about twenty feet off to Keegan's right, the barrel of his heavy Sharps rifle propped up in the "V" of his shooting sticks, the stock braced against his right shoulder, and Breen's right eye staring through the long brass telescopic sight affixed to the barrel of the .50-caliber cannon.

"I mean it," Breen said. His head never moved from the Sharps. Had he not spoken, Keegan could not have determined if his "ol' pardner" in this affair were still living. A man couldn't even tell if Jed Breen was breathing. He resembled some old juniper, dead but standing till Judgment Day.

"I didn't join up with you to get my head shot off," Keegan said.

"That's a Winchester," Breen said, still not looking away from the brass scope. "Not even a .44 caliber. Must be .38-40. We're a hundred and thirty, forty, no more than a hundred and fifty yards away. And he's shooting uphill. Not very much chance that he'll shoot your head off. Thick as your skull is."

Keegan felt his blood rushing again, the way it was prone to do when he found himself working alongside Jed Breen. That blood pressure might blow off his head.

"He still might kill me," Keegan said.

"Didn't say he wouldn't kill you," Breen said, still focusing on the dugout. "What I said was he wouldn't shoot your head off."

After choking down the curse, Keegan gathered his rifle and crossed his legs to see if that bullet fragment had done any damage to his boot. He could just make out a dent in the heel, but he had seen rougher damage done by mesquite and stones. So he twisted around, wiped his palms on his shirt front, and decided to look around the left corner of his boulder. Wetting his lips, he brought the Springfield's barrel over, bracing it against a natural groove in the side of the granite, and aimed at the dugout.

He saw the flash below, the white smoke, heard the report of the Winchester, and felt the heat as the bullet screamed past his ear. That slug tore through a heart-shaped prickly pear and whined off another rock. No, not quite a whine. Just a ping.

But Keegan had pulled himself back, shaking his head, feeling the blood roaring like an express train, and tried to catch his breath.

"That must be Billy Ray," Breen said. "Darn good shot, Billy Ray. Much better than his brother. With a rifle, anyway. Six-shooter, too. I don't think Jim Bob was ever good at anything except with a running iron on other men's cattle."

"You told me that rustlers usually don't put up much of a fight!" Keegan yelled.

"They aren't just rustlers anymore. They are escaped convicts."

Keegan's mouth tasted like sand. He wanted to spit, but his tongue was drier than this patch of misery. "You could at least take a shot at those outlaws," he growled. "So they wouldn't keep taking potshots at me."

Suddenly, Keegan got mad. He crouched, brought the Springfield to his shoulder, pulled back the hammer, and quickly spun around, fired, and ducked back behind the rock. The carbine's report drowned out any satisfaction he might have gotten by hearing the bullet strike anything— man, dugout, tree, cactus, boulder, or even one of the two horses in the corral about twenty yards east of the dugout.

A moment later, he heard laughter from below. Then a Texas drawl: "That the best you can do, pardner?"

"No. Don't have a shot." Breen was calm as a night sky. And it took a moment before Keegan realized the bounty hunter was addressing Sean Keegan. "Dugout's walls must be three feet thick, probably with some stone in there. Only one opening, the door, and whoever's shooting is too far back for me to hit him. So I figure, let him waste his lead. I know what they say about a repeating rifle, that you can load it on Monday and shoot till Sunday. But that's not true. And .38-40 cartridges are hard to find in this country."

Five days earlier, Jed Breen had found Keegan outside a grog shop in Purgatory City. Keegan had known the bounty hunter mostly by sight and reputation until a few years ago when fate had brought the two together in a stage-coach station with Matt McCulloch, a horseman who had been kicked out of the Texas Rangers. Keegan had just been kicked out of the US Army, and Breen had always managed to rile citizens because of his occupation. A newspaper editor had labeled the three "Jackals." 'Course, that news-paper editor was now dead and buried—but the name stuck.

Breen informed Keegan that the Hardwick brothers had escaped from prison, and the warden and state had posted a two-hundred-dollar reward for their capture and return.

"Huntsville," Keegan had reminded Breen, "is a long way to go for two hundred bucks."

"Not Huntsville," Breen had said. "The Peering Farm."

Keegan wasn't quite drunk. "Peering Farm is not what I'd call close." The farm was a cotton plantation, about as far into the Texas Panhandle as white settlers would dare go, even though most Comanches were now pinned up on the reservation near Fort Sill in Indian Territory.

"My guess is that the Hardwicks will ride south. Mexico."

That made sense, at least it did at the time, so Keegan had asked: "What's the split?"

"Fifty-fifty."

A hundred bucks could keep a man drunk for a whale of a good time.

Now, with Keegan being shot at and sober, he began thinking about why he was here.

"What made you think those outlaws would try for Mexico?" he asked.

"Just a hunch."

"Indian Territory's a hell of a lot closer."

"Indian Territory's still in the United States."

"But . . ." Keegan wiped his mouth. "It ain't like ye, being a bounty hunter, got to get a warrant or a writ or whatever to haul two owlhoots back to Texas."

Now, Breen moved. He lowered the rifle from his shoulder—he had to be stiff from keeping it aimed all this time—sat up, brought the big rifle beside him and stared across the hard canyon rim at his partner.

"What the hell do you care? We found them. Didn't we?"

Keegan sniffed. "One of them . . . maybe."

Breen rubbed the beard stubble on his chin. *One of them.* His whisper almost escaped Keegan's ears.

"What are you getting at, laddie?" Keegan asked.

"Only one is shooting at us," Breen said.

Keegan ejected the brass casing from his Springfield, thumbed a .45-70 shell out of the bandolier that hung across his chest, and set that round into the chamber. "You said Billy Ray's the best with a long gun of them two."

"Better," Breen whispered. "Not best."

"Huh?"

"Ramona's been working on me to talk more like the educated man I am."

"Huh." Keegan brought the carbine closer. Ramona would be Ramona Bonderhoff, daughter of Purgatory City's noted gunsmith. Keegan tried to picture Ramona and Breen together, found the image disgusting, and spit, though there wasn't much to spit out of his parched mouth.

"One rifle, one man, one dugout. Two horses in the corral." Breen talked as though he wanted to just hear the thoughts aloud.

"Like ye said . . . he's the best shot," Keegan said. "And those boys just escaped from a prison farm up at the southern edge of the Panhandle. Maybe they don't got but one rifle. Maybe they—"

"Maybes," Breen interrupted, "get a lot of men killed in this country."

Keegan realized that Jed Breen was educated in many ways. So was Sean Keegan.

"Man trapped in a dugout wouldn't be wasting his powder and lead." Now Keegan started testing theories aloud himself. He had never tried that, but then he had always been the man of action, not the planning type. Jump into the fire and see what happens. He would not question how hot the fire might be. Or how much Irish whiskey he had consumed before making the jump. "He'd know, good of a shot as he is, the chance of hitting one of us would be slim." He pulled off his hat, and sneaked a quick peek at the dugout. One of the horses in the corral was saddled, the other not. He wished he had thought to bring a spyglass with him. Breen had one, but it was hanging on the horn of his saddle. And they had left their horses at the top of the ridge, climbed down, and found themselves here.

When the first shot from the dugout sent Keegan to this spot and Breen to the other, both men figured they had been seen. Just a chance thing. Bad luck on their part. But the man with the rifle had scooted back into the dugout. And the standoff began.

"He didn't yell for his brother," Breen started talking now, and looked up the canyon wall. Where they had left their horses.

"And he didn't try for the corral," Keegan said. "Where one of those horses is saddled. Brush is thick down there. Some mighty big boulders, too. We both have single-shots. Good rider could have gotten away on a saddled horse."

Breen peeked cautiously down the slope, came back to his position, and looked back at Keegan.

"Just one horse saddled," he said.

"Aye, laddie. Aye."

Now both were staring at the canyon.

"Those horses might be played out," Breen said.

"Aye, they probably are," Keegan said. "If they didn't steal any riding south."

"Not much chance to steal anything between Purgatory City and the Peering Farm," Breen pointed out.

Except ours. The thought hit Keegan like one of Paddy Fitzsimmons's haymakers back in those glorious days of the Rebellion, when the Irish boys would put on prize-fighting exhibitions for those not blessed to have been born in paradise.

They heard the hoofbeats then. Both men sprang to their feet, brought their weapons up, pulled back the hammers, and saw one man—Jim Bob Hardwick riding Breen's dun, pulling Keegan's sorrel behind him—and aimed. Then ducked, falling flat on their faces, when Billy Ray Hardwick stepped out of the dugout and began sending .38-40 slugs as quick as Paddy Fitzsimmons's punches in the ring. One slug tore at the yellow silk kerchief around his neck. Another punched off Breen's high-crowned black hat. Both men fell to the ground, letting out the vilest curses about their own stupidity.

CHAPTER 2

Blithering idiot.

Jed Breen spit dirt out of his mouth. Cursed and cursed again when he saw the hole through his brand new hat, which had cost him two dollars and thirty-seven cents at Pendergrass's mercantile in Purgatory City. Felt blood on his lips from the tough sand. He had bitten his tongue, to boot.

Everything had looked so perfect. Made to order. They had seen the smoke rising into the colorless sky late that morning, coming out of Fool Fassbinder's Folly. That's the name someone, thirty years or so earlier, had given this canyon. After the German settler, Fassbinder (the first name had long been forgotten), had settled in the canyon. No one knew, or remembered, his reason. There was no gold, no silver, nothing but granite and prickly pear, a few hardwoods, and a lot of hardships. But his dugout would always be a welcoming spot for travelers in this harsh country. Fassbinder, though, never knew about it, for the hostile Comanches—some say Kiowas—killed him shortly after he built his first fire.

Or so the legend went.

But Breen and Keegan knew of the canyon, and the smoke meant someone might be visiting. They wanted to make sure the fool at the dead fool's dugout wasn't the Hardwick boys. So they found the goat trail that led up the canyon, left their horses in a shady spot with some grain, and good, secure hobbles, and climbed down to the flat spot, found the cabin, and almost caught a bullet.

Now, however, Breen could picture in his mind exactly what had happened. Jim Bob Hardwick, always considered the better cowboy, had left his older brother in the dugout, ridden to the canyon's exit, and waited. When he spotted two men riding toward him, he mounted his horse, galloped back to the corral, told his brother, and then he ran, afoot, to the canyon's exit. Billy Ray started a fire, got the chimney puffing out smoke like a locomotive pulling a freight train up a steep mountain grade on a cold December morning. And while Keegan and Breen, two greedy sons of guns acting like two greenhorns, climbed down to get the drop on the outlaws, Jim Bob found their horses and stole them.

While Billy Ray, a fine shot with a puny little Winchester toy gun, kept Keegan and Breen pinned down with nothing much to do but pontificate. That would give Jim Bob time enough to find the horses, ride down the slope, come back to the canyon's entrance, gallop back to the dugout to save his brother, and ride away, free to push on to the Rio Grande, swim that creek of a river this time of year, and live happily ever after in Mexico.

And it wasn't like those boys were leaving two idiots to join Fool Fassbinder buried in this lonely canyon. The Hardwick boys weren't leaving them afoot. They had two horses in the corral, which might or might not be lame. They even had a fire going, though it had to be ninety-one degrees right about now. They might be able to nurse their way back to Purgatory City, or maybe even up to Peering Farm.

Which made Jed Breen madder than a rattlesnake. The Hardwick boys were raising dust for the border—on Breen's and Keegan's horses. Two hundred dollars getting away—on mounts Breen and Keegan had paid good money for. Well, Jed Breen knew he had paid thirty bucks for his. Keegan might have won his in a boxing match, or found it and claimed it for his own.

Two hundred dollars did not amount to much. Jed Breen had brought in men worth far heftier rewards. But it was the principle that mattered. He dropped to his knee and brought the Sharps up tight against his shoulder.

"What the hell are you doing?" Keegan shouted. "You might hit one of the horses and not those English-loving dogs."

"So?"

"Them's our horses."

"No," Breen said calmly. He made the adjustments in his head. Shooting at a galloping target. Shooting downhill. Factoring in the wind. Always aim high. "I'm shooting your pile of glue bait."

He let out a slight breath, smiled, relaxed, touched the set trigger, then shifted his index finger to the trigger that did the rest of the work. Smiling, Jed Breen squeezed. He was a professional. He ejected the massive brass casing, fished another from the pocket in his vest, and glanced at Keegan.

"My hundred dollars is heading for those rocks," he said as he calmly reloaded. The Sharps had quite the range. "Yours is getting away. On my horse."

That was all the motivation he needed to give the pesky, but good, Irishman.

Swearing, Sean Keegan brought his Springfield to his shoulder, pulled back the heavy hammer, and aimed at the fleeing rider.

"Remember . . ." Breen let the barrel of the Sharps cool slightly, then settled the big rifle to that familiar position. "You're shooting a carbine. And a .45-70. You don't have my range. And you're shooting downhill."

"And if I want to hire someone to teach me how to shoot a mad-dog killer, I won't be hiring a low-down cur like you, pard." Keegan had to calm himself down. He started taking so long to adjust his composure, Breen thought he might have to take the shot himself.

Just as he put his right eye near the telescopic sight, Sean Keegan's Springfield roared. Breen lowered his rifle and looked over the brass. His horse was somersaulting off toward Mexico. In fact, it looked like it might roll all the way to the Rio Grande, which was four or five hard days' ride from here. He saw the figure on the ground get up, turn, stagger, and fall. He saw the other escaped convict come from a small depression, run to his brother, and drag him behind a small rock.

Jed Breen nodded, and used the Sharps to push himself to his feet.

Sean Keegan did the same, the professional that he was despite a taste for barley and whatever grain they used in Irish whiskey. He thought it might also be barley, but it didn't matter.

"Let's go collect our bounty," Breen said.

"What do we do for horses?" Keegan was reloading.

"I imagine the two nags they left behind will manage to get us to London's ranch. That's on the way to the prison farm."

"They might still resist."

Breen grinned. "They just got two horses shot from under them while riding at a full gallop. On a hard-packed, Texas-tough floor. I think they'll enjoy being back in a prison where all they have to do is plant and pick cotton."

He tucked the heavy rifle under his arm. But he kept his right hand on the holstered .38-caliber Colt Lightning—just in case.

CHAPTER 3

How many times do I reckon I've done this?

Those kind of thoughts rarely entered Matthew McCulloch's brain, and because of that, he stopped reaching underneath the brown mare's belly for the cinch.

His pa once told him that Matt had saddled his first horse when he was five years old. His ma countered, *No, he was six.* His pa had said something like, *Darn it, woman, I reckon I know when my son saddled his first hoss*, and his mother had sung out something like, *I begat you five boys and two daughters, and you can't even get their names right half the time.* And so it had gone till they yelled each other hoarse.

Five or six? Matt couldn't recall. It just seemed like forever. He didn't want to think about how old he was. The door to what passed for a home in West Texas shut, and the mare snorted and shook her head.

Hearing footsteps, Matt found the cinch and resumed his chore.

"I can saddle my own horse, Pa," Cynthia called out. She was probably stamping her own feet right about then.

Matt finished the job without comment, then tugged on the horn to make sure the saddle felt secure. He looked over the saddle and smiled at the blonde he would always picture as a little girl, even though she was a woman full grown. And as pretty as her mother, God rest her soul. Maybe prettier.

He grabbed the reins and walked in front of the mare, extending the leather to Cynthia.

"You wouldn't begrudge an old man for saddling his baby girl's horse?" Matt smiled. Smiles, like thoughts about how many times he had saddled a horse, came rare to Matt McCulloch. But the look on his daughter's face told him this was one habit he might get used to.

"As long as it's not a sidesaddle," Cynthia said.

He laughed out loud and pushed back the brim of his big Texas hat. "I ain't seen a sidesaddle in this country in six years," he said. "It belonged to Blanchefleur Boudoir. And she was . . ."

"A French lady?"

"Never you mind." Blanchefleur Boudoir certainly wasn't a lady. Ladies didn't ride palomino horses sidesaddle wearing nothing but silk hose, thongs, and a delicate ribbon around her ponytail. And Matt didn't think she had an ounce of French blood in her—not as thick as he remembered that Texas drawl sounded.

He extended his arm, and she took the reins.

"You got that pepperbox?" he asked.

Cynthia rolled her eyes. "Yes, Papa." She carried a purse that hung over her shoulder. She opened it and let him see the well-worn handle of walnut. The pistol had to be twenty years old, maybe even twenty-five, and he wished he had something modern. Something that might not shoot off all six barrels instead of one when you touched the trigger. It was an Allen & Thurber pistol, .31 caliber. Matt couldn't remember where he had gotten it, probably from an arrest back when he was Rangering. Next time he made it into Purgatory City, he'd visit Bondy the gunsmith and see if he

had something more suitable, a Remington over-and-under
.41-caliber derringer seemed better.

"You know how to use it, right?" he asked.

"And I know when to use it," she told him. Her eyes
twinkled.

"Well . . ." He bit his lower lip and debated if he ought
to accompany her to town.

She read his mind.

"You've got work to do here, Papa," she said. "And if
you had dinner with Ramona and me, you'd be so bored
you'd fall asleep in your bowl of soup."

"Soup?" Matt shook his head. "For dinner? I don't
reckon I'd be ordering soup."

She smiled, until he pointed at the purse. "Now, Cynthia,
just remember—"

His daughter cut him off, and slowly lifted the left side
of her skirt. Above the boot he saw the Apache knife
sheathed against the unmentionables around the calf.

"I can use this better," she said. "And I will."

Matt found himself at a loss for words. Fathers, he
thought, never lost their tongue when warning daughters
about all the dangers in this world.

"I'll be fine, Papa," she told him. "Purgatory City is becoming civilized."

That'll be the day, he thought, but kept his lips flattened.

The skirt dropped back over the boot. Cynthia had been
kidnapped as a child during a murderous Apache raid. She
had lived with the Apaches up until not quite a year ago,
when Matt and his friends, Sean Keegan and Jed Breen,
had helped rescue her deep in Mexico. She had been home
since, reluctantly going to a school in Purgatory City until
the teacher, Schoolmaster Markum, said she ought to be
teaching him and the schoolkids. Now Matt looked at the
miserable home he had been sleeping in for years. It was,

he told himself, time to rebuild this ranch. And put his daughter in a real home. Not some hovel.

"All right," he said. "Need . . . ?"

He didn't have time to say "help" before Cynthia was in the saddle, smiling down at him.

"Have fun," he told her. "Tell Bondy I'll be in town in a day or week or so. Tell him howdy. And stay out of the saloons."

She laughed.

"Get to the garden," she told him. "Stay off of any widow-making broncs today."

She let out a whistle, turned the horse around on a dime, and kicked the mare into a trot. By the time she rounded the corrals and found the trail to town, the dust from the galloping horse hid both daughter and mare from view.

Cynthia McCulloch, her papa marveled, rode like the wind.

Like her old man.

He cupped his hands over his mouth and cried out: "Make sure you're back before dark!"

She probably couldn't hear him over the pounding of the mare's hooves, but she would be back before dark. She was a good girl. She'd always been a good girl. He told himself that Purgatory City wasn't that far—not that it was close— and maybe Cynthia was right. This part of West Texas was, ever so slowly, getting close to being civilized.

He pulled off his hat and used it to slap the dust off his chaps.

He told himself: Close to civilized ain't exactly civilized.

He ran his free hand through his hair.

When was the last time he had looked into a mirror? He ran his fingers across the stubble on his cheek. Last time he shaved, most likely, he answered to himself. Three days. Maybe four from the feel of the beard. And how many more gray hairs have sprung up since Cynthia returned home?

I'll be white-haired like Jed Breen, he thought, before I know it.

Daughters. He shook his head. They had a way of aging a daddy.

But it was a mighty good way to grow old.

Two hours later, he found himself hoeing weeds in his garden.

Gardening. Like a farmer. Yes, the newspapers in the great state of Texas would have a run of sensationally sarcastic stories for a month at the least if one of those ink-blooded fools learned that the famed jackal named McCulloch was armed with a hoe and attacking weeds.

McCulloch had tried to grow hay for a few summers during the good years, before that Apache raid, but he just wasn't cut out to grow much of anything. His wife? Now that was another story. She could find a way to make a flower bloom when the rain didn't fall and the sun never wanted to set, just scorched the already-dried earth. But here he was trying to make that thick-muscled, callused thumb turn to a color that resembled green.

Potatoes mostly. The clerk at the general store told him those grew easier. The clerk had also suggested turnips, but Matt had smiled and said a soft, "Not on my land." Cynthia had laughed when she heard that story. Neither one of them cared for turnips. McCulloch said he would rather eat prickly pear. He hoed another weed, stopped and leaned against the long handle, wiped his brow with a shirtsleeve, and studied his garden.

Pinto beans. The tomato vines already looked dead. But the corn seemed to be coming right along. At least that's what Cynthia had told him a few days back.

That's when McCulloch heard the metal shoes clanging on the hard patch of ground, and he saw two riders round the corner. His Adam's apple bobbed and he took a sidelong glance at the Winchester carbine he had leaned against the well. He hadn't even buckled on his gun belt this morning. That long-barreled Colt remained inside, sitting on the seat for any guest for supper. Like they ever had visitors out here.

The horses, a bay and a sorrel, were practically played out. Breathing heavily. Caked with lather. The riders didn't look much better, dust-covered dark hats—the dark-bearded man wore one of those tall silk hats, tied with a bandanna from top to chin to keep the wind from taking it away—and dusters that had seen better days.

Both held their reins in their left hands. The one with the silk hat had a good enough reason. His right arm was in a sling made from a purple silk bandanna. The bandanna holding his hat on was yellow. The other man, sunburned with long brown sideburns, kept his right hand near his stomach, the thumb apparently stuck in his waistband. He wore a gun belt, but even from the distance, McCulloch could tell that the holster was empty. But he wondered if the man had a revolver stuck near his thumb.

Both had rifles in the scabbards. The man with the silk hat and the bum arm wore no holster, but now as they drew closer, McCulloch saw the sawed-off shotgun hanging from his shoulder by a rawhide cord. Matt didn't think he could recall seeing a shotgun barrel sawed that far down. Hell, the pepperbox he had given Cynthia wasn't much bigger than this man's scatter-gun.

"Mornin'." Silk Hat's grin revealed stained and rotted teeth.

The horseman considered the leader of "The Jackals" leaned against the hoe. "Past morning," he said. "But good day to you."

"We was tol'," Silk Hat continued, "that you gots horses to trade."

"I do. You don't."

"That ain't neighborly," the second rider said.

"Just the truth." McCulloch swallowed. "I'm not sure your mounts would bring much money at a glue factory."

Silk Hat laughed. "You gots a good eye for horseflesh, mister. You surely do. Buster an' me run up ag'in some injuns. Comanch, I figgered. They was after our hosses, but we outrun 'em."

"Lucky." McCulloch didn't believe a word the man said.

The man nodded and raised his head toward the pale blue sky. "Blessed, suh. Blessed by the Lord. He shore looked after Buster and me this fine, glorious day."

The wind stopped blowing. The horses breathed as if they might keel over in a minute.

"Maybe," Silk Hat said, "you gots horses to . . . sell?"

McCulloch tilted his head backward. "I haven't been mustanging for some months now," he said. "What you see in the corral is all that I have. For sale. I have a couple in the barn over yonder." He tilted his head.

When the two men looked at the barn, McCulloch took a few steps toward them, stopping when they turned back toward him.

"How much for the roan?" Buster asked.

McCulloch tilted his head, thinking. He took a few steps closer to Buster's horse, and held out his left hand—his right still gripped the hoe—and let the horse catch his scent. Its eyes were dull, the breaths ragged, but it had been a good horse before being ridden by a fool. He could see the outline of the gelding's ribs.

"My horses sell for forty dollars," he said.

"Fer a mustang?" Silk Hat whined.

"Mustangs are fine horses," McCulloch said. "You ought to know. You're riding one."

Silk Hat cackled. "This ain't no hoss, partner. It's a toy."

"Forty bucks," Buster said, "seems on the steep side."

McCulloch had kept Buster in his peripheral vision. Now he took a step toward the rider so that he could look at him and not miss any movement by Silk Hat.

"You must have asked someone about me," McCulloch said, "if you came looking to buy horses."

"Feller on the road to Hugh's Town," Silk Hat told him.

"Hugh's Town." McCulloch nodded. "Makes sense. I've sold a few horses in Hugh's Town. Forty dollars. But I'll knock off five bucks for your horses."

"Generous." Buster's voice turned icy in the heat.

"Yes. It's mighty generous. Seeing I might be burying both of these horses in the morning."

"So . . ." Silk Hat said. "Thirty-five bucks for two hosses."

McCulloch laughed. "No. Seventy-five dollars plus your two horses. It's forty bucks for one horse. I knocked off five."

Buster laughed without humor. "You ain't much of a horse trader, pardner."

McCulloch nodded. "You ain't much of a liar, either," he said. "Seeing that Hugh's Town is east of here, and you rode in from the west. And seeing that those horses you're riding are ones I sold to Jim Ketchum. His place is twenty miles west of here."

The wind blew. The horses breathed heavily. The mustangs in the corral began milling around nervously.

"I'd say you've been running these horses for about twenty miles," McCulloch said. "Those horses wouldn't be in such ragged condition if you'd ever stopped to let them rest a mite."

"We bought these horses from Jim Ketchum," Silk Hat said. "Let me show you the bill of sale."

He was reaching for the sawed-off twelve-gauge, and Buster started to pull a belly gun. But McCulloch was already swinging the hoe. That hoe had been attacking the hard ground of West Texas since spring, so it was tough and sharp and savage. Buster's eyes widened from penny size to goose eggs, and he dropped the derringer and grabbed at the throat that was gushing blood. His sorrel bolted, and Buster fell out of the saddle and knocked Silk Hat aside. Silk Hat accidentally touched a trigger of his shotgun, and that sent his exhausted horse in a frightened lope.

The bay, frightened enough to run till he died, likely would have dragged Silk Hat with him. But McCulloch had dropped the hoe and stepped over and grabbed the bridle. Played out from a hard ride, the horse still wanted to run after the sorrel, but McCulloch kept a firm grip, and the horse ceased fighting.

Silk Hat whined and cursed, then cursed and whined. Buster wasn't making any noise. At least, not on this side of Hell. He had bled out rather quickly. But he had dropped his derringer, and Silk Hat kept slapping his good hand toward the silver-plated Remington.

Until McCulloch crushed the man's fingers with his left boot.

"Bill . . . of . . . sale. . . ." Silk Hat grimaced. "I . . . gots . . . one."

"From Jim Ketchum?" McCulloch demanded.

"Yes. I swear on a stack of Good Books."

He screamed when that boot pressed down harder. "Mister," McCulloch said when he released the pressure. "I was pallbearer at Jim's funeral six months ago."

His boot rose, hooked underneath the yellow scarf and pulled it off. The silk hat rolled away. McCulloch gripped the purple piece of silk and jerked it away. The man's arm bounced one way and another, and he screamed. The horse dragged him a few feet, and McCulloch didn't stop it this time. It stopped on its own ten yards later.

McCulloch grabbed the shotgun, opened the breech, checked to make sure one barrel hadn't been fired. He snapped the sawed-off barrels into place, and covered the distance to the hung-up rider and the worn-out horse. Tears filled Silk Hat's eyes, but he could see well enough.

At least, he saw the scatter-gun.

"For the . . . love . . . of God . . . mistah . . ," the ugly man whined.

"I knew Mary, Jim's wife, longer than I knew Jim." McCulloch hardly recognized his own voice. "Her favorite colors were purple and yellow. And, God, how she loved silk. Jim must have bought her twenty scarves, bandannas, kerchiefs, whatever you want to call them. She loved wearing them, mister. Said when she wore them, it was like Jim was right with her."

He pulled back one hammer.

"Wait, now . . . you . . . can't . . . I gots . . ."

"I reckon they're together now." He put the shotgun's right barrel next to the horse's hindquarters.

The man's eyes cleared. He gasped. "No." The plea was just audible.

McCulloch's pointer finger went inside the trigger guard.

"It was Buster. He done it!" The man's screams almost sent the horse into a lope. "He killed her. I didn't do nothin'."

"I bet." He felt sick. He had hoped Mary wasn't dead.

"Buster!" Silk Hat shouted. "Buster!"

"Buster's dead," Matt told him. "But he'll hear you soon enough."

"No!" Silk Hat shouted. "You're a good man. You . . . raise fine horse. Mister, you . . . ain't no . . . jackal!"

"Oh, yes." The words came out as barely a dry whisper. "Oh, yes. I most certainly am."

He did not hear the horse's hooves on the hard ground, or Silk Hat's brief screams. His ears rang from the roar of the shotgun, which he flung to the ground. The horses ran around the corral. A few snorted and kicked the stalls in the barn.

McCulloch looked off west, toward the Ketchum ranch. His heart pounded. What was it Cynthia had said?

Purgatory City is becoming civilized.

"That'll be the day," he said. "Civilized? Not in my lifetime."

CHAPTER 4

Cynthia McCulloch liked the way the brown mare loped. She liked the way the horse trotted, too, and she had never cared much for a trot. She'd much rather feel the wind blowing her hair, burning her face—which remained a deep tan from all of her years living with the Apaches in Mexico. A little wind wouldn't hurt her now, and the mare seemed ready for a real ride, so she leaned forward, grinning like she was ten years old again, and kicked.

The mare exploded out of a lope into a full gallop.

Feeling like a child again, she laughed as the hooves tore the ground and kicked up dust clouds. She remembered once, a lifetime earlier, when she had scared her father out of twenty years—at least, that's what he said later—when she dared race him. He probably let her win. But he never made the mistake of racing her after that. Fathers, she eventually realized, thought their daughters were fragile things, like her mother's crystal vases. They'd push their sons as hard as they pushed themselves and their horses, but they never seemed to understand that the women of the frontier had to be stronger than the men.

Still, she began to sit up in the saddle and pull the reins till the mare slowed. Matt McCulloch had taught Cynthia better than running a horse too hard, too long, too foolishly.

She didn't think he would spank her for acting like a child—not after all she had been through, not after all those years away from her father after being kidnapped by Apaches—but she could remember her mother's spankings. And she didn't want to go through that again. Matt McCulloch, her oldest brother once told her, hit a whole lot harder than their ma.

When she saw the beginnings of Purgatory City, she brought the horse to a walk. West Texas towns weren't much to look at, she remembered, but townspeople sure liked looking at anyone coming into town. Strangers or folks they knew, none of that mattered. *You pay attention in this country,* her pa would have told her. That's what keeps a person alive and healthy. But Cynthia figured there was another reason people stared from the boardwalks or out of windows. They were just plain nosy. And while most folks said drinking and debauchery were the two biggest vices in Purgatory City, Cynthia thought at least one foible topped those two.

Gossip.

Cynthia had learned that from Ramona Bonderhoff, her best friend—well, her only friend—in this ramshackle assembly of homes and businesses and dirt and heat and violence. My, how folks loved to gossip in this town. Not just women. Men were bona fide champion gossips. She thought Sean Keegan was at the top of the class, but Keegan, her father had told her, was out with Jed Breen on some bounty-hunting job.

She made her way past the jacales on the edge of town where most of the Mexican laborers lived and where the Catholic church stood and the two graveyards, the small one for the good citizens, the massive one for paupers, killers, and no-accounts. Past the stagecoach station and the livery stable, then turned onto the main street—some called it the only street—passing The Palace of Purgatory City on her left and the marshal's office and jail on her right.

Immediately, she felt the stares.

The lawyer who hung his shingle on the corner frowned. Two cowhands riding out of town gave her the drunken looks she had never seen while living with the Apaches. One started to tip his hat, but his pardner whispered, "Don't bother"—just louder than he had meant.

She didn't care.

The women standing outside the bakery straightened from all their self-righteousness.

That didn't bother her, either.

Down on the right, though, she spotted the carved wooden rifle that marked the location of the town's gunsmith. There was an opening at the hitch rail, and she reined the mare to a stop, swung out of the saddle, and led her horse between a piebald gelding and a saddled mule. After wrapping the reins around the rail, she dipped underneath it, slid past the water trough, nodded at two school-age kids who were running and singing, but now stopped to stare.

"Howdy," she told the freckled, corn-haired boy.

He grinned, and let out an exaggerated wave. "Howdy!" Two front teeth were missing. Cynthia laughed, till the girl, in a blue gingham dress, scowled at her companion and said, "I'll tell Ma!"

"Tell her what?" the boy blurted.

"Just hush." She glared at Cynthia as though she was the cause of this squabble.

She let the children pass, then stepped onto the warped, sunbeaten, and Texas-battered planks. The children kept walking, and Cynthia stared. She hoped the boy might turn around to give her one more look-see. But he just hung his head and moped along while his sister told him everything he had done wrong.

"You jes don't speak to the likes of her. She lived with injuns."

The mirthless laugh came out like a cough, and she shook her head. Well, since her father was considered an outcast by the social elite of this miserable town, she should feel some pride that she was considered even lower than Matthew McCulloch.

"Don't let them spoil our fun day."

The voice made Cynthia smile. She turned to find Ramona Bonderhoff standing underneath the rifle sign. Ramona had to be the prettiest girl Cynthia had ever seen— excepting her mother, or what she remembered of her mother. Wearing a red-and-green checked dress, the gunsmith's daughter walked over and put an arm around Cynthia's shoulder.

"We're here to eat like pigs and have fun. And we can gossip about those ol' sows and the swine they're bringing up." She turned Cynthia around, and they walked back down the boardwalk and turned inside the shop, which smelled of metal and gunpowder and grease and warmth.

Bondy, Ramona's father, wearing sleeve garters and an apron, grinned over his spectacles.

"I suppose," he said, "you two have nefarious schemes to plan, so I won't have a helper the rest of this afternoon."

"All right if I put dinner on your tab at The Alamo Café?" Ramona asked.

"Why don't y'all try Dos Amigos?" Her father looked down at the Smith & Wesson revolver he was working on. "The enchiladas are the best this side of San Antonio."

Ramona frowned. "If you like grease."

Bondy looked up, and faked a grin. "I work with grease. But there's something about the grease at Dos Amigos that is quite tasty. You may not like the enchiladas, but don't forget their sopapillas."

His daughter grinned, and she turned to her guest. "The sopapillas are wonderful. I think it's the one thing that might keep me in this town when I become eighteen."

"I could eat the grease your father is using on that six-shooter," Cynthia said.

"Good." Ramona steered Cynthia back toward the door and turned and told her father they would be back before closing time, that she would check on her dress at Miss Katharine's and at the post office and would tell Felix, the man at the livery, that his shotgun was ready."

"Have fun," Bondy told them with a wave. "Don't eat too much."

They stepped outside, and Cynthia glanced down the street at the café on the corner. The one Bondy had suggested they skip in favor of the Mexican café. She had a strong feeling that Bondy was just trying to keep the two girls from the kind of hostility Cynthia had seen and heard riding to the gunsmith's store. But the owner of The Alamo Café, Miss Clarabelle, had always been kind to Cynthia and her father. The patrons? Well, that was another matter.

They headed toward the Mexican place.

The food turned out to be much more inviting than hot grease. Cynthia had not tasted Mexican food in years, and she had forgotten the wonder of a sopapilla topped with powdered sugar and honey. When the owner asked if they would like another sopapilla, Ramona and Cynthia gave each other conspiratorial glances, and broke out laughing.

"No," Ramona said at last, "but gracias, señora. There is a dance a week from Saturday at The X-Bar Ranch. I don't want to be fat by then."

"Honey," the old Mexican woman said, "you're too skinny to ever be fat. So's your friend, here." She gathered the dishes, and ambled away.

"I hope Jed Breen is back in town by next Saturday," Ramona said.

"Why?"

"So he can take me to the dance. They have a really good fiddler at the X-Bar."

Cynthia tilted her head. "Do you think Jed Breen would ask you?"

"He'd better ask my father first," the girl sang out. "If he doesn't want his head blown off." She sounded just like her father then, or even Cynthia's dad.

Cynthia's face made Ramona burst out laughing. "Oh, Cynthia, you're just so funny. Haven't you noticed the way Jed looks at me?"

Her head shook.

"I know he's older. And his hair makes him look even much, much older, but he's a man, and I'm a woman. Even if Papa says I'm a little girl." She stopped. "Oh, I'm being silly. I know. And you didn't ride all the way out here just to hear me talk about men."

So they went to see the dressmaker, who was courteous and told Cynthia that any time she wanted a dress to come see her, that she and Matt McCulloch were old friends, and that Cynthia's father wasn't a jackal like all those no-accounts and busybodies in Purgatory City said. The old man at the livery stable was pleasant enough too, for a livery man anyway, and he was polite enough not to spit out tobacco juice until the girls had left.

They were walking back up the boardwalk, looking into windows, full of Mexican food and avoiding eye contact with anyone they met, when Cynthia looked up and stopped suddenly.

Just up the street, she spotted one of her father's horses, well lathered from a hard run. She saw her father, too, standing in front of a small stone building, talking to a tall man in black broadcloth.

Ramona backed up to her friend and followed Cynthia's line of vision.

"Who's that Pa is talking to?" Cynthia asked.

"J.J.K. Hollister," Ramona said in a faraway voice. "They haven't spoken in years."

"Hollister." Cynthia shook her head.

"He came after you were . . . well . . . he's the captain of the Texas Rangers in charge of this part of the country."

The tall man in black nodded, shook her father's hand, and went behind the stone building, while Matt McCulloch grabbed the reins, led his horse to the street, and swung into the saddle. He didn't ride away, just waited, letting the horse drink now that it had cooled off. Two minutes later, the Ranger captain rounded the building on a black thorough-bred. He spoke briefly to McCulloch, and then they rode down the street.

Seeing Cynthia and Ramona, Matthew McCulloch guided the horse to the boardwalk.

"Ramona," he said, tipping his hat. The Ranger captain stopped in the middle of the street, but he also nodded at the two girls and touched the brim of his big black Stetson. "Reckon you can put up with this firebrand of a girl of mine for the night?"

Ramona's face and voice bounced with joy. "It would be like Christmas," she said. "Of course."

"What's the matter, Papa?" Cynthia asked.

"Capt'n Hollister and I got some mess to clear up," he said. "Don't worry. I see that look on your face. We've got . . . burying to do."

"Oh." Ramona gasped and took Cynthia's hand.

"Just stay in town. It's all over. The capt'n and I just have to ride back to my place, then over to check on Mary Ketchum."

"I see." Ramona didn't see, but Cynthia thought she did. She didn't remember Mary Ketchum, either, but the last name rang a slight bell.

"Don't go back to the ranch, Cynthia," her father said. "Just stay put." He made himself try to smile. "You and Ramona can stir up enough trouble here on your own. The capt'n and I'll be back tomorrow night, most likely. Maybe early morning after."

He stared down with those firm eyes.

"Understood?"

"Yes, Papa."

He nodded, then smiled, and this time the look was genuine. "Y'all got powdered sugar on your cheeks."

Laughing as the girls busied themselves wiping their faces while Ramona moaned that they had looked like fools before Miss Katharine and the livery man and half of the town they met on the boardwalks, McCulloch turned his horse back to the Texas Ranger. Then both kicked their horses into trots and rode out of town, toward the McCulloch spread.

"They'll be all right," Ramona whispered.

"I know," Cynthia said. "But somebody else isn't all right. I've seen that look on Papa's face before."

CHAPTER 5

Sean Keegan was still talking.

"Generally, I believe that any fool who is elected into office is nothing but a bloody fool, and a confounded idiot. And any citizen who does business with the government is a confounded idiot."

When the Irishman stopped to find his canteen and take a drink of water, Jed Breen took advantage and made two observations.

"I work for the government. Not full time. But the government pays me to bring in wanted felons. And you might not have noticed these kind of things, Sean, but when you were fighting to preserve the Union and then to protect citizens in this state, it was the United States government that was paying you. And you're working for me to bring in these two scoundrels."

Jim Bob Hardwick and Billy Ray Hardwick, their hands bound to their saddle horns, said nothing.

Keegan screwed on the cap of his canteen and hung the canvas strap over his saddle scabbard.

"Ye ain't the government, laddie," he said, and wiped his mouth with the back of his sleeve.

"But the government is paying me, and I'm paying you from what the state pays me."

"The warden's paying you."

"But the state's paying the warden to pay me."

"Ye be hurting my head with all this kind of tomfoolery." Keegan wiped his forehead. "And not letting me get to the point."

"Please." Breen grinned. "*Please* get to the point."

"The point be this, laddie. What's the name of the guy who owns this cotton patch?"

"Peering. It's called the Peering Farm."

"Aye. Here be me point. Warden Peering—"

"Peering's not the warden. He just owns the farm."

"All right. Peterson—"

"No, Peering. You had it right—"

"It don't matter what be the man's name. Quit interrupting me. Peering, he gets his cotton planted, picked, and sold, and he don't have to pay for the labor. Sorta like what he was doing before the boys and me helped take his slaves away from him."

"Darned right," Billy Ray Hardwick said. "We ain't nothin' but slaves."

"Billy Ray. . ." Jim Bob sighed at his brother.

"I'm sure the state, or at least the prison officials, get some money," Breen said. "Not sure about if these field hands see any of it, if they ever get out of prison. But we're splitting two hundred dollars—paid by the government of Texas."

The hooves clopped. "This is dry country," Breen said, unable to keep quiet for too long. "Surprised they can grow cotton in this country."

"This is about as far north as they can," Jim Bob Hardwick said.

Both Keegan and Breen shot the rustler a glance.

"About as far north as it's safe, too, I would expect," Keegan said when he turned back. "I imagine some Co-

manches and Kiowas get homesick up on that reservation
and come back to visit."

"Comanchero country," Breen said.

Keegan spit. "Comancheros. Now them heathens be worse
than the government."

"God help me," Billy Ray Hardwick said, "I never thought
I'd be glad to get back to Peering Farm, but damnation if I
ain't. That mick hasn't shut up for a hundred miles."

Breen laughed. "Salvation awaits." He pointed ahead at
a small track that led off the trail. "If a cotton sack is salvation to you. By my map, yonder is the road to Peering Farm."

Keegan slapped his thigh. "Ye reckon they got a sutler's
store beyond the walls that sells good whiskey, Jed?"

"Criminy, Sean. This is a state prison farm, not an army
post."

"Aye. But prisons got guards, and guarding scoundrels
the likes of these two can work up a powerful thirst. And
I've been dry for, like that scoundrel ahead of us just said,
a hundred miles."

There were no walls at this prison, and Jed Breen knew
why. You didn't need walls here, except for protection—and
most of the Indians had given up. Just a few Comanche and
Kiowa holdouts remained, and the US Army kept busy
chasing down those who had jumped the reservation north
of the Red River in Indian Territory.

Breen, Keegan, and the two escapees climbed the road
and the country flattened before them. The red earth turned
green and white for about as far as a body could see. Cotton
balls looked like clouds, and men in the striped uniforms
of convicts dragged huge sacks and did not bother to look
up as the four riders eased down a path between two fields.
A few guards, in their own uniforms but with wide-brimmed

straw hats to protect their faces and necks from the blistering sun, eyed the riders, but most, holding shotguns or repeating rifles over their shoulders, kept their eyes on the workers. The workers wore shabby wool caps. Black wool. Which had to make the tops of their heads feel like they were baking in an oven.

"I gots water," a big black man said as he walked down a row, maybe a half-dozen canteens hanging over his shoulder. "Who's thirsty? Who's thirsty?"

When a hand shot up, the giant man eased through the cotton plants and let a thirsty man drink.

"I see why you boys made a break," Breen said softly.

"Might've made it," Billy Ray said. "You say a hundred miles. That be the record. Moze Blackstone only got four miles before they dragged him back to the fields."

A guard finally took interest in the newcomers, probably because they were riding toward him, and he brought his Henry rifle around, keeping it in front of him, and pulling back the hammer, but not raising the repeater.

"It's enough to make a body think that maybe he ought not break the law," Jim Bob said.

"Shut up," his brother barked. And Jim Bob Hardwick sunk in his saddle, defeat, and what he could expect for the next several years of hard labor, staring at him, even though only that one guard looked at the riders.

That guard stepped out into the middle of the path.

"Stop your horses," Breen ordered, and the Hardwick boys obeyed.

"Sean."

That's all Breen needed to say. Keegan drew his Remington, and cocked it, just so the Hardwick brothers could hear the sound, after which Breen eased his horse between the two convicts, and approached the guard.

He reined up a few yards before the man with the Henry and the scowl.

"Got a couple of deliveries for you," Breen said.

"Appears like." The guard kept his eyes on the brothers. "Where do I take them?"

The guard tilted his head to the left.

"Big house. Warden and Capt'n Peerin' should be there."

"Gots water," the big convict began singing again. "Hot water. Who wants a drink of hot water?"

"Where'd you find 'em?" the guard asked.

"Fool Fassbinder's Folly." Breen noted the man's eyebrows arch.

"Hell's fire," he said, relaxing. "They covered a lot of territory."

"That was their mistake. Wore out their horses. And came mighty close to getting away with ours."

"Hot water," the Negro trusty yelled. "Who wants hot water?"

"You want us to leave these two boys with you, or take them in to see the warden?"

The guard glanced at the sun. "Day's about done. Take 'em on in. They look plumb tuckered out anyhow. Besides, the warden'll likely want to see what he's payin' for. You boys done good."

"Sean," Breen called. "Bring them on ahead."

The horses began moving, and Breen nodded at the guard and kicked his down the trail. Behind him, Keegan said, "Laddie, by chance would there be a store of some sort on this here lovely plantation? Where a hard-working servant of the government might be able to wet his tongue with just a wee drop of whiskey, or even a nice porter?"

"Mister," the guard said, "the only thing to drink around here is . . ."

The man working a few rows over finished the sentence.

"Hot water. Who wants a drink of hot water? It be free. Hot water. Gets your free hot water!"

"What do ya think of my little ol' farm, pardners?" Peter Peering said. Without waiting for an answer, he picked up the silver bell and rang it. "Confound it, Marcus. We got guests here, sugar. Now c'mon, these kindhearted gents have come a right far piece for a visit."

The white-haired trusty pushed open the screen door. "Sorry, boss man," he said, and, arms shaking, glasses and decanter rattling, backed out, turned, and moved toward the fancy table on the porch.

The screen door slammed, and Peering let out a string of curses. "Marcus, if that screen door slams again, son, it'll come off its hinges. And then you know where you're going." He pointed to the stocks that lined the curved red-earthen path in front of the big house.

The trusty said nothing. He didn't have to. Breen could read the fear in the man's eyes, and that tray kept rattling until he set it on the table and removed all of the glasses and the decanter.

"Will that be all, boss man?" the sweating man said nervously.

"For the time bein', Marcus. Now, you get right back in the kitchen and fix up a good helping of grits and sowbelly. Our visitors come far, gots a long way to go home, and, well, we want them to eat high on the hog."

"Oh, Captain Peering." Sean Keegan was already drinking the cotton king's Kentucky bourbon. Captain might be an honorary title for the farmer, though his thick Southern drawl sounded like it would have fit a Confederate officer from cotton country during the late rebellion. "This'll do just fine, sir. Yes, sir. Just fine."

"Probably tastes better than hot water," Breen said.

The three men laughed.

The man in the prison uniform, who had been introduced as Warden Franklin Plummer, said nothing. He did not even drink the glass of bourbon in front of him.

"Yeah," Breen said. "Thanks for the offer of supper, Captain, but Sean and I would like to start for home. It's a long way south."

"I see, I see, but you won't insult me by turnin' down my offer of Kentucky's best? Would ya? It's a hundred and fifty proof, son. Mighty fine."

Breen contained the sigh, and the curse, but picked up the glass and sipped.

"Fine view, don't you boys think so?" Peering found the decanter, refilled his glass, then topped off the others, except for the warden's. That glass had not been touched.

Jed Breen was a man who enjoyed good whiskey, and could not deny that this bourbon had a kick but went down the throat as sweet as honey, with just a hint of fire afterward. But the view?

The Hardwick boys were in two of the stocks, about as miserable as anything Breen had seen in a while.

"Oh, now, boys, I see." Peering sipped more from his glass and chuckled. He set his glass down and turned toward the warden. "Franky, my fine fellow, it appears my guests are havin' a hard time drinkin' with me because of the view. And you know how I detest drinkin' alone. I guess we can hold off on punishin' them Hardwick boys till tomorrow. Besides, they look all tuckered out from the ride." His head whipped back to Breen. "How fer did you say you come?"

"Hundred miles," Breen said. "Or in the neighborhood."

He clucked his tongue. "Well, that isn't that far in a state as big as Texas. But it sure ain't no Sunday stroll. Let 'em go, Franky. We shall resume their proper place in the morn."

Warden Franklin Plummer just stared into the horizon, eyes fixed like a dead man's.

"Franky."

When the warden refused to acknowledge, Peering laughed, cupped his hands over his mouth, and called out to one of the two guards standing beside the stocks occupied by the two brothers. "Lex. Get them boys out of the stocks and take 'em back to the fields."

"If you say so, sir, but they only have another hour of work before it's chow time."

"But I say so, Lex. And an hour of work is an hour of work. Cotton prices are high this year, too."

The guards moved to the racks. Peering sipped his bourbon, then reached over and took the glass in front of the warden.

Warden Plummer came alive. "Damnation!"

Which caused Peering to break out into a coyote-like laugh. "I thought you was sleepin' with your eyes wide op—"

But Plummer wasn't looking at the plantation owner. He was staring at the fields.

Two inmates were rolling across the rows, cursing. Other inmates moved away from the cotton plants or the heavy sacks filled with white balls, watching. Some cheered. Guards cursed. Whistles sang out.

"Fight!" one inmate yelled.

A pair of guards hurried toward the brawlers.

"No, gosh darn it, no!" Warden Plummer screamed. He pointed.

Peering was yelling, too, but he was staring at the brawling inmates.

"Stop 'em. Kill 'em. They's ruinin' fair to middlin' cotton!"

Fights held no interest to Sean Keegan, if he wasn't in the middle of the brawl, so he reached for the glass of bourbon that the warden had not touched. But Breen's eyes followed Plummer's. He saw the rising red dust from the far edge of the cotton fields.

"Captain Peering," he called out, but the farm's owner kept yelling at the guards to break up the fight before more cotton was ruined.

"Sean!"

That at least got the Irishman's attention. Breen pointed at the rising—and fast approaching—cloud of dust.

Keegan left the bourbon on the table. He leaped over the balustrade and found the saddles. He jerked out Breen's heavy Sharps, and tossed it. Breen caught it. Then Keegan pulled his Springfield from the sheath.

"It's a trick, boys!" Warden Plummer had found his voice. "We're being attacked!"

"What the Sam Hill are you talkin' about, Franky?" Captain Peering said.

Two explosions rang out from the cotton field.

The two guards running to break up the fight dropped behind the plants. The two prisoners who had been, presumably, fighting, came up and fired their revolvers, while two other field hands dived toward the downed guards. Within seconds, they came up with the dead or wounded guards' shotguns.

Closer to the big house, the Hardwick boys, freed from the stocks, took advantage of their situation. The two guards who had just unlocked them from the hard, hot wood, were staring either at the brawling in the fields or that fast-moving cloud of dust. Whichever, they weren't looking at the two returned escapees. The guards went down, the prisoners on top of them.

Jed Breen swung the big Sharps toward them, but he cursed, and brought the rifle back against his shoulder, aiming at the dust cloud that was almost halfway through the field. He couldn't shoot at the Hardwicks because he might kill a guard.

"By thunder, what is that comin' right at us?" Peering had finally seen the cloud of dust.

"Hell," Breen answered. And the Sharps roared.

CHAPTER 6

Sean Keegan braced the Springfield against the column. Drawing a bead on one of the riders galloping toward him, he let out his breath, paused, and knew in the next few seconds he would be sending some dirty rotten ambusher to meet Lucifer in that toasty pit. Just let the horse carry the fool a wee bit farther.

Before his pointer finger pressed the trigger, though, a slug of lead tore into the column, just inches above his head. Splinters flew, Keegan cursed and dropped onto the flooring, his ears ringing and a few splinters stuck in his neck.

He heard the roar of Jed Breen's Sharps rifle, but just barely. Sensing—not seeing, and barely hearing anything— Keegan rolled over. He had not punched the trigger. A rider came around the front of Peering's out-of-place plantation home. He looked like a Mexican, with a big sombrero, bearded face, and twin bandoliers of rifle cartridges criss-crossing his chest. Reins in his teeth, and a double-action revolver in his right hand, the rifle he had just fired at Keegan in his left, held out.

It was a single-shot, like Breen's Sharps and Keegan's .45-70. A bullet from the bandit's Smith & Wesson broke a window behind Keegan. Another thudded into the wall.

The horse kept galloping, and Keegan rolled away from the column, stopped on his belly in front of the steps. The rider was past the house and turning toward the fields. He was between two of the stocks when Keegan fired.

The man sailed over his horse's head, and the horse did not attempt to avoid trampling him before it reached the cotton fields. Keegan felt certain that that hombre did not feel the horse's hooves, though. From the spray of blood that came out of the outlaw's chest with the heavy chunk of lead, that man was likely dead before he ever flew out of the saddle.

Now Keegan rolled again till he reached the column on the far side of the steps. He sat up, bracing his back against the whitewashed cottonwood, opened the Springfield's breech, and reached into his pocket for another .45-70 cartridge.

On the other side of the porch, Jed Breen let his Sharps speak forcefully.

Keegan finished loading the rifle. He rose now, and aimed his rifle where he thought he'd find the Hardwick brothers. That was two hundred bucks to Breen and Keegan, and the bounty hunter had promised an even split. Keegan wasn't about to let that reward money slip through his fingers now on some governmental technicality. They had delivered the escapees, sure, but those old boys hadn't even been on the prison grounds for an hour before they were gone.

And they were gone.

Keegan lowered the rifle, and strained to see.

Two guards were lying on the ground, one faceup, the other facedown.

Nothing. Billy Ray and Jim Bob Hardwick had vanished.

He looked at the rows of cotton, but not for long. Two more riders came into view from the other side of the porch.

These two held revolvers in both hands, and two bullets tore off Keegan's old hat.

He dropped, his eardrums hurting from the whining that appeared to be ricocheting in his brain.

Another bullet carved a gash in the floorboards just inches from the heels of Keegan's worn-out army boots.

He let the riders pass, then came up and killed one of the raiders' horses. He didn't mean to kill the poor beast, but he had no time to make sure of his aim. And it worked out anyway. That rider went sailing as the horse somersaulted toward the white picket fence that surrounded a vegetable garden. The rider went screaming into the side of the stone well. The crunch of bone could be heard despite Keegan's still-ringing ears, and the man crumpled into a heap. The other rider did not look back, and Keegan retreated against the white-painted balustrade and searched for another .45-70 shell.

"Where are the Hardwicks?" he yelled at Breen, although he could not be certain the bounty hunter heard.

The warden had, however. He came up with a revolver and yelled. "Don't concern yourself with those Hardwicks! Cullen Brice is escaping!"

"Cullen Brice!" Jed Breen slid on his knees to the front right corner of the porch. The Sharps came up. "Where?"

The warden started to aim his pistol but a fusillade of gunfire sent him diving for cover. More glass shattered. The plantation owner covered his head and ears and balled up into the fetal position as glass shards and chunks of wood rained down on him.

Keegan rose to his knees. He saw two riders on one horse galloping toward the far field. That had to be the Hardwicks. He drew a bead. He'd have to shoot the horse, this time intentionally, but now thundering hooves and screaming horses came from his left. He turned the rifle's barrel in that direction, expecting to see a full regiment of charging bandits, but found a dozen or so horses, eyes filled with fright, their bodies coming at a gallop. Riderless horses. No saddles. Some of the animals looking like fine-blooded stallions and excellent broodmares—the quality of horses one didn't see often in Texas—even at Matt McCulloch's horse ranch.

They were being driven by more black-bearded, buckskin-dressed men with big hats—and plenty of weapons.

A bullet zipped past Keegan's ear.

He fell again, filling his lungs with scalding air.

"My horses!" Captain Peering seemed to regain his senses. He sat up, even started to stand, yelling now, "They are stealin' my prized thoroughbreds!"

Peering came to his knees, then stood erect, and he began running for the front steps. Bullets rained everywhere, and now Jed Breen dropped his Sharps, lowered his shoulder, and plowed into the plantation owner's thighs. His arms wrapped around the man's upper legs, and both crashed to the porch floor, then rolled down the steps.

"Blasted idiot." Keegan added a few foul words to that accurate description of Captain Peering. Another bullet shaved some hairs the back of Keegan's neck. He brought the Springfield to his shoulder, found the back of a fleeing bandit, and aimed at the spot where the bandoliers crossed right between the man's shoulder blades.

He touched the trigger, then made himself as small of a target as he could, and searched for another cartridge.

Breen's Sharps roared again. Keegan thought he heard a few shots from the nether regions of the cotton fields. The pounding of hooves slowly died down. The curses, on the other hand, grew louder.

Cautiously, he rose. Breen strode away from the porch steps, the smoking Sharps in his left hand, his right holding the double-action Colt .38. The warden rose from his knees, his face seemingly asking, "What the hell just happened?"

Which was a question in Keegan's mind. He had never heard of anyone, redskin or outlaw, raiding a prison. Granted, this wasn't exactly a prison, but a cotton operation, but it had plenty of guards. Just not as many as a while back. Jed Breen knelt over a couple of bodies.

In the fields, prisoners were moving toward the big house. Some of them carried bodies—bodies of prisoners, bodies of guards. Others helped wounded men with them. Guards helped prisoners, and prisoners assisted guards. One guard leaned over a body, stood up, shook his head, and made the sign of the cross.

Breen rose, found Keegan, and said, "These two are still breathing, but the Hardwicks did a good job of knocking them out. You got a doctor at this farm, Captain?"

The answer came from near the livery.

"Those sons of dogs murdered Doc Stacker!"

"They stole my best horses," Captain Peering whined. He didn't seem to have heard that they had murdered a sawbones. "They stole my best horses." Now he noticed something else. "Oh, goodness. Oh Lord. Look what they've done. Trampled rows and rows of cotton. This is . . . a disaster. A terrible disaster."

The warden loaded his revolver, and when Keegan stood beside Breen, Franklin Plummer tried to spit, but found no moisture in his mouth, so he wiped his lips, tried to swallow, and said, "Did you notice the two leaders?"

Breen blinked. "I couldn't tell a leader from a follower. They were all shooting at us."

"Well, I've seen the posters of Wild Kent and Mal Martínez. And as God as my witness, I saw those two."

"It makes sense." The leader of the guards who had greeted Keegan and Breen earlier nodded. Blood ran down a crease above his left ear, and another bullet must have creased the right hand just below the pinky finger. "Cullen Brice was one of the men they rode out with."

"Shoot," Breen whispered.

"And those two prisoners you brought in."

Breen looked at the fading dust, then at the horses the raiders had left behind—Keegan's and Breen's mounts, the horses they'd brought the prisoners in on, and a few strays that managed to get away from those the killers had stolen.

"Cullen Brice." Keegan spit and wiped his mouth.

He stood over the body of one of the men he had killed. Using the toe of his boot, he rolled the corpse over.

"I don't recognize him," Breen said, and only now did he holster his Colt.

"You don't have to. His outfit tells the story."

Breen nodded. "I know that."

"Comanchero," Keegan said.

"But not just any Comanchero. This piece of slime rode for Boss Linden."

Boss Linden. The last of the Comancheros. The most daring of them all. Wild Kent Montgomery and Mal Martínez were two of his lieutenants, so that explained why they had raided the prison farm.

"Those Hardwick boys . . ." Breen shook his head. "They might regret riding out with that bunch. There's a big difference between rustling cattle and trading . . ." He turned to spit out the gall in his mouth.

Keegan cursed, and found Peering. "Why in the devil's name did you bring Cullen Brice to this place? He should have been locked in the sweat box in Huntsville for the rest of his life."

"I did not ask for him," the Southerner said. "They send me who they send me, and they happened to send him."

"He was supposed to have hanged," the warden said, shaking his head. "When that sentence got commuted . . . well, it doesn't matter now."

Breen spit again.

"That's a hell of a thing," Warden Plummer said. "A raid like this. Cullen Brice freed. Men, prisoners and guards, killed, wounded. The Hardwick boys escape. We'll have to do a roll call to see if anyone else managed to break out. And we're in no business to go out after those renegades."

"Well, I'm out two hundred bucks," Breen said. "We'll be going after the Hardwicks. And I'll be bringing Wild Kent, Martínez, Cullen Brice, and, by thunder, Boss Linden in, too."

"Not right now." The warden drew his gun. He didn't aim it, not yet, but his face said he would if he had to.

"What the hell—" Breen started.

"I need your help," the warden said. "I've got wounded guards, and not enough to keep these prisoners from escaping. We're in a fix."

"You're in a fix," Breen said.

"Matt McCulloch's in a fix," Keegan said.

He waited till everyone looked at him.

"Matt killed Brice's brother. And that was after Matt caught Brice and put him in Huntsville. Remember? And I remember all the newspapers in Texas printed what Cullen Brice said when he got sentenced to hang. He said he'd be damned if he swung until after he had killed Matt McCulloch."

CHAPTER 7

Boots drove spades into the hard, West Texas ground, but only after a pickaxe had broken up enough of the rocky ground to make digging possible. Matt McCulloch and J.K.K. Hollister dug a grave without comment behind the remains of a West Texas home. Mary Ketchum would have company, resting beside her husband, and that might be of some comfort. They'd all be together now. Two daughters had died in infancy, and a son had died at age twelve, bucked off a horse. Mary kept those graves free of weeds, and kept the three crosses straight—hard doing in this country.

McCulloch left the spade in the dirt and began adjusting his gloves. Even with the leather protection, his fingers and palms were aching. He wiped his face and kept looking at Jim's grave, then the smaller ones.

"What are you thinking, Matt?" The Texas Ranger captain had paused to catch his breath and rest his aching muscles, too.

After wetting his lips with his tongue, McCulloch nodded in the general direction of the children's graves.

"Just wondering who'll look after the graves now that Mary's gone."

Hollister turned and focused on the well-pruned mounds, the perfect crosses, even the prickly pear cactus Mary had planted near the base of the crosses. A cactus wasn't a rose, but the prickly pear sure was pretty when it bloomed.

"I will," J.K.K. Hollister answered, and he pushed back his hat, let his hands find the right spots on the shovel, and dug up another pound of dirt and rocks and misery.

McCulloch studied the Texas Ranger closer now. The answer had surprised the horseman. Hollister, McCulloch had figured for years, was nothing but a politician, not one of the hard-riding Rangers that McCulloch had ridden with over the years. Maybe McCulloch had a beef with Hollister since he had been the captain that had driven McCulloch out of the Rangers. Yet there was one fact that McCulloch had finally learned to accept. J.K.K. Hollister really didn't have much of a choice in the matter, and McCulloch had grown to accept that he actually wanted to be freed from the Rangers.

Texas Rangers had laws they had to uphold and obey. A jackal had no such restrictions.

He started digging again.

They kept it up till they hit bedrock, roughly four feet down, and when the pickaxes made no progress, the two men looked at each other.

"Deep enough?" Hollister asked from his grave. "We won't get any deeper without dynamite."

McCulloch smiled. Dynamite. He started to tell a story about old Jim Hollister, but stopped. He pitched the pickaxe out of the hole.

The Ranger laid his pickaxe on the mound of dirt and rocks beside his shovel. "We can lay some stones on top." After flexing his gloved hands to get the feeling back in his fingers, he shielded his eyes and looked at the sun. "Well . . ."

Both men climbed out of the grave, and walked to the body they had wrapped and laid in the barn. Now they carried it, so light—and Mary Hollister had been stout, hard and stubborn—laying it into the grave as gently as possible.

Hollister said the prayer. McCulloch stood with his hat in his hand and mumbled an amen afterward. They covered the grave with the dirt they had moved, then searched another hour and topped the mound with stones. The cross wasn't as professionally carved as Jim's nor the children's, but maybe someone would put a real marker, and not planks from the barn with just a name crudely carved with knives.

"I guess . . ." McCulloch said as the two men saddled their horses in the barn. "Guess we ought to head back to my spread." He paused. *Spread* was an exaggeration. Years ago, maybe. But not since . . . He blocked that from his mind. "Find the bodies of the two men who did this that I sent to hell. Before someone finds them and starts raising a ruckus."

"No need." The Ranger pulled on the horn to make sure the saddle was straight and cinched tightly. "I left instructions on my desk for Sergeant Butler to see to that." He moved to the reins, grabbed them, and led the horse out into the sunlight.

When McCulloch finished, he did the same, starting again to alter his opinion about the captain. They walked their horses to the corrals and looked at the Ketchum horses, which they had grained and watered before starting the gravedigging jobs.

"Not much of an inheritance," Hollister said.

"No one left for the inheritance." McCulloch retightened the cinch.

"You want the horses?" the captain asked.

McCulloch shook his head. "I got no right to them."

"More than anybody else, I'd say. You killed the scum that murdered her."

"I got enough horses."

"Yeah. I'll send Butler back out here. He can drive them to Purgatory City. Let the courts settle ownership."

They knew they would not reach Purgatory City that day, and with a new moon both men knew better than to travel at night, so they made camp about ten miles from the old horse trader's place. Hollister cooked pretty good coffee, and the salt pork wasn't swimming in grease.

He stared at his hands and shook his head while offering a soft chuckle. "I didn't tell you what I found in Jim's tool shed, did I?"

McCulloch shook his head.

"Dynamite. Probably a full box. Hope it didn't leak and turn into nitroglycerin." He stared at his sore palms. "We could've used it to blast those graves."

It was a joke, but McCulloch did not laugh. "He bought that to make his well deeper."

Hollister's face showed doubt. "I don't reckon he ever used one stick."

Now McCulloch laughed softly. "Mary wouldn't let him. Said it might break the good china."

"I'll send some boys out with a buckboard," the Ranger said, changing the subject. "Fetch it back. Don't need that falling in the wrong hands."

"Good idea." McCulloch thought about the Ketchums. The dynamite was never used, he thought, not because of any fancy plates and saucers, but because neither Mary nor Jim would have wanted to disturb their children's graves.

They ate the meat with their fingers, which they wiped on their chaps, and finished the coffee over a small campfire, kicked out the fire, and dug into their bedrolls.

"Matt," the Ranger said.

"Yeah."

"I got a report from the Rurale captain in Agua Medianoche day before yesterday."

McCulloch waited without speaking.

"He reported that Boss Linden had skirted around the village and was heading with his men for the border."

"Well," McCulloch said when the Ranger added no more information. "I don't reckon Boss Linden skirted around that town. Not in his nature. Probably drank all the tequila in Agua Medianoche with his Comancheros till the village was dry, then those swine crossed the river into Texas."

He looked at the blackness overhead.

"That Mexican say when Linden crossed?"

"Two weeks ago."

McCulloch turned his hat and spit. "Nice of him to let you know as soon as he could."

The silence stretched.

"Not many Comanches left to trade with." McCulloch ended the silence. "What would bring him out of hiding in Mexico?"

"Apaches," Hollister said. "Maybe."

"He could trade with the Apaches south of the Rio Grande."

"But he couldn't get the guns the Apaches would want. And there are a few holdout Comanche bucks who would still want to do some trading."

McCulloch considered that theory, and offered a noncommittal grunt.

"What else?" he said after a long silence.

"Yesterday the major at Fort Elliott telegraphed that a shipment of Springfield rifles and Colt revolvers had been hijacked."

"That's the army's concern."

"For now. If Boss Linden got his hands on those weapons, though, it's my concern. Comancheros trading whiskey to Indians is one thing. But firearms? Indian wars aren't over yet. And this could be a bad one."

"Not yet." McCulloch turned toward the man he could not see but could hear. "Your concern, I mean. That would be the concern of the Ranger company closer to the Panhandle."

"Captain Brisbane hasn't even seen a Comanchero in two years."

"Because he hasn't left the saloons in Mobeetie from what I gather."

"Most likely. Most Rangers are solid men. Most leaders know what they're doing. But there's always one bad apple."

McCulloch wondered if he had been a bad apple. No, not really. He just did things his own way. He breathed in and out, and rolled back to look at the nothingness overhead. Then he asked, "What are you trying to get at, Captain?"

"I can't order my Rangers after someone we have not seen. If we were in pursuit, I could make a case. But by the time I got word of Linden being back in Texas, he had to be near the Panhandle if not already in his stronghold."

"And nobody has ever found Linden's stronghold," McCulloch pointed out, "and he's been heading the Comancheros for as long as I can recollect."

"Yep. But I thought a few private citizens might be up for the job."

McCulloch chuckled. "You mean three jackals."

"I didn't say a word."

"Well, Captain, next time Jed Breen rides into town, you ask him. He might be game. Last I checked, the state had put out a five-thousand-dollar reward for Linden. But I got no quarrel with Linden these days. He's left me alone."

"And Cullen Brice?"

"Brice is in prison. He's not getting out."

"Well." The captain shifted into a comfortable position. "It was just a thought."

And McCulloch was thinking. "Would Apaches be willing to ride that far up? The Texas Panhandle's a long way from their range."

"They blow through country like the West Texas wind. And rifles and revolvers—and women—would be to their liking. Besides, have you thought what kind of hell could be unleashed upon this country if Comanches and Apaches formed an alliance?"

"Ain't my department, Captain. I got my daughter to think about. She's home. And I'm trying to make something out of my life again. For her."

"It's her that I was thinking about," the Ranger said. "Her and every woman in Texas."

"Still no sale, Captain. I'd like to try to be a father again. Put all these years behind me, start new. Get back to horses. Get back to being something other than a jackal."

"Matt," the Ranger said, and then yawned. "You never were a jackal. You just got every deplorable job handed to you. And you saw to it that those jobs got done. Just like how you took care of those two fiends that murdered that good horse trader's lovely widow. You're about as decent as a man gets."

"Like hell." He laughed, and pulled his hat brim over his eyes.

That night, McCulloch dreamed.

* * *

"What you doing, Papa?" Cynthia Jane asks. She's six years old. No more. The ranch is in good shape, or getting in shape. McCulloch puts a boot on the shovel and pushes down.

"You digging a well?" Cynthia asks.

"No," he answers, and tosses dirt onto a pile.

"Well, what you digging?"

"A grave."

"Whose?"

"Everybody's."

And now he stands over the grave, or rather a trench, only he's no longer wearing the gravedigging outfit of a summer undershirt, tan britches, boots, bandanna, and hat. He's in his black Sunday-go-to-meeting duds. The beard stubble has been shaved off, and he holds his black bowler in his hands. He's standing on the mound of dirt he had been digging, and watching as faceless figures drop the bodies into the trench.

First, his oldest son. Then the younger. Then his mother. His father. The soldiers he served with during the War Between the States that had died of dysentery, malaria, smallpox, grapeshot, rifle fire, saber cuts, or just bad luck. His grandma on his mother's side, the one he never met. His littlest sister who lived only six weeks. The Rangers who had died performing their duty. Then Sean Keegan.

He gasps when he realizes that old Irishman is dead.

Then Captain J.K.K. Hollister.

Bondy, the gunsmith in Purgatory City.

His pretty daughter.

Another figure, but this one rolls over, so he cannot see the face. But he doesn't have to see the face. He can see the dozen exit wounds in the man's coat. And no one had hair that white other than Jed Breen.

Then he sees the men he has killed, or just some of them. And now Mary Ketchum. Her children. Her husband.

They keep piling on, and he wonders how he managed to dig a grave this deep, this wide, that can hold the bodies of almost everyone he has heard of or known. John Bell Hood of the Confederacy. Sam Houston of Texas glory. The newspaper editor from Purgatory City who had first branded McCulloch a jackal. The Apache leader who had kept Cynthia Jane McCulloch alive for all those years when she was a captive, when she had learned to be Apache, but never forgot all of her McCulloch blood.

More and more the bodies fall.

And then, through the tears, he sees Cynthia. Hands folded across her breasts, eyes closed. Suddenly they open, and she screams.

McCulloch woke, chilled from the sweat, shaking from the nightmare. He waited till his breathing became steady. Then he picked up the hat he must have knocked off. He stared up at the still black skies. Nearby, Captain J.K.K. Hollister snored.

One of the horses snorted.

He tried to laugh it off. *Who would think that a jackal has nightmares?* McCulloch closed his eyes. Over the course of his life—especially in the months immediately following the Indian massacre of his family—he had been awakened many times by bad dreams. They meant nothing.

But he did not even try to fall asleep again.

CHAPTER 8

Like a lot of merchants in West Texas—and through-out many frontier towns in the western United States and territories—the Bonderhoffs lived above the gun shop on what passed for the main street in Purgatory City.

Although Cynthia McCulloch had spent most of her young adult life living with Apaches, she had always been a bright girl. Unlike her brothers, she knew a lot more than just about horses, saddles, guns, and cattle. Even at a young age, her mother would often shake her head, grin, and say, "Child, you've got a head for business. Your father could sure take lessons from you."

The Bonderhoffs had a head for business, too, Cynthia thought when she woke up in the trundle bed in the upper story. Ramona slept in the main bed, and across the small hallway, Cynthia could hear the snores from Ramona's pa. They owned the store outright. Bondy had paid off his mortgage early, and could thank all the gunmen, bounty hunters like Jed Breen, soldiers—at least the officers—stationed at the nearby fort, Texas Rangers and other lawmen, and drunken cowboys for giving him a lot of business. It made good business sense to live above the store. No rent to pay for a place in town, or a mortgage on a home.

And in a town like Purgatory City, a savvy businessman had another reason to live above where he or she worked. A man or a woman who ran a business wanted to protect their investment.

Glass shattered below. Cynthia might not have heard the sound if the window had not been open to cool off the bedroom.

She had been lying atop the sheets and blankets, head on the pillow, eyes closed with the hopes that she might drift back to sleep. Now, her eyes opened. She thought she heard glass falling onto the wooden floor downstairs.

Quickly she realized her hands were balled into fists, and that sleep would not come again anytime soon.

Something else had changed. Cynthia strained to hear, but no noise came. No noise at all. She couldn't even hear Ramona breathing. And across the hall? Mr. Bonderhoff wasn't snoring anymore.

By the amount of light creeping through the open window, Cynthia guessed it had to be just past dawn. No horses clopping down the street. No businesses opening their doors. No thumps of this week's *New Weekly Herald Leader* smacking against walls. No "Good Morning, Missus So-And-So," and no boots stomping on boardwalks.

She waited for the next sound, expecting it, but praying she would not hear anything except the regular sounds of a West Texas town beginning a new day.

The bell above the door to Bonderhoff's Gun Shop jingled.

Someone had broken the glass, unlatched the lock, and now was starting to come inside.

Yet before Cynthia could sit up or cry out the alarm, Ramona had thrown off her covers, and swung her legs off the bed.

Cynthia's mouth opened, but she choked back any words and just let out a small breath.

The door downstairs opened.

Ramona stood quietly. "Stay here, Cynthia," she whispered and tiptoed toward the window.

There was nothing to see. The awning and the sign carved into a big gun covered the boardwalk. Cynthia had looked out the window enough the previous night to understand that.

Ramona picked up a sawed-off shotgun that leaned against the windowsill. Quietly, she opened the breech to check the loads, then clicked the barrels back into place. Cynthia sat up, but Ramona stopped her with a hard stare.

Her lips moved, but she said nothing, just mouthed the warning, or orders, again:

Stay . . . here.

Then she stepped out of the window, onto the little catwalk, and inched her way down to the corner.

Below, Cynthia thought she heard the sound of glass breaking on the store's floor, likely crushed by boots. She might have imagined it, but she knew the next sound—the door to Mr. Bonderhoff's room opening—was all too real. She could picture the older gent inching his way to the stairs. He probably held a gun, too.

A muffled thud came outside.

That would be Ramona dropping to the ground in the alley.

Stay here, Cynthia told herself.

"Like hell," she heard herself whisper, and she rose. Barefooted, dressed only in a camisole, she covered the length between bed and outer wall in no time. But she was Apache. Maybe not by blood, but one did not live with that tribe down in Mexico for more years than she wanted to remember and not become one. And she had had many good teachers. And before those Indians had kidnapped her and slaughtered her mother and brothers, she had had another excellent instructor in how to stay alive in a lawless frontier.

Matt McCulloch was a good teacher when it came to lessons like that.

She leaned against the wall and peered outside. That was something Ramona Bonderhoff had not done.

Downstairs, Mr. Bonderhoff yelled, "Stand still, boys, or you'll feel both barrels of buckshot."

"Don't shoot!" came a high-pitched squeal.

More glass crunched, the bell above the door sang out, and then, outside, came Ramona's voice.

"Didn't you hear what my papa said, boy? I've got a sawed-off Parker .10-gauge, and both barrels have double-aught in them."

That would have been it. There would be nothing for Cynthia to do except come downstairs and congratulate the Bonderhoffs for thwarting a burglary. But from her perch upstairs, she saw that these boys had an accomplice. A young lad dressed like a cowboy, except for a gunnysack pulled over his hat and face with holes cut out so he could see, made his way from across the street. He moved quietly, too. Like an Apache. And he was smart. The sack covered not just his head and face, but his hat. She had often heard her father say that he often recognized a person too far away to see the face, but, by Jehovah, a man might be recognized by the hat he wore.

"Hold it, missy," the man said, and he had to have stopped just near the awning. Cynthia couldn't see him now, but his voice sounded to be just below the window.

The cowhand raised his voice. "Hey, Gunsmith! I've got a .44 Remington aimed at this girly's back. So how about you both lower those scatter-guns and go back to sleep." That was not a question.

"You hurt my daughter—"

The man below cut off Mr. Bonderhoff's challenge.

"I won't hurt her, old man. I'll cut her in half."

Cynthia looked for a weapon. Nothing. Bondy had taken Cynthia's old revolver to clean and her knife to sharpen. Here she was in the bedroom of a gunsmith's daughter, and the only weapon—a formidable shotgun—had been taken by Ramona. No Colts. No Smith & Wessons. Neither Winchester nor bowie knife. She grabbed the only thing she could think of and stepped onto the catwalk.

And jumped.

Three Dogs, the Apache chieftain who had been like a father during Cynthia's captivity, had often said she was more catamount than child.

She landed lightly, bending her knees, springing up and turning around in one movement.

The cowboy who had stopped right behind Ramona spun around, opened his mouth, tried to bring his Remington's barrel so it would put a .44 round in Cynthia's middle, and then screamed and tried to duck. But he was far too slow.

The jar of mostly pennies smashed against his head, and down he went like he had been poleaxed. He managed to squeeze the trigger, but the bullet just blew a hole in the street, about ten yards to Cynthia's right and three feet behind her. The jar shattered. Coins scattered. The boy hit the ground hard and did not budge.

Inside, Bondy yelled, "Stand still!"

Ramona dropped to her knees, grabbed the shotgun, spun around toward the door and echoed: "You heard him. Move and you're dead!"

Cynthia shook the feeling back into her throbbing fingers, stepped over the sea of copper coins, and picked up the revolver the unconscious accomplice had dropped. She glanced at the barrel, making sure it wasn't clogged with Purgatory City dirt or horse droppings, and thumbed back the hammer.

"Is Pete . . . d-d-d-dead?" one of the burglars stammered.

"He'll live to hang," Cynthia said.

"H-h-h-hang?" The boy started sobbing.

Ramona laughed.

The gunshot had sounded the alarm. A Texas Ranger sergeant, the deputy marshal, and three businessmen who also lodged upstairs or in a room behind their store came charging from up and down the street. A few others pushed open their doors and watched with curiosity and from the safety of their wooden, stone, or adobe walls. The most adventurous spectators were the glassy-eyed drunks who wandered from the two saloons and one gambling hall that bragged that they had never closed their doors since opening.

The Texas Ranger took charge.

"What happened, Mr. Bonderhoff?"

"These two busted into my place," the gunsmith said. Ramona and I got the drop on the danged fools, but then that one—that scum—he must have been a lookout in the alley over there. He sneaked up on Ramona and threatened to kill her if I didn't lower my Greener. The girl there . . . she's staying with us. She's Matt McCulloch's daughter. She leaped down, and, well, hell's fire, Jimmy, I don't know what happened next. I was halfway upstairs. Couldn't see. But I dang sure could hear. And when that gun went off . . . Oh. . . . I thought my heart was gonna bust into a billion parts."

"She jumped," Ramona told the Ranger. "From the bedroom window." She pointed up. "I guess she found my savings." Now Ramona smiled. "That was money well worth saving, Cynthia! Thanks!"

The Ranger pushed up the brim of his big hat. "What about that gunshot?"

Cynthia reversed the grip on the Remington, and handed the long-barreled .44, butt forward, toward the lawman.

"He pulled the trigger," she said. "After I broke the jar against his noggin."

She stared at her bare feet.

The woman who sold the fancy hats cried out something that Cynthia did not catch, and then she forced her way past the deputy and a clerk at the general store wearing green sleeve garters, and held out a robe.

"Goodness gracious, child, you'll catch your death out here dressed in nothing but . . . that . . ." She slipped the pink garment over Cynthia's shoulders. "And you drunken loafers, stop with those leers. What kind of men are you? If you want to see a girl's unmentionables, I'm sure you know where you can go to find them. Sergeant Butler!"

"All right, boys. Move on. Move on or you'll be dealing with the Rangers."

The big man stared again at the one sprawled on the street, surrounded by coins.

"Milt. Fetch the doctor," the Ranger said. "Let's patch this boy's head up before you take him to jail." He turned to the deputy. "This is a matter for the town law, Johnson, not the Rangers." He glared at the others. "I said let's move on, folks. There's nothing here to see. It's all over. Harry. Why don't you fetch a pitcher from that saloon you run? Let Miss Bonderhoff pick up her money. Your fingers are bleeding, Miss McCulloch. Would you like the ol' sawbones to have a look at those."

Cynthia realized the Texas Ranger was talking to her. Only then did she glance at the fingers on her right hand and see the blood trickling down from where the glass shards must have cut them.

"I'll take care of that, Sergeant Butler," Ramona said.

"These boys must pay for the glass they broke," Mr. Bonderhoff said.

"That'll be up to the judge, Bondy," the Ranger said. "I said, break this up, folks. You got businesses to tend to, and I got a pot of coffee waiting to be drunk."

Slowly, the people disappeared. The two boys who had been caught inside the gun shop were roughly pushed toward the jail. The one with a bloodied temple and a knot rising on his head like a mushroom was hauled to the doctor's office. The Texas Ranger nodded at Cynthia and Ramona and went back to his office. And most of the people moved toward the café or the closest saloon and did their eyeballing from across the street.

Ramona guided Cynthia, still wearing the pink robe, into the office.

"Watch where you step!" Mr. Bonderhoff commanded. "Let me sweep up that glass." He muttered a few choice words of profanity underneath his breath.

"After I patch up those cuts," Ramona said, "how about you and me going to the café to get us some breakfast?"

Cynthia managed to smile. Now that she thought about it, she was quite hungry.

CHAPTER 9

With hardly a moon to guide their way, they rode all night. Jim Bob Hardwick couldn't believe how hard these men rode, how the horses managed to continue at such a pace. They did not bother to hide their trail. They just rode.

Rode.

Rode.

When dawn broke, the horses stopped, snorted, hanging their heads, lathered and breathing heavily. Jim Bob Hardwick's thighs ached, his backbone felt as if it had been acting like a hammer for several hours, and his shoulders hurt. So did his teeth from clacking against each other most of the night.

A black-bearded Mexican walked his palomino gelding up to him and grinned.

"Amigo," he said. "Follow me, *por favor.*"

"Have you seen my brother?" Hardwick asked.

"Follow me," the man replied, his tone cheery, and his rock-hard, sunbaked, beard-covered face as close to charitable as possible. *"Vamanos. Por favor."*

"I asked you a question, mister." Jim Bob Hardwick tried to sound as menacing as he could after being roughly handled by Jed Breen and his ex-soldier partner from that miserable canyon all the way back to that brutal prison farm, and then somehow surviving a bloody prison riot—no a prison break—and the hardest ride he had ever endured.

The Mexican sighed, and quickly palmed his handgun. "Amigo, I do not know your brother. And if you do not wish to follow me, I will gladly kill you now. Then you will find your brother whenever he arrives in Hell. It is your choice. You call the tune. Follow me, *por favor.* Or die." He grinned.

"Reckon I'll follow you." Somehow, Jim Bob Hardwick found enough saliva to force down a swallow.

The Mexican laughed and waved his gun barrel. "It is just an expression, amigo. I do not want you behind me. When I say follow me, what I mean is, I follow you. I tell you where to go. You obey. Or I blow your head off. So, follow me. *Por favor.*"

He kicked his worn-out horse into a walk, came out of the line of the other raiders, and rode south. He studied all the men he passed, but found no sign of Billy Ray.

It was light enough now that he could make out the country. Red earth with some tan and even paler patches. Rough hills. Stunted trees, mostly juniper, cactus, rocks.

They were in some valley, with a creek, mud-colored like the rest of the country, cutting a winding path, but the Mexican told Jim Bob to ride up the hill, and he let his horse follow a rabbit path—not much wider for anything else, and they followed something resembling a switchback till they crested the ridge.

He breathed a sigh of relief. There was Billy Ray, mounted on another winded horse.

The relief did not last long, though.

Another prisoner who had escaped Peering Farm was on his knees. A lariat was tight across his upper arms and chest, the rope held behind the prisoner by a man in dark brown leather. Jim Bob Hardwick had worked alongside that prisoner at the farm in the cotton fields, but darn if he could recall the old boy's name.

In front of the prisoner, a man sat on his horse. He, too, had been a field hand, but more often was confined to the blacksmith's shop on the farm, where the guards could keep a better eye on him, and make sure he was chained and enclosed by walls, not cotton plants. Everybody at Peering Farm knew his name. Cullen Brice.

"You can trust me, boss man," the old prisoner cried out.

"Trust you." Brice slid out of the saddle. "Yeah, I can trust you. Trust you to tell the warden anything you might have thought you heard me say. Trust you to get easy work while I sweated twelve hours a day, and even nights when they'd stick me in the sweat box for fun. How many times did you ever spend in the sweat box, amigo?"

"Boss, now, I know things."

Cullen Brice stepped behind the man, and when he tried to turn his head around, another Comanchero slapped it hard and snapped. "You look that way, hombre. You look. You listen."

"Harry's good at both looking and listening, Emilio." Brice put a hand atop the balding man's head. "He'd listen to whatever I might say. And he'd look out for his own worthless hide."

"No, boss." The man was sobbing now. "No. I know things."

"What do you know, Harry?"

"I . . . I . . . I . . . kno-no-no-know. . . ."

"Why in hell did you ride out with us, Harry? What did you have left on your sentence? Three years? Two?"

"Eighteen months." The man laughed and shook his head, then began sobbing again. "I just saw the horses, boss. Saw one with no rider. I dunno, boss. Somethin' come over me. And . . . well . . . I know I can help you."

"Help me, Harry. Tell me something I don't know."

Brice held out an empty left hand. A Comanchero unsheathed a Bowie knife and passed it, handle first, to Linden.

"I—I—I . . . I kno-no-no-know where . . . where . . . where M-M-M-Matt M-M-Mc-Cul-loch is."

Brice was bringing the big blade toward the sobbing prisoner's neck. Now he paused.

"Go on, Harry. You got my interest."

"Pu-Pu-Pu—"

"Purgatory City." Brice laughed. "Hell, boy, everybody knows that. He was there when he sent me to Huntsville."

"B-b-but . . . hi-his . . . d-d-d . . . daugh-ter. She's w-w-with h-him."

"His daughter got killed. Or at least taken by injuns years ago."

"H-h-he . . . f-f-found her."

The knife lowered. "The hell you say."

"I swear, Cullen, on my ma's grave." That came out without any hesitation. "I-i-it's t-t-true."

"It's true, Brice."

Jim Bob Hardwick drew a deep breath. He wanted to curse. He wanted to whisper a soft warning to his brother, who had just spoken up: *Keep your mouth shut, Billy Ray. You want to get all our throats slit?*

Brice spun around and found the speaker.

"Hardwick, ain't it?" Cullen Brice said.

"That's right. Billy Ray."

"Where's your brother, Hardwick?" Brice asked.

"He was with me when we left the farm. Don't know now."

Jim Bob decided not to speak up yet. He liked being incognito.

"So you've been picking cotton for a while now, bub. How the hell would you know anything about Matt McCulloch, that renegade lawman, or his girl."

"The library," Billy Ray said.

"The library?" Cullen Brice howled with laughter, and several renegades laughed, too.

"Y-y-yeah," the man on his knees cried. "N-n-news-p-p-pa-p-pers."

The Comanchero paused. He glanced at the man named Harry, then back at Billy Ray. "I'll be darned. Newspapers. In the library." He shook his head. "Almost makes me wish I'd learned my letters more than just writing my own name. Big letters, though. Capitals. Never bothered with them little puny letters. C-U-L-L-E-N . . . B-R-I-C-E. That's enough to get by in this country."

"I-I-I c-c-can . . . r-r-read—for you!" Harry managed to say.

"I bet you could, Harry. I bet you're a fine reader. But the thing is, Harry. I got this Hardwick boy to do my reading for me now."

The knife shot out savagely, expertly, quickly. Blood sprayed in front of the man on his knees. He reached out to stop the flow, but was falling. The man who held the lariat let it go. And Harry fell into a pool of his own blood and began twitching.

"His daughter, eh?" Cullen Brice held out the knife to its owner, who took it with great reluctance. Brice began walking toward Billy Ray Hardwick. "Newspapers. Which ones?"

Billy Ray breathed in and out. "Whatever Capt'n Peering or the warden could get, after they were done with 'em."

"But the Purgatory City paper was one?"

"Sometimes," Billy Ray Hardwick said. "It depends. A stage runs from El Paso through Purgatory City and then up through Fort Griffin and all the way to Fort Elliott in Mobeetie. Military road mostly, but the stage goes for the hide business mostly, and the bluebelly business."

"Passengers?"

"Usually businessmen. Men doing business with the army. And . . ." Billy Ray grinned. "Some hurdy-gurdy girls or . . . you know . . . ladies *de la noche.*"

"I might have use for you, Billy Ray Hardwick. Maybe your brother, too."

Well, Jim Bob Hardwick thought, a man can't live forever. He kicked his horse forward. The Comanchero behind him followed.

"Here I am," Jim Bob said. He saw the relief sweeping over his brother's face, but Jim Bob just glanced at his brother. He kept his eyes on Cullen Brice.

Brice did not speak until Hardwick reined up.

"You're the quiet one, eh?" Brice said.

"I speak when I got something to say."

"Can you read good?"

"Good enough. Capital and baby letters."

Brice smiled. "I like a man who knows when to talk and when to keep quiet. And I like a man with a wit, and one who ain't afraid to show that wit." He looked at his belt. "Seems I handed away that knife. I could have cut your throat, you know, for insulting me like that."

"If you would have kept the knife," Jim Bob Hardwick decided to gamble, "I might have kept mute."

This time the Comanchero laughed out loud.

"Like I say, you got wit. You got guts. And you can read. So if Billy Ray happens to get killed on our next raid, I'll let you take his place."

"My pleasure," Jim Bob said. He did not even look at his brother to let him know this was a joke. Because, hell, it probably wasn't a joke.

"Cullen." That came from one of the leaders of the Comanchero raid on Peering Farm.

"What is it, Montgomery?" Brice said.

"We ought to be moving to the canyon."

"You in a hurry?"

"There's a telegraph wire that runs from that prison farm," Wild Kent Montgomery said. "Remember?"

"I figured you boys were savvy enough to cut the wire."

"We did," said the other Comanchero leader, Mal Martínez. "In four places. Spliced it with rawhide to make it harder to spot than just a downed talking wire."

"See what I mean," Brice said.

"Yeah," Wild Kent Montgomery said. "But rawhide don't hold wire too good in this wind. And they ain't all fools who work at that farm. There were professionals doing a good job at shooting. Which is one reason we're well mounted. We left a bunch of good shots lying dead or dying to get you out of that prison. And we just got you out of that cotton patch." He pointed at the Hardwicks. "And them."

Cullen turned toward Billy Ray, reconsidered, and found Jim Bob Hardwick.

"You two broke out. I started to think you might have made it, or maybe died and got eaten by buzzards. Would you say you were captured and returned by *pro-fessionals*?"

"Jed Breen," Billy Ray said. "And Sean Keegan."

"I've heard of Breen. Bounty hunter." He spit. "How I hate a bounty hunter. Never heard of no mick named Sean Keegan."

"Former bluebelly," Billy Ray said. "But he and Breen are what have become known as 'The Jackals.'"

"Jackals. All right. Well, if they come after us, those two will be dead jackals."

"There's a third Jackal," Billy Ray Hardwick chimed in. "Matt McCulloch."

Cullen Brice paused, spat, then shrugged.

"Well, you can kill Breen and the mick. I'll take care of McCulloch. But right now, my business is finding a stagecoach. We'll stop it. Take what we can, money, guns, mules . . . and . . . if we're lucky . . . some women to sell."

"Cullen," Wild Kent Montgomery said, "Boss Linden sent us to bring you back. You and—"

Mal Martínez cut him off. "Amigo, Boss Linden, he did not order us to rob any stagecoach or find any women. And Boss is the boss for a good reason."

"That's right. And I'm his right-hand man. And I know that the only way I stay in his good favor is by honoring him. You got, as you've already said, a bunch of good men killed. Boss Linden. He won't like that. But if we bring him something he can sell to renegade injuns or even worse white men, then, hell, all of us might live to see next year."

He found the reins to his horse and swung into the saddle. "The buzzards and wolves will take care of Harry. Let's ride. You Hardwick boys, you find us a good place to ambush a stage. Mal Martínez, you take half the boys and the horses we got, and you head back to the Canyon of Weeping Women. Tell Boss that we'll be coming in as soon as we can. With gifts galore."

CHAPTER 10

He had never been a town man. Even when he had been stationed at the Texas Ranger company headquarters in Purgatory City, he had felt penned in by buildings. Purgatory City called itself a city, but it was only a town—and not much of one by most standards. But it was too big for Matt McCulloch. He preferred a ranch, even a small horse outfit like his, where he could see for miles. He didn't have to worry about neighbors, since the neighbors were miles away.

Yet he could see the advantages of living in a city. Especially for a young girl. If you didn't kill anything for supper, you could eat in a restaurant. If you got sick, you could find a doctor. If you wanted a new dress, there was more than one store, and at least one dressmaker in town. You could read a newspaper; there might not be much happening in Purgatory City or the county, but the paper often reprinted writings from other newspapers in the big cities back east, sometimes even across the Atlantic Ocean. Books—not just the Bible—could be found at a mercantile. Most of those stores carried catalogs, so you could see what the newest fashions were in New Orleans, Paris, London, or New York City. There were people you could talk to, about just about anything. You didn't have to make conversation to

your horse just to hear human words spoken. Buildings—
not fence posts—served as windbreaks. The telegraph
office could link you with friends or relatives in El Paso or
Dallas, even Little Rock or San Francisco. And if you
wanted to see something new, a stagecoach could carry you
to El Paso or Dallas, to a railroad, to just about anywhere.
There was even a schoolhouse, paid for by subscriptions,
and a smart young schoolmaster. All McCulloch had were
three of McGuffey's Readers. Cynthia had devoured them
in a month.

Well, she always had been a fast learner. Unlike her
brothers, who had been well on their way to becoming just
as mule-headed as . . .

McCulloch stopped that thought.

He rode into Purgatory City with Ranger Captain J.K.K.
Hollister, hearing the pounding of hammer on iron at the
blacksmith's shop, the cheers at a roulette wheel or faro
layout at The Palace of Purgatory City; smelling the hash
browns frying at that popular Alamo Café and the enchiladas cooking at the Mexican grub down the street.

Both men reined up in front of Bonderhoff's Gun Shop
and noticed the piece of wood nailed up over the glass in
the front door.

"Looks like Bondy had some trouble," the Texas Ranger
said.

McCulloch swung down and secured his horse to the
hitch rail. "Might have been testing one of the guns he was
cleaning and shot out the glass," he said.

The Ranger chuckled.

With a grin, McCulloch ducked underneath the reins
and his horse's head, and came up, extending his right hand
toward Hollister. Even a year earlier, McCulloch never
could have envisioned him doing that. Or the lawman
beaming as they shook firm and fast.

"Will you think about what I asked you, Matt?" Hollister asked.

"I thought about it, Captain. But I wish you luck."

"Take care of yourself, Matt. And keep an eye on that daughter. Were I a younger man, and didn't have a wife in Galveston, I'd be tempted to call on you."

"And I'd be tempted to fill your backside with birdshot."

They laughed, shook hands again, and Captain J.K.K. Hollister turned his horse and rode toward the company headquarters.

McCulloch watched him go, then turned, frowning at the door to the gun shop. He tipped his hat toward a middle-aged lady who walked down the boardwalk, hurrying when she spotted McCulloch. She did not acknowledge the greeting, but he was used to that. He stepped to the door, found the handle, and pulled the door open. The bell chimed as it always did.

But behind the counter, Bonderhoff, who was busy ramming a greased rag down the barrel of an army Colt, stepped back, dropped the gun on the newspapers he had covered his workspace with, and reached for a double-action revolver next to the cash register.

Standing still, McCulloch waited.

"Oh, hell, Matt." Bondy immediately lowered the pistol, and wiped his fingers on his badly stained apron.

McCulloch closed the door. He saw the broken pane, and figured out that this had not been an accident.

"You're jumpy." McCulloch turned around and walked to the counter, which Bondy reached over and came up with a jug of his homemade corn liquor. After cleaning his hands with a rag, he pulled out the cork, lifted the jug, and held it out toward McCulloch.

"No, but thank you," McCulloch said, and watched the gunsmith take a pull, smack his lips, and set the brown-and-tan container next to the register, return the cork, and wipe his lips.

McCulloch hooked his thumb toward the door.

"Trouble."

Bondy started his answer with a shrug. He then returned the liquor to its hiding place, and when he rose, he saw McCulloch's face.

"Some punk kids. Tried to break in this morning. Well, hell, they did break in. We took care of it in a hurry. They're over in the jail now. Well, two of them. The third, I think, might still be at the doc's."

McCulloch said: "We?"

Bondy's shoulders sagged as he sighed. "Ramona. Not the first time she's had to do something like this. And . . . well . . . yeah, Cynthia took a hand." He seemed to toy with the thought of smiling, just to ease the tension he had to read in McCulloch's eyes.

"How big of a hand?"

Bondy could sigh like no one else. "She clubbed the guy that was still at the doc's, at least right before the girls went off to eat." He laughed. "I thought boys had big appetites, but Ramona and Cynthia, they can put away a steak and not get any fatter." He rubbed his stomach.

"She pistol-whipped him?"

Bondy wet his lips and glanced down at that shelf that held his bracer. But he didn't drink again, because the gunsmith had a reputation for not drinking more than he should.

"Hell's fire, Matt," he said at length. "There were three of them. Two came in the store. Ramona jumped down." He motioned with his head toward the ceiling. "Came up behind them and got them covered. That's the third, no fourth, time she has had to do that. But those other times, there was just one, maybe two. Drunks usually. I supposed these boys were glassy-eyed, too. Except, these boys had another one keeping a lookout. He got the drop on Ramona. Had her covered with a shotgun, Matt. A shotgun. So your daughter, she jumped from the window, that little bit of trim, the four-by-four the carpenters put up there, for decoration, and to hold up my big sign. Sprang up like a panther, and put that third boy on the ground before he knew what hit him. Then had the shotgun on the other two. It happened so fast, hell, I don't rightly reckon I would have known what happened had Cynthia not explained it to Sergeant Butler and Deputy Collins."

McCulloch tried to comprehend everything he had just heard. He thought he might ask the gunsmith to explain that one more time, but at a slower gait.

"The girls are fine, Matt. Fine. Oh, Cynthia had some cuts on her fingers."

"From . . . ?"

"Oh." This time Bondy returned with the jug. He had another sip, and left it, uncorked, near the register. "I guess I didn't tell you that. Ramona saves a lot of change. Pennies. Half dimes. You know. Keeps them in a jar on her dresser. I guess that's the only thing Cynthia could find to use as a weapon, seeing how Ramona jumped down with the scatter-gun she keeps in her room. So she bounced up like a panther when she hit the street, and smacked that son of a gun on the head with the jar so hard it shattered."

He drank another sip.

"That's why the doc wouldn't let Deputy Collins take the third punk to jail. Wants to keep him overnight, maybe tomorrow, too. Something about a concussion. Or maybe a fractured skull."

Matt McCulloch didn't remember reaching over and dragging the jug of Bondy's personal brew off the counter, or even drinking it. He saw his hand return the stoneware to the counter, and saw Bondy pick up the cork, but just play with it in his fingers instead of ramming it into the mouthpiece of the clay jug.

"The girls are fine, Matt. Those cuts weren't deep. And, like I say, they done good. Chips off both of their daddy's blocks, I'd say. Stopped me from getting robbed. And maybe, the boys being as young as they look, this might be an end to their criminal ways. I was thinking that I wouldn't press charges, you see. If they would maybe work it off. Enough to pay for the glass in the door. You know what they charge for window glass these days, Matt? Well, you wouldn't believe it. Two of them, I mean. The two in jail. That third punk, though. I think he's gonna spend some time behind bars. Maybe not prison. Not on a first offense, if it is his first offense, but here in jail. You don't point a shotgun at my daughter, Matt, and threaten to kill her. No, sir. It could have had a far worse ending, Matt. I'm sure glad Cynthia was staying with us. Mighty glad."

Both men spun around when that little bell sang out and the door swung open.

Bondy moved the fastest. He had that cork rammed in the jug and the jug out of sight before the door closed.

"Papa!" Cynthia ran and leaped into her father's arms, but not before McCulloch glimpsed the bandages over two fingers and the back of her right hand. "When did you get back?"

"Just now." He made himself smile. He jerked a thumb as Bondy rose from behind the counter. "Mr. Bonderhoff was filling me in on your—"

"Oh, Papa, I see that look in your eyes. It was nothing. Ramona and Mr. Bonderhoff did all the work. And this." He wiggled her fingers. "You've cut yourself worse shaving. Which you wouldn't do if you'd come to town for a proper shaving with a sharp razor."

McCulloch wiped his beard-stubbled face with the back of his hand.

"Well." He smiled. But that faded when he saw the yellow piece of telegraph paper in his daughter's left hand.

"What's that?" he asked.

She seemed to have forgotten it was there.

"Oh." Cynthia held it toward him. "That boy, Oscar. The freckled-face fellow who works at the depot. He got this and saw Ramona and me in the dress shop. Said it was for you. I paid him."

"With the pennies from Ramona's jar you busted?" He made himself smile, but he wasn't finding much levity in the story Bonderhoff had just told him.

"No, Papa. Quit your joshing. From the allowance you gave me. Remember?"

He nodded. Then he took the telegram, unfolded it, and looked at her.

"Did you read it first?"

She hesitated. "Ramona and I just glanced at it. Accidentally."

"Uh-huh."

His eyes went down to the paper.

"It didn't make sense to us. Just names."

"The only ones we recognized were Jed's . . ." Ramona swallowed. "Mr. Breen's. And Sergeant Keegan's."

Matthew McCulloch, on the other hand, recognized all the names. And it made perfect sense to him.

CHAPTER 11

"Hey, Boss."

Jed Breen had just stepped out of the telegraph office at Peering Farm. Immediately, he pulled the .38 Colt from his holster and aimed it at the man in prison clothes.

Breen had seen dead cactus skeletons bigger than this cuss. Or so it seemed. He would have suspected the inmate to have been sick with consumption except for his bronzed, wrinkled face. And those green eyes were full of life, vinegar, and deadly menace. But his hands were empty, spread out from his hips, and his weathered face cracked with a grin. Thin as he might be, small as he stood, Breen figured it wise to keep the Lightning aimed at the man for the moment.

"You want something?" Breen asked.

The man's teeth shone white. So clean and straight, Breen thought they had to be ivory dentures, but, hell, even ivory yellowed with age. And this man had seen some years. The teeth didn't wiggle, and the man didn't whistle when he spoke. Maybe he still had a full set of chompers. The face was hard, the smile was friendly, but those eyes . . . those green eyes were as deadly as a rattlesnake.

"Just wondering if you got a reply yet?"

"What do you mean?"

"Now, boss, I've been in this farm for thirteen months, and in the big house down in Huntsville for three years before that. You sent a telegraph to your pard, Matt McCulloch. I just want to know if you've heard back from him."

"How do you know I wired McCulloch?"

The man's thin neck shook his hard head. "Because he's your pard. And you would make sure he knew Cullen Brice got away."

"All right. So what makes it your business?"

"Not what. *Who*. I make it my business."

"It's not your business. And there's cotton to be picked."

He nodded. "Well, you just let me know when you hear from McCulloch. If you'd be so kind. And if you don't. You'd be smart to tell him about this here conversation."

Breen waved the revolver. "Cotton. Remember."

"I remember, boss."

It wasn't much of a conversation, and hardly even an argument. The man tipped his cap, turned, and walked his bowlegged walk back toward the fields. Breen saw Sean Keegan standing at the edge of the field, shotgun in his hand, staring at the leathery little man who walked past the old cavalryman, tipping his hat with respect, and grabbing a sack, then heading toward the other inmates who were back at work.

Breen watched him for a long time, then went back into the telegraph office.

"You know how to sign it, Karl," the warden said, and the telegrapher nodded and started clicking.

Keegan, two trustees and two guards had found the various places where the Comanchero raiders had cut the wires, then spliced them with rawhide. They had done it in pretty good time, too, and the warden and Captain Peering had let Breen send his telegraph. They might not have liked doing that—the warden was particular about his budget, and telegrams cost money—but they figured it was in their best interest.

Besides, the warden, the plantation owner, all the surviving guards, and most of the inmates knew how much worse things could have turned out when the Comancheros hit the prison farm had Breen and Keegan not been here.

"Warden." Breen waited till the telegrapher had finished his clicking.

Franklin Plummer looked about ten years older than he had when Breen and Keegan arrived at the farm. "Yeah?" he said in a hoarse whisper.

"You got a prisoner here," Breen said. He held his arm out to his shoulder. "About this high. Sunburned face. Green eyes. About a thin as a strand of barbed wire."

The warden sighed. "Green Clayton. He give you any trouble?"

"No. Not exactly. He was just asking about the wire we sent."

The wire clicked. Plummer turned to the telegrapher, who struck a few clicks himself. "Just acknowledging receipt, Warden, sir," the man said.

Plummer looked back at Breen. "If you work in prisons long enough, Mr. Breen, you will know that you cannot keep a secret from an inmate. No matter how hard you try." He pointed at a window in the back. "These walls are thin—Captain Peering is business minded, and not prone to spend money on thick walls or windows that you can't hear through. Some of the prisoners know the code and can probably work a telegraph better than Herr Lamsdorf here. And some of my guards are just like the prisoners. They'll exchange information for the fruitcake some inmate's mother mailed him from Nacogdoches."

Breen had been in the bounty-hunting business long enough to know that. "What's this . . . Green Clayton . . . in for?"

"Twenty years hard labor. I'd guess seventeen or eighteen left to serve. Robbery, possession of stolen property, kidnapping, attempted murder." Franklin's head shook. "Maybe a few other charges. Undoubtedly not charged with some crimes he most certainly has done."

"He mentioned Matt McCulloch."

The warden shook his head. "I don't know that their paths ever crossed. Clayton was arrested by deputy sheriffs in Shackelford County. The Texas Rangers had nothing to do with his arrest, trial, conviction, or sentence."

Breen's lips flattened. He had hoped to learn more.

"Clayton's no fool, Mr. Breen," the warden explained. "He knows who you are, and your sergeant friend. He knows McCulloch's reputation as the third jackal of Purgatory City." He paused just for a moment. "No offense."

Breen nodded. He still wasn't satisfied.

"Undoubtedly, Green Clayton—I don't know if that's his real name or if it was just given to him because of those eyes he has. But, undoubtedly, Green Clayton is working on a scheme. He'd like to get away from this cotton patch in the middle of Hades. Figures you might get him out."

"Why? What does he have to offer?"

"Boss Linden. Cullen Brice. And the murderous fiends who are the reason you have not left Peering Farm yet."

"He's a Comanchero?" Breen asked.

"He was. Hence the kidnapping and most of the other charges. Rode for Boss Linden. I'm surprised, with your occupation, that you've never heard of Green Clayton."

"Texas is a big state. Too many wanted posters for one man to read."

The warden nodded with a smile. "Well, I expect Green Clayton might have a motive now to help the law out. If the law ever comes here. Since Wild Kent Montgomery and Mal Martínez apparently rode here to free Cullen Brice, and only Cullen Brice, and left Clayton here to finish his sentence."

That made some sense. Enough to satisfy Breen for now.

"Thanks, Warden," he said. He turned around and started to open the door.

"I should thank you and Sergeant Keegan," the warden said.

Breen looked back over his shoulder.

The warden offered a tired smile. "You two agreed to stay here. Help us guard the prisoners. We're short on hands and eyes and men who know how to pull a trigger after that raid. And will be till we get help from the army, the Rangers, or the county."

"Not like we could have done anything else, Warden," Breen said. "I believe we were conscripted into this job." He sighed. "But, I understand. Too many bad guys would have gotten out."

"And every one would have had a reward on his head."

Breen smiled. This time he opened the door.

"I'm not that bounty-hungry, Warden." Stepping outside, he closed the door, and walked to Keegan. The former cavalry trooper pushed his hat brim up and shook his head as Breen approached.

"I was standing here hoping, laddie, that you might have thought about bringing me a nice lager to quench me thirst. It be tedious and hot work here, looking at these swine, and not even a cool breeze blowing in a country where I thought the wind always showed its fierceness."

Breen got to the point. "You ever hear Matt mention an owlhoot by name of Green Clayton?"

"Nay, laddie. But conversing with Matt McCulloch isn't the easiest thing in this part of the country to do. He lacks the gift of gab that I possess."

"Hell." Breen spit onto a plucked cotton plant.

"Who be this Clayton Green?" Keegan asked.

"Green Clayton," Breen corrected, and he pointed at the small convict who wasn't doing much work at picking cotton.

"Puny lad," Keegan remarked. "Don't look like much to worry yourself over, and I would gladly bet on Matt McCulloch whipping him in a fight—gun, fists, knives."

"He rode with Boss Linden," Breen said.

"Aye." Keegan reappraised the runt. "Well, why didn't that terror free him during the raid?"

"I don't know."

Keegan changed the subject. "Did ye happen to get that telegram off to Matt, laddie?"

Breen nodded. "I told him what had happened. That Cullen Brice broke out of the farm here. That Boss Linden's lieutenants led the raid. That we were stuck here till we got some guard help."

"Did ye tell him that we would be willing to ride with him?"

Breen shook his head.

"Wasn't that the point?"

"No," Breen said. "The point was to warn Matt that Cullen Brice wasn't behind bars—or cotton balls. If Matt wants help from us, he'll . . ."

"Ask for it?" Keegan spit and shook his head. "Ye know Matt McCulloch better than that, Jed, me lad. You think the two of us could bring in Boss Linden and his gang by ourselves?"

"Not if we don't get out of this prison-guard duty in a hurry." Breen cursed underneath his breath. "Hell, those boys are likely back in their stronghold by now. It'd take a month of Sundays just to find a trail. And then more just to luck our way into that camp. We'd need Comanches to lead us to that place."

"Aye, and Comanches wouldn't be so inclined to take us to the place that brings them guns and powder and lead and . . ."

"Women," Breen said.

"Aye." Keegan frowned. "That's what galls me. It's bad to trade guns and bullets to those Indians, but that is just business. We gave guns to the Mexicans to overthrow that emperor ruling Mexico right after the Rebellion. And trading for weapons has been going on since the first fight on our Mother Earth. But that other. Enslaving good women. That's just . . . wrong."

"Comancheros have been doing it for thirty years," Breen said.

"Or longer."

Breen looked around the cotton fields, then stared right at Keegan. "I'd like to end it. Put Boss Linden out of business. And not for the reward, either."

"I hear ye, laddie. And I'd be right willing to work alongside ye." Keegan grinned. "But I wouldn't turn down any reward the good citizens of Texas and the government of this Lone Star State might offer us."

Breen put his hand on his holstered revolver's handle. Keegan took a few steps to the bounty hunter's left.

The little runt, Green Clayton, had left his cotton sack and was walking straight for the pair.

He stopped in front of Keegan.

"You the Irish jackal I've heard about?" the little man asked.

"Irish, I proudly admit." Keegan grinned. "Jackal is a matter of opinion. But what business do you have with me?"

"This."

The little man buried the foot of his left work boot in Keegan's groin.

CHAPTER 12

Having been in a number of brawls—more than most enlisted men in the old man's army could count—in which the Marquess of Queensberry rules were not followed, but ridiculed, Sean Keegan managed to twist his body just enough to avoid taking a breath-sucking blow below the belt. That didn't mean the boot did not hurt. It hurt like blazes, and Sean Keegan groaned, felt that he might vomit, and sank to his knees. He tried to block out the pain, and worked even harder not to let his vision blur.

He had to keep that little cuss in sight.

Well, he saw this Green Clayton cuss. Saw him grinning like a punk who had just swallowed the last of his ma's Irish pasties. Pastie. That's about what Keegan felt his face must have looked like. He saw the fist, but Keegan remained too numb to do anything about it.

Then he saw stars, a flashing bright light, and felt as though he could see himself falling to his left, like he had been coldcocked. Which he had. He figured that out when he hit the dirt.

His brain cleared the way it did during a fight. Now that he had been kicked below the belt and allowed a haymaker to knock him to the dirt, Sean Keegan let those instincts take over. He drew in a deep breath and pushed his face and chest out of the plowed earth.

"Hold it, Clayton."

That sounded like Jed Breen's voice. If Jed Breen were five hundred yards away. But Jed Breen, Keegan knew, was just a few feet from where Keegan was smelling the churned earth.

The next sound was Green Clayton's laughter.

"Nay," Keegan felt his lips move and thought he heard his own voice. "Nay, Jed."

He came to his knees. It hurt to breathe. Hurt his head. Hurt his private parts. Hurt his dignity.

"Laddie." It hurt to even say that. "I shall handle . . . this."

Footsteps sounded all around Keegan. He saw guards rushing toward him. They probably feared a riot, or another breakout was starting. He saw prisoners running through the cotton rows. They probably knew this was a fight between a fellow inmate and some Irish pig who had volunteered to be a guard for a wee bit. They just wanted to see the show. That was something Keegan understood.

He realized he was standing on his own two feet. Maybe not steadily. Maybe a hard gust could knock him down. But he'd never let that scrawny little cuss put him on the dirt again.

"Is . . . that . . . ?" Keegan wondered if the words reached anyone. He wasn't even sure he was saying them. That blow to his noggin, after that dirty low blow, had put reality at a precarious position. "Is that . . . the best . . . ye can do . . . shorty?"

Aye, now that wasn't an illusion. He saw Green Clayton's grin disappear, and those verdant eyes turn black.

"Sean . . ." Jed Breen sounded skeptical. If the man would just stand still for a moment, keep from becoming two or three white-haired bounty hunters, stop falling out of focus, and if his voice wouldn't sound like he was a frog forty feet down a hole, Keegan might have heard the rest of what his partner said.

But the runt was walking toward Keegan now, and the Irishman made fists in both hands.

Breen came into clear focus for a moment. He did not holster his Colt, but he turned his head toward the closest guards and said, "Hold up there, boys. This is a personal fight between these two hombres. Let them have at it."

Keegan almost smiled, but he saw the runt. Keegan swung, a hard blow that caught air. The momentum almost drove Keegan into a twisted knot. He felt himself staggering, swaying, but he kept his feet, spun back and sent another punch at this Clayton Green or Green Clayton or whatever his name was.

He missed again.

The little punk laughed.

Jed Breen yelled, "You're swinging over his head, Sean. You're swinging over his head."

Aye, Keegan thought. *Of course I am. But that's because this little devil hasn't grown to man-size yet.*

He saw the attacker standing in front of him now. Saw that mocking grin on his ugly face. And then he saw the work boot, coming up, right for the same precious spot.

But this time Keegan twisted around. The midget's leg caught nothing but air, and Keegan spun, and swung again. This time his fist was almost low enough to make contact, but he only skimmed through the hair atop Clayton's noggin.

And Clayton ducked, coughed, and threw a series of jabs. One hit the holster. And the crack and curse told Keegan that Green Clayton had punched the revolver, and not Keegan's privates. And the revolver hurt the punk's knuckles.

When Keegan found the attacker again, the Comanchero was sucking on his knuckles. The smile was long gone.

"Ha!" Keegan snorted in triumph.

That made the little cuss mad. The hand dropped, the lips formed a snarling curse, and he lowered his shoulder and charged. Keegan spun, but stuck his leg out, and Green Clayton tripped and went flying toward some of the prison guards. Keegan himself went to the ground, but he rolled over and started to push himself up.

He found Clayton coming right back at him. There was no time to stand up, so Keegan did what he liked to call his barrel roll. He rolled over toward the charging attacker. The mad-dog fool's knees connected with Keegan's sides— hurt like the dickens against his ribs—and Clayton let out a yip like a puppy dog when he went flying over the Irishman. Keegan stopped rolling, flattened his palms against the dirt, and pushed himself up.

Clayton was already on his feet, and he came charging at Keegan, eyes mad, lips bleeding, cussing like a mad dog. Keegan swung, but again, caught nothing but air. He felt two blows in his side, but his ribs were too hard to break. Clayton spun away. Keegan tried swinging down, thought he might be able to drive the punk to the roots of the cotton plants if he could just connect. But his arm just glanced off the small guy's shoulder.

There was something like victory, though. Green Clayton cried out in pain, and fell back, cussing, then wiping his bloodied lips with the back of his hand.

Both men where wheezing now, fighting for breath. Both seemed to have trouble standing.

The guards cheered for Keegan.

Some prisoners cheered for Keegan.

Green Clayton, Keegan was learning, didn't have many friends on this farm.

"I'm gonna put you . . . on . . . your . . . arse." Green Clayton managed to say.

The fists clenched, and the arms came up in a pugilist's stance. His feet began dancing a jig, and the little man was bouncing all around Keegan, moving in a circle. Keegan turned with the punk, around and around, then stopped. The fool was trying to make him dizzy or seasick. Something like that.

Keegan kicked. He usually didn't like to fight with boots and toes. It didn't seem sporting. But this fool had started this ruckus by trying to castrate Keegan or at least shove his valuables up to his voice box.

The toe caught the little fiend's thigh. Probably would leave quite the bruise, and Clayton stumbled but did not fall to the ground. Only because he staggered into Jed Breen.

Clayton cursed, grabbed Breen's gunbelt, and tried to pull the bounty hunter to the ground. Instead, Jed Breen clipped the inmate's head with the barrel of the .38 Colt.

Grabbing the top of his head with his left hand, the leathery Comanchero staggered back, groaned, and for a second looked as if he were going to charge Jed Breen.

That's when Captain Peering raised a big black cane with an ivory grip, and smashed it atop Green Clayton's head.

Sean Keegan tried to understand what he had just seen. He also wondered when the plantation king had arrived at the large, makeshift boxing arena. Keegan shook his head, put up his fists again, and walked to end this fight. But he couldn't find the punk.

Until he tripped over the body, and fell in front of Jed Breen's boots.

"Neither of you are Jack Broughton, and I will not stand to watch you ruin my cotton fields. Those renegades have already cost me a fortune."

Keegan realized Captain Peering was talking.

"You guards are paid to make sure these prisoners work. Not show the poorest exhibition of prizefightin' ever staged in the entire globe. You prisoners are here to pick cotton. So get pickin'. My word. I could have whipped these two fools with one hand tied behind my back." He turned around and stormed back to the comfort of his porch.

Keegan stared down at the unconscious Comanchero. "What set this runt off on me? I was just minding me own business."

One of the inmates answered. "He's a mean man. Wants to show he can whup anybody."

"Aye. Well, he met his match. Let that be a lesson to ye all. I . . ." He found Breen shaking his head, giving Keegan that soulful you-must-be-kidding-me look.

"You prisoners!" a guard snapped. "You heard what Capt'n Peering said. Back to the cotton plants, you scum. Back. Quit burnin' daylight and let's get the last of this cotton picked."

Keegan didn't bother watching the men go. He was still trying to catch his breath. He was still wondering how the hell he could still be standing. He looked down at the unconscious Comanchero.

"Ye didn't have to do that," Keegan said. "And neither did Captain Peering."

Breen kept shaking his head.

"I was wearing him down." Keegan had to let everyone know that he had not been fought to a draw by a man more than a foot shorter than he was. That he would have won handily if Breen and that plantation owner had not interfered. "I would have taken him in a few minutes. Would have knocked his head off had he not delivered that low blow."

"Sean," Breen said. "You wouldn't have knocked his head off until he grew another fourteen or fifteen inches."

CHAPTER 13

CABLE MESSAGE
The West Texas Telegraph Co.
TO: McCulloch, Matt, General Delivery
Purgatory City, Texas
Received at: Purgatory City, Tex.

MESSAGE: *Comanchero raiders struck Peering
Farm yesterday. Part of Boss Linden group. Led by
Wild Kent and M. Martinez. Killed 4. 8 wounded.
Freed 2 no-account rustlers. And Cullen Brice.
Rode into Comanchero country. Keegan and me
must guard inmates till replacements for guards
arrive. Then we will pursue killers. Watch yourself.
Cullen Brice.*

> Signed:
> Jed Breen

"I'm sure glad Jed wasn't hurt," Ramona said. She
quickly added, "And Sergeant Keegan, too."

"Papa?" Cynthia asked.

She asked again.

On the third time, McCulloch looked up from the telegram he had crumpled into his hand.

"Are you all right, Papa?" his daughter asked.

He made himself smile. The telegraph paper, he almost tossed into the street, but thought better of that and shoved it into his pants pocket. "Yeah. I'm hungry." He wasn't even close to hungry, and doubted if he could swallow half a biscuit washed down with good coffee. "You two girls want to eat?"

They frowned, which was what McCulloch hoped they would do. "We just ate, Mr. McCulloch," Ramona said. "But . . ."

"Oh, that's all right," he said, smiling again. "I forgot. Y'all better help Bondy get that door pane fixed up. You two seemed to have done more damage than Sean Keegan could in a saloon."

Ramona giggled, but Cynthia wasn't buying anything her father said or any way he acted. "I don't think so," the gunsmith's daughter said.

"Anyway. I'll eat. Round up some supplies. Meet you two girls at the gun shop. That sound all right?"

"Sure," they answered as one.

McCulloch put his hand on Cynthia's shoulder. "Try to stay out of trouble," he told her, smiling to show that he was filled with such frivolity.

Cynthia said nothing, just looked at him oddly, and McCulloch made his head bob. He turned toward Pendergrass's mercantile and made his legs carry him to the boardwalk and toward the open door.

"Who's Cullen Brice, Papa?" he heard his daughter ask.

He turned back. "An unpleasant outlaw. Got sent to prison some years back." He thought up a lie. "The state will put up a reward now that he has broken out of prison, and you can bet Jed will go after him and bring him in.

Don't fret over the likes of Cullen Brice. He isn't worth the time or the lip-biting. And he's no match for Jed Breen. Or Sean Keegan. I'll see y'all at Bondy's in a little bit."

It wasn't all a lie, he told himself. Unpleasant might be an understatement, but the state certainly would put a price tag on that sidewinder's head, and Jed Breen absolutely would go hunting Brice. But not for the reward. But because he knew what Brice was capable of. Keegan would go, too, and also not for the reward. Those two fools would risk their necks to try to protect Matt McCulloch because they knew despite everything Cullen Brice was, every horrible thing he had done in his thirty-odd years, he was also a man of his word.

Cullen Brice said he would have his revenge on Matt McCulloch. And he most certainly intended to see that done.

"Got any .44-40s?" McCulloch asked the kid with the apron and the sleeve garters behind the counter. He didn't see the owner of the shop, and didn't know the boy by face or name.

The kid turned around, went to the ammunition, and said, "Yes, sir. Winchesters." He brought a box and set it in front of McCulloch.

"This all you got?"

The kid paled. "No, sir." He turned around and glanced at the shelf, and said, "Looks like eight or nine more boxes, sir."

"Bring them."

"All of them?" The clerk blinked rapidly.

"All of them."

Generally, McCulloch gave Bonderhoff his business, but the prices were a bit cheaper at the mercantile. Bondy would get McCulloch's business, too.

There were only six boxes. Seven counting the one the boy had fetched. That was a start.

"That'll be . . ." The kid pulled out a paper and started multiplying the price of a box of Winchester .44-40s times seven.

"I'm not finished." McCulloch didn't want to sound brusque, but he wouldn't apologize for that, either.

"Six sacks of beef jerky. Two jars of that new horse liniment you got in two months ago. You know the ones I mean?"

"I think so." The boy kept paling.

"I'll tell you if it's not what I want."

The boy scribbled.

"That canteen over there. Yes. That's the one. Those two sacks of coffee. A half-dozen horseshoes, a hammer, some nails for the shoes." Just in case. He'd be riding into some tough country. "Pound of salt pork. No, forget the meat." He would have to live on jerky and off the land. "Sack of grain for the horse." He pointed at the bolts of cloth for ladies to make shirts and dresses and pretty things like that. "Four yards of that white cotton." Bandages would undoubtedly be necessary. "And that bottle of elixir yonder." It had to have alcohol in it, and alcohol was mighty good medicine for gunshot wounds and knife cuts.

"Is that all?"

It wasn't anywhere near enough, but McCulloch nodded. Then he turned and pointed through the open door.

"There's a horse tethered right yonder. Grab the saddle-bags off the back, and pack everything up that you can in there. So that the bags are balanced. I'll be back in a few minutes and I'll settle up." He leaned and scowled. "Is that all right with you, son?"

The boy had no voice. He simply nodded.

McCulloch found a dollar in his pocket, underneath the telegram. He tossed it onto the counter. "That's for you. Not to cover the price of the goods. That's for your help.

For dealing with an ornery son of a . . . Well, for your trouble. And your help."

And he was out the door.

"Lord help us all."

Captain J.K.K. Hollister slid the telegram across his desk to McCulloch. Then he reached down, opened a drawer, and pulled out a bottle. He didn't bother with glasses, just pulled out the cork and slid the rye toward McCulloch.

"No, thanks, Captain," McCulloch said.

The Texas Ranger retrieved the bottle and started to take a snort, only to think better of it and return the cork. The bottle, though, remained on the top of the desk.

He found his sergeant and barked an order. "Get to the telegraph, inform Captain Brisbane in Mobeetie that Cullen Brice is out of prison, that the Peering Farm has been raided, and that he most certainly can expect Comanchero activity . . . practically . . . hell . . . immediately." He looked back at McCulloch. "Boss Linden wouldn't break Brice out unless he really needed him."

McCulloch nodded. That was exactly what he had been thinking. The Comanchero leader had let his lieutenant stay in prison for years. And Cullen Brice could have been busted out of that stupid cotton farm experiment months ago. Something was brewing in the Texas Panhandle. Something that involved the recent hijacking of Springfield rifles and Colt revolvers bound for the fort in the Panhandle near Mobeetie.

"What will your Captain Brisbane do?" McCulloch hated wasting time asking a question that he already knew how Hollister would answer.

"Not a thing, Matt. Not a thing." Again Hollister reached for the rye, and again he stopped, cursed, and brought back an empty hand. "Oh, he'll send out some scouting patrols. Hell, he might even get lucky and cut a trail. But he'll never get anywhere close to that Canyon of Weeping Women."

"No one ever has," McCulloch agreed. "And lived to tell about it. Except for Comancheros and Indians. And some white men who ought to be dragged to death through cactus."

Hollister sighed. "I read that a couple of white women were found up along the Pease River," Hollister said. "But they were insane by then. Couldn't do a thing but scream and drool and cry."

Now McCulloch was tempted to reach for that whiskey.

"You still need that concerned citizen to head north, get those weapons back?"

The captain's face showed no emotion. "Or destroy them."

McCulloch was like a mirror reflecting Hollister's face.

"Those thieves," McCulloch said. "How many Colts? How many Springfields?"

The captain reached for a stack of papers on his left, shoved two aside, dragged the third toward him.

"Four crates of .45-caliber Colts. Seventeen crates of Springfields in .45-70 caliber."

"Two hundred revolvers then," McCulloch said, "and . . ." He started to cipher in his head.

"Two hundred. Twelve per case. Sixteen cases. The other case holds only eight." He shrugged. "It's the way the factories and the United States Army like to do things."

"Hell." McCulloch frowned. "Two hundred revolvers. Two hundred Springfields. Put those in the hands of Indians or anybody, and that adds up to . . ."

"A lot of dead Texans."

McCulloch glanced at the bottle of whiskey, but his eyes shot back to Hollister.

"What about ammunition?"

The Ranger's face lightened just a shade. "That's where we got a break. No ammunition was in that wagon train. So they got the guns, but nothing for the weapons to shoot. But—"

McCulloch nodded and cut him off. "But cartridges are easy to come by—if you've got the money."

"Or the men to steal what they need."

"Maybe." McCulloch started thinking again.

"Indians can rob gun stores and hardware stores and, hell, even military arsenals, too, Matt," Hollister said.

"I know. You didn't answer my question, Captain. Not directly anyway. Do you—"

Hollister cut McCulloch off this time. "I need a volunteer, or three volunteers, to head into the Panhandle, make contact with Boss Linden's Comancheros, and get back two hundred stolen Colt revolvers and two hundred stolen Springfield rifles. Or destroy them. And preferably kill every mother's son of those Comancheros."

"You got one of them, Captain. And I might be able to hire two partners."

"You sure you want to do this, Matt?" He tilted his head toward the window. "You got a daughter to think about."

"That's why I'm doing it, Captain. I'm thinking about my little girl."

"All right." He started to extend his hand. "But you have to understand one thing. We never had this conversation."

A tired grin stretched across the beard stubble. "J.K.K. Nobody in this part of the country would believe you and I could even have a civil conversation."

This time, Captain Hollister's hand found the bottle, and he uncorked it again, and this time, when he extended the rye, McCulloch accepted and took a quick swallow. The Texas Ranger's drink took a few gulps longer.

"There's just one more thing, Captain," McCulloch said after Hollister corked the bottle. "I need some money."

"How much?"

"Enough to buy every round of .45-caliber Colt cartridges and every round of .45-70s that I can find in Purgatory City." The Ranger's face lost its color.

"And a pack mule, probably two, to carry the load."

Seconds ticked by. Captain Hollister's head shook, but he was starting to grin first. "You're going to drive me to some serious drinking, Matt."

They shook hands.

"Matt?" Hollister called when McCulloch rose and turned for the door.

"What are you going to do with Cynthia?"

McCulloch felt his body tense.

"We're a far ride from the Panhandle, Matt. Chances are Linden won't ride down here . . . at least not until his deal is done."

"Linden wouldn't." Matt saw his hands were now fists. "Can't say the same about Cullen Brice."

"I can put guards at your place. Good men. I'll send Sergeant Butler and the best Rangers I have. Hell, they'd enjoy getting away from Purgatory City and looking at a pretty girl. But don't worry. Butler's married, and I'll make sure the men he picks keep their distance." He laughed. "Well, that wouldn't be necessary. Your daughter knows how to handle herself."

McCulloch just stared, so the Ranger went on. "That's one thing we have here. Good men. Can't say that about Brisbane's bunch in Mobeetie."

"I appreciate the offer, Jaime." McCulloch nodded. "I really do. But that's too dangerous. And I'm not leaving Cynthia at my place alone, or sending her to town to stay with Bondy or in a hotel for who knows how long. I got something else in mind."

CHAPTER 14

She was upstairs, packing her grip, when the bell chimed downstairs. Cynthia smiled. She recognized her father's boots on the floor and the song his spurs sang. They would be going home soon, and that made her happy. She started hurrying. It had been a short visit, so there wasn't much to pack. And, well, it wasn't like Cynthia Jane McCulloch had too many dresses to count in the armoire and trunk. The armoire was new. Her father had traded a high-stepping bay mare for it.

She started breathing fast, smiling, wishing Ramona were here so they could laugh together. She closed the grip, took it in her hand, ran to the door, stopped, and came back to pick up her straw hat. Quickly, she scanned the small room, just to make sure she didn't forget anything, and then out the door, down the hall, and before her feet felt like they touched the wooden stairs, she was at the small entrance and in the shop.

Mr. Bonderhoff was sliding a handful of boxes toward Cynthia's father, who stood by the door.

"That's all I got, Matt. Sorry." Mr. Bonderhoff saw her father turn, and he looked at Cynthia, too.

"That'll do," her father said. He smiled at Cynthia, but it was not the gentle smile she was starting to get used to.

There was no laughter in his eyes, and those lips did not stay curved for more than a couple of seconds.

"What you got there?" he asked.

"My things." She watched his eyes dull. "We're going home, ain't we?" When he did not respond, she realized her mistake. "Aren't we?"

"You in a hurry to eat my cooking?" She could have smiled, but his tone was not the same. And those eyes had not changed.

Mr. Bonderhoff cleared his throat. "I'll put these on your bill, Matt."

"No." He turned back, reached into his vest pocket, and pulled out money. "I'll pay now." He cleared his throat. "You know how I am with money. Get it. Spend it. And I sold a dozen half-broke geldings to the Diamond Seven for more money than I should have gotten. How much?"

"For the bullets?" Mr. Bonderhoff started staring at the ceiling, moving his lips but not even whispering, the way he always did when he was ciphering in his head. "Let's see . . ."

"My whole bill, Bondy," her father said. "How much?"

The gunsmith stared at the man as if he had never seen him before. Cynthia knew then that something was terribly wrong.

"You got a problem getting paid in full, Bondy?" Again, Matthew McCulloch tried to sound . . . jocular. That was the word Ramona Bonderhoff had used at breakfast that morning. And, one more time, McCulloch did not sound funny at all.

Mr. Bonderhoff's eyes shot once more at Cynthia, and now he tried the false comedy.

"Well, I do enjoy the half-percent interest I charge." He found his ledger, opened it, and went back to figuring out math in his head. "Counting the .45-70s and the .45 Colts, sixteen dollars, and nineteen cents."

A coin rattled on the counter.

The gunsmith opened the register, which chimed louder than the bell above the door, and counted out change for her father.

"You might try Carter's hardware store, Matt," Mr. Bonderhoff said. "And Pendergrass probably has a few more boxes of cartridges."

"I will, Bondy. Thanks." He shoved the boxes of ammunition into a potato sack. Now he looked at Cynthia.

"You hungry, girl?"

"I just ate." She wet her lips.

"I'm hungry. Want to eat with your old man?"

"I thought you were going to eat."

"I was. Got busy. Now I'm hungrier."

"All right."

Now she heard the strain in her voice. It matched the uncertainty in her father's.

"I'll be seeing you, Bondy." Her father held the door open for his daughter.

"Why don't you leave your possibles with Bondy?" her father said. He looked back at the gunsmith. "Is that all right, Bondy."

The perplexed man was staring at the gold piece he had just received. His Adam's apple bobbed and he looked up, as though the words were slow to reach his brain.

"Oh, sure."

Cynthia put the grip on the counter, returned to her father. When they stepped outside, he started to cross the street, but looked through the window. His face changed again, debating something in his head. He made the decision.

"Can you go grab us a table, darling?" He did not wait for an answer. "Tell Clarabelle the usual for me. Get whatever you want. I need to discuss one more matter with Bondy."

He must have noticed the fear in her eyes, or the confusion.

"It's all right, Cynthia. Ask Clarabelle for a double helping of those hash browns. For me. And get what you want."

"I just ate, Papa," she said. But he didn't hear. He was already stepping back inside the gun shop, and the little bell was ringing, echoed by the cash register which Mr. Bonderhoff was closing.

She turned, head down, and walked without much feeling, and hardly an ounce of hope, to the café again.

When he sat down, he stared at the cup of steaming black coffee Clarabelle had placed before him within seconds after he sat down. She said, "I'll get ya yer vittles in a minute or two. Y'all need anything else, hon?"

He acted as if he hadn't heard a word.

"Nothing, thank you, ma'am," said Cynthia, and Clarabelle's eyes showed concern. For Matthew McCulloch. But the waitress knew how to put up a brave façade—another word Cynthia had learned from Ramona Bonderhoff—as well as Matt McCulloch.

"Oh, you ain't gotta thank me, hon. I get pleasure servin' some folks. Some folks." She scowled at the two blue-coated soldiers singing a bawdy tune in the corner, and hurried away from the table and bawled out the two wannabe singers, who fell silent and went back to sipping their coffee and shoveling their eggs into their mouths.

At length, he noticed the coffee before him, and picked it up. Took a sip. Pulled it away. Blew on it. Sipped again.

Looked over the piece of battered tin, and stared hard at Cynthia.

When the cup lowered, his mouth opened, but no words came out. But that was because Clarabelle was back with a plate of food that she sat in front of Matthew McCulloch.

"Thanks, Clarabelle." At least he had noticed her this time. She smiled, walked away, and he looked at the empty table in front of Cynthia. "Where's your grub?"

"I told you, Papa," she said, "Ramona and me already et." She frowned. "Ate."

"Oh. Yeah." He found a fork, speared the hash browns, and made himself eat. Just three bites later, he lowered the utensil, and stared at the coffee cup, but made no move for it.

He wiped his mouth with his shirtsleeve, and looked again at his daughter. Still, no words came.

So she spoke.

"It's Cullen Brice, isn't it?"

The eyes changed, a flash of anger—no, something much more than anger—and then recognition. This time he found the cup and drank a lot of coffee.

"Brice is a dangerous man," he said. "Captain Hollister asked me to go after him."

That was a lie. So she said, "Don't lie to me, Papa. I'm a woman. Not a baby. Not a little girl. And you know I can handle myself."

"Not against Cullen Brice."

She laughed, and saw the shock, then anger, in his eyes. Before he could say anything, she leaned forward and whispered.

"I wasn't living in a convent all those years, Papa. I was living with the Apaches. Chiricahua Apaches, Papa. You remember what happened when those scalp hunters came into our camp. You tried to send me away. But I came back.

Remember. I can fight. I have fought. How do you think I survived living with the Apaches all those years?"

His lips flattened. He just sat there, eyes burning with an intensity she had never seen—in any man.

"All right," he said. "You're a big girl. You're a McCulloch, though you'll likely regret that before long." His laugh held no mirth. "Hell, I regret it a lot." He found the fork, started for an egg, moved back to the hash browns, left the fork on the plate and found the coffee cup. He drank. Not much, but a bit.

When the cup rested again on the table, he cleared his throat.

"Didn't mean that, Daughter. About regretting to be a McCulloch." His face softened just a hair. "I put Cullen Brice in the state prison years ago," he said. "He promised that he'd get out, and when he got out, he'd make me pay. Well, he's out. And sometime, don't know when, don't know where, he'll come, and when he comes, he'll come for killing. And he'll kill anyone who gets in his way."

She figured it had to be something like that.

"He's a Comanchero. Rode with, and rides with again, an hombre called Boss Linden. They don't come any worse than that bunch. And that bunch just robbed an army patrol of two hundred rifles and two hundred revolvers. They sell them to the Indians, they sell them to some white cutthroats, they use them themselves, that'll mean a hell of a lot of blood spilled over this country."

Cynthia tried to comprehend those words. He had a few more words to add.

"It's not going to be your blood."

There was a change, then. Humanity returned to his eyes, and his smile seemed genuine.

"You can fight me if you want, sweetheart, but this fight you won't win." He reached inside his vest and pulled out a ticket. "You're going to Little Rock. See your kinfolk."

She blinked rapidly. "I got . . . kinfolk?"

He nodded. "Your ma and me weren't orphans. Weren't only children, either. Yeah, I got kin. You got kin. And I got a big sister who teaches school. Little Rock, it ain't much, but it's years ahead of Purgatory City. She'll teach you better than them McGuffey's will. And I'd like you to see what the world is like outside of this lawless, godforsaken patch of nothing in the middle of even less. Those papers will take you out tomorrow night. Take you all the way to Fort Griffin near Albany. From there another ticket will take you to Dallas. Then that last one will get you to Little Rock."

"Am . . ." She stopped the tear that wanted to form. "Am I coming back, Papa?"

"Hell, yeah, Daughter. Of course, you're coming back. If you want to. I mean, once you see a fine city like Little Rock, Arkansas, you might have no wish to see your old man or that ramshackle place I call home again."

"But I don't know—"

"You know Ramona Bonderhoff."

She studied him.

"Ramona?"

"Bondy wants her to see something different, too." He glanced again at the coffee and the plate, but seemed surprised now to find there was something to eat and drink in front of him—as if he had not tasted the hash browns and the scrambled eggs or sipped the scalding brew. "I think that fight y'all had with those dumb burglars made him decide to get Ramona out of here—but just for a while. Rest of the summer maybe. Into the fall. Maybe my sister will want you to stay with them for Christmas. And New Year's."

Now he drank a bit more coffee.

"I'm not getting rid of you, kid." He grinned. "Just loaning you out. You know. Just like I'll let someone take one of the mustangs I've broke for a day or two. Get a feel for the animal, I tell them. See if you two can get along. But what I'm doing is selling them on the fact that they can't find a better horse than what I'm selling them. And they won't dicker too much at the price I want. And, I make them jealous. That's really what I'm doing by letting you visit my sister for a couple of months or thereabouts. Letting some other folks get jealous at what I got."

She smiled. But Cynthia Jane McCulloch really wanted to cry.

He wasn't certain he would see her again. He wasn't sure he would see anyone again. That's why he had insisted that he pay Mr. Bonderhoff every dime he owed.

Just in case. In case Cullen Brice wound up killing him.

CHAPTER 15

Jed Breen always thought the grub served at a prison wasn't fit for hogs, but at Peering Farm, he learned, well, what they dished out on a plate tasted better than anything you could find in Purgatory City—except, possibly, Clarabelle's hash browns or her biscuits at the Alamo Café.

The guards ate first in the long, narrow dining hall. The trustees served as cooks and waiters. The guards got to eat with forks and knives. The prisoners had spoons only. Trustees made sure the forks and knives were washed and locked up after the guards ate, and two guards made sure the trustees actually made sure.

Breen wasn't much for breakfast. Coffee and a biscuit would suit him, maybe bacon. This morning, breakfast was coffee and corn pone. Supplies were running low, so Breen decided that between corn pone and coffee, he'd just drink coffee. Sean Keegan, sitting across from the bounty hunter, had no such reservations. That Irishman could, and would, eat anything.

When Keegan asked a trustee for seconds, Breen sighed, drained his cup, and rose. "I'll be in the telegraph office," he told his partner. He found his hat, dropped the cup in the tin pail at the end of the table, nodded at the two guards who had already eaten and were at their lookout spots by the door, and stepped into the morning light.

Other guards were making their way to either their duty posts or to fill their bellies. He saw Captain Peering and the warden talking on the front porch of Peering's big house.

Breen made his way to the small telegraph office, opened the door, and stepped into the room.

The German telegraph clerk was testing the lines.

Breen and Keegan had done good work, they were told, spotting the places where Boss Linden's Comancheros had cut the wires and spliced them with rawhide. Had they used heavy rubber bands or something like that, it would have taken them longer to find the cuts. But then they had to splice the wires together, and with the wind blowing the way it did in this country, the German clerk had warned that there was no guarantee how long that doctoring would hold.

The telegrapher finished clicking, waited, and smiled when the reply came. He tapped again, then slid back in his chair and found the coffee someone had brought him.

"Still good," the bespectacled man said in a German accent. "Good."

"Any news?" Breen asked.

"*Nein.*" He answered too quickly. More importantly, he glanced at the trash bucket beside his desk.

Which wasn't the thing to do to a bounty hunter who had been conscripted into guard duty while thousands of dollars in reward money escaped into the rugged frontier of the Texas Panhandle. So Breen walked up, picked up the bucket, and emptied the crumpled papers on the counter.

"*Sie dürfen nicht . . .*" the German began, but Breen's stare had always managed to end any protest from any gent who worked behind a desk.

The first telegram was a bunch of nothing. The second was worse, because the clerk had written it all down in German. He thought about asking the man to translate, and maybe he would, but he found the next paper, and that was written in English. Maybe the other message had been personal. Maybe that's why the telegrapher had been worried. The one in English was brief, but it came from a Captain Anderson at the army post near Mobeetie.

MESSAGE RECEIVED. FORWARDED TO
MAJOR. EXPECT REPLY SOON.

But the last telegram was interesting, and it came from a deputy US marshal down south in Albany.

RAID OF PRISON ESCAPE OF BRICE MIGHT
BE TIED IN WITH ROBBERY OF ARMY
RIFLES AND REVOLVERS. WILL KEEP
WATCH HERE. SEND POSSE OF ARMY
RANGERS OR MARSHALS AFTER ESCAPEES
NOW. TO PREVENT BLOODBATH.

Breen frowned. He picked up the message in German and handed it to the clerk. "Read that to me. In English."

"Ich will nicht!" The fellow looked practically indignant. *"Sie haben—"*

His expression changed when Breen put his right hand on the butt of his revolver.

"And don't lie to me," Breen said. "You've got German prisoners here. And they'll tell me the truth for four bits. Or a sack of Bull Durham."

The man sighed. He was sweating, and not just because the sun was up now and the day promised to be another scorcher. He glanced at the paper, looked into Breen's eyes, and said, "It is from Huntsville. Says to keep you and your *freund* here as long as possible. Says they vill send their own posse. To prevent huge payments of bounties."

Breen chuckled. "The state of Texas is getting cheap." He looked at the paper. "But I don't see my name there. Or Sean Keegan's. You mean to tell me you have to translate our names into your Hun tongue?" He inched the revolver out of the holster just enough to get the man's attention."

He pointed to a word.

"*Schakale*," he said.

"Does that mean Breen or Keegan?"

The man blinked. "*Weder. Schakale* means . . . jackals."

The door opened, Breen dropped the revolver back into the leather and turned around. The warden walked in, and at that moment, the machine began clicking. Breen turned, watched the timid German slide closer to the metal and wires, grab pencil and pad, and when the clicking stopped, he tapped out a reply. Then the machine started making a racket, and the telegrapher started writing at a furious pace.

Breen found his Sharps and headed for the door.

"Morning," he whispered to the warden.

"Mr. Breen," Plummer said.

"Where's Keegan?"

"He was walking to the fields when I passed the commissary."

"Best join him."

Warden Plummer nodded, and Breen stepped out the open door but stopped when the clacking stopped and the German called out, *"Warte!"*

Breen looked back.

The cowardly little man waved the paper. "This is for you," he said in English.

* * *

All this guard duty had changed Sean Keegan's thinking. He felt a bit of respect, newfound respect, for all those guards who had been ordered to watch over Keegan in the guardhouse, or while he was digging new latrines, or cleaning out some of the old ones. Peeling potatoes. Walking around carrying a twenty-pound cannonball that was shackled to his ankle. All those years, all those sentences, all that time in the army, and he had figured that a guard was the lowest duty a fellow could pull, so the guards had to be about as lazy as Keegan's Uncle Paddy in County Cork. But now?

It was hard work watching over prisoners. There was something grand about galloping across the plains on a good horse. There was glory in firing at an enemy who was firing at you. But there wasn't anything grand or an ounce of glory in standing in the sun watching tired men work like draft horses on a farm. A guard sure worked up a thirst, especially here, on the edge of nowhere, where the only liquor could be found at owner Peter Peering's fancy house—and he wasn't all that gracious when it came to sharing his best bourbon. And bourbon was a long way from that grand Irish whiskey.

Water would have to do. Brackish water. Tepid in the morning. Scalding hot by the time the prisoners headed out of the fields and back to their locked quarters.

Today looked to be about the same as yesterday and the day before yesterday and the day before that.

The prisoners were falling in now, being told what to do, who to do this, who would do that, how many pounds of cotton Captain Peering expected. While others would get to break the boredom of picking white fluffy balls that could prick you if you didn't pay attention to where you put your hands. They would get the glorious assignment of hitching the mules to plows and discing up the plants that had already been cropped.

They had started that yesterday—or maybe the day before—and that made Keegan mighty proud he had never dreamed of becoming a farmer.

Well, at least he'd have some company. Jed Breen was walking this way. Keegan climbed into the back of a farm wagon, letting his legs dangle over the tailgate, and laid the Springfield rifle over his thighs. The sun was behind him. That was a blessing. So he'd just sit here, try not to get too many splinters in his backside, and watch till the sun was making its way to the butte in front of him, about thirty miles away.

He never thought he would miss Purgatory City—but, my, did he—and not just the grog shops and the buckets of blood that served the worst whiskey a man could ever get down and not drop dead from poison. He missed the comfort, the smells, a few of the people, and the fact that it was . . .

"Jed," he said when Breen stopped in front of him, "have ye ever been homesick?"

"Sun's gotten to you already, Sean. You want to go lay down? See the inmate now acting as the prison sawbones?"

"Nay, laddie. I'm just bored out of my mind."

"Get used to it. I just found out that the prison superintendent in Huntsville wants to reap all the glory, and all the reward, or all the reward the state won't have to pay, by sending its own posse of guards after Cullen Brice and that wild bunch."

Keegan felt the blood rushing. "They cannot do such a thing."

"Easy," Breen said. "Do you know how long it will take a posse to be formed in Huntsville and make it all the way up here?" The bounty hunter did not wait for an answer. "We've got plenty of time."

"They'll move faster than ye expect, laddie. Cullen Brice. Boss Linden. That's a pair to draw to." Keegan shook his head. "Any idea when we're getting our relief?"

Breen swore softly. "That's another thing I learned. They're all dragging their feet. Marshals down south don't want to ride north. Marshals and Rangers up north don't want to ride south."

"Aye, well, that's why this Panhandle country has always been a no-man's-land. No men here, but Comancheros and Indians, and they're mighty stubborn about letting anyone who isn't Comanchero or Comanche stay here, unless they're buried here."

Breen nodded.

"So why don't we say *'Slán abhaile'* to our fine hosts and get after those dirty curs?"

"Can't." Breen pulled a folded paper from the pocket of his vest. He extended it toward Keegan, who took it, read it, and scowled.

STAY PUT. ON MY WAY. BRINGING AMMUNITION ON TWO PACK MULES. HOPE YOU WILL JOIN ME. PLAN TO DO BUSINESS WITH COMANCHEROS.

Keegan blinked and let Breen take the telegram paper out of his hand.

"Has Matt gone daft?"

"No." Breen shoved the paper back into the vest pocket. "That army train that got ambushed. The warden told me that the bandits got guns, but no bullets."

"Matt wouldn't sell powder and lead to those scoundrels."

"But he'd do whatever it takes to get us in their camp."

Keegan swallowed. "Us?" Then he grinned, but only for a second. "It's a bloody long way from Purgatory City to this hellhole, Jed, me friend. You know that better than I do. And a man with two mules. It will take him a week to get here, and that's if he pushes it."

"Matt," Breen said, "will push it."

CHAPTER 16

The Apaches, Cynthia McCulloch kept thinking, made better time than a stagecoach. And the Apaches preferred to move by foot, in higher and much rougher country than this. She also noticed something else.

Stagecoaches rocked this way and that, that way and this, and Cynthia and Ramona Bonderhoff had grown tired of grown men throwing up their sowbelly, beans, and coffee. The messenger riding up top with the driver kept having to throw a bucket of water on the flooring, and threatening to empty both barrels of his shotgun into the belly of the next gent who couldn't hold his breakfast. Or at least have the common courtesy to stick his head out of the window or door and send his breakfast to help tar the path that stretched from one station to the next.

Then there were delays caused by nature. Bridges washed out. Sandstorms that forced the driver to stop, and for passengers to close the leather drapes and ride out the storm with stinking men and choking dust that nothing could keep from finding openings in cracks. At one stop, a drunken tender apparently forgot how to hitch a fresh team of mules. The coffee served at these stations was more tar than liquid, the biscuits could break a tooth, even if you dunked it repeatedly in the undrinkable coffee. And the hash browns certainly didn't resemble the ones Clarabelle made. The beans, on the other hand, were always filling, and always good, till they came out on the rear extremes of the drummers and tinhorns and bankers moving with Ramona and Cynthia.

Yet sometimes the two young women laughed. Ramona said she felt as though she would write a letter to the Purgatory newspaper about their experiences, or maybe forget about a small-town press, and send it to Joseph Pulitzer himself or Horace Greeley. She'd make Cynthia McCulloch and Ramona Bonderhoff as famous as Mark Twain.

Cynthia smiled—as though she knew about Pulitzer, Greeley, and Twain. It was hard, sometimes, trying to learn what everyone else had learned while you were trying to survive with Apache Indians.

The coach pulled into Fort Savage, and the driver called out, "Changing teams and moving north. Get your coffee. See the privy. Just be ready to load up when I shout, 'Load up!'"

He didn't have to yell. The only passengers for the last thirty miles were Cynthia and Ramona.

Once the coach slid to a stop, the messenger opened the door. He was a gentleman, though he looked fierce— almost as intimidating as Cynthia's father—and he pointed the barrel of his shotgun toward the station.

Ramona looked around, her face showing shock. "Where's . . . the fort?"

The leathery man with the thick mustache and dust-covered face laughed. "Never was much of a fort to begin with," he said. "Army moved out in the 'fifties, before the late War. Folks hereabouts took the stones the bluebellies had quarried for their own use. That station's the only thing left, practically. Old Morse, he built the corrals and the barns. Get some chow. It's better than—"

He stopped, stared.

Two Mexicans were hauling away the worn-out team of mules, and two more men were bringing the fresh animals toward the stagecoach.

From his perch in the driver's box, the ornery old man who knew little except how to throw out cuss words and whip a team, barked, "Passengers? Passengers at Fort Savage! Jorge, we ain't taken on passengers here in four years."

The fat man in the apron said, "Well, you are taking these on, confound it. All of 'em."

Four women, who might have been younger than Cynthia and Ramona, walked by. Three of them carried a valise. The redhead had a pillow case. They weren't dressed for travel. They were hardly dressed at all. It looked as though they had been roused out of bed, given a robe or a coat or a duster, told to pack what they could in what they could find, and get the hell out of town.

Which, Cynthia soon learned, was pretty much exactly what had happened.

"You tellin' me we gots to haul them four hurdy-gurdy girls all the way to Albany?" the old-timer with the sharp tongue yelled.

"I ain't tellin' you nothin'," the stationmaster said. "But Sheriff Yardley might have words with you, or let his pistol barrel do it's talking when he clubs sense into you."

"Ladies . . ." The messenger tucked his shotgun underneath his left armpit, tipped his hat, and dropped his voice to a whisper. "I'm sorry, but looks like you'll have to share the last leg of this ride with these . . ." He swallowed down the word.

But Cynthia remembered some words. And one of them was *prostitute*. Besides, she had seen enough of those women since she had been taken away from the Apaches. She felt her skin bristling, not at having to share a stagecoach with four ladies *a de la noche*, but at the attitudes taken by these men.

"It's all right," Ramona said.

The messenger thought she was talking to him. Cynthia knew Ramona had seen that flash of anger—that Apache look—in Cynthia's eyes.

"That ain't all you got, Pritchard," the stationmaster told the driver. "You got them, too." He hooked his thumb.

Everyone except the stationmaster and the four prostitutes looked back at the stone building that had been an army structure and now was a way station.

The woman, prim, proper, and perhaps middle aged, stood holding a parasol in her left hand and the trembling hand of a young boy in her right. The boy was twelve years old or thereabouts, and he held the hand of another boy, the spitting image of himself. Twins.

Emilio stopped. The four prostitutes did not even acknowledge the driver, the messenger, Cynthia or Ramona. They opened the door to the coach, and crawled right in.

The stationmaster lowered his voice. He had to have seen the two female passengers standing right there. Maybe he didn't care. Or maybe he thought two fare-paying passengers deserved to know exactly what was going on in this part of the country.

"Reform."

That's what was going on in this part of Shackelford County.

"Whole county's taken to reform." Emilio spit. "Don't ask me why. Or how. But the good citizens of Savageborough decided that burgh was too good to have a cathouse. Sheriff Yardley brung them over. Said for me to take 'em to the county seat or else. Said he'd get them out of Albany as quick as he could. The fool had to ride over to Red Mound to collect the two soiled doves there." He spit, wiped his mouth, and shook his head. "Curses, all them churchgoers and haughty women and weak-livered businessmen haven't any heart when it comes to what us bachelors is gonna face."

The messenger nodded discreetly toward the stone building.

Emilio sighed. "Well, that's a different story. That Missus O'Leary. Her husband was a surveyor in Savageborough. They was sitting at their supper table—this is what the widow told us—and he just let out a gasp, clutched his chest, and fell to the floor. Poor twins was at the table, one of them saying grace, and the ol' missus was pumping water into a pitcher. Turned around, she done, and there her man lay right there on the floor. Deader than a doornail."

"Pump broke," the driver said.

"No," Emilio said. "Well was full. Pump was working."

"He meant the surveyor's heart," the messenger said.

"Oh." The fat man spit, wiped his mouth, and smiled. "Pump. Yeah. I get it. I'll have to remember that one." The smile faded. The man's head shook. "Well, she couldn't stay there. Not with them two boys and no money. Folks taken up a collection—and your section manager agreed to let the widow and her twin boys travel to Albany." He pulled out some papers, walked closer to the stage, and held them up toward the driver.

"This is the tickets for the . . . well . . . girls. And here's the pass signed by Connard for the Widow O'Leary and her two boys."

When he walked back, he seemed to notice the two women.

"Oh. Ladies." He cleared his throat, glanced over his shoulder and said, "The facilities is over yonder. You might have time for some coffee. I got good beans. Ground squirrel in 'em. Flavorful. I can have two bowls ready for you when you're done . . ." He nodded at the ramshackle privy. "With . . . you know . . . Good beans. Ground squirrel makes 'em even better."

"That's all right," Ramona said.

Cynthia added, "We're just stretching our . . ."

"Limbs!" Ramona sang out before Cynthia could say "legs."

"Bring us some coffee, Emilio," the driver yelled.

Emilio walked back toward the widow and the children. The messenger tossed his shotgun up to the driver, tipped his hat at Ramona and Cynthia, and headed to the station, probably, Cynthia figured, to escort the widow and her children to the coach.

"That's so sad," Ramona whispered, and let her chin silently point at the bereaved family.

Cynthia tried to grasp, as the messenger walked the woman and her twins to the coach, that this widow had not chopped off a finger, or cut off all her hair and sliced gashes into her arms or legs to mourn the sudden loss of her man. She shook her head. She had to remember that she was no longer Apache, that Americans did not show grief that way. She had to remember that her father might be called a jackal, but that she had to be civilized.

Civilized. She watched Emilio spit in front of himself as he carried two steaming cups of coffee away from the station. She heard the men working the mules and the crotchety old driver curse. The woman nodded stiffly as she passed Cynthia and Ramona, and the boys stared. The messenger stopped before he reached the station.

"Jorge," he said softly, and the stationmaster stopped. Now the messenger spoke to the driver. "Toss me that scatter-gun."

The driver picked it up, pitched it, and looked in the direction the messenger's eyes had locked on. So did Cynthia.

"How long has that rider been on that hill?" the messenger asked.

Now Cynthia and Ramona looked at the lone butte off to the southeast.

"Hell, Mort, I don't see no rider. I don't . . ."

"There." Cynthia pointed. "A flash of sunlight."

It was gone.

"Spyglass," the messenger said.

"I saw him yesterday," one of the men working the mules said. "Around sundown. I figured he was hunting."

"You can see that far?" Cynthia didn't know if Ramona was asking the messenger or her.

"If he's hunting," Emilio said, "he will be mighty hungry. The only thing on that butte is buzzards and scorpions."

"Maybe he's signaling us," another worker suggested. "Maybe he needs help."

"No," Cynthia said. "It is no signal. He mounts his horse now."

Emilio laughed and spit in the dirt. "Maybe this gal can tell us what color that hoss is. Or if it's stallion, mare, or gelding."

"Don't be a fool, Emilio," the messenger said. "You haven't seen clearly in fifteen years."

"Can you really see that far?" Ramona whispered.

"It is not that far." She frowned. She could not see the horse and rider now.

"He's gone." But the messenger had eyes as good as Cynthia's. "Rode down the far side."

The driver spit. "Hand me that coffee, Emilio." He wrapped the leather lines around the stagecoach's brake, looked over at the butte, and reached down for the coffee cup. "You two are joshing us. You didn't see a thing."

"You've been living out here too long," the messenger said, and he took the other cup of coffee. "Trees block your view."

Ramona let out a breath. She smiled at Cynthia. "I guess I've been living in town too long. Buildings block my view." She stared at her friend. "Isn't that right, Cynthia."

Cynthia smiled, but her gut tightened.

The Apaches had taught her how to see far. And your long-distance vision was a lot better when your life depended on what you could see and what you didn't notice.

"Probably a hunter," Emilio said. His head bobbed as if trying to convince himself.

"Yeah," said one of the mule handlers.

The messenger cracked open his shotgun, examined both shells, and closed the breech. He handed the gun up to Harry, the driver, and downed his coffee quickly.

"All right, ladies!" Harry yelled. "Climb back inside. I gots a schedule to keep, hunter or no hunter."

Cynthia's mouth moved, but she made no sound.

That was no hunter.

And she followed that with a silent thought.

At least, he was not hunting for wild game.

CHAPTER 17

They called the place Pale Canyon. Matt McCulloch hadn't been here in years, but the place never changed. The wind blew dust on the best days; on the worst, it would whip sand that could scald a man's skin if he didn't protect himself. This day, pushing noon, seemed to be somewhere in between.

One bandanna covered his nose and mouth. Another tied on his hat to keep it from being blown all the way to the Gulf of Mexico. The hat's brim had been pulled down low enough to keep from being blinded. The horse held its head down, but kept plodding along. He let the gelding pick its own path, knowing it somehow would follow the trail. It was a good horse, with a keen instinct for survival.

When the sand, dust, and wind slackened, he breathed a little easier. The horse had found Pale Canyon, and turned in. The wind still blew hard, just not enough to drive man and beast insane, or suffocate them.

It was more of a depression than a true canyon, probably a river that had dried up centuries ago, and the wind had kept digging the banks down. That meant the wind blew over the canyon as it dug ten, fifteen, then thirty-five feet below the plains above. Dust fell like misting rain.

A hundred yards into the canyon, McCulloch reined in the horse, dropped the lead rope he had been holding, pushed up the hat brim, and pulled down the bandanna. He sucked in air that might not have passed as fresh, but at least it wasn't like filling one's lungs with burning sand. He untied the other bandanna, then shook the dust off them. After that, he swung from the saddle, found the canteen, blew dust off the cap, took off his hat, placed it in front of the horse, and splashed some water into it.

The horse deserved a drink. So did McCulloch, but his thirst would have to wait. There was a well about a quarter mile deeper into the canyon, just before it ended, with six or seven trails horses and men could climb to escape. A box canyon that wasn't quite boxed in. A pretty good hideout, even though just about every lawman in Texas knew of its existence.

Few lawmen knew how to find Pale Canyon. Those who had learned the location knew better than to ride into Pale Canyon.

As the horse drank, McCulloch unholstered his Colt, then used an oiled rag to clean it of dust. He blew on the cylinder and hammer repeatedly, making sure the action worked. He blew down the barrel until he thought it was clean enough. Satisfied, he thumbed a brass cartridge from the shell belt, wiped it clean, and filled the empty chamber with it.

Six beans in the wheel.

The gelding had finished, so McCulloch picked up the hat and walked to the two mules he had been pulling. They were brown animals, but now looked as pale as the canyon. He splashed a bit of water on one of the bandannas, and wiped the eyes of both animals, then set his hat on the ground again, and this time emptied the canteen. The mules had been trained well enough to share water. While they alternated drinking, McCulloch drew the Winchester from the saddle scabbard and wiped it down. The .44-40 had been protected from most of the blowing sand, but a smart man took no chances in a place like Pale Canyon.

He checked the packs on both animals, picked up his hat, pulled it on his head. The dampness felt better right now than a bath in one of those fancy houses in towns bigger than Purgatory City. He did not return the Winchester to the scabbard.

Instead, he wrapped the lead rope around the horn, mounted the horse, and spurred it into a walk. He rode on, rifle braced against his thigh, to the sod hut near the end of the canyon. He counted five horses in the corral, all saddled. He spotted no lookout, but that he had expected.

Nobody dared ride into Pale Canyon unless they had business here, and were expected here.

A door opened in the privy, and a man in a big black sombrero stopped and stared. He cupped his hands and whistled, but McCulloch paid no mind. The horse and two mules clopped along. Dust still rained from the sky, and he stopped again, in front of the soddy. He nodded at the Mexican with the black hat, and dismounted, keeping the horse in front of him.

The Mexican licked his lips and walked forward, hands spread far enough from the holstered revolver and the sheathed machete.

"Buenos días," the Mexican said.

McCulloch nodded.

The man's eyes turned to the mules. A smile peeked through the dark mustache and beard.

"¿Vienes a comerciar, muchacho?"

He nodded. "What else would bring me here?"

The Mexican laughed, so he understood English. He stepped to the door, opened it, and waved his hand. "Come in," he said, eyes dancing with delight. *"Bienvenidos."*

McCulloch let the rifle barrel point in the general direction of the man's belly.

"After you."

He followed the Mexican into the small, dark room.

It hadn't changed since the last time he was here. The man behind the bar was new, younger than the one McCulloch remembered. He figured the old man with the woolen cap was dead now. The whiskey being drunk was all clear. Tequila. Three men played cards at a table. The other one stood at the bar. Now everyone stared at McCulloch as the Mexican walked to the bar to the glass of whiskey he had left to visit the outhouse.

The Mexican hooked a thumb toward McCulloch, spoke in Spanish—too fast, for McCulloch to catch most of it— but the man picked up the tequila, held it out toward the man at the end of the bar and says, "Two mules. Boxes and kegs. He says he comes to trade."

The man at the end of the bar was silver-haired, and sported a two-gun rig. His eyes were the pale color of a killer, and he eyed McCulloch, sizing him up.

"What are you selling, hombre?"

"I'm selling to Boss Linden," McCulloch said.

"Who?" The silver-haired man smiled.

McCulloch looked at the Mexican. "You tell Boss Linden I'm coming."

The man smiled and pretended to try to recall the name. *"¿Quién es este hombre Lin-deeeen?"*

"Tell him if he wants bullets for those Colts and Springfields he stole, he'll deal with me. Tell him in four days he can find me on the trail from Peering Farm. Tell him."

The Mexican laughed. "Why do I get this honor to find this Boss Linden man who I do not know?"

"Because," McCulloch said, "you're the only one getting out of this pigsty alive, other than me—and the barkeep, unless he's a fool."

He was holding the Winchester with his left hand, keeping the barrel aimed at the Mexican's big belly.

His right whipped out the Colt and put a bullet in the silver-haired man's chest. The man was grabbing for the revolver on his left when he was knocked against the wall, eyes showing shock, then nothing at all.

McCulloch twisted just enough, bringing his right arm over his left, thumbing back the hammer, squeezing the trigger again and taking the top off the head of one of the card players. The other man was trying to stand, pawing for a big Dragoon in a red sash. The .44-40 slug took him in the brisket, and he staggered back against the wall, and accidentally touched the trigger. The old .44-caliber relic, still in the sash, boomed and set the silk and the duck trousers smoldering as he groaned and fell sideways to the floor.

The Winchester's barrel remained trained on the big Mexican's belly. Now McCulloch turned the Colt to the bar, and the bartender, his face pale, slowly raised his empty hands toward the ceiling that was now cloudy with gun smoke.

"That's good," McCulloch told them. His eyes quickly scanned the floor, but it did not take him long to understand that the three men lying on that side of the room were dead. The Winchester's barrel never budged.

The gun smoke had faded, but the acrid smell of gunpowder was now being replaced by that of blood and death. They were all smells McCulloch had grown used to, and so had the Mexican and the bartender.

McCulloch's eyes briefly shot to the barkeep.

"Go outside, grab the canteens, and fill them with water."

The man nodded. "Would you like a drink of whiskey?" He tried to smile. "On the house."

"Just fill the canteens. And if you're not quick about it, you'll join these three. And if I think you put something in my canteens other than water, you're dead. And if my cinch is loosened or if there's a burr put under my saddle, you're dead. So what are you going to do?"

"I'm going to fill your canteens with water from the well. And I'm going to do it quickly."

"Good. Leave the door open. So I can hear exactly what you're doing."

When the bartender returned, with his hands over his head, he walked back to the bar, found the drink of tequila the silver-haired man had not finished, and gulped it down.

McCulloch focused his attention on the Mexican.

"You know what to do?"

The Mexican nodded gravely. "I will deliver your message to Boss Linden, señor. But I can make no promises to what he will do to you." He tilted his head to the dead card players. "Rafael and Cummings were not much, but worked real hard." He nodded in the general direction of the silver-haired corpse. "But Gentleman Phil, he was good."

"No, he wasn't," McCulloch said. "That's why he's dead."

"We all die, *señor*."

McCulloch grinned. "I don't." This time, he lowered the Winchester and stepped toward the door.

It had been a bold play, but McCulloch knew it had to be done. A lone man leading two pack mules would be easy pickings for Comancheros in the country to which he was heading. So he needed to get word to Boss Linden what he was bringing. It was still risky. Comancheros did not like dealing with rogues. In fact, they didn't like dealing with anyone.

"And tell Boss Linden this," McCulloch told the Mexican. "If he tries anything, everything goes up in smoke."

"Including you, señor."

McCulloch nodded. "Including me."

"So . . . even you don't live forever."

McCulloch grinned. "Yes, I do. Because you'll tell Linden that. And Linden's no fool. That's just a warning. And security to make sure Boss Linden deals with me."

He looked out the door.

"I'll be taking my leave, gentlemen. If the door opens before I'm gone, I'll kill both of you. If you come after me, I'll kill you. So, barkeep, you busy yourself burying your patrons, or feeding them to the coyotes. And you raise dust for Boss Linden. But not for two hours." He smiled. "Maybe I'll be raising dust. Maybe I'll be waiting to see just how honest you can be. That's your gamble. Savvy?"

"Sí," the Mexican said.

The barkeep wiped his mouth with his apron and nodded. His Adam's apple moved and he cleared his throat. "You're the one . . . ain't you?"

"The one what?" McCulloch had started backing out of the hut. Now he stopped.

"The Ranger who came here . . . alone . . . three-four years ago?"

"I'm not a Ranger anymore," McCulloch told him.

"They say you killed three men that time."

"They say it right. So I tied my record today. You don't want to make me break it."

He pulled the door shut, and hurried for the horse and mules.

CHAPTER 18

None of the women, not even the twin boys, got seasick despite the swaying of the coach. But the driver or the mules seemed intent on hitting every rock and every hole in the road. Cynthia felt as though her kneecaps would break, her legs would come out of the hip sockets, and her arms would both be dislocated. Her neck already ached. But the Apache still in her told her not to let anyone know just how much she suffered.

No one talked. The mother's red-rimmed eyes blinked constantly. She looked as though she did not know where she was. The two boys stared at their brogans. The women who had been run out of whatever that town was named almost looked relaxed. This probably wasn't the first time they had been relocated. One of them had made a cigarette but she never brought it to her mouth, just rolled it between her pointer finger and thumb. Maybe she had too much respect for the widow and the twin boys. Probably she just didn't have a match.

Ramona stared out the window at the passing dust.

Cynthia and Ramona sat on the front bench, their backs against the coach's wall. The fallen women were on the back bench, facing forward. The mother and the two boys sat in the middle bench, and Cynthia thought about asking the boys and the widow if they would care to change places. The middle bench had no backrest. And that's the seat that generally produced the most vomiting passengers.

When Ramona turned away from the window, she smiled at Cynthia. She started to say something, but noticed that the widow's mouth had started moving. Cynthia listened, but nothing audible came out. Maybe she was praying silently. Then, she cleared her throat, and asked, "How . . . much . . . farther?"

She was looking directly at Cynthia. Asking her. Asking the woman who had never ridden in a stagecoach, not as a little girl in Texas, and certainly not as an Apache squaw.

Ramona came to Cynthia's rescue. "Three hours to Albany. If nothing happens."

The woman's eyes widened in fright. "What . . . ? What could happen?" The twin boys, sitting on either side of their ma, looked up at the woman whose face paled and whose lips trembled.

"Oh." Ramona realized her mistake. "Nothing terrible. A road might be washed out. Or a bridge. Nothing to worry about. In fact, that means the coach has to stop, and we can get out and stretch our limbs."

Or get out, Cynthia remembered, to help push the coach through a muddy bog, or up a hill, or maybe lift the coach up so the driver and the messenger can replace a busted wheel. She had not realized how lucky she had been never to have ridden one of these neck-breaking contraptions.

Apaches had the right idea. Walk . . . run . . . ride only when you have to.

The woman stopped trembling. "Oh," she said in a whisper Cynthia could just hear over the pounding hooves, curses from the driver, snapping whip, and rocking wheels.

"If you'd like to change places. . . ?" Ramona must have had the same idea. She looked at Cynthia, who smiled and nodded.

"This isn't comfortable," Ramona said. "But it's easier on your back. And sometimes . . ." She winked at one of the twins. "On your buttocks."

The boy grinned at the word *buttocks*.

"I . . ." The mother seemed confused.

"Take 'em up on that offer, missy," said the prostitute with the unlighted cigarette. "Four hours is like forty in this torture chamber."

"The boys might be able to take a nap," Ramona said.

The other kid stiffened. "We're too old for naps, lady."

"Oh." Ramona grinned. "My mistake, sir."

The woman swallowed. She licked her lips. "I wouldn't want to impose."

"You're not," Ramona said.

"But we should wait till the driver stops," the mother said.

"Lady," said the prostitute who appeared to be trying to sleep. "This wreck won't stop till we get to the county seat."

"Are you sure it's safe?" the mother asked.

That's when the wood above the door splintered, and the gunshot sounded an instant later.

Cynthia felt the bullet as it whistled past her nose and punched through the leather curtain on the far side of the coach.

"What the devil!" the driver, shouted.

If the messenger answered, the next rifle shot drowned him out.

"Get down!" Ramona dropped to her knees, grabbed the boy in front of her, and pulled him to the floor.

"Ladies!" That came from the messenger.

Another bullet hit something.

"Take cover!"

Cynthia grabbed the second twin and covered him with her body. The boy struggled. Cynthia looked up, pressing her weight against the twisting, turning, clawing kid. She saw the mother still sitting there. Three of the prostitutes had fallen onto the floor, one covering her head, another saying a prayer that seemed vaguely familiar. The soiled dove who held the cigarette just sat where she was.

"Get down!" one of her companions yelled.

"All a bullet can do," the woman said, still rolling the cigarette without a concern or a match, "is kill me. What the hell. It'd be a change of pace."

The coach lurched suddenly to the right, sending the woman onto two of her companions.

The mother still sat there. A bullet splintered wood again and thudded through the roof.

Cynthia and Ramona came up on their knees at the same time, each grabbing one of the widow's arms, while they tried desperately to keep the twins on the floor between the middle and front benches, and pulled her forward, diving back on top of the writhing bodies of two boys and a stunned, but now shrieking, widow.

Just as another bullet punched a bigger hole in a door.

Gunfire sounded from atop the roof. Not from the guard's shotgun. Those came from a repeating rifle. He must have had a Winchester or a Henry hidden in the driver's box. The coach bounded furiously. Then came a yell:

"God help us all!"

The coach swayed, bounced high. Cynthia couldn't hear the hooves from the mules anymore, and she sucked in a breath as she understood. The team had broken free. The coach was sailing out of control.

Screamed the driver: "Hang on, folks!"

"Hang on—hell!" That was the messenger. "Everybody jump! Jump now!"

But Cynthia knew they would never get out of the coach in time. They were huddled on the floor, and the coach bounced and bucked at such a furious rate, she didn't think anyone could even climb onto their knees and find the handle to open the door.

She held onto the squirming boy underneath her, and then came the mother's scream: "We're all going to die!"

A sickening crash, crunching wood, dust and grime filling the coach as if it had gotten caught in an avalanche. Twisting over. Falling to the side of the coach, onto the roof, feeling splintered wood jabbing her back, her thighs, her arms. Slamming onto bodies, back to the side, hitting the bench, all the while hanging on to the squirming kid. Then she felt the door against her back. The coach bounced. She realized she was sitting up, but the coach was still rolling. She took a chance, somehow found the handle, pushed hard.

She thought she saw the coach's wheels flipping past her. But that had to be her imagination. When she could see, when she could breathe, when she realized she wasn't dead, she saw mostly thick dust.

On the far side of that cloud of dust, wood crunched, women screamed. There was another sound, too.

Horses. At a gallop.

Blinking hurt. Her toes wiggled. Then her fingers. She felt something on her chest, looked down, saw the boy. He wasn't moving. He wasn't yelling.

She sat up. The kid's head was bleeding, as were his lips. His coat and shirt were ripped. One of his fingers was bent at an ugly angle.

He's dead!

Her heart burst.

But then she saw the sand on her skirt moving. Air came from his nostrils. He was breathing. He was still alive.

Those horses grew louder. Coming closer.

The stagecoach must have settled.

"Ramo—" but she bit off the cry.

If she stayed here, whoever was attacking the stagecoach would have her and the boy. If she ran away, she might save the boy, might save herself. And then she would have a chance, slim certainly, but at least a chance to save Ramona.

Her heart sank. If Ramona were alive.

If the boy's twin and their mother were alive.

She stood, holding the limp boy in her arms. Cynthia had no idea how she managed that. She looked around. Trees. There were trees. That was her only hope.

Her legs worked, though the left one worked better than the right. Every step she took sent agony from her ankle to her thigh. But she made it to the trees, into the dry creek bed. She wasn't big, but she was Apache—at least for the time being. She'd have to be Apache to get away. The horses were already there. Voices shouted in Spanish and English. Guttural grunts. A few cheers, but mostly curses.

A rifle shot fired.

"¡Alto!" said another man. "¡Alto!"

Then, in English, a Texas drawl warned: "Don't shoot, you fools. You might kill a dance-hall gal."

The boy was over her left shoulder. Cynthia staggered. She followed the creek bed. By the time she rounded the bend, she was dragging her right foot. They'd be able to follow this trail. By thunder, a city slicker who needed spectacles to see could follow the trail.

And the bed turned again, and when it turned, the covering of trees ended. She could blame that on the white settlers who had cleared timber for firewood, for corral posts, for rafters and such. But she also saw a butte about four hundred yards to the west. That was her hope. She had to make it to that butte. There was timber there, and maybe she could hide. Hide just long enough to see what happened. To see what these white and Mexican cutthroats wanted to do with the passengers they had captured.

If the passengers weren't just corpses.

The boy she slung over her shoulder—like she had been made to carry dead animals when she first joined the Apaches. Or poles that carried large gourds filled with water. Or anything the women did to make her work and sweat.

Her ankle throbbed. Broken? Maybe. It didn't matter. All that mattered was reaching the butte. Her only hope to get there, she understood, would be if the outlaws were too busy checking on the stagecoach. She tried to run, but couldn't. And that butte looked like it was moving farther away from her.

Mirage?

No. It is there. Those words she thought in the dialect of the Chiricahuas.

It well better be there. That, she heard in her father's voice.

Every step made her cringe. But she did not stop. She did not give up. She walked, carrying the dead weight, moving, moving, moving.

A rifle shot sounded, but it had the echo of a shot being fired in the air.

She was all right. Just keep moving.

And then she heard a voice that did not come from her brain.

"Hell. One of them is gettin' away!"

CHAPTER 19

Jim Bob Hardwick told himself over and over again that he was an outlaw. A cutthroat. He and his brother paid no attention to laws or, in general, human decency. He had cheated at cards, he had taken money from the tin cup the preacher had passed during those Sunday go-to-meetings. He had slapped another brand on the hides of horses and cattle. He had stolen with stealth. Once he even had robbed with a gun, enjoying the frightened look of the man whose railroad-grade Illinois watch and chain he was stealing along with his billfold and that fancy diamond stickpin. He had done an awful lot of what the lawyers referred to as assault and battery, and he had slept off countless drunks in calabooses from New Orleans to Tucson.

But he was no animal.

Until right now. Right this minute, he felt like some rabid coyote. The Comancheros he and his brother Billy Ray had somehow joined were screaming in the Mex tongue and English. Three women huddled over a fourth, whose legs—both of them—had to be pretty badly busted. Those women were soiled doves. Jim Bob could see that despite the dust and the Comancheros dancing all around them.

A little boy and a pretty city woman stood over another woman, and that one wasn't in good shape, either.

Well, hell, Jim Bob thought, who would be in good shape after the wreck the Hardwick boys and Cullen Brice's renegades had wrought?

Cullen Brice was not too happy.

"Is that how you stop a stagecoach?" he screamed, even as he shoved the hot barrel of his rifle into the buckskin-clad man's chest. "The idea was to fetch some women to sell. Alive women. Not half-dead and crippled petticoats!"

The Comanchero said, pointing to the crumpled trash that once had been a Concord stagecoach. "He drive like crazy man. He cause all this. Not me."

Cullen Brice spit.

The Comanchero laughed and pointed. "But he will no longer drive like a crazy man."

Two other Comancheros came around the splintered wood and broken wheels of the wrecked stage. They had taken a spoke from one of the wheels and propped a bloody head on one end.

"You cut his head off?" Another Comanchero laughed.

"It was practically off already," said the man.

Jim Bob Hardwick turned away. He found his brother, and to his surprise, he saw his brother laughing, pointing the barrel of his still-smoking revolver at the head of a man. Well, Billy Ray always had a peculiar sense of humor.

"Where's the messenger?" Cullen Brice demanded.

A Mexican pointed at the crumpled mess. He said something in Spanish that Brice understood.

"Set it on fire. If he's still alive, we can hear him scream."

One man splashed the rotgut whiskey from the jug he had just uncorked on the wood. Another struck a match, knelt, and tossed on the wood. After a loud *woosh*, the fire began crackling.

Cullen Brice walked to Jim Bob, put his arm around Jim Bob's shoulder and pointed the gun barrel at the survivors.

"You found the women, Hardwick. I didn't believe you could do it, but you sure did a fine job. Mighty fine. It's not your fault that these imbeciles of Boss Linden's botched the raid. You can have your pick of the girls. Just don't pick the crippled one."

"Thanks." Jim Bob did not know how he managed to say that.

Laughing, Brice walked up to the unconscious woman being cared for by a handsome lass and a little kid, who was sobbing.

"She dead?" Brice asked.

"No. But no thanks to you and your scum."

The young woman had sass.

"Yeah." Brice nodded. "They are scum. You nailed that one right on the head." He pointed the barrel at the woman. "She gonna live?"

"I think so," the woman said.

Brice nodded. "Good." He looked at the boy. "Unfortunately, I don't see no market for busted-up children."

"The mines in Mexico." Jim Bob didn't know why he said that. The words just came out. He hadn't even know there were mines in Mexico until he had found himself picking cotton for that vindictive cotton king Peering in that hellhole. One of the men working near him liked to talk. Talked all the time. The windy never would shut up, but he had said that the mines in Mexico were filled with slaves. Black slaves. Red slaves. White slaves. Brown slaves. Slaves from seven years old to seventy. So the owl-hoots working at Peering Farm didn't have nothing to worry about. They had it pretty good. They got real scratchy wool uniforms to wear, and a hat to cover their heads, and three squares and a hard cot. *Try working as a slave in a Mexican mine,* he had said. *You don't live too long doing that.*

Brice turned and stared. "What's that you say?"

Jim Bob Hardwick wondered if he was about to be shot dead.

He swallowed, and found his voice. He had to say this with conviction. But he did not know if that windy inmate knew what he was talking about.

"Mexico mine owners," Jim Bob said. He could see the frown appearing on his brother's face. "They'll buy slaves to work, and they don't care what age they are."

"He's too puny to work in a mine anywhere," Cullen Brice said.

"But not too young to carry water to the other slaves." Cullen Brice, Jim Bob could tell, was not convinced. "They want to keep the men who can work a mine alive as long as they can."

"How do you know that?"

Jim Bob made himself smile. "I know lots of things. I've only been in prison eight months. So I've heard and read and—"

"Es verdad," said a graybeard with a brown leather patch over his left eye and no right ear.

Cullen Brice looked at the Mexican, who said, "We have sold slaves to many miners when in Ciudad de Tierra."

"Kids, too?" Brice asked.

"Sí."

"How much you get for a puny cuss like this one?" The gun barrel again trained on the boy.

"¿Quién sabe?" The Mexican shrugged. *"¿Cien pesos? ¿Doscientos?"*

"Hell's fire." Brice laughed. "Economy sure has changed since I got locked up." He started for the prostitutes. "Keep talking, Jim Bob. You have interesting and informative things to say."

Now the ruthless outlaw stood over the unconscious prostitute. He clucked his tongue, turned, spit, wiped his mouth with his dirty shirtsleeve, and looked at one of the other ladies *de la noche*. "Two busted legs, eh?" His head shook. "That's a shame. Left one looks real bad."

The fire was raging. One of the Comancheros suggested that they should ride out now, in case someone saw the smoke.

"You're as gutless as you were before Matt McCulloch sent me to Huntsville," Brice said. "She can't ride a horse with two busted legs, can she?"

One of the women sobbed. "You can pull her in one of those . . ."

"Travois?" Brice chuckled. "That would slow us down. And leave a trail real easy for some lawman or soldier boy to follow."

From where he stood, Jim Bob Hardwick heard the sound of a hammer being drawn back on Cullen Brice's rifle. "And we ain't got no ambulances."

"How do you know she can't ride?" The dark-haired gal tending to the boy and his mother—at least Jim Bob figured it was the boy's ma, though the girl was too old, and too dark-haired, and too dang pretty to be the lad's sister—was standing now. Jim Bob guessed that she had heard the rifle's hammer, too.

Cullen Brice turned to the outspoken, and sharp-tongued girl.

"You ever rode a hoss with two busted legs, girlie?"

"No." She still had sand. "Have you?"

Brice shook his head.

"Then how do you know it can't be done?"

The Comanchero tossed the decapitated head into the destroyed coach, but too far from the flames—for now.

"She will scream her head off. We travel far. We travel fast. Kill her now. Kill her and let us *vamanos*."

Jim Bob started walking away. He couldn't ride away. Not now. They would shoot him down like Cullen Brice was about to kill the gravely injured prostitute. He wanted to be as far away from these men—and as far away from his brother, right now—and he didn't want to see the poor woman murdered. Besides, Cullen Brice probably would gun down the plainspoken brunette, too.

"She can't scream if you stick a gag in her mouth," the dark-haired girl said. "And she'll pass out from the pain quickly enough."

Jim Bob stood on the edge of the road, staring ahead, not really looking for anything. He just wanted to look away from what was about to happen. But nothing happened. No gunshot rang out. No one spoke. All he heard was the panting horses, and the crackling of a burning stagecoach.

Then . . . he saw it. He saw something moving. Out on the flats. Heading toward . . . toward that little butte.

The messenger? Maybe that guard had been thrown clear of the crashing Concord. Like the women had been. Maybe his neck hadn't been badly broken like the driver's.

Jim Bob removed his hat and held it above his eyes. He wet his lips. He strained to see. It was a small figure. What he needed was . . .

"Fernando." Cullen Brice stood right next to Jim Bob. He moved quietly. Or maybe Jim Bob had been in prison too long and his senses had dulled. The Comanchero saw the moving figure, too. "Your telescope, *por favor*."

One of the Comancheros hurried over, opening a leather cylinder that hung over his left shoulder. He removed the brass scope, extended it, and handed it to his boss.

Cullen Brice stared silently for almost a minute. Jim Bob kept watching till the figure disappeared. Whoever it was had reached the butte. Might have been hiding behind a boulder, or had found a sinkhole, or cutbank, something to hide in.

"I'll be gobsmacked." Brice compacted the spyglass and handed it back to the man named Fernando. "Did you see that, Jim Bob?"

Jim Bob nodded. "Just now. You think it's the guard?"

Brice laughed. "Son, that ain't close to no guard—unless times have *really* changed since I got sent away." He spun around. "All right. We're riding out. Jenkins. Gag the cripple and put her on that mule. Strap her in good. Missy, you better hope she don't scream too loud. 'Cause if she does, I'll leave both of you for the buzzards. Let's get the others tied up and put on mounts, and let's ride. Jim Bob, we'll go slow. Give you time to catch up with us."

Jim Bob turned around, confused.

Cullen Brice laughed and pointed to the butte. "You found that one, pardner. You got dibs. But don't take your good sweet time. We'll ride slow to let our hosses catch their breath. Then we ride hard to the Canyon of Weeping Women. Get to it, pard. She's all yours."

She? Jim Bob Hardwick thought.

Chapter 20

Cynthia preferred the calf-high moccasins she wore when she lived with the Apaches. You could run with those on your feet. But these awful "ladies" shoes. These were called "fine needle buttons," and they took an eternity to button—or unbutton. She laid the boy in the shadiest part behind the boulder, then, biting her lip, pulled up her dress, and began getting the leather over the buttons. It hurt like blazes, and she cringed when she turned her right foot one way or the other. But, she figured, they might come in handy. The narrow patent leather toes were pointed like a knife tip. And the heel had some heft to it.

But first her attention turned to the ankle. Leaning over, she took her foot and began turning it, just to see how far she could go. She sucked in a breath.

All right. It didn't feel broken. Sprain, but a bad one. She ripped off the left sleeve of her blouse. Her arm remained tan, darker than any Anglo she had seen in Purgatory City. That came from those years in Mexico, but she thought she had paled some in the months she had been away from the Chiricahuas. But this was no time to think about skin color.

She went about wrapping the ankle as tight as possible, and since she had been blessed with long arms, she covered the rest of her foot, too. Walking across this hard country barefoot was not for the soft in heart, or soft in foot. Cynthia wrapped her left foot, too, after tearing off the other sleeve. Yeah, Apache moccasins would have been a big help. But she didn't think she could get a quarter of a mile with that ankle of hers, at least not in those patent-leather shoes. With her feet wrapped, though, and the ankle bound, she would be able to cover some ground.

A lot more, she knew, if she hadn't brought the boy with her.

Now, she turned her attention to the kid, but she kept that brief. There was a pecan-size knot on his head . . . lots of little cuts, but those had already clotted—and bruises were starting to form. She figured the underside of his right arm would be completely purple. Well, from what she remembered about her brothers, the boy would show that off like it was a medal or a buck with a perfect set of antlers he had bagged with a clean arrow—no, a clean rifle shot.

She still felt his hot breath on the back of her hand.

The kid was alive, but she knew she would have to carry him.

After pushing the young boy's yellow bangs out of his eyes, she smiled at his hair, then touched her own golden curls. He had to be hurting, but he was sleeping. Sleep blocked the senses. Sleep let the body heal itself.

Water would help. She didn't know this country, but she did know water could be found. There was enough green to be spotted from here, and trees did not grow without water. Cottonwoods, especially. And that stagecoach stop. There was well water there. If she could keep away from those outlaws, she could double back easily to the station. In fact, that's as far as she needed to go. Get to the station. Hide till her father . . . or a white man she could trust . . . arrived.

A white man she could trust.

That was the problem. Who did she trust after a few months back with her father's and mother's kind?

Her father.

Mr. Bonderhoff.

Jed Breen.

Sean Keegan.

Do not, she told herself, *think ahead. You're a long way from finding help. You're a long way from getting the boy and yourself out of here alive.*

She looked up. The sun was too high. Nightfall had to be hours away. There was something else, now, too.

Smoke. She saw it, and she smelled it.

Grimacing, she carried her shoes and moved with stealth, like the Apaches had taught her, making little sound, raising no dust. She became a snail, hardly moving, till she could see.

Smoke came from where the stagecoach had crashed: burning wood, leather, and all that luggage. Her father had just bought her that grip. Not that she would miss it, or her clothes. She also realized that that poor woman and her two boys had lost everything they owned. Bad luck was following that family. A dead husband. Now this.

But they were alive.

Well, at least the boy was alive.

Maybe, she realized, not for long. Her eyes found the man, a white man, moving one way, then the other. Had to be running, but crouching, hoping no one would see him, and nobody would shoot at him.

A horse would have gotten him closer in a hurry, but a horse would also be easy to see. And hear. This man was not stupid. Well, not completely stupid. He moved swiftly, and quietly, and he was not coming at this part of the butte in a direct fashion. He had figured his best chance would be to circle around.

Once she had a good idea about where he was headed, she turned back to the smoke. She remembered what Three Dogs, the Apache leader, had taught her. Don't look for anything in particular. Look for everything. See everything. Watch for the unnatural. The men had finished with the stagecoach—and maybe the passengers. She had not heard much gunfire, but these men could have easily used their knives to kill . . .

Ramona?

The boy's twin?

It did not matter. There was nothing she could do about that. Focus. See . . . everything.

Cynthia did not look at the man coming toward her. She trained her attention the other way. If one man came at her from her right, surely another would come at her from the left. It would have helped had she known this land, its contours, its low points, its high spots, the tree lines. She had to guess, though.

Nothing—nothing obvious, nothing unnatural, nothing different—came into her vision. She looked again at the smoke, and below. The dots were moving away from her.

Wetting her lips, she looked back at the man who was coming for her.

He is . . . alone.

She bit her bottom lip.

He must be very brave.

She hated to kill a brave man. But she would.

She hefted one of the shoes.

Then she lowered herself and crawled back to the boy. Still on her stomach, she took in every detail, every possibility.

Going up the butte was pointless. There would be no cover—and the man would be able to see her—if he paid attention—and, undoubtedly, he would.

The obvious path the man would take would be up the side of the butte. Looking down. But that would be too obvious. She sensed that this man would not try that, which was good. She would have no place to attack him, armed as she was with just two city women's shoes. But the man coming after her did not know that.

He would be cautious.

He would have left his horse a few hundred yards away. Toward that clump of cactus she had spotted. She tried to visualize where it was from here, since the rocks blocked her view. There. Would he come from the left or the right. He had been riding toward the right. So . . . he would come from the left.

Cynthia smiled.

And that was perfect . . . for her.

She looked at the boy, rubbed the hair off his forehead, smiled. Cynthia had the blond hair. Her brothers had taken their father's dark hair. This boy, she imagined, looked a little like her brothers—if they had been given golden hair, too. No, that was her imagination. Wishing. Wishing she could see her brothers again.

Leaning over the kid's face, she whispered an Apache blessing. Then she left him. And hurried to the rocks. Reaching them she stopped, studied the path animals— most likely skunks and rabbits, coyotes, maybe a badger— had traveled. She turned.

Perfect. She could see the boy from there. So could the man hunting her—if, indeed, he came this way. She moved to the edge of the rock, studying the signs she might have left behind. The sleeves of her blouse had done her well. Nothing anyone other than an Apache might see.

What if this man is Apache?

No. Her head shook. An Apache would not have ridden with such trash. These men who had attacked the stagecoach, they were no better than the Mexican and pale-eyed scalp hunters who tracked down Apaches—men, women, children—killed them, lifted their hair, and sometimes entire heads, and sold them for bounties paid by the Mexican government.

She braced her back against the rock.

No. Too close. She backed up four more steps. Yes. This would be perfect. The man would come. He would stop there, look around the corner, but see nothing. The sun was perfect. It would cast no shadow that he would see. He would see the boy. He would move slowly, silently, and step right . . . there.

She slid her hand into one of the shoes. The other she held like a club. Jab the pointed end into his neck as hard as she could, start clubbing him with the heel in her other hand. They would fall to the dirt. And she would beat his head with the heel, jab the pointed toe into every soft place she could find. Adam's apple. Mouth. Ears. Eyes.

It would be a hard fight. And for the man coming after them, it would be a hard death.

She looked at the boy, still unconscious. She tried to see the smoke, but the rocks here obstructed the view.

Cynthia waited. No, not Cynthia. She was no longer Cynthia. She was Litsog. She was Chiricahua.

Ten minutes passed. She might have made a mistake. He might not be as smart as she thought. He might be coming from the side of the hill. Or even this side of the rock. No, no, that would be too noisy. Too many stones to knock loose. But he could have come in from the other side. That would be really smart. Follow Litsog's trail. He might be . . .

She heard the noise, faint, but not faint enough for a wild animal.

Her breathing became controlled, silent. Her eyes slitted but did not blink. She made sure both shoes were firm.

The wind did not blow. The earth became still.

There. On the ground in front of the rocks. A darkness that had not been there before. It moved half an inch. It was a shadow. Where the rock, the butte, and the sun protected Litsog, it gave away the man's position. He came closer.

Soon—Litsog grinned—he would be dead.

The shadow grew longer. His next step tipped a small stone. She heard him catch his breath, then nothing at all for five full minutes.

Closer.

Closer.

"Mama!"

Litsog almost gasped. Her eyes shot out to the boy.

"Mama!" he screamed again. She saw him rise, yell, and fall back. "Mama! Where are you?" The boy cried. "Danny? Danny, where are you?"

He wailed. He prayed to his God. He said he did not want to die. He rolled over and screamed in agony. Litsog felt her heart, and her will, shatter.

She told herself that the boy meant nothing to her. He was a white boy and she was . . .

She was Cynthia Jane McCulloch. And the boy looked like her. The boy looked like . . .

The boy was just a boy. A helpless kid who had seen his father drop dead. Who was suddenly all alone in a strange country and gravely injured.

"Ma'am!"

The voice came from the other side of the rock. English. With a drawl. A younger version of her father.

"Ma'am. You best show yourself."

The boy yelled, "Who are you? I can't see you? Help me, mister. Please, God, don't leave me here alone. . . . *Mama! Danny!* Papa. Papa. Where are you, Papa?"

"Lady." The voice cracked a bit. Weakness. Or just the nerves of a brave man. "Lady. I got a repeating rifle, and if you don't show yourself, I'll shoot the kid."

She looked at the boy.

"I'll shoot him dead."

Litsog was gone. Cynthia Jane McCulloch felt like she might just crumple into a ball and sob till her tear ducts ran dry.

"I'm gonna count to five, ma'am," the voice on the other side of the rock called out. "Then I'll kill the kid."

He called out only one, then *uno,* in case Cynthia was Mexican. Then Cynthia threw one of the shoes into the dirt on the path. She tossed the next one near it.

She limped down the incline, and did not look behind her at the man. Instead she walked to the sobbing little white boy.

It was over.

CHAPTER 21

Jed Breen took the glass of bourbon Captain Peering had poured him and walked to the wallpapered wall in his library and the big map of Texas framed in well-carved, well-oiled wood. The cotton king finished pouring his own drink and walked across the room.

"A prisoner did that," Peering said in his soft drawl. "It is part cartography and much artistry, would not you agree?"

The colors were vivid, and the inmate had also painted in figures of steamboats in the eastern river towns, Apaches in the regions from the Big Bend to New Mexico, Comanches in the Panhandle, deer and limestone in the Hill Country. There was Sam Houston, and—what else—but the red-bricked walls of the state prison in Huntsville; the Alamo in San Antonio; crosses and an angel at Goliad, where those Texans, prisoners of war, had been massacred by Antonio López de Santa Anna's Mexican army shortly after the fall of the Alamo during the war for Texas liberty. There were sailboats and steamships along the coast from Houston to Indianola to Corpus Christi. And longhorn cattle as if in a trail herd from east of Austin to Fort Worth. He found cotton bales on a wharf in the riverboat town of Jefferson, pine forests so thick and tall in the eastern part of the state; and more cotton, not baled but growing in red-earth country, balls as white as the clouds, blanketed by dark green leaves and white balls about right where Breen and the plantation owner were standing right this minute.

"How accurate is it?" Breen asked, and took another sip. He hadn't tasted bourbon this good in a long, long time.

"Well, Nacogdoches is spelled right." Peering laughed at his own joke. Breen, since he liked this bourbon, smiled politely.

"It looks accurate," Peering finally said. "The Brazos River, the Trinity. The Colorado. They appear to flow where they should be flowing." He pointed to the topography, pretty pictures. "And the land looks like what I have seen in the places I have gone. Now, I cannot attest to the veracity of the Guadalupe Mountains, or the courses of the Rio Grande, Neuces, or the Pecos—"

"I can," Breen said, and smiled at the cotton king.

Breen had ridden along both sides of the river that separated Texas from Mexico. He had crossed the Nueces River in search of outlaws before the Texas Rangers had been reinstituted, years after the Civil War, back in the days where few lawmen dared to travel into that part of the country; and the Pecos, dangerous and deadly, flowed not far from Purgatory City, where Breen had made headquarters some years back.

The warden came over, and the chimes rang on the bell that the Comancheros had not shot to pieces during their raid. A Mexican trustee, dressed in black and white—but not stripes—headed for the door.

Peering had invited Breen, Keegan, the warden, and a few of the highest-ranking guards to supper. Breen had accepted, but he had not been looking forward to this. He had lost track of how long he and Keegan had been stuck out here in the middle of nowhere, when he could be chasing bounties and making a living. He had been conscripted into becoming a prison guard, and no one—not Peering, not the warden, and not in any of the telegrams Breen had read—had mentioned a thing about money.

But . . . He took another small sip of bourbon, making it last, savoring the hint of oak and barley. But the liquor was pretty good.

"And what in the bloody hell be that ye is planting ye eyes upon, laddie?"

Sean Keegan had made it after all.

"I had hoped Captain Peering would have locked the front door," Breen said without giving the Irishman a glance.

"Well, he didn't, did he, me white-haired friend? Now cut with the jokes and tell me what exactly it is."

"It's a map of Texas."

"I see that. But it looks like no map I've ever seen." Keegan gulped down his sipping liquor and handed it to an inmate wearing tails. "Be quick with another, me good man," he said. "And don't spare the whiskey."

Breen turned this time and looked at his partner. Keegan held a glass in his right hand, but his left was bandaged around the bottom knuckles up to the fingernails.

"What happened to you?" Breen asked.

"Aye. Nothing really. I been practicing, ye see."

Breen didn't see at all, and his expression must have relayed that to the former cavalry sergeant.

"Well, that little runt. The prisoner. I've been practicing me swings, me punches, so the next time I beat the cur to the brink of death, I shan't be swinging over his head."

Breen blinked. His face was turning blank, like the fresh page of an artist's sketchpad.

"I hit the side of the hitch post in front of Captain Peering's fine house."

"So that's what happened to my carved stallion's head," Peering declared, and laughed.

"I did little damage to the head," Keegan said.

"That is true," the cotton king said. "But you almost knocked the post over."

Keegan laughed. "And that will be what this hand does once I meet up with that little weasel next time."

"And your hand will likely look like it does this time, too," the warden said, laughing.

Breen laughed with him, as did the warden, and, finally, Keegan joined them. But only after he had replaced an empty glass with a full one.

Jed Breen looked again at the colorful and brilliantly detailed map. It had been painted on canvas. With oil paints. The canvas had been professionally stretched. Breen guessed that the frame had been built by likely the same prisoner who had carved the stallion's head for the top of the hitch post. Sometimes he wondered how a man who had this type of artistry at his fingertips could wind up in a place like Huntsville or Yuma or here at Peering Farm.

He raised his glass toward the map and told Peering:

"Maps I've seen be in black-and-white, or black ink on yellowed papers. This one . . . it be . . ."

"Quite artistic." The warden had joined the two conscripts.

"It's big and it's beautiful," Breen said.

"Jed, me fine old pard, never did I know you had an eye for the arts." Keegan quickly turned and took a glass of something brown off a tray that another inmate was carrying toward the fireplace, unlighted, in this summer Sunday.

Breen looked around, found an umbrella in a bin next to a coat rack, pulled it out and pointed it.

Peering gasped.

Breen said, "I'm not going to touch it, sir. I wouldn't harm anything this beautiful."

"Unless it had a price on its head." Keegan laughed and took another mouthful of liquor.

"The Panhandle," he said. "Till the buffalo became fair game, that was all Indian territory."

"Not just any Indians, either," the warden said. "Comanches. Kiowas. Even the Southern Cheyenne, from time to time."

"What's this canyon?"

"It sure be colorful," Keegan said.

It was, too, yellow and red earth—a stream sometimes blue, sometimes muddy—dark green trees and light green cactus, and blooms of red and yellow and lavender, with prairie dogs dancing alongside Indians in front of their teepees.

"I would not know." The warden looked at Peering, who shrugged. "That is far north and west of where we are." He held his glass to the illustration of Peering Farm.

Breen brought the tip of the umbrella down to a winding blue line that led from near the canyon to just north of the vibrant representation of the cotton plantation.

"Hey, I see the bars this rascal has drawn." Keegan snorted. "It's like the cotton has been locked up." He slapped his thigh, and handed his empty glass to a man carrying a tray.

"The river?" Breen asked, trying not to lose his temper and tell his Irish pard to shut up.

"That," Peering said, "is what I have been told is Eroded Plains Fork of the Red River."

Breen nodded. "All right. I've heard of it. But that's about all." He lowered the umbrella and looked at Keegan.

"Too far north for me, laddie. I was always stationed in the southwestern hell of this part of the world." He craned his neck and stared. "But, by thunder, that man sure got the country right where Purgatory City ought to be." He drew in a breath and straightened. "Why isn't Purgatory City and Fort Spalding shown? There is nothing but tan paint, a buffalo skull, and a pair of beaten-up wooden crosses!"

"Looks like Purgatory City to me," Breen said.

"What ails ye, Breen me pal?" Keegan looked to be truly concerned. "'Tis not like you to been attracted to a drawing that is not the likeness of a felon."

"Whoever painted this knows this country better than any white man I've met," Breen said.

Keegan shook his head and grinned. "And how in the name of Patrick Vincent Duffy, grand artist of Dublin, would ye know what this country looks like? Ye being a white man yeself, Jed, me friend?"

The Irishman had a point. Breen knew that. But he saw something in this ten-by-eighteen-foot painting that others must have missed. Honesty. Detail. A convict at Peering Farm painted this? That was amazing.

"The cutthroat that did this made the most of it," the warden said. "How long did you have him painting this instead of planting, hoeing, or picking cotton."

"Five months," Peering answered.

"Who painted this, sir?" Breen waited for Peering's reply. But the cotton man seemed at a loss for words. Perhaps no one had ever pointed out just how remarkable this map, this piece of gorgeous art, was.

"Jeddie." Keegan snorted. "Like any fine artist, the bloody defamer of Fort Stanton and our adopted hometown signed it right there in the corner. In green paint."

Breen moved closer. Keegan seemed to figure it out before anyone else.

"*Green* paint. Green!"

Yes. Even Breen did not believe it when he read the name. The signature was rough, childlike, like a six-year-old just learning how to write his own name. The painting was brilliant.

gReeN

CLaYToN

Breen turned and stared at Peering and the warden. "Green Clayton?"

CHAPTER 22

Sean Keegan unwrapped his bandaged fingers that morning. The cuts had scabbed over, and he could flex those digits just fine. No piece of walnut carved into an ugly horse's head would break his fingers or keep him from putting a sorry cuss like Green Clayton in his place one of these days. He dipped his hand in the water trough, tossed the cotton strip into the garbage pail and started whistling as he walked to eat his morning chow.

That wasn't going to happen quite yet.

England Joe said something to Wild Hawg Harvey on their way to the cook shed, and the two went to brawling in the red clay.

Keegan looked for some guards, but most of them were either having their breakfast or on their assigned duties elsewhere. Well, Blubber Bill was closer than Keegan, but Blubber Bill was just blowing his whistle. Fat as he was, he couldn't blow that whistle louder than a bluebird, and he also quickly ran out of breath. He put one hand on the side of his mouth, and wheezed out a timid, "Sean . . . stop . . . 'em."

Keegan made a beeline, checking his holster, making sure the flap was down and secured. A guard didn't want any criminals getting their hands on a Remington .44. Wild Hawg was no Wild Kent Montgomery and England Joe was a forger. How dangerous could a forger be?

It appeared that Wild Hawg had the better, but just as Keegan reached over to grab the collar of the stagecoach robber's shirt, England Joe flipped him over. That impressed Keegan. He let the forger climb to his feet before grabbing that weasel's collar. He jerked England Joe to the ground and saw Wild Hawg up and running, cutting loose with a Rebel war cry. Keegan considered his best course of action, and then stuck out his leg.

His timing was great. Wild Hawg tripped and landed in the sand with a curse and an oomph.

England Joe stood up, found a piece of firewood someone had dropped, likely on the way to the cook fires behind the eating place. Now that could do some damage, even in the hands of a forger who wasn't used to nothing but pens and pencils.

Keegan stepped in front, and said, "Stop, ye bloody fool."

England Joe stopped, but Wild Hawg was coming to his feet behind Keegan, and the forger screamed and took a swing with the log at Keegan.

It knocked off Keegan's campaign hat, and pulled out quite a few hairs. The man spun around; he swung so hard, but kept upright, and started at Keegan again.

The punch stopped him. England Joe stood there, blinking, then dropped the wood, ran his tongue across his upper lip, but Keegan hadn't hit the man's mouth. He'd planted his banged-up fist right between the man's eyes.

England Dan sat down all of a sudden, listed to the left, and capsized.

"I'll kill that inky-fingered son of a—"

Wild Hawg came plodding like an upright bear wanting all the honey in that hive.

"Stop, ye—"

Keegan could not finish because he had to duck. Wild Hawg sent a haymaker that likely would have reduced the number of teeth on that side of the Irishman's mouth. Squatting, Keegan swung his left and caught the big man in the side. The man grunted, stopped, and focused on Keegan.

Seeing the blow coming, Keegan dropped to his knees and rolled to his right. He felt the air that Wild Hawg split when he brought both of his arms down, intending to drive Keegan deeper into the sod than that post that held that carved stallion's head in front of Captain Peering's fancy house.

Keegan rolled over, pushed himself up with both hands, and took the pugilist's stance.

"Is that how you fight, you ignorant . . ."

Wild Hawg did not finish, either.

Keegan flattened the man's cauliflower left ear with his right. His left took him under the chin. Then it was two quick punches to the ribs, another under the chin, and then one, two, three in the belly. Wild Hawg, however, did not seem to be feeling any of that.

So Keegan kicked the man in the groin.

Wild Hawg felt that. He likely also felt it when Keegan brought up his knee into the man's face. The stagecoach robber went to his knees, and Keegan balled his right into another tight fist and slammed it as hard as he could into Wild Hawg's head.

The man's eyes glazed over and he fell into the dirt.

Breathing heavily, Keegan turned toward the forger, glanced over his shoulder at the stagecoach bandit, found his hat and walked to the water trough.

"You boys take them two curs to the hospital," Keegan ordered the first four inmates he saw.

After dropping the hat he had not put back on, Keegan dipped his right hand in the cold water. He followed with his left. Then he cupped his hands and dunked them into the trough, came and splashed away the grime and the dust, a wee bit of pain, and a few beads of sweat. Next, he dunked his whole head under the water, came up spitting and blinking and shaking his head.

When he was satisfied that he felt dry enough, he bent, snagged the hat, returned it to its proper place after slapping it against his trousers, and looked at that cotton field.

How long was he going to be stuck here, playing nursemaid to a bunch of pettifogging forgers and robbers and cutthroats and mean rapscallions like Green Clayton?

"Capt'n Keegan!"

Sean Keegan sighed. Another inmate—but this one a kind old Negro trustee—stood near a hayrick and beckoned him.

"A man can never get breakfast in this place," he said to himself, and walked the forty yards to the old store thief.

"What is it, Mike?" Keegan asked.

The old man pointed. The rider was coming from the southwest. Keegan wished he had a pair of binoculars.

"We ain't expectin' nobody," the old-timer said. "Is we, Capt'n?"

"I wish you'd quit calling me Capt'n, Mikey," Keegan told him. "I was a sergeant. Can't you call me sergeant?"

"If that's what you want, Capt'n."

Other guards were noticing the rider.

"Thanks for spotting him, Mikey," Keegan said and walked toward the approaching rider. Actually he was walking toward his bunking place, where he would find his Springfield under the bunk. A man couldn't take too many chances in this place. Keegan had already been through brawls and one murderous raid.

Strangers did not always mean friendly visits.

"You be welcome, Capt'n," the inmate called after him.

When Keegan came out with his .45-70, he saw three guards pointing. The rider was closer, but still a good ways off. That was one good thing about a place like Peering Farm. Nobody really sneaked in on you—unless they were well-seasoned Comancheros from Boss Linden's bunch.

One of the guards had a spyglass.

Keegan stopped beside that one.

"Make anything out?" Keegan asked.

"Looks like just one man, Sean," the man said without lowering the telescope.

"Lookout? Some sort of sentry? Lost soul?" Keegan didn't think any of those were likely. He flexed his fingers and then stared at his right hand. The scabs were gone, and he was bleeding again, but he wiggled the fingers. By grab, he thought with Irish glory, nothing like a brawl to make a man's busted hand mend itself.

Nothing could make him happier on a day like this.

"One rider," the guard said. "But he's pulling one . . . no, two spare horses. No. Those aren't horses. Those are . . ."

"Pack mules," Keegan said. "Let me see that piece of brass."

He took the telescope from the guard and focused. It did not take him long. He handed the glass back to the guard and said, "Ye will likely find Jed Breen sipping coffee and looking like a vainglorious man. In the mess hall. Run fetch him for me, laddie. And tell him to be quick."

"Should I tell him to bring his Sharps?" the guard asked.

"Nay." Keegan grinned. "He'll have that with him anyway. Just tell him to come. Tell him . . ." He laughed. "Tell him I think we're being relieved."

He walked away, passing three other staring guards who looked without telescopes, but held their weapons tightly.

"Should we prepare for an assault, Sergeant?" one of them asked.

"Nay. But be a kind soul and saddle me horse. And Master Breen's, as well."

He pushed down the rifle of a Henry .44 one of the guards was holding, though not aiming, at the rider. "Ye'll have no need of that, me fine friend. That rider is no enemy of ours."

He met Matthew McCulloch at the edge of the cleared land a hundred yards away.

"You win the fight?" McCulloch asked as he reined in.

"Don't I always?" Keegan extended his hand.

"That hand strong enough to take my grip?" McCulloch asked.

"Always, me friend. Always."

They shook, and McCulloch grunted as he swung down from the saddle. Keegan followed the former Texas Ranger as he walked toward the barn and corrals. As Keegan followed, he glanced at the two packsaddles on the mules. He had seen enough ammunition crates, and these were not hiding what they carried. Cartridges for Springfield rifles—the same army caliber that would fit in Keegan's long gun. And .45-caliber cartridges for Colt revolvers. But the letters were crudely painted on, not marked by stencils. It was crude advertising. That ammunition would be of no use for Keegan, who carried a Remington .44. Or McCulloch, whose Winchester repeater fired the same

.44-40s as his long-barreled Colt. Or Jed Breen's .50-caliber Sharps or his .38 Colt.

Breen met the two men near Captain Peering's big house.

"You made it," Breen said, and shook hands with McCulloch.

"You ever doubt it?" McCulloch smiled without much humor.

"No, I never doubted that you'd get here," Breen said, "but you're a day early. I sure didn't expect that."

"Well." McCulloch wiped his mouth and jaw. "This ain't country to tarry in."

"Hungry?" Breen asked.

"I won't lie to you. I've had nothing but stale crackers and jerky and little water. Didn't stay anywhere long enough to boil coffee."

Keegan whistled. "Ye trustees and ye guards. Take these mules and these hosses. I want two guards in the stables. No one comes near the crates and stuff. No one. And no guard tries to see what's in them. Or he'll be spending time in . . ." He pointed to the stocks. "Those. Ye have me bloody word on it."

McCulloch handed the reins to the old black gentleman. Breen led them to the dining hall, where he introduced McCulloch to the warden and a few of the guards. Captain Peering was taking his breakfast, as he usually did, in his big home, alone, except for the trustees that served as his manservants.

After his third cup of coffee, McCulloch went to work on the salt pork and scrambled eggs. One plate. Then another. Then he tried another cup of coffee.

"Well, you're here," Keegan told his friend. "Jed and I waited for you."

"I appreciate that." McCulloch finished the coffee and wiped his lips and bearded face.

"How's . . . ?" Keegan didn't know if he should ask, but he had started it. Might as well finish it. "Your baby girl?"

"Out of harm's way." McCulloch sounded relieved. "Sent her to Arkansas to visit my sister. Till I kill Cullen Brice."

Kill. Keegan heard that. So did Breen. Kill. Not capture. Well, Keegan wouldn't blame the man for that.

"How's . . . ?" Now Breen hesitated. "Bondy's . . . daughter?"

Keegan could not help but grin.

"She went to Little Rock with Cynthia," McCulloch replied.

Breen's face saddened instantly. "Oh."

Keegan didn't know if that had been a sigh or a query.

"We be with ye, Matt," Keegan said.

"Thank you." Matt McCulloch nodded. "I'd say I don't want you. And I don't want you. But against the bunch we'll be going after, I sure need you."

"We haven't seen or heard from any Texas Rangers, any soldiers," Keegan said.

"And it appears that the prison superintendent at Huntsville wants to send his own men after Linden and Brice."

McCulloch snorted and shook his head.

"I don't expect the warden or Captain Peering will be willing to spare a guard or two to help us," Keegan said.

"Amateurs?" McCulloch shook his head. "I'm not taking any volunteers. I'm taking me. And you two if you want to come."

The faces on all three men formed that bond. No handshakes were needed. No verbal approval. This deal had been forged the moment Cullen Brice rode away from this cotton plantation.

"You got a plan, Matt?" Breen asked. "About finding Brice?"

"Yeah, Jed, I got a plan all right." McCulloch looked like he had aged ten years.

CHAPTER 23

"Problem is," Matt McCulloch said, "my plan most likely will get us all killed."

He lowered his voice, and laid it out as simply as he could. Hell, it had to be simple. There wasn't anything complex to his idea.

The expressions on Jed Breen's and Sean Keegan's faces were about the way McCulloch had imagined.

Breen bit his bottom lip, then spoke with measured tones. "If Boss Linden and his Comancheros get their hands on those cartridges, we will have company in the boneyards."

"Aye," Keegan said. "This whole country would be running red with blood."

McCulloch nodded. "You don't have to go. Won't be any hard feelings. I know the risks. But I got to take them."

Breen started to speak again, but someone shouted, and all three men turned. A puny man was running toward them, waving something in his right hand.

"Karl Lamsdorf," Breen said. "He's the telegraph operator here."

The man slowed down and lowered his hand holding the flimsy telegraph paper. He swallowed and tried to catch his breath, glancing at Breen and Keegan before wetting his lips and locking his eyes on McCulloch.

"Are you Matthew McCulloch, sir?"

"I am." He held his stare on the little man. Would not, could not, look at the paper. He had never cared for telegrams. They were too cold, too informal. He wasn't much for letters, either, though at least they felt personal. Truth was, McCulloch preferred to do his talking face-to-face. A man rarely misunderstood the message when words were spoken, or if he did, he could ask for a better explanation. And you could read in the man's words, his breathing, his eyes what he was saying, know if he happened to be lying to your face.

"This . . . sir . . . it's for you."

His hand held the paper tightly that fluttered in the brisk wind.

McCulloch stared at it for a second, then took it into his own.

"It sounds like a piano, Papa."

Matt laughs out loud, then looks down at the little girl standing beside him.

"I don't reckon I ever heard a piano that sounded like that, Cynthia," he tells her.

The telegraph rattles away, with the clerk sitting down, ear close to the device, his right hand scribbling letters at a furious pace.

"I just think it's musical," she says.

The sound stops.

"Ohhhh," she cries. "I want to hear—"

He holds a finger to his lips. She falls silent. The machine starts clicking again.

"Hurrah!" she yells. "More music!"

"Shuuuuuussh," he pleads.

The telegraph clerk keeps listening, keeps writing, and can't help but smile at the young girl.

Now, all these years later, Matt McCulloch could not remember what that telegram said, or why he had brought his daughter into Purgatory City. He wasn't a Ranger in those days, just a mustanger trying to make something out of a hardscrabble ranch for his wife, daughter, and sons. He just recalled how beautiful, how innocent, the girl was. What had she been? Six? Seven? Ten? That would have been the first telegraph line that connected Purgatory City with Dallas and Austin and all points east. Probably wouldn't have gotten here had it not been for Fort Spalding.

"Hurrah! More music!"

He read the words, but they made no sense to him. Just words. Read them again. He wondered if he would wake up. Another nightmare that jackals like Matthew McCulloch were not supposed to have.

"Vud you like to reply, sir?" the clerk asked. "Captain Hollister has asked for an acknowledgement."

"Yeah." McCulloch handed the paper to Keegan. "Let's go."

CABLE MESSAGE
The West Texas Telegraph Co.
TO: McCulloch, Matt, C/O Peering Prison Farm
Young Territory, Llano Estacado, Texas
Received at: Purgatory City, Tex.
Received at: Peering Prison Farm

MESSAGE: *Comancheros hit stagecoach at Fort Savage station. Stage found wrecked burned half-mile away. Driver dead. Messenger gravely wounded but crawled till sheepherder found him. Your daughter must be alive. But taken by raiders. Bonderhoff's daughter taken too. Messenger said widow and two small twins also gone and four prostitutes. Willing to dispatch all men to help if needed. Will also get the Mobeetie Rangers off their hides. This is now too big for just you. Give me the word. Good luck. Respond quickly.*

Keegan swore savagely as McCulloch followed Ledbetter to the farm's telegraph office. Breen said nothing, but McCulloch heard the hard intake of breath. That bounty hunter likely never would admit to it, but half the population in Purgatory City knew how he fancied Bonderhoff's daughter.

Inside the shack, the clerk went to the machine, found a pad, and laid it on the counter next to a tin cup filled with pencils.

"Your reply, sir," he said, "and—"

"I'll tell you what to send on that contraption," McCulloch said. "To Captain Hollister, Texas Rangers, in Purgatory City."

The man bit his lower lip, too, but that was out of nerves.

"*Herr* sir, the Vest Texas Telegraph Company and Vestern Union, our parent company, both require—"

"Clear the line, son, and start sending out your code."

The man hit a few keys.

"Forget Mobeetie," McCulloch said. "Stay put. You'll be needed there if I don't succeed. I've sent word ahead to Linden. According to plan. If you don't hear from me in a week—no, make that two weeks—assume I am dead."

The clerk tapped. Stopped. Got a reply. Struck out another message, then swung around and swallowed.

"Vill that be all, sir?"

"Yeah."

"I am sorry to deliver the bad news, sir." The clerk sounded sincere.

"Don't be. I appreciate it. Linden and those weasels— they're the ones who are going to be sorry."

The door opened and two strangers entered, one dressed like he owned the place, the other in the prison uniform of a fancy guard. Breen introduced them as Captain Peering, owner of the farm, and Warden Franklin Plummer.

"What in heaven's name are in those boxes on those two mules you brought here?" the warden demanded. "The letters on them—"

"That's my business," McCulloch told him. "But don't worry. I'm riding out as soon as I can water my animals."

"I'll be riding with him, Warden," Breen said.

Keegan spit into the trash can. "Aye. And I tender my resignation as your conscripted guard, thank ye, kindly."

"You men cannot leave," Plummer said. "We remain short on guards."

"Maybe so," Breen said. "But you don't have enough guards to stop us."

The warden stared at Captain Peering. They appeared to be stunned.

And Matt McCulloch? He had never quite understood the value of having friends. Good friends. McCulloch, Breen, and Keegan had been thrown together several times over the past few years—often not by their own choice, but by happenstance, and luck, good or bad. But this time . . . it felt different. And Matt McCulloch wanted to look after the two jackals he now realized were good friends.

"You boys ought to stay here," he said. "I appreciate—"

"And, laddie." Keegan cut him off. "We'd appreciate it if ye just kept your mouth shut. We're coming with ye."

"No argument," Breen added. He was speaking to McCulloch, but now he extended his left hand toward the warden. Matt couldn't see the bounty hunter, but figured Breen's right hand was on the butt of his holstered Colt. The right held the telegram.

Franklin Plummer took it and read it, and his face slackened. He passed the paper to Captain Peering, who paled when he read the message, and then whispered, "Dear God."

McCulloch looked at the clerk. "Telegraph the Ranger captain in Mobeetie. Tell him that if he does not get four Texas Rangers to Peering Farm he will be looking for a new job, after his trial in Austin for dereliction of duty."

The man just blinked repeatedly, like he was using his code with his eyes.

"And sign the governor's name," McCulloch said.

The man wet his lips, looked at Warden Plummer and Captain Peering for help.

"Do it," Captain Peering told him.

"Now," the warden added.

The message was sent. The clerk looked like he might keel over from heart failure.

"Four extra men," Captain Peering said in a whisper, "is nowhere near what we need."

"Like hell," McCulloch said. "You only got one prison here."

After the message was sent and acknowledged and the clerk seemed to realize that the worst had passed, McCulloch moved to the door, Breen and Keegan behind him, followed by Peering and Plummer.

"I'll have my orderlies pack some grub for you."

The offer from Warden Plummer surprised McCulloch, and he thanked the man for the generosity but said he wanted to ride out now.

"Slow down, Matt," Breen said. "That horse and those mules need rest. And we'll need some food. You've been living on jerky and your hard head for a week now. Think straight."

They stopped in front of the big house that looked about four hundred miles from where it should have been. The prisoners were at work now, most of them cropping the last of the cotton. He could see splinters in the wood from the Comanchero raid, and fresh graves for the prisoners and the guards. Most of the latter seemed to be fitted with bandages.

"I'll treat you to a drink while my orderlies get the grub packed," Peering said.

"Breen's right," Keegan whispered. "An hour won't make any difference."

"You wouldn't say that if that it was your daughter who had been taken by Boss Linden's bunch," McCulloch barked.

"Aye," the Irishman replied. "That I wouldn't be saying at all. But, laddie, I sure would hope I had a friend who would tell me that. And threaten to bash in me head if I didn't listen to good sense and solid reason."

McCulloch frowned.

"Warden." Now Breen was talking. "Could you do us one more favor, sir?"

"I suppose so. We owe you two. What do you need?"

"While Captain Peering's servants are fixing us some chow, and Matt, Sean, and me are having a bourbon 'fore we hit the trail, do you think you could fetch Green Clayton, bring him in." He glanced at the plantation owner. "If you don't mind, sir." But Breen did not wait for a reply. "Let Clayton join us. For a bit of a parley. And a proposition."

McCulloch frowned. Jed Breen was speaking in tongues, or some sort of code. McCulloch had never heard of anyone named Green Clayton.

"I see." The warden seemed suspicious.

"Do it, Franklin," Captain Peering said. "I've got a keg of Kentucky's finest. And the next shipment I get should have another case. Bring Clayton with you. We'll all have a toast."

Peering started climbing the steps. The warden headed toward the fields. Keegan nodded, wet his lips, and bounded the steps like a younger man, passed the owner, and opened the door for him, then followed him inside.

McCulloch stared at Breen, who smiled and started up the steps, too.

"Come on, Matt. There's something you have to see before we set out to get Ramona and Cynthia back. And Green Clayton is someone you really need to meet."

CHAPTER 24

The country here flattened. Purgatory City might be far from any hills, though a good rider could reach the stunning Davis Mountains in a day or so if he had a good horse. But from Cynthia McCulloch's father's horse ranch, a small hill or larger butte could be seen off to the west, east, and south. And when the wind wasn't blowing up too much dust, you could even see the faint purple outlines of those Davis Mountains, where Cynthia's father usually found most of the mustangs he caught, tamed—but never breaking their spirits—trained, and sold.

This country was like riding atop a pancake.

The grass grew high, but had been browned by a lack of moisture, a relentless sun, and a hard, warm wind. The Comancheros followed no trail that Cynthia could see, but knew where they were going.

She rode alongside the mother, now conscious but still addled. Her two sons rode alongside her, for comfort, but the Comancheros had made it clear that no one was to speak. And if they coughed or sneezed, they had better do it as softly as possible.

The boys did not ride alone. One was mounted in front of the Comanchero who called himself Wild Kent—who might have been the leader of this group were it not for the meaner one named Cullen Brice. He rode near the point. Cynthia and the prisoners were in the middle. The other boy rode in front of Cynthia. The Comancheros had tried to get him to ride with a man, but the kid cried so hard Cynthia feared the boy might rile the killers to the point one would slice his throat.

Cullen Brice refused to let that happen. He said one hundred pesos or more was worth the inconvenience, but he warned Cynthia. "Unlike my greed, woman, my patience is not unlimited. Keep him quiet, or he dies."

The way to keep him quiet, she told the evil man, is to keep him close to his mother.

So he would reach out and hold his mother's hand every once in a while, and the mother would sob, and so would the boy. But they did that quietly. And Cynthia always kept one arm on the boy, around his stomach or chest, or gripping his shoulder, or brushing the tears off his cheeks.

She could count her blessings. She rode with the mother and the two twins. Ramona Bonderhoff, she had the hard job. She rode alongside the badly injured prostitute. Sometimes Cynthia wondered if she had not helped that poor girl, who was tied to the horse with two busted legs. Usually, the pain made the woman pass out, but when she was awake, her agony was apparent. Ramona, riding or walking alongside her, wore herself out, and her nerves had to be shot after this hard traveling. But she was tough. In fact, Cynthia thought the gunsmith's daughter was tougher than she was.

Caring for a frightened child and a mother in shock was one thing. Looking after a city woman forced to ride across hard country with broken legs and heading to a fate that would likely be a hundred times worse . . . that was . . . that had to be . . .

Nothing short of hell.

"Oh, my God!"

That came from up ahead. One of the prostitutes had shouted.

"*Silencio,*" a Comanchero barked in Spanish.

The boy's name was Darnell. That's about all Cynthia had managed to get out of him, other than that his brother's name was Danny. Danny and Darnell. Cute names for twins.

He leaned over to the right, and Cynthia moved her arm to his shoulder to make sure he didn't topple out of the saddle.

"What is it?" he whispered.

"I don't know," she told him softly. "Sit up straight."

Then she saw it. The boy gasped.

One of the prostitutes muttered something quite profane. The Comancheros did not rebuke her for speaking loudly. They laughed with delight.

The canyon appeared out of nowhere. Flat, dismal land ended and dropped off into a world of color—of red and yellow rocks, bordered with pockets of green, trimmed with streaks of white. It had to dip five hundred feet below—maybe twice that distance.

She could not see how far the canyon reached, but it might have gone on for a mile, likely farther, perhaps forever. Maybe this was another mirage.

Hooves sounded, and the Comanchero who had captured her and Darnell and the twins' mother, reined up hard, and turned his horse around as he rode beside Cynthia and the kid, near the edge of the canyon they had just found.

"Ma'am." He tipped the brim of his hat. He always did that. An outlaw with manners. Cynthia did not know what to think of him. He had told her that his name was Jim Bob. She had not let him learn her name.

"Brice says we'll reach the entrance in a quarter mile. You'll have to ride single file. And there will be places where you will have to get off and walk the horses."

Cynthia tried to find Ramona and the prostitute who could not walk—who might not ever be able to walk again, especially if she did not get out of that saddle soon.

Jim Bob . . . Hardin? No. Harvey? Hardwick. That was his last name. Jim Bob Hardwick must have read her mind.

"Someone will have to take the reins to her horse and lead the animal," he said. He cursed, then sighed, and glanced between Cynthia and the boy and the horse's head. "Hell, someone will have to lead that poor lady down, too."

"I will," Cynthia said.

"No. No, ma'am. You look after them twins." He turned his horse, rode a few yards back, and cut between the Comancheros behind her, and to the other side where Danny now rode in front of Jim Bob's brother.

"When we start going down this trail, Billy Ray, I need you to take my horse."

"I'm taking my own horse, Brother," the meaner of the Hardwick brothers said.

"I gotta guide their ma down," Jim Bob argued.

"Let her take her own horse down. I ain't riskin' my life for no crazy petticoat."

"She can't do that. She'll go over the edge and take the horse with her."

"It'll be a blessing," Billy Ray said, but this time not as a shout, but almost a prayer. "For her and the horse."

"I'll do it."

Cynthia leaned over and realized that Danny had spoken.

"There," Billy Ray said. "It's settled."

"The kid can't do this," Jim Bob argued.

"He better. And he better be smart. Or, from what I been hearing, he'll be feeding buzzards and wolves at the bottom. He'll just be dessert, though. The horse will be supper."

Jim Bob cursed his brother and rode back to the side, precariously close to the edge.

"Whoa!" came a shout from ahead, and Cynthia, Jim Bob, and everyone else stopped their horses.

"Rest five minutes," came another command.

That order was repeated in Spanish.

"Then single file. Keep at least twenty feet apart. Try not to die."

No one laughed at the joke, which also was translated into Spanish.

"I want to help my mother," Darnell said after Cynthia helped him dismount.

"You need to help me," Cynthia told him.

"I'll help Danny," he said. "You don't need no help."

She smiled, and nodded. "All right. Be careful."

Jim Bob held the reins to his horse, and when the twin boys walked over, he shook his head.

"Walk alongside your ma for the time being," he said. "We got a ways before we'll hit the trail down. Then I'll take your ma down, your lady pal will take her hoss down, and you boys will take my hoss down. He's a good hoss. He likes boys, too." He cleared his throat. "But if he rears, kids, you let go of them reins. I've stolen a lot of good mounts, owned a few my ownself, but I ain't never yet found a hoss that was worth dyin' for. You boys savvy?"

They nodded.

Jim Bob smiled and took his horse into the line, but as he passed Cynthia he whispered, "That goes the same for you, Miss Cynthia."

* * *

She kept passing places that looked to be decent paths, but stayed in line, following the horse Jim Bob Hardwick was leading.

The wind blew harder, but she expected it to die when they disappeared over the rim. She pulled the horse she had been riding, and kept glancing back at the two boys. They kept looking over the side, as the depth deepened and deepened.

"Watch where you are going," she said. Of course, she had to remind herself of that. Behind the boys came Billy Ray Hardwick. Behind him more Comancheros, some leading mules, some horses. One man, she saw, stopped long enough to say a prayer and cross himself. And he, unless he was a new recruit—and he certainly did not look like a newcomer to this life—had been down this trail before. Maybe many times.

She whispered, *"From battle and murder, and from sudden death, Good Lord, deliver us."* And wondered where that had come from, how far back in her mind did she have to reach to pull it out.

Hooves thundered, and she gasped as a raider loped off to the side, where the prairie still stretched out, a bleak, and unbroken, world. He reined up and slid from his saddle. Jim Bob Hardwick stopped his horse now, turned, and motioned Cynthia ahead.

She said that prayer again, but louder this time.

"You go on," he said. "I'll be right behind you."

Cynthia stared.

He smiled and shrugged. "This way, if you get in trouble, I'm right behind you. And if the boys find trouble, I'm right in front of them."

When she hesitated, he cursed, and said, "I don't get to pretend to be some dime-novel hero every day, Miss Cynthia. Give me that, won't you?"

Turning, she found Darnell and Danny. Their faces had paled. Their mother seemed oblivious to everything. Maybe she was blessed.

"Be careful," she whispered, and saw Darnell smile. "Watch your step."

The boy's lips moved, and she felt a sudden warmth.

You . . . too.

She tried to swallow, and turned back and stared ahead. She gave Jim Bob Hardwick a curt nod, and led her horse around his.

Then she saw Cullen Brice, standing at the rim, holding the reins to his horse. He nodded at the rider who had cut in line, and that man and his horse stepped off the edge of the world and vanished.

She looked back at Jim Bob, who smiled. His lips moved, but she could not read his words. Maybe *Good Luck.* Maybe *Fare Thee Well.* Maybe the same prayer she had just repeated.

Cullen Brice nodded at the Mexican rider, and let him go. Once that man had disappeared, Brice nodded and Cynthia started walking. The horse she led began fighting, sensing the danger, but Cynthia jerked his head, and he fell into obedience—for now. The Comanchero butcher before her raised his hand, and Cynthia stopped.

"Hold up, missy," Brice said as he lowered his hand. He was chewing on a long stem of brown grass that he had pulled from the ground. "Let Miguel get a good distance from you." He looked down, and Cynthia did, too. She studied the ground. The pebbles were many, and she heard stones rolling off the side.

Cullen Brice was watching below. His hand absently rose and plucked the chewed grass from his mouth. He let the wind carry it away before he looked up and nodded at Cynthia.

"Move on," he said. "Keep your distance. And try not to get yourself killed. You'll fetch a good price when we sell you to some big redskin chief. Comanch' would love to have you for one of his squaws."

CHAPTER 25

The wind picked up and almost blew the hat off Jim Bob Hardwick's head. He stood on his tiptoes, looking down, but could not see Miss Cynthia or the horse she was leading.

"She's still on the path, boy," the Comanchero leader said. He squatted, plucked another long blade of dried-up grass and stuck it between his teeth. "You would have heard her scream if she fell."

Now he saw her, being smart, not making the mistake of bringing the horse too close to the canyon's wall. Actually, he had not thought about that, so now he turned to the twin boys and said, "Kids. Listen to me. When you climb down, stay in the center of the path. Not too close—"

"Shut up, Hardwick," Cullen Brice said. "Sound travels far in this country, and nobody likes getting ordered by no novice. Not even stupid kids."

Jim Bob reined in his temper. "Not too close," he said, but lowered his voice. "And tell my—"

"I'll tell Billy Ray," Brice said. "Come on. Let your horse see the trail. Few steps forward. And you might want to lash the widow's hands to the horn." He grinned. "Don't want her falling a *long* way down."

Jim Bob took a few steps, stopped when Brice's head moved, and he watched the girl round a sharp turn. The horse followed. Then he saw nothing but a few men leading their horses farther down the trail. He was suddenly thirsty, but he did not know if his fingers and hands were steady enough to hold a canteen or unscrew the cap.

"Did you hear me, Hardwick?"

Jim Bob blinked. He nodded, and the words Brice had spoken finally registered. He looked at the saddle, surprised to see a woman sitting there. Then he remembered the mother of the twins.

He started to unloosen his bandanna, but turned back toward Brice. "But if the horse goes over, it'll take her with him."

"If that horse goes over, you'll go over after it does," Brice said. He shook his head and whispered a curse. "The woman's more likely to come to her senses and fling herself to a merciful end. Tie her to the horn, Hardwick. That's the safest thing to do."

Maybe Brice was right. Jim Bob went to work, but told the twins behind him what he was doing. "This is for your mother's protection. This is so—"

"Can't you just shut the hell up?" Cullen Brice growled.

Jim Bob tied the last knot. The woman still looked like she was lost.

"All right, Hardwick. Your turn. Don't rush. Take your time. You'll get down there when you get down there. Then we got to ride a ways to camp."

"How far down is it?" Jim Bob asked.

Cullen Brice smiled. "Eight hundred feet. Or so I been told. Not all at once. Hell, you fall off right here, I don't think you'd drop more than a hundred, hundred and twenty-five. And the treetops would stop you from hitting the ground. Maybe."

When Jim Bob turned back to the twin boys, Brice barked, "Get movin', kid. I'll tell them snot-nosed punks what to do. But be smart. This ain't no race. And you got the boys' ma to think about."

He swallowed, wrapped the reins around his right hand, then thought better of it. He held the reins loosely.

"That's wise, Jim Bob. You ain't the idiot I been takin' you fer." Cullen Brice spit out the grass. "Seen a lot of smarter men go over because they couldn't get loose of that leather they was holdin'. Move. I'll see you at the base."

When Jim Bob and the horse were maybe twenty feet down the trail, the Comanchero yelled. "I'll see you. Wonder if you'll see me." He laughed.

Jim Bob managed not to look back up. He kept his eyes on where he was walking. But he smiled, and called back, "That depends on if you're dead or alive, Brice."

When he reached the first turn, he heard Brice chuckling, then telling the twins. "Hold up. I don't care a whit if one of you falls over the edge. But don't take that hoss with you. Savvy that, boys?"

He breathed easier when he saw Miss Cynthia and her horse. They were moving down a steep incline, the woman inching down sideways, sliding sometimes. At least she wore real moccasins now. She had been given those by a silver-bearded Mexican when they had arrived back at that station called Fort Savage. Jim Bob looked at his own boots, and now began to wonder if he should have bought, likely on credit, a pair of moccasins for himself.

Cynthia fell to her knees, and Jim Bob gasped. He started to cry out, raising his hand to issue a warning—to whom, he wasn't sure. But the horse shied at the sudden movement, and Jim Bob cut off his shout, and turned suddenly back toward the horse.

"Easy," he whispered. "Easy."

The mother did not seem to notice anything. She just stared.

Jim Bob made himself think now, let his mind clear. He had a goal. That was something Pa always told the boys. Set yourself a goal, big goal, small goal, middle-of-the-road goal. And focus on making that one. When you reach that, then get your next goal. Of course, their pa's goal had usually been *Find a jug.* The next goal would be: *Get drunker than hell.* And after that, *Let's do 'er ag'in.*

"Make it to that next cut," he said softly, and turned to the horse and the mother. "Let's make it to that next cut," he said. "You ready, ma'am?" He started moving, keeping in the center of the trail.

At some point, he could not tell where the center of the path was. It was that narrow. He thought about stopping, going back to warn the twin boys. But he couldn't stop now. He couldn't turn the horse around. There was just one way to go. Down. Down.

I'm climbing down to hell, he thought.

He found the path where he remembered seeing Cynthia slide. The pebbles were slick here, and the reddish-orange clay slick and damp. Slippery like soap. Here, whatever moisture came into the canyon remained. Not enough sunlight to dry it. And the wind did not blow here.

"Easy," he told the horse when it fought the bit and reins. "Easy."

Or maybe he was telling himself.

"You all right there, ma'am?"

No answer. The eyes rarely blinked.

He could not swallow. There was no moisture in his mouth. And he wasn't about to sidle up to the horse and find his canteen.

So he put one foot in front of him, standing sideways now, looking where he stepped, testing the hold, then turning back to study the horse and the poor woman. When he straightened, he slowly exhaled. He did not slip. This time. He brought his other foot down, tried to swallow, and put his weight on his legs.

Again.

Inching down. Inching down.

No longer did he look for Miss Cynthia. He could not look up the trail at the boys. He stepped again. Right foot. Left foot. Right. Left. He did not even look at the woman lashed to the saddle horn with his bandanna. Jim Bob stopped to catch his breath, and he saw the cross carved into the sandstone wall. Jim Bob thought in awe about God. God had carved a cross here, as a reminder to Jim Bob of His power. God had carved it with his finger, or with rain, or maybe lightning, or wind over years. Hundreds and hundreds of years. Or thousands of years. Or . . .

Blinking, he saw another carving at the foot of the rude cross. No, God had not carved this for Jim Bob Hardwick.

S. REVELLES
D: 1859

Some Comanchero had likely gone over the edge here. The horse began to fight again, and Jim Bob barked, and glared. "No. Come on. We got to get around this edge. And you ain't pulling me and Missus O'Leary down to keep Señor Revelles company."

He was amazed that he remembered the mother's last name.

"All right, Missus O'Leary," he said. "We got a bit of a turn here. You just relax." The next words weren't quite as friendly. "Maybe just close your eyes." They were so unnerving, staring, but not seeing.

Mrs. O'Leary did not close her eyes, of course. She just stared.

When the horse appeared around the sharp turn, Jim Bob felt like praying. The path became twice as wide. It moved now at less of a grade. The trail seemed harder, firmer, and he found Miss Cynthia moving with ease, a Mexican ahead of her.

He had trouble guessing how long this part of the trail went. Maybe one hundred and fifty yards. The men ahead of Miss Cynthia moved quicker, but she kept the same pace. So that's what Jim Bob decided to do. He also stopped every now and then, and stepped toward the edge, looking at the twins. Behind them he could see his brother. And another Comanchero leading a horse and a mule behind Billy Ray.

Jim Bob turned around and walked forward, keeping a firm, but loose, hold on the reins. He saw Miss Cynthia as she reached the next turn. Ahead of her, where the world dropped off again, he saw a cone-shaped sandhill, striped with white and orange, and a little stream with water that reflected the colors of the hills. Probably no reflection. Probably the water was just that muddy.

And he thought: *Could one little stream like that carve this canyon by itself?*

He led the horse down. By now, his shirt stuck to his skin with sweat. His heart pounded like a steam-driven hammer. He thought he would plunge into that muddy stream when he reached bottom, and drink it, mud and all, till he felt done. Cynthia was gone now, making the next turn. He forgot about patience and quickened his pace, came to the bend, and peered around it.

His heart sank. Cynthia was ahead, still working her way down, but the canyon now looked steeper, even deeper.

Maybe he was going crazy. Perhaps it was just the lay of the land. But he understood, as he looked back and found the twins and his brother and the Mexican with the two mules, that they still had a long way to go.

"Ma'am," he told Mrs. O'Leary. "We got another turn to make." He had stopped looking at her. "We're almost home," he said, lying, and wishing he had never run away from his home.

Eight hundred feet. That's what Cullen Brice had told him. Just eight hundred feet. But that was from the flat plains to the base of the canyon. Eight hundred feet down, but a man didn't go eight hundred feet straight down. Not and live to tell about it. This part of the trail had been a respite. The one Miss Cynthia was on now seemed steeper, sharper, and the ground was so uneven. The width seemed hardly enough for a horse. And the drop was a long, long way down.

This would be the dangerous part of the journey.

"Hell," Jim Bob heard himself say. "How do you know? The next bend might be longer, narrower and a hell of a drop to nowhere."

He realized now why the Comancheros had picked this for their hideout. First, a traveler had to happen upon it. The plains ended and the canyon began. And if someone happened to find it, by thunder, then he would have to find a way to get to the bottom. And there was no reason to go into a place like this. It did not appear to be gold country. Hell, how many mines had ever produced anything that amounted to pay dirt in this state? All the buffalo a Kiowa or Comanche needed could be found on the grassy prairies. There was nothing likely down here, except death.

He pulled his horse and unspeaking rider easy, talking like he was preaching to a baby, maybe even singing one of the hymns that had always comforted his mother. The horse made it, snorted, and Jim Bob turned around. He saw Miss Cynthia again.

She gave him hope.

But then he heard the scream.

CHAPTER 26

There was a map of Texas that Matthew McCulloch had seen in Austin once. Capitol building maybe, or it could have been the governor's mansion after Texas had pulled out of the Union, Sam Houston had been kicked out as governor, and everybody thought the war would be over in months. And an old Ranger McCulloch had known had a crackerjack map tacked to the old building down in the Nueces Strip.

But he hadn't seen anything like this.

And really didn't care to be looking at it right now.

"It's a map of Texas," he said, and sipped his glass of water, having turned down the offer of fine Kentucky bourbon. "It's real pretty, Jed, but . . ."

"Look at it closer, Matt." The bounty hunter walked toward the big desk, seemingly pulled an umbrella out of nowhere, and pointed toward the ceiling. "You've been into the Panhandle before," he said. "This is no-man's country. Does this look right to you?"

"It's a drawing," McCulloch said, losing his patience. "It's . . ."

Then he understood.

He set the glass of water on a table, and walked closer. He stopped. Don't get too close. He stepped back until he could take everything in. He looked at the Panhandle's depiction, then focused on the Davis Mountains, country he knew like the back of his hand. He saw where Purgatory City would have been. He measured the distance, and knew that, in scale, the distance from Fort Stockton to Fort Davis looked about right. Fort Spalding wasn't on the map, but Spalding wasn't much of a post, and Purgatory City really wasn't big enough to rival those towns included.

His eyes traced the Pecos River. That was right, too.

He found the Hill Country, and found the small river that had to be the Perdenales, traced it to where it joined the Colorado. He remembered Cynthia playing in the water after he had made it back after the fall of the Confederacy. He could almost see his daughter splashing, picking up a chunk of limestone, and throwing it at one of her bullying brothers. He knew that river—had known it anyway.

So he looked at the map as a whole, then stared at the Panhandle.

"I don't know of any canyon like that one," he said. He hadn't meant to say that aloud, but it was what was running through his mind. "But you got to understand, when I was riding through that—no-man's country, that's a right fine description. When I was riding there, I was usually running my horse hard to keep from getting scalped. Or riding hard after some hombre that the state of Texas wanted real bad."

"I always thought that country was just as flat as the crown of a Spaniard's hat," Sean Keegan said to McCulloch's right.

"It is," McCulloch said. "And it ain't." He pointed just below the Panhandle, to a spot where Texas curved eastward, a bit below the Red River. "See those hills. That's the Copper Breaks. Big power to Comanches and Kiowas. Almost got killed there back in '68. On the Pease River."

He nodded. "That line of blue looks about right, too. Though rivers change their courses."

He found another spot. "This was before my time, but Old Man Horseshoe said that's where the largest Comanche camp he ever saw was." Teepees were crowded in the illustration, along with a white buffalo. "And that's where Chief Black Forehead saw a white buff." He shook his head. "Old Man Horseshoe died in '63—in bed, in his sleep—never thought that would happen. Wife's letter reached me in . . . well . . . wherever the hell we were that autumn. And Old Man Horseshoe, he taught me a lot, and he knew this country better than most white men. But he couldn't draw worth a tinker's cuss."

"The man who painted this," Breen said, "knows this country even better than you, Matt."

"Knows?" McCulloch asked.

Breen nodded.

McCulloch considered that, then said, "Or he has some imagination."

Now Breen shook his head. "I've met him. Imagination isn't his strong suit."

"He's a fool," Sean Keegan sang out. "And too little to whip soundly in a fistfight." Keegan drained his whiskey.

"Well, what do you think he's going to do?" McCulloch said. "Draw us a better map? Write down the directions so we can find it? We're burning time, pards. And we don't have any time to spare. Nor does Cynthia. Nor does Ramona, Jed."

Now McCulloch saw something in Jed Breen's eyes. The anger. The intensity. And he knew immediately that he had made a mistake, bringing Ramona Bonderhoff's name into this. But McCulloch couldn't back down. Couldn't apologize. He stared at Breen, and saw his own reflection in the pupils. Suddenly, all those miles from Purgatory City to Peering Farm caught up with him. He had been wrong. Wrongheaded. Acting like a fool.

He picked up his glass, took another long sip, and looked at Breen. "All right, Jed. Who the hell painted this?"

The door opened, and the Warden Franklin Plummer shoved a tiny man through the door. "Don't dally, Clayton," the warden said.

He didn't look like an artist, not this rough-faced man. He snorted, and turned to spit on the Oriental rug when he spied the decanter of bourbon. Now he wet his lips.

"This appears to be a meetin' of minds," the man said in a hard Texas accent. "And whiskey is always a good way to start a meetin'."

"Not you, Clayton," the warden said.

The prisoner stopped and laughed.

"Let him have a drink, Franklin," Captain Peering said.

The warden frowned. The little man headed to the decanter, pulled off the stopper, and drank without bothering to dirty up a glass. He coughed, shook his head, and laughed. "Must be rusty. I been drinkin' the brew some of the boys make. Not used to cutting the dust with any of the good stuff." He took another swallow.

"I know these two gents," he said, staring at McCulloch. "But don't reckon I had the pleasure of makin' yer acquaintance."

The eyes. Those green eyes. McCulloch had to look away. They were like emeralds, but hard, deadly. Yet they also reminded him of Cynthia's green eyes. McCulloch emptied his glass of water.

"I reckon you'd have to be Matthew McCulloch," the prisoner said. "The third jackal."

He had enough bourbon, and walked over and poured two fingers into McCulloch's glass.

"But you wouldn't know me," he said.

McCulloch looked at the painting, saw the rude signature, and remembered the name.

"You'd be Green Clayton."

The man bowed. He turned to the painting and nodded. "It ain't half bad. My ma said I had talent. She wanted to send me off to Paris. Or some place in Germany. I wasn't gonna be no sissy painter. I wanted something bigger than some da Vinci. Nobody knew him from Jesse James till he was dead."

"Nobody has ever heard of Green Clayton," McCulloch said, "except maybe a couple of Texas Rangers and some prison guards."

He laughed. "Oh, Mister Ranger, but they will. They will and they shall remember the name for a long time. Longer than they'll remember Sir David Wilkie."

McCulloch took a small taste of the bourbon. He had never heard of da Vinci or anyone named Wilkie.

"Well, here I am, in the presence of three notorious jackals. What the hell do you want with me?"

McCulloch held his glass toward the painted map.

"You're taking us to the Canyon of Weeping Women."

Green Clayton laughed. "You breakin' me out of this cotton-pickin' cotton farm?"

"That's right." McCulloch did not even look at Peering or the warden.

For the first time, Green Clayton looked surprised. He brought the decanter up, took two more swallows, and wiped his mouth with his other arm. "The hell you say."

Breen cleared his throat. "I thought you wanted to take revenge on Boss Linden."

"Aye," Sean Keegan added. "Boss Linden likes Cullen Brice a whole lot more than—"

"Boss Linden's mama is a pig," Clayton said. "He'd be dead by now if I hadn't showed him where the Canyon of Weepin' Women is. He wouldn't have met Chief Black Forehead. He wouldn't have nothin' without me. I get caught just because I helped him after his hoss got shot from under him. He'd be dead, then, too. Man like that ain't fit to live. And I aim to kill him."

He laughed, returned the decanter, and spun around.

"And I will kill him. But I'll kill him myself. I won't be helpin' no stinkin' law dogs who just want the reward."

He headed for the door, but made sure he walked past McCulloch. "The only thing you'll find if you head out there on your own, boys, is your graves. But that's fine with me. You'll just be three men that I don't have to kill."

He stopped in front of McCulloch.

"Go to hell," he said, looking up into the former Texas Ranger's eyes.

McCulloch laid him out with one punch.

Then he turned around to the warden and Peering. "You gents ought to excuse yourselves," he said. "Maybe see if any new messages have come in to the telegraph building. Maybe stay there for a couple of hours. Maybe not take notice if Green Clayton isn't here till we get back."

"Maybe." Captain Peering nodded. "Maybe . . . that's . . . reasonable."

The warden, on the other hand, was flustered.

McCulloch wasn't sure which way the man would turn, but Captain Peering cleared his throat and said in a voice barely above a whisper. "Franklin. Don't . . ."

"These jackals," the warden said hoarsely, "are delivering ammunition to Boss Linden's Comancheros. If that ammunition gets to Black Forehead . . . or any outlaw, red or white . . . Texas will be set back fifty years. Not only that, but I'm warden here. I took an oath. I—"

"Franklin," Peering said. "You've got a daughter of your own. What is she now, sixteen? What the hell would you do if that was your girl . . . taken by Comancheros? Taken by Boss Linden's Comancheros? And you haven't forgotten Cullen Brice. That's probably why Linden had him busted out of jail. Brice can deal with Black Forehead. He's the last Comanche holdout since he ran off the reservation. Think of your daughter, man. Or just, dang blast it, think!"

CHAPTER 27

The man was cursing, the horse snorting, and that made the horse Cynthia was leading begin fighting rein and bit. She tightened her grip, turned. The horse tried to rear, but she held firm, and the gelding must have sensed the surroundings, and knew that rearing would be more dangerous than jerking his head one way, then the other.

She whispered to the horse, in Apache, then English.

"You ignorant son of a—"

"Help!" That came from one of the twins. Darnell. Cynthia released the reins, and the horse snorted, saw freedom and started running. Cynthia dived out of the animal's way. She saw the twins, one on his knees, the other being jerked up and down, tossed this way and that way as he refused to let go of the reins.

"Let go!" Cynthia yelled, but realized she had screamed the order in the Apache tongue. She yelled hard, this time in English. "Let go, Darnell!"

Instead, Danny dived and wrapped his arms around his brother's legs. The horse's hooves came down. Cynthia cringed. Then she was running, singing an Apache horse song. The horse whipped its head, and both boys went toward the edge of the path.

"Noooo!" Cynthia cried.

But the horse jerked its head the other way, and this time the boys were freed from the reins, from that childish sense of duty. They crashed against the red-and-yellow sandstone wall. The horse reared, snorted, turned to run, but saw another horse rearing, screaming, its hooves crashing toward the man leading it.

The man. Jim Bob Hardwick's brother.

Cynthia stopped and slid by the twins.

Darnell was sobbing. Danny was sucking two fingers.

"Are you—" She had to catch her breath. "All . . . right?"

Darnell tried to stop crying. Danny timidly withdrew his bloody fingers. "Are they . . . ?" He sniffed. "Still there."

"Yes." She looked at Darnell. "Stop it. Do not cry. A Chiricahua warrior does not cry. Our enemies might hear you."

Tears still streamed down the boy's cheeks, but he made no more sound.

"Stay here." She saw the horses, the one she had been leading, and Jim Bob Hardwick's, which the boys had been pulling. They had stopped, seeing the difficulty of the turn ahead, and now slowed, stopped, twisted their heads. The horse behind her—Billy Ray Hardwick's—kept fighting. Jim Bob's brother kept cursing at it. That seemed to stop the two horses from doing anything.

She looked past the dancing horse and the fighting man, and saw other men holding their horses by the reins tight, almost up to the bridle's bit. No one dared to help Billy Ray Hardwick.

"Stay here," she said, pushed to her feet, and hurried toward the rearing, twisting, snorting horse and the evil white man who had wrapped one rein around his left hand, and was whipping the horse's face with the rein in his right.

She tried to sing the horse song again, but stopped now. The horse reared. The man stopped lashing. His face turned white, and he desperately tried to free his left hand from the looped-over leather rein.

Cynthia bolted for him. She dived, reaching out. Then the horse was gone. And so was Billy Ray Hardwick. The screams—the animal's and the man's—melded into one.

She hit the ground, reached out, lost her breath, bounced, and felt herself going over the edge, too.

But she would not scream. The wife of Killer of Cougars. Nor would Litsog shame Three Dogs, who had taught the white girl the ways of the Chiricahuas. Billy Ray Hardwick was a coward. Litsog would die with honor, without a word. She closed her eyes and saw the kind face of a dark-eyed, dark-bearded white man.

"Why do you do that, Papa?"

She is in the barn. Her father dips his left hand in a bucket of something with the consistency between honey and muddy water, but smells like old guts. He smears this mess on the bay filly's right front leg. Then begins wrapping it with a sheet from a bed.

"Ohhhh." She cringes. "Ma will be madder than a wet hen when she finds out what you done to y'all's bed!"

He keeps wrapping, ties the end, and pushes back. He wipes his hand with what's left of the sheet.

"Ma would tan my hide," she says.

He holds out his still-reeking hand. She backs away. He laughs and wipes it some more.

"I'll explain it to your ma," he says, and studies the young bay.

"Why'd you do it, Papa?"

"She's hurt." He watches as she moves gingerly to the bay mare in the corner. The mother horse remains suspicious, but begins to nuzzle her daughter.

"Eddie Stryker says there ain't nothing to do to a horse with a bad leg but put it out of its misery," she tells him.

"Well, with luck, that medicine will end that little girl's misery," he tells her. He uses straw to scrub his hand. He isn't even wearing gloves.

"Eddie Stryker means you shoot the horse."

Her father nods. "That's what Eddie's pa would have done. Guaranteed."

"So why didn't you?"

"She was hurt. Needed help. You help someone who's hurt."

"Eddie Stryker says you and his pa killed about five thousand Yankees when you was out fighting in the war."

"Does he, now?"

Her head bobs with vigor. "He does." Her head tilts. He's watching the mare and the filly closer. "Did you?"

His eyes soften, and he smiles beneath that hairy face that has not shaved since the filly started favoring its right foreleg.

"Did I what?"

"Did you and Eddie's papa kill five thousand
Yankees?"

He chuckles. "If we had, I expect we might have won
the war. Don't you?"

She shrugs.

"Does Eddie Stryker say anything nice?" he asks.

"Not much."

"That figures. Apple don't fall far from the tree, does
it, sweetheart?"

Her face squinches. "Eddie never said nothing about
having an apple tree. I like apples."

He laughs and holds out his stinking hand. "Want to
help your papa up?"

She takes a step, but nods with her chin. "Let me pull
you up with your left hand."

"Oh." He finds his hat, plants it on his head, and
brings the right hand down and the left one up. "This
better?"

"I think so."

She leans back, and he grunts, but he comes to his
feet, and turns and studies the two horses at the far
end of the stall.

"We'll check on her tomorrow. See how she walks."
He heads toward the barn door, and they step into the
sunshine.

"I don't know about you, Papa . . ." she says.

He laughs, shaking his head, and stares down at her.

"What don't you know about me?"

"Well." She figures out the words. "You take care of a baby horse that Eddie Stryker's pa would have put out of its misery. That's what Eddie says, anyhow. But you went to war, and maybe didn't kill five thousand Yanks, but I reckon you killed . . . I don't know . . . two thousand."

"Might not have killed a single one," he says. "I wasn't as good a shot as Eddie Stryker's pa."

"I seen you shoot, Papa."

"Well, the war's over. And that filly's life . . . it's just beginning. Same as yours."

"Hmmmm." She considers this. "Well . . . I'm glad you didn't kill that baby horse."

"So am I."

She sighs and shakes her head. "Eddie Stryker won't believe a word of it."

"You don't have to tell him. Keep my reputation intact."

"Huh?"

He laughs. "Want to help me saddle Ginger?"

"Sure. But where you going?"

He takes her hand with his right, the one that had smeared all that stinky medicine on the bay's leg. But that's okay now. There's some hay sticking to it, but the hand's warm, and not smelling or feeling icky. They walk to the corral.

*"Town," he answers. "Going to see if I can find a new
bedsheet at Pendergrass's before your ma gets back
from that quilting bee at Missus Ketchum's."*

She slid over the edge. Her eyes remained closed, but
she felt the rushing air, the emptiness, and the screams of
the man and the horse no longer echoed. They had reached
bottom. Both were dead.

Then something bit into her left calf. Another hold tightened on her right ankle. The injured ankle almost made her
scream.

Her eyes opened. She spotted the treetops below. The
boulders. And the crumpled mess of a horse. The man, the
mean, vindictive Billy Ray Hardwick, she could not see.
Just his hat, which was perched atop a tree. Branches had
been sheared off. The trees still swayed from the intrusion.
Billy Ray Hardwick? Where was he? Then she knew. He
was under the horse.

And she would soon be on top of it.

"We . . . got you . . .!"

That was Darnell's voice. Danny said something else, a
word that most white mothers would have punished a son
for saying, or even thinking about saying.

"Let go!" she yelled. "Let go of me!"

She kept sliding. All the boys were doing was slowing
the inevitable. And if they did not let go, she would take
them to their deaths, too.

"Let go! Do you not hear me? Let go. Let go, or you will
die and—"

She screamed at the pain. Something heavy had crashed
down on her legs just below the knees.

Her chin bounced against the sandstone. A tooth
cracked. Both lips began to bleed. But she wasn't moving.

"Move back!" She heard the voice, more grunt than English. "Get away! Get away! I've . . . got . . . her."

She yelled again, as the weight rolled over her ankles. Then strong hands latched onto the ankles. "I'm pulling you . . ." The sentence stopped, but the grip on her tightened. "What the hell are you two . . . ? Let go of me."

"No!" Darnell's voice.

"We're helping!" That sounded like Danny.

"Let go!"

She knew that voice. For a moment, it sounded like her father's. A much younger man, though.

"Hang on!"

"Don't let her die!" That was Darnell, and he was sobbing again.

"Hang on!"

Her head hit a long-dead tree root. Another cut began to bleed. She saw the dead horse. The hat that had belonged to Billy Ray Hardwick. She saw the smashed branches. Then she saw the far side of the canyon, the rugged red walls, the green of juniper and piñon and maybe oaks or elms. And the endless blue sky.

And then her chin scraped against red earth, and she stopped moving. The weight left her ankles, and she breathed in dust and air, and felt herself being rolled over.

She saw her father.

But then the face became paler, younger . . . Jim Bob Hardwick. He gasped for breath. On his left she saw Darnell. On his right, knelt Danny.

"Are . . . you . . . all . . . right?" Jim Bob Hardwick asked.

"I . . . think . . . so . . ." She did not sound like Litsog. She did not even sound like Cynthia Jane McCulloch. She sounded like a frightened schoolgirl, like the time they huddled behind the schoolmaster's desk while the wind roared like a train, hail pounded the tin roof, and the twister uprooted elm trees all around them, ripping off planks from the wall, smashing windows, spinning McGuffey's Readers, pieces of chalk, papers, and lunch pails around the dark, dangerous room.

Jim Bob Hardwick rolled away. He sprang to his feet, looking down the trail, then up it.

"Billy!" he screamed, and the echo bounced all over the canyon. "Billy! Billy Ray!"

Cynthia blinked, sat up. She let the boys hug her, then she kissed each twin's cheek. As she rose to her knees, she put her hands on the boys' shoulders. "Thank you," she said. "Thank you for my life. You were very brave. Very brave. Now . . . *stay here!*"

She looked down the trail at two Comancheros who had made their way around the sharp turn. Up the trail, she saw the horses. And other men holding their mounts or mules close and tight. And, of course, here came Cullen Brice, cursing, barking at the men he passed. He did not pull his horse. He walked alone.

It would take him a few minutes to reach them.

Favoring the bad ankle, she limped to the edge, reached out, and took Jim Bob Hardwick by his right arm.

"Come on," she whispered. "Don't look anymore. There is nothing you can do."

CHAPTER 28

"Don't throw water on him. But wake him up."

Having finished removing the rope that tied Green Clayton's hands and legs underneath the saddle of a chestnut gelding, Matthew McCulloch rose and pushed the unconscious Comanchero off the saddle. He landed with a thud on the high, but dead, grass. The horse twisted a bit, but McCulloch grabbed the reins and pulled the gelding away, wrapping the leather around a small stone underneath a cottonwood tree on the banks of a small stream. He removed the lariat from the saddle and then walked back to the spread-eagled body of the little killer.

Sean Keegan knelt and slapped Clayton's face. Jed Breen stood near the three other horses, holding his Sharps, scanning the ridgeline. Occasionally, the bounty hunter would study their back trail. Not that anyone expected the warden or Captain Peering to follow them, but Breen hadn't stayed alive as long as he had by underestimating anyone.

"Wake up, ye piece of trash." Keegan slapped the face again.

The man groaned, blinked, and finally got his eyes to focus on the Irishman.

"You dirty rotten pig," the killer seethed.

Keegan grinned, slapped the man again, then rolled him over.

"What—"

Clayton raised his head, but Keegan grabbed a handful of greasy hair, jerked the head up till he heard cartilage cracking, and slammed the face into the red clay.

While the Comanchero groaned, Keegan grabbed the man's left hand, pulled it over to the lower backbone, did the same with the right hand, and used wet rawhide to bind the man's hands together. He wasn't satisfied till Clayton cried out in pain at the tightness of the rope.

Then he found the man's hair again, and jerked him up to his knees.

The man spit out dirt, saliva, and curses.

"I'll kill you—you son of a—"

Keegan slapped the man's head with his hat.

"Quiet with ye," Keegan barked, and then stepped away, slapping the dust and grime from his campaign hat before settling it on his head.

McCulloch picked up his canteen, walked over till he stood next to Keegan, and extended the canteen.

"Give him some water," the horseman ordered.

Without a word of protest, Keegan uncorked the container and took the few steps to the fiery-eyed killer. Not wishing to drink after the likes of the pig on his knees, Keegan took a quick swallow himself before he tipped the canteen toward Clayton's mouth.

The man guzzled a few swallows, wanting more, but Keegan withdrew the canteen, letting some of the water splash over the man's forehead, hair, and face.

"Ye be lucky, laddie," he said as he slammed the cork back into place with the palm of his left hand. "There be water right here." He stepped back. "He's all yours, Matt."

McCulloch was uncoiling the rope. He stepped forward and let the small loop of the lariat dangle in front of Clayton.

"You're taking us to the Canyon of Weeping Women," he said. His voice sounded dead.

"The hell I am."

"You have two choices. You take us to that canyon. Or I send you to hell."

The man spit. His laugh sounded dry, callous.

"You want Boss Linden dead," McCulloch said. "He's all yours. I just want my daughter back. Ramona Bonderhoff back. And those other women those sons of bitches took at the Fort Savage stagecoach station."

"I'll kill Boss Linden myself." The man's throat was already dry. "And after that, if your daughter looks a lot better than you do, I'll give her a—"

The lariat caught Clayton's face hard, ripping a gash in the cheek, and toppling him to the hard clay.

"Pick him up again, Sean," McCulloch said.

The old horse soldier did, and when he unloosened a bandanna, McCulloch said, "Let him bleed."

Keegan stepped back. Jed Breen studied the ridgelines to the west, and to the east.

"I don't have time or patience, you piece of dung," McCulloch said as he rolled up the lariat a bit, but still left the loop dangle. "You're taking us. Or we find it ourselves."

"Find it, you cur dog. Find it." The Comanchero tried to spit but didn't have enough moisture in his mouth. "Many a fool has tried. And many—"

He stopped, blinked, and stared at the leathery Ranger.

"What the hell are you smiling at, you—"

McCulloch faked another lashing with the lariat. The man flinched, and cursed when he was not struck again.

"Anybody can find that canyon now, you stupid jackass. That big painting you did for Peering shows us the easiest path to it." He pointed to the north. "All we have to do is find the Eroded Plains Fork of the Red, and that'll take us right there."

Green Clayton's silence lasted twenty seconds.

"I thought so." McCulloch laughed without any humor.

"You bas—" The Comanchero drew in another breath, and laughed. "If you ride in like that, you'll be dead and never hear the arrow or ball the sends you to the devil. Not that many white men have made the mistake of trying to find buffalo or antelope in that part of the country, and not many scouts have stumbled onto it. But they got one thing in common. They're all dead. The only people that get there, hardcase, are those that got dealings with Boss Linden's bunch. And that's Comancheros and injuns."

McCulloch's nod was brief. "I've got dealings with Boss Linden. He's expecting me." He pointed his free hand toward the horses and pack mules. "And that ammunition."

"You're a liar." Spittle leaked from the Comanchero's mouth. "And a fool."

"You're going to be the fool if you don't decide to join us. A dead fool."

"No one's expecting you. And I'm not a fool. Because—"

"I sent word to Boss Linden." McCulloch's words silenced the green-eyed killer. "By way of Pale Canyon."

The wind began to pick up. The silence stretched a full two minutes.

"You couldn't have gotten out of there alive." This time, Green Clayton didn't sound confident. He spoke like a man trying to convince himself of something that he knew was not true.

"But I did." McCulloch let the wind carry the loop a bit, before twisting his wrist to let the hemp swing back and be carried southeast by the wind. Back and forth. Back and forth. Like the pendulum on a rich man's clock. "Some of your companions, though, didn't."

Clayton's verdant eyes studied the tall man.

"From what I've heard," Sean Keegan said, "that wasn't the first time you rode in and out of Pale Canyon."

McCulloch nodded. "That time was state business. I was a Ranger. This time was personal."

"That was . . ." Clayton tried to picture the man standing before him. ". . . you?"

"That was me. Now I'm done wasting time."

The man regained his courage. "No." He tried to laugh, but it came out more like a dry cough. "No. No luck, Ranger."

"I'm not a Ranger anymore. Just a father protecting his daughter and his daughter's friends, and daughters of folks I don't rightly know."

"Once a Ranger, always a Ranger." Clayton tried to spit again. "But, no. You might have gotten in and out of Pale Canyon. But they won't let you in alive to the Canyon of Weeping . . ." His eyes found the mules. Again he started to lose that hard-edged confidence.

"Take him to that horse, Sean." McCulloch turned away from the prisoner and pointed at the horse underneath the cottonwood. "Put him back in the saddle. We'll be riding on. Alone. Just the three of us . . . unless you want to back out. Won't blame you a bit."

He turned toward Breen, who just stared at McCulloch.

McCulloch nodded, and led the way toward the cottonwood. He threw the looped end of the lariat over a thick, low branch, then tied the end around the trunk. And he waited there, his boots ankle deep in the creek. He reached up, and grabbed the end of the loop, and pulled it tight.

Breen walked to the three other horses and the pack mules. He shoved his Sharps in the scabbard, grabbed the reins to his horse, and swung into the saddle. He let the horse keep drinking from the stream, but turned around to watch.

Keegan shoved Green Clayton forward, and the man tripped and splashed in the water. The chestnut snorted, started to kick out at the strange noise, but McCulloch, holding the reins tightened, pulled the animal's head toward him and whispered a few soothing words.

"Don't let him drown," he told Keegan, who grabbed the man's collar, and jerked him to his knees.

A few moments later, McCulloch and Keegan had the little man—he wasn't that hard to lift—in the saddle, with the loop of the lariat around his head. Keegan reached up and tightened it, making a snug fit over Green Clayton's neck.

McCulloch let the reins slacken in his hand. The gelding started to drink again. He glanced at the country, and recalled the illustrations on Green Clayton's map of Texas that hung in Captain Peering's fancy home. Pale Canyon looked like Hell. But this place, with its vibrant colors, its peaceful setting, it really was raw, but beautiful. Most folks thought this country was worthless, but they had thought the same of the Great Plains to the north. The Great American Desert they called it. But now it was no desert at all. It was farmland. Rich, glorious farmland. Being settled every day by newcomers from the east, from countries on the other side of the Atlantic Ocean that Matt McCulloch had never even heard of.

But it didn't matter what the country looked like, uninhabitable, unimaginable, ugly, or something like this, where a man could feel the touch of God.

This was Texas, and no matter where a man set foot in Texas, he'd find death. Ugly, everlasting death. It was a country where you sometimes had to be a jackal to survive. He looked up at the man he was about to hang.

McCulloch waited till those green eyes, now reflecting complete fear, made contact with his.

"Now I figure your pals in the Canyon of Weeping Women might be expecting me, but have no plans other than ambushing us and trying to take that ammunition for themselves. But I also figure if they see you, they might have another notion."

"You can't kill me," Green Clayton pleaded. "You're a Texas Ranger."

"*Was* a Texas Ranger, buster. *Was.* Past tense." McCulloch let out a dry laugh. "And your memory isn't that good. Have you forgotten how many outlaws we hanged south of the Nueces Strip in those early days? No trial. No jury. They were wanted. They were captured. They were executed. And the politicians and lawyers in Austin never said one word against it. Summary justice, that's what our capt'n called it. Summary justice." He smiled without humor. "I've become a big believer in summary justice."

The man almost sobbed. "If they . . . wanted me . . . they'd . . . have taken me out with . . . Cullen Brice."

"Maybe so. More than likely, they didn't expect Sean and Jed to be there. They had to get out quickly, or they would have all been buried there."

The green eyes blinked.

McCulloch laughed. "You really are stupid, Clayton. That never struck you as a possibility?"

The short Comanchero wet his lips.

"You want to play this my way?" McCulloch asked.

The killer found new nerve. "Go to hell. You're lyin'. I was double-crossed. Go to hell."

"You'll be there in a few minutes. Kicking and choking. Tell your friends I left dead at Pale Canyon that I said, "Happy suffering."

He led the chestnut away.

CHAPTER 29

So this, Cynthia McCulloch thought, *is the Canyon of Weeping Women.* She looked over at Ramona Bonderhoff and wondered if the gunsmith's daughter was remembering the same thing that flashed through Cynthia's mind.

They sit in the stifling hot one-room schoolhouse in Purgatory City, then nothing much more than a crossroads with three saloons, one livery, a loosely defined mercantile where Mr. Bonderhoff rents a corner and works on guns and clocks and watches and anything else he thinks he could make better, and a stagecoach station attached to a six-room hotel—and some smaller shacks behind the saloons that schoolchildren aren't allowed to look at and no decent person talks about.

The schoolmaster will quit at the end of the term—"running for his life back to Baton Rouge," Cynthia's mother will say—but on this autumn day, he is letting the class draw a picture that tells the story of Purgatory City, their new home.

Cynthia sits across from Ramona. Most of the students today are girls. All of the boys, except two sons of officers at Fort Spalding, which is just now sod huts, tents, corrals, and a flagpole, are skipping school. Even Cynthia's brothers are watching the branding, or helping the branding, at the Bar M spread, where her father is breaking horses.

"That's enough time, children," Master Beery says. "Joanna, you first. Show us your drawing and tell us what it represents and why you decided to draw it."

Of course, it's the hotel. Her dad owns the place, which means he has to check in the guests, check out the guests, empty the chamber pots, while his wife washes the sheets every month. Joanna can't draw, either, and is horrible at keeping the colors in the lines. But Master Beery praises it as beautiful and says that hotels are key to a town's future.

Ramona is shy then. She blushes when her name is called, but holds up a nice little drawing of colorful blue mountains, the moon rising behind them, cactus plants and stunted trees growing in the foreground.

"Mountains, child." Master Beery shakes his head. "There are no mountains in Purgatory City."

She hangs her head. "I know. But I can see them from here. And they are so beautiful. I always look at them. I always want to see them closer. We came from Pennsylvania. I used to look at the Alleghenies. But they were green and smoky looking. These West Texas mountains, they look different."

Master Beery smiles. "That's lovely, Ramona. Lovely, indeed."

Cynthia has drawn horses. Horses in a corral. They look more like dogs, but Master Beery, he sighs, shakes his head, and says, "I guess that's probably the only thing you could draw."

Half the class laughs. Cynthia closes her fingers and grinds her teeth.

"Class," Master Beery says with false admonishment. "I think all of you understand the importance of horses in this country."

He looks to one of the sons of a Fort Spalding captain. "Preston, let us see what you have drawn."

He stands up, holds the parchment close to his chest, and turns right and left so everyone can see what he has drawn. There are red figures with white and black feathers dancing around a fire. A corpse is lying in the foreground while one red figure holds up a head, blood dripping from the neck that has been cut free of the body. And all around the perimeter of the painting are the faces of women, all of them crying, some of them looking wretchedly pathetic.

She will see that painting over and over in a few months, after she has watched her mother and brothers killed, after she has been picked up, slammed into unconsciousness against a horse's head, thrown over in front of a red figure, and taken away. Taken so far away.

"My God!" Master Beery steps back. A few girls gasp. "What, Preston!? What the devil is this?"

"It's the Canyon of Weeping Women," he says proudly. "It's where all these girls will wind up if they are not careful and are bad girls. It's the ugliest place on the face of the earth. That's what my pa says. He tells my mama that if she isn't good to him, that's where she'll wind up. And it's where all them chippies that live behind the saloons ought to be. That's what my pa says. It's the Canyon of Weeping Women." He smiles gleefully at Ramona, then shoves the painting out toward Cynthia as if it might frighten her. "It's where all bad girls go."

Well, Cynthia thought now, *no wonder poor Jubal Beery ran away from Purgatory City.*

Once they reached the bottom, she realized how vast this place was. It was not just one canyon, but a series of canyons carved by this little stream and the branches of the little stream that went off in opposite directions.

"Can I see to my brother?" Jim Bob Hardwick asked when they gathered at the stream and let their horses drink.

"No," Cullen Brice said. "You'd never find your way out."

Jim Bob seemed to understand any argument would be futile, and that Cullen Brice might even shoot him out of the saddle if he asked again. Besides, a quick glance at the terrain that spread out toward where the horse and man had gone over the side made Cynthia, and likely Jim Bob, think that Brice was not exaggerating about never coming out of that inhospitable thicket.

Brice nudged his horse toward the women prisoners and the two boys.

"Know this. You stay here, you are fed, you are clothed, you are alive, and you get out of here when we sell you." He let those words sink in. "Hell, there's a half-decent chance you'll wind up in the teepee of some buck who don't beat you senseless, treats you better than your favorite beau."

He looked every woman in the eye, even the addled mother of Darnell and Danny. Cynthia held his stare and was pleased when he looked away first.

After spitting and wiping his mouth, Brice added: "But if you try to escape, you will not get another chance." He laughed and pointed up the ridge.

"Do you think any of you could make it back up there before we ran you down? And let's say you somehow made it out at night, without being struck by a rattlesnake. Or mauled to death by a badger. Or walked off the edge and joined this poor sap's brother. Let's say you made it back to the plains above. The Llano Estacado."

He laughed and shook his head.

"Well, bully for you. But where the hell would you go from there? There ain't nothin'. There ain't nothin' but a hell of a lot of nothin'." He pointed west. "Santa Fe. Better than three hundred miles." The hand shot north. "Dodge City? Just a day's ride closer." He nodded due east. "Fort Smith? Hell, that's nigh five hundred miles." And at last he gestured to the south. "Fort Spalding? That's better than two hundred."

His smile widened, and triumph shone in his eyes.

"Country filled with every sidewinder, man and beast. Red devils that will take your scalps after they take you for all they think you can handle. And the white men you'd meet—they ain't no better than a Kiowa or Comanch'. Here? You'll be fed. You'll work. You won't be touched. Most importantly . . . you'll live."

He stared hard at Ramona. "So don't be a fool."

And the eyes stopped on Cynthia. "Or you'll suffer a long time before you die. We Comancheros . . . we've learned a lot from the injuns we deal with. And the white men, or the Mexicans, that deal with us. They make us look like . . ." He laughed. "Saints!"

He turned the horse, crossed the stream, and found a trail.

They followed. No one spoke. Even the horses fell into a long silence.

The trail left the stream at a dry bed that cut about two feet below the surface and meandered easterly, eventually narrowing into another steep canyon. Cynthia looked up, guessing that it had to be some three hundred feet to the top here. She knew there had to be trails. Comancheros were not stupid. This might be a box canyon, but these traders, these outlaws, these scum of the earth would not let themselves be trapped in a box canyon. There would be escape routes out.

She sighed.

But how do I find one?

Something reflected off the northern wall. She stared. Ahead of her she saw Cullen Brice holding out his repeating rifle, letting the sun catch the brass frame, signaling the lookout above. On the other side, another Comanchero did the same to the lookout perched to the southwest.

If there is an escape route out, she thought, *then there is a way in. And my father . . .*

No. No, she knew better than to hope to be rescued. She would have to save herself. She saw the twins, and their mother, the crippled prostitute, and even Jim Bob Hardwick. No . . . they must save themselves.

The Comancheros kept their rifles across their legs and let their horses resume a slow walk.

The canyon spread open, and she spotted a few fires. She smelled coffee, and fried pork, and realized how famished she was. Beans. Glorious beans. The scent filled the air along with that of bluebonnets and wildflowers, of jasmine and horse dung. She heard music, and found a man leaning underneath a blackjack tree, playing a mouth harp.

Some of the raiders pulled off here, and she spotted a circle of teepees. But no Indians. Many Comancheros had adapted the lodgings of those they might deal with.

"Hardwick!" Cullen Brice pulled his horse off to the north. Other men rode on. Jim Bob Hardwick kicked his horse, passed Cynthia and Ramona, and trotted up to the Comanchero. He reined in. "You're coming with me." He pointed the barrel of his Yellow Boy toward a log cabin, built from cottonwood and sporting a thatched roof. "Time you met my pard, my boss, the famous Boss Linden. So vile, so contemptible, so gawd-awful the devil hisself don't want him in Hell."

Brice nodded at a Mexican bandit.

"Carlito, take the others to their place. Who's the grand dame these days?"

"A Mexican." The Comanchero seemed to be bragging. "Paulita. She is fine, amigo. *Muy bien.* Much pleasure just to look at her, *hombre.*"

Brice grinned. "As long as you just look, amigo."

He pointed at the captives. "Take 'em," he told the one named Carlito. "But you." Brice nodded at Cynthia. "You come with me. And bring your good-lookin' friend."

He meant Ramona.

Cynthia turned in the saddle and stared at the twin boys, who were now leading the horse their mother rode.

"Darnell," she said softly, smiling. "Danny. You go on now, just go on. I'll be along . . . we'll be along directly. Go on. Look after your ma."

But the kids began to sob. Cynthia swung out of the saddle, handed the reins to Ramona, and hurried. She reached up and squeezed Darnell's hand.

"Listen to me, sugar," she pleaded. "You can't cry. Just don't cry. You got to take care of your mother. You've got to grow up now. I mean right now. You cry like this, they'll kill you. And they'll kill your mother, too." She nodded. "Look at her. She's not crying."

Because, God help the poor woman, her mind must be gone.

Darnell was the first to stop crying.

Cynthia caught her breath. She tried to smile at him, give him some encouragement. "I'll be back. I promise you. Ramona and I'll be back. We just got to go meet someone."

"That's right," Cullen Brice said. "She's right. About everything. Same goes to you that I said about your ma, your friend here, her friend, and all them other young . . ." He snorted. ". . . ladies."

"Go on, boys," Jim Bob Hardwick said. "Look after your ma."

"Come on, Danny." Darnell picked up the reins he had dropped. He smiled up at his mother. "We're almost . . . *home*."

The poor woman just blinked.

"Take 'em," Cullen Brice told Carlito.

Cynthia watched the women, the boys, and a handful of Comancheros head down the trail, farther back into the canyon. She grabbed her reins, and eased into the saddle.

Cullen Brice laughed. "Comanches teach you to ride, girl? You sure know your way around horses."

"No."

He grinned. "Word's been goin' around that you lived with Apaches for a spell. They must've taught you, though I always think Apaches would rather eat a hoss than ride one."

"They didn't teach me, either."

Brice reined up beside Jim Bob Hardwick.

"Well, you had a good teacher." The killer tipped his hat.

"I did," she said, and smiled at the cold-blooded wretch. "He taught me a lot of things."

CHAPTER 30

Green Clayton had quit kicking and choking and had fallen unconscious when Matthew McCulloch sliced the lariat with a big bowie knife. The Comanchero's legs hit the creek, and he fell facedown into the cold water.

That revived the foul man, who raised his head, coughed, and dropped back under the reddish water.

"Turn him over," McCulloch ordered. "Before he drowns."

Sean Keegan swung off his horse, splashed through the shallow water—about as fast as he had ever moved without anyone offering him a free whiskey or someone had been shooting at him—reached down, grabbed the rope that bound the mad-dog killer's hands behind his back, and rolled Clayton over.

His nose was bleeding, the muddy water washing the redness into the stream. The man wheezed, blinked, and fought for breath. Keegan reached down and loosened the coil so the man might catch his breath a little quicker. The rope burn around the tiny outlaw's throat would be there a long, long time.

When Keegan started to pull the rope over Clayton's head, McCulloch said, "Leave it on him."

The Irishman looked up. McCulloch had wrapped the reins of his horse around a piece of driftwood.

"We might hang him again." McCulloch walked into the water.

Keegan glanced again at the rope, and then the killer, who still coughed, still bled, but appeared to be slowly regaining control of his faculties. But he stared hard at the former Texas Ranger who stopped on the other side of the coughing, wheezing, despicable man. Sean Keegan had lived a hard life, and always considered himself to be a hard, hard man. But Matt McCulloch? He had never seen the horseman like this. Hard, yes? You had to be hard in this part of the United States. It was a hard place to survive. But Matt McCulloch, he always had been the most reserved of the men dubbed "The Jackals." He's the one who once had a family, and now had his daughter again—or had her—till the Comancheros had hit Fort Savage. McCulloch was the only one of the three who had worn a badge. He'd always been the . . . well . . . most human of the lot.

But now . . . he seemed harder than the Comancheros.

Green Clayton's eyes finally focused, and his breathing started to slow.

"Sit him up," McCulloch ordered.

Keegan straddled the man, leaned forward, grabbed his shoulders, and jerked the killer to a seated position. Then he backed away, the water soaking his boots, but at least cooling his feet.

A minute passed, then another. The Comanchero fought the binds that held his hands behind his back, but they were on too tight, and the water would make them even tighter. Blood still leaked from both nostrils and a cut over the bridge of his nose. But the man finally grinned.

"I knew . . ." He struggled just a moment longer. "I knew you wouldn't leave me to die. You're . . . too . . . soft. You're—"

McCulloch's backhand sent the little killer into the water.

As the weasel coughed, spat, and cursed, McCulloch bent forward, rolled the man over, and shoved him to the bottom of the creek bed. It wasn't deep, probably no more than eight or nine inches, but that was enough for a little man, or even a big one, to drown in—and McCulloch slammed the man's head so hard, it might have sunk into the mud. He jerked the man up by his hair, then shoved him back in after he managed to suck in a lungful of air.

McCulloch did not let the man stay under longer, this time. He jerked him up, sat him up, then knelt beside him.

The man spit out water, wheezing. Another cut appeared over his forehead. When the man's breathing returned to normal, and his eyes were clear of most of the water, McCulloch delivered another savage slap.

"Listen to me, you miserable piece of filth." The horseman's voice was sharper than a barber's straight razor. The slap sounded like a gunshot. "You got one more chance. I'm not playing around. I'm not wasting my time with you. That first hanging. That was just a warning." He slapped him again, knocking him to the ground, then stepped on the side of the killer's neck, holding him down, his face half-submerged.

"Next time, you swing. You stay swinging. Till the buzzards pick your bones clean."

McCulloch moved his boot slowly, sliding off the side of the man's neck, then letting the rowels of his spur carve a trench down the back of the neck.

Green Clayton screamed, and gagged from the water he swallowed.

Sean Keegan felt mighty glad that he did not have a lot of whiskey or bad food in his stomach.

McCulloch turned around, grabbed the Comanchero by his hair, and jerked him to a seated position again. As the man coughed, swore, and continued to bleed, McCulloch splashed around him, then squatted in front of the man's shoes.

He waited till Clayton stopped coughing.

"You're taking us to Boss Linden's camp in the Canyon of Weeping Women," McCulloch said evenly. "I don't have time to waste. Either you agree to this. Or, like I said, I follow the fork there myself, and take my chances. They got my daughter." He stood.

Green Clayton whimpered. "I got . . . my . . . rights."

"They've got other innocent women, including my daughter's best friend. Hell, her only friend. You think I give a tinker's cuss about your *rights*?"

One of the horseman's boots caught the Comanchero's chest, almost at his throat, and he fell backward. McCulloch splashed over and pressed the heel of his other boot on Clayton's forehead.

Sean Keegan always considered himself to be a man of action. But right now, he just felt as though he could do nothing but watch. He couldn't stop McCulloch. He wasn't even sure he wanted to. Keegan glanced at Jed Breen, but the bounty hunter appeared to be looking for any sign that they might have company. Or maybe even Breen didn't want to see what was happening.

The army, Keegan thought, could be hard. He had been ordered to flog men, even ordered once during the Rebellion to form a firing squad to kill two deserters. And he had seen two spies, Confederates wearing the blue of the Union, hanged. One's neck had broken at the drop, but the other had strangled. An ugly way to die. Kicking, twisting, the only blessing being that the black piece of cotton covered the spy's face so no one could see the fear and pain in the dying man's eyes.

But those deaths were executions. Those men had been tried and found guilty. That had been during a war. The general in command had confirmed the sentences. A priest had been summoned to hear the confessions and pray with the two spies and perform the sacraments. And those members of the firing squad? Those young boys Keegan had picked for the detail? They never knew which one's rifle was loaded with just powder or a leaden ball that would take another man's life. While Sean Keegan did not squeeze a trigger. He just raised his saber, looked at the captain, and brought it down when the officer nodded.

This was different. This was raw and ugly. This was the work of a jackal. Sean Keegan was supposed to be a jackal. Right now he just felt like a little boy. A sick kid. But he also knew that there was nothing he could do to stop it. And if that was his daughter, or his sweetheart, taken by Comancheros, he'd be acting just like Matt McCulloch.

Besides, McCulloch was a friend.

"Yes or no, Clayton?" McCulloch said. "Last chance."

When the man made no response, McCulloch stepped off him. He took the end of the rope, brought it over his shoulder, and gripping it with both hands started moving toward the bank, and the cottonwood tree with the low, thick branch where the lynching had started. Where the beautiful tree with the light green leaves had become a gallows.

The coil tightened against the man's neck. He fell backward, eyes now frightened, and McCulloch leaned forward, gripping the rope with both hands, churning like an ox breaking hard prairie earth, dragging the killer toward the hanging tree.

Green Clayton's head hit the bank. He was out of the water up to his shoulders, but the rope had tightened so much he couldn't breathe, and Matt McCulloch was so out of his mind with rage, he didn't notice. He threw the end of the lariat over the low branch.

Keegan charged through the stream, dropped to his knees, and grasped desperately at the wet hemp before the Comanchero choked to death.

"Easy, Matt. Easy." His fingers pulled the rope free just enough. McCulloch turned, stopped, looked Keegan in the eyes, and then stepped back into the creek. He straddled over the gasping, terrified man.

"I meant what I said, Clayton," McCulloch warned. "You help me, or you die right now. Slowly." He knelt again, so he could let the killer see his own eyes, and hear the truth in his words. "And if you think you can lie to me, say you'll take me there, say you'll do exactly what I tell you to do, this is what I'm going to do. I'm going to tie your hands and feet. I'm going to put this loop over your neck again, and tie the other end to the horn on your saddle. Then I'm drawing this Colt." He pulled the .44-40 from the holster and let the man stare down the long barrel. "I'm putting it against the rump of your horse. And I'm cocking the hammer and pulling the trigger."

The Colt fell back into the leather.

"If you're lucky, your neck breaks when the horse first jumps. It'll be a quicker death than me leaving you swinging here, but you're just as dead. Your head most likely will be decapitated. Either way, you die here strangling, or you die somewhere in the Panhandle. And buzzards pick you clean."

He stood.

"Or, you and me. And my two pards. You help us. I get my daughter back. I get Ramona Bonderhoff back. I let you go."

Green Clayton just blinked. His mind might have already been reduced to porridge.

"Get his horse." McCulloch looked at Keegan with those savage, fiery eyes. "We'll leave him swinging. I'll pin a note on his body that says, 'This is what happens to Comancheros in this country.' And we'll do this without him."

Keegan started for the animal, but stopped. Jed Breen was already bringing it. Jed Breen looked like he was just as hard and determined and inhuman as Matt McCulloch. But then Jed Breen had always had a soft spot for that gunsmith's daughter.

CHAPTER 31

Most of the Comancheros Jim Bob Hardwick had seen wore buckskins, or woolen britches reinforced on the thighs and backside with leather. Their hats were Mexican sombreros or wide-brimmed, high-crowned Stetsons favored by cowhands. They wore clothes that fit the country—woolen vests, cotton shirts, some with bib fronts for extra protection against the wind. Their six-shooters were holstered low on their hips, for easier access, and most often they carried at least two. Some had a third gun in a shoulder holster or secured near the small of their backs. Scarves were colorful silk or cotton. Boots and moccasins were about even, half the killers going for the harder, firmer footwear, and the others—favored more among the Mexicans and half-breeds—wore moccasins, some to their ankles, most of them calf-high, but almost none decorated with beads. Jim Bob saw a few St. Christopher medallions and plenty of crucifixes among the Mexicans. The white men, on the other hand, had likely given up on their souls, and perhaps the Mexicans just wore those for decorations, for color, or maybe to let their women captives think that they might still have an ounce of sympathy, a bit of compassion.

The man who stepped onto the porch in front of the cottonwood cabin was different.

The boots were high heeled with the tops stretching all the way to his knees. Black boots. No spurs. His pants were clean, gray with pinstripes, tucked inside the tall boots. The sash around his waist was bright red, and two pearl-handled revolvers—Smith & Wesson double-actions from the looks of them—were stuck inside, butts facing opposite. The tall man must have been ambidextrous. His shirt appeared to be silk, with mother-of-pearl buttons from waist to paper collar. The coat was green, woolen, probably out of fashion, but what the hell did Jim Bob Hardwick know about the latest fashion? It was the kind of coat Jim Bob and Billy Ray's father had worn—the one his dad had stolen from a Shreveport politician after knocking him out while, allegedly, luring him to a fancy woman's house.

The hat was as black as an ace of spades, the crown flat as the prairie they had crossed before stumbling into the canyon, and the narrow brim just as flat, stiff as the man's back. He leaned on a cane in his right hand, and stepped off the short porch. The right knee, Jim Bob noticed, did not bend.

Nor, he suspected, did his iron will.

"What have we here?" the man said when he stopped.

A woman, young, dark-haired, wearing white cotton rags and sandals, stepped out behind him. She stared at her sandals.

"Figured I owed you somethin' for breakin' me out of that cotton farm, Boss," Cullen Brice said.

Boss Linden leaned on the cane and eyed the two women Brice had brought along.

"That's why I always liked you, Cullen. You pay your debts."

The young Mexican girl walked behind him. She never raised her head.

He limped over to the fair-haired girl first. Boss Linden pushed back the stiff hat, and smiled. "How old are you?"

When she did not answer, he straightened, laughed, and raised the cane to his shoulder. "Missy," he said, "I can use this cane to lean on, and look dashing, or I can use it to beat your face into a bloody pulp. Now." He brought the cane lower, holding the curved end in his right, and the bottom in his left. "Shall we try that again? How old are you?"

"Seventeen." Her voice cracked. Jim Bob couldn't blame her for that. Those gray eyes in that sun-burned face looked just like the eyes of a timber rattlesnake.

"Hmmmm. I like mine younger. But that's all right. You look . . . Greek?"

"Texan."

He grinned. "Well, the drawl's there. And the uppity attitude. You a virgin?"

She blushed. Jim Bob went rigid. *The audacity* . . .

"That's what I thought." The tall man lowered the cane, and moved over toward the blonde.

The Mexican girl just stood there, not looking, barely breathing, never talking.

"Well, now." Boss Linden clucked his tongue. "Blond hair. Green eyes." He stepped back, turned to Brice and said. "Green eyes. Where's Green Clayton?"

Brice shrugged.

Boss Linden's face darkened. "Martínez, when he got back the other day, said my raiding party ran into a force to be reckoned with. Where's Montgomery? Don't tell me he got killed when you decided to bring me a black-haired virgin with a Texas tongue for a gift. And this hard-rock of a gal with pretty curls and green eyes and a face that's been bronzed like she's been living with Comanches for ten years."

"Apaches," Miss Cynthia, bold as brass, said. "And not quite seven years."

Linden whirled toward Miss Cynthia and raised the cane over his shoulder as though he intended to strike. "You speak when I speak to you and ask you a question. Otherwise, like the ol' Paul says, you 'keep silence in the churches—'cause it ain't 'permitted unto 'em to speak.'" The cane rose higher, and Jim Bob moved his hand toward his revolver. "'They are commanded to be under obedience, *as also saith the law!'"*

He whirled, the eyes now fiery. "Where's Wild Kent?"

"He's delivering the rest of the merchandise."

Boss Linden leaned against the cane. His breathing slowed, and his eyes glinted with delight.

"Women?"

"Loose women," Cullen Brice said. "One's half crippled. I don't know how she even got this far." He pointed at Miss Cynthia. "But she somehow kept the other woman alive."

"Old?" Brice frowned.

"Not ancient. She's got twin boys. Maybe not yet in their teens, but they could fetch three hundred pesos in some Mexican slave mine."

"Three hundred?" Linden shook his head with a snort.

"No one can drive a harder bargain than you, Boss."

The crippled man laughed at his lieutenant, but the smile in the eyes did not last long. "Green Clayton?"

Brice shook his head. "I don't know. I never saw him. It appears a couple of bounty hunters brought this young turd and his brother in to the prison farm." He pointed at Jim Bob, who moved his hand away from the butt of his revolver. "He and his brother run off from the farm. I thought they might make it, gone as long as they were. Where did you get caught?"

Jim Bob wished he had been mute, like the young Mexican girl who must have been Boss Linden's kept woman.

He looked for help, and found himself looking at the Mexican girl.

"She can't tell you, boy," he heard Boss Linden said. "Deaf and dumb, she is. That's why I like her. Now, boy, look at me. Didn't your mammie teach you to look at your elders, respect them, and look 'em in the eye when they ask you somethin'? So they know if you're lyin' or not."

Jim Bob made himself look into Boss Linden's deadly eyes. "Fool Fassbinder's Folly."

"That far?"

Jim Bob forced a grin. "Wish it had been farther. Like on the other side of the Rio Grande."

"Brice said you and your brother. Where's he at?"

Jim Bob stared at his saddle horn. He felt that chill, that emptiness.

"He and his horse went over the side comin' down here, Boss," Cullen Brice said.

"Good horse?" Boss Linden asked, but did not look away from Jim Bob.

"Not particularly," Brice said.

"That's a shame." Boss Linden snorted, spat, and looked away from Jim Bob and back at Brice. "Since Wild Kent Montgomery tells me six to eight of our boys will wind up being planted next to those poor slobs that died at that cotton patch in the middle of nowhere."

"I wasn't leading that raid, Boss," Brice said steadily. "It's not my fault they got killed. You take that up with Mal Martínez and Wild Kent Montgomery. I robbed a stagecoach at Fort Savage. I brought you women you can sell, and two boys you can sell as slaves. I think I've repaid you in full."

Boss Linden stared a full two minutes, and those minutes stretched on for what felt a whole lot longer. Then the man laughed, lifted his cane and started tapping it against the palm of his left hand. He spun around so fast, the horse Miss Cynthia was riding shied, but she quickly got the gelding under control, holding the reins like she had been born with both in her hands, and singing a soft song that was not in English.

"You handle that horse mighty fine, missy," Boss Linden said. "Now let's start this conversation again, and see if you live through it. How old are you?"

"What year is it?" Having the horse steady, she turned to stare right into that rattlesnake's eyes. Only Miss Cynthia's were almost an even match.

"Fifty-four years after my birth," Boss Linden said. He laughed. "You were singing an Apache song. So I guess you ain't lying about having lived with them. Maybe you'll be going back to them. That suit you?"

"It would be a hell of a lot better than staying with you, you . . ." Jim Bob did not know the words that followed, for they were guttural, hard, monosyllabic and, obviously, an Apache curse. An obscenity that Boss Linden understood.

"Oh, little lady, I don't think you will like the Apache I am dealing with. It's Dog Heart."

That got Miss Cynthia's attention, and Cullen Brice drew in a sharp breath. But it was Jim Bob Hardwick who gasped, "My god!"

Laughing, Boss Linden turned to Jim Bob. "You heard of him, boy? I reckon you must have a good library in that cotton-picking prison, get plenty of newspapers from Arizona and New Mexico territories. Is that it?"

"Everybody's heard of Dog Heart," Jim Bob managed to say. "From San Francisco to New York City, I suspect."

"I suspect so, too, boy."

Cullen Brice cleared his throat. "I thought you were dealing with Black Forehead, Boss."

The Comanchero leader laughed, and leaned again on his cane. "I am. I'm dealing with Dog Heart of the Warm Springs Apaches. I'm dealing with Black Forehead of the Comanches. I'm dealing with Pony Soldier Killer of the Kiowas. And I'm dealing with Bad Buffalo of the Southern Cheyennes. I got two hundred Springfields and two hundred Colt revolvers. And I'm selling them all to the highest bidder."

"You sell that many guns to those injuns," Cullen Brice said in a faint whisper, "and they'll likely cut our throats and take our scalps before they kill every white man, woman, and child in the Southwest."

"No. They won't kill us. Because they know I'm an honest businessman. And if they kill everybody in Texas, why should I care? Because for the price those Indians will pay me in stolen horses, stolen cattle, and stolen gold—for this gift of glory and guns—I'll be resting my ol' stiff leg in the Pacific Ocean or the Gulf of Mexico, with *señoritas* taking care of me and keeping me filled with tequila and spicy food. Fifty-four years is time for this ol' Comanchero to retire to a life of leisure. I think a combined army of Apaches and Southern Plains tribes could do a whole lot of killin' of Texans and Yankee soldiers."

Cullen Brice was won over. He laughed.

"You won't get the price you think you will . . ." Jim Bob Hardwick could not believe he spoke those words aloud.

Boss Linden spun around, but kept leaning on the cane, and his face was not flushed with anger, but those hard, evil eyes now danced with what appeared to be amusement.

"Go on, boy," Linden said, and waved his hand as if encouraging completion of the thought. "I like a man— even a half-growed knucklehead—who thinks before he acts. Rather than raid a worn-out stagecoach station in the middle of the Big Nothing and try to bribe his way back into my good graces by fetching me whores, one of them crippled, two worthless punk kids, their idiot of a mute mama, a Greek goddess who speaks like a Texas biddy, and a girl who is pretty but has already been spoiled by some murderous Apache buck. Or bucks."

Jim Bob swallowed down bile and fear. He found strength in the way Miss Cynthia looked at him. Even the brunette, Mona—no Ramona—stared at him hopefully. He wondered if the mute Mexican girl were somehow looking at him, too, though she seemed to be focused on the sandals she wore.

"When you raided that army pack train," Jim Bob said, "did you get powder and shot?"

"Powder and shot?" Linden laughed. "You're speaking about old relics, boy. You got a modern Colt there. Ain't you heard the news? It ain't powder and shot no more. It's self-contained loads, brass cartridges loaded with primer and powder and a bullet—.45 caliber for the revolvers, and .45-70 for those long-range Springfields."

Jim Bob shrugged. "Word at Peering Farm—we get telegrams fair to regular, you understand—is that weapons were stolen, but no bullets."

Boss Linden laughed again. "I'm startin' to like you, kid. You got a name?"

"Hardwick," he said. "Jim Bob Hardwick."

"Well, Jim Bob Hardwick, you might have a brief career as a Comanchero, if it suits you. And if it don't suit you, let me know, so I can cut your throat before I get attached to you." He winked. "Or you get attached to Sweet Alyvia yonder." He chuckled again. "She don't say nothin'. Good quality in a female."

Linden drew a breath, exhaled, and resumed his speech.

"Well, the word you got at Peering Farm would be absolutely correct. Absolutely. But, while Cullen Brice, my *segundo,* was out riling up Texas Rangers and lawmen and good citizens south of here where white men ain't scared to tread, I got word—via courier from Pale Canyon—that someone wants to come here to sell me bullets that will conveniently fit those Colts and Springfields."

The crippled killer laughed. "That be a man who's got guts. And ambition."

"Pale Canyon?" Cullen Brice said in complete bewilderment.

"That's only the second time someone has ridden into that hideout, uninvited, and left alone. I figure a man like that is worth listening to. Before I kill him and take the ammunition to sell to those redskins for my last deal. The deal that'll send me to a life of leisure in Mexico."

CHAPTER 32

Jed Breen rode drag, keeping the Sharps across the pommel, taking his eyes off Green Clayton just to scan the ridges. Breen didn't bother looking behind him. Taking the eyes off Green Clayton, he figured, would be a mistake that could leave a man dead. Besides, Sean Keegan rode off about a hundred yards ahead and to the south. Keegan kept an eye on the back trail. Matt McCulloch rode point.

No one spoke. Even the horses stayed relatively quiet—as though they knew how far sound could travel—and that if they were heard by Comancheros or Indians, death could come swiftly.

He was having trouble comprehending everything he had just done over the past couple of weeks. He had returned two men, relatively minor outlaws, prison escapees, for a decent reward but nothing like some of the bounties he had collected. That was Jed Breen's job, one he was good at, one he had been doing for more years than he cared to count.

So . . . I, with Sean Keegan's help (and for 50 percent of the reward), return two convicted felons to the work farm to resume their sentence, with probably another six months tacked on for trying to escape.

*Then . . . I, with assistance from Sean Keegan and
Matthew McCulloch—that would be former Texas Ranger
Matthew McCulloch—when you get right down to the plain
and dirty facts, pretty much helped spring Green Clayton
from prison. And Green Clayton is a much harder hardcase
than the Hardwick brothers combined.*

Oddly enough, Jed Breen felt no remorse. He had not
said much, to McCulloch or Keegan. He could tell Sean
Keegan, a wild Irishman, certainly, but a soldier who knew
about sworn oaths and devotion to duty, felt that pull. Felt
that Matt McCulloch, jackal or not, had crossed a line that
men of his reputation were not supposed to cross.

Bounty hunters had lines, too. At least Jed Breen did. He
had shot and killed plenty of outlaws. Turned in their
bodies, collected the rewards that paid for "dead or alive,"
but he had never killed anyone in cold blood. Most of them
had been facing him when he pulled the trigger. Maybe a
few were running away and he had missed his aim, but
those were hardened killers facing a rope if they were
brought in alive.

None of that mattered anymore to Jed Breen. He felt as
hard and as cold as the horseman riding ahead. The only
thing Jed Breen wanted was to see Ramona Bonderhoff
safe and tucked inside that stupid gun shop her father ran
in Purgatory City. Far away from Boss Linden's Comancheros. And he didn't care what he had to do, who he had
to kill, or how many he had to kill to see that done.

Folks called him a jackal. Maybe he had always been one.

He was one now. He had to be one now. It was the only
chance Ramona Bonderhoff had. And Matt's daughter,
too. And those other women the blackhearted butchers
had kidnapped.

They dipped over a ridge as the sun disappeared behind
the next one, and found the chalky edge of an old riverbed.

Water had to be somewhere around here, because there were cottonwoods. McCulloch turned his horse north and rode to a natural cut in the small canyon wall. It would keep the four men dry if it rained, though the lack of clouds said rainfall wasn't likely. It would also keep them out of some of the wind. Wind, out here, was always likely.

McCulloch removed his hat, waved it toward Keegan, who waved his as an acknowledgement. Then McCulloch stepped out of the saddle and began loosening the horse's cinch.

Spurring his gelding slightly, Breen trotted the horse until he rode alongside Green Clayton. The Comanchero's hands had been lashed to the pommel. The reins were draped over the horse's neck. Breen shoved the Sharps into the scabbard, and reached over with his left hand for the reins.

That's when Green Clayton swung his right hand up. His left grabbed a rein. The rawhide bindings fell away.

Both horses shied.

Breen dodged the fist. The outlaw cursed, kicked the horse while grabbing for the reins.

Breen put the weight of his left boot into the stirrup, kicked his right free, and dived.

His right arm wrapped around the runt's waist. Hooves of both horses pounded the ground. And Breen saw the red-and-white earth rushing up to greet him. He also heard Green Clayton's curse.

They hit hard. Horses ran in opposite directions. Breen pushed himself up.

He saw Green Clayton's right hand coming up for his throat. But where was the left?

That's when he felt the holster turn lighter.

The Comanchero had grabbed the .38-caliber Lightning.

Breen had to move fast or he was dead. So he rammed his knee into Clayton's crotch.

He heard a thud. That had to be the Colt landing on the ground. Those green eyes shut in agony, and Breen shoved the knee in tighter. He jabbed a punch that split the killer's lips, then pressed all his weight down on the cold-blooded butcher as he pushed himself up. On his knees, Breen caught his breath, found the .38, picked it up, and began wiping it off on his britches as he stood.

Green Clayton rolled over, pushed himself up on hands and knees, and vomited.

Matt McCulloch strode over, stopped, and waved at Keegan, telling the trooper to catch both horses before they took off. McCulloch could do that much quicker than Keegan, but the ex-Ranger made a beeline. His Colt was in his right hand, and when he stopped and the Comanchero started to push himself up, McCulloch's left caught him under the chin and toppled him down the rocky incline about three feet, where he landed on a patch of prickly pear.

The man groaned, gasped, and spit out a busted tooth.

"You've run out of chances, Clayton," Matt McCulloch whispered. "I'm sending you to Hell."

"Nooo." The man could barely talk, but he held out his left hand, fingers extended. "You win."

McCulloch dropped to his knees, and slammed the barrel into the man's gut.

"You've seen a man die from a belly wound, Clayton. That's what you'll be doing. Screaming. Screaming to die, but it'll take a long time."

"I . . . I . . . no . . . more."

McCulloch stood, lowered the hammer and shoved the Colt back into the leather. He leaned forward and jerked the tiny man to his feet, and then shoved him forward. Clayton staggered, stumbled, then fell onto softer clay. He was gasping, and when Breen reached the old Comanchero, he saw the patches of prickly pear stuck through the back of the man's shirt. Entire pads were rammed into him.

Matt McCulloch kicked the man practically all the way to the shelter. Jed Breen took the reins to McCulloch's horse and followed in silence.

Darkness was slow to come in this country. The air cooled because the sun was going down, and the wind stopped. A coyote yipped off in the distance, and another answered somewhere to the south. The bullbats would be out before long. Then the world would go black until the moon decided to rise.

Jed Breen ached all over. His thighs, his backside, both shoulders, in the lower neck, and his stomach felt empty. What he needed was a hot bath, new clothes, and a fresh shave. No. He needed none of that. What he needed was a young woman who had to be scared out of her wits, stuck somewhere in a hideout no one had been able to find for thirty years or more. A long way from home. With death staring her in her face.

He never had any desire to be a doctor, but Jed Breen used his pocket knife to pull away the pads. He let Green Clayton take off his own shirt, and then Breen went about plucking out the cactus tines. He had a bar of soap in a saddlebag, and washed the wounds with that, and poured horse liniment over the wounds for as good of a cleansing as a body could get in this savage wilderness.

After that, the three jackals passed around a bag of jerky, which they washed down with water from their canteens. When they were done, Breen handed the bag to the little man, who ate greedily.

"Coffee?" the man whispered. His face was a mess. Probably battered more than the back. But his eyes finally registered defeat.

"No coffee," McCulloch said. "No fire."

"Smart," Clayton whispered.

McCulloch drew his revolver but did not cock it. He said, "You talk. But know this. I'm not playing around with you. I'm not going to let you get another chance at killing one of my friends. You give the wrong answer—or if it's the right answer but I think it's wrong—I'm blowing your guts out. This is it. You either deal yourself in with us, or you die."

The Comanchero nodded.

CHAPTER 33

As Cullen Brice and Jim Bob Hardwick led Ramona and Cynthia away from the log cabin, Cynthia studied the canyon. Now she could see fingers of other canyons, two of which had to hold more horses than her father had ever dreamed of catching and breaking.

"Money on the hoof," Brice said, pointing out the herd to Hardwick. "Comanches like to trade in horses. They steal horses better than any tribe. We take them to New Mexico, or Mexico, sell them. It's just the cycle of business." The man laughed. "I guess Boss Linden ain't dreaming like I thought he was. He's been saving up horses to make a killing. And with what he'll get for those guns, it'll be even bigger."

A rider loped up, but the party did not stop. The rider in buckskins slid his horse to a stop, turned it around, and rode next to Brice.

"Amigo," he said.

"Mal." So this was the Mal Martínez the Comancheros mentioned.

Brice pointed at the horses in the canyon. "Lots of trading, I see."

The Mexican laughed. "You have been gone a long time, my friend."

Brice whistled. "When's the last time you've been paid?"

He shrugged. "In whiskey? Yesterday." He laughed. "But we take some gold and paper money from those we have killed. As long as we bring horses or something of value. I must say, business was not as good while Boss was in Mexico. But we did as Boss told us, knowing he would return. A little business with Kiowas, a few Comanche. Trade with the New Mexicans—they hate Texans almost as much as I do." He turned to wink at the two women. "Boss Linden stays in good spirits. Now that he is back, we all are in good spirits."

"What's this Paulita like?"

"She is the devil."

Brice turned and winked at Cynthia. "Well, the devil might be about to meet her better."

The O'Leary twins ran from a lean-to, yelling Cynthia's name, so she reined her horse to a stop and swung down easily. She heard the mirthless chuckle from Cullen Brice, but the other riders stopped, too.

Darnell and Danny almost knocked her onto her backside, but she returned the embrace.

"We thought they'd murder you!" Danny said.

"Are you all right?" Darnell asked.

"I am fine." She turned and stared hard at Brice.

"This is far enough," the Comanchero said. He pointed at the lean-to and other huts. "That's your new residence, ladies. There are only a couple of rules. Don't try to escape. There's no use. That's already been pointed out to you. Don't kill one another. If you kill a woman or a kid, we kill you. It's not good business because instead of being out just one sale of a woman or slave, we're out the price of two. But . . ." He shrugged and yawned. "But, Boss Linden's rule does seem to keep down the number of catfights."

Mal Martínez giggled.

Cullen Brice turned to Jim Bob Hardwick. "Boss gives you the easy duty, boy. You get to look after this merchandise. Just remember what they say in fancy and cheap stores. 'Lookin' at the wares is fine. Tryin' out the wares means you pay for 'em.' He put his hand on the handle of his revolver. "In this case, you pay the hard way. Tell him, Mal."

The Mexican seemed to delight in his description. He pointed to a flat butte maybe a half mile to the north. "We strip you naked and drag you up there. But we do not drag you hard. Just enough to tear most of the skin off your body. Then we stake you." He removed his hat and began to fan himself. "It is very hot up there. So much closer to the sun, you see. We slice off your eyelids so you can see the buzzards that will begin to circle over you, waiting for you to die. Don't worry. You will not see them for long. Because there are big ants that live on the top of that mesa. They will be drawn to your body. By the blood, amigo. By your blood." He laughed, stopped waving the big hat, and returned it to his head. "You might scream, but the wind blows your cries away. You might swallow some ants. I hear they are tasty. They will eat out your eyes so you no longer see the buzzards. They—"

"If you're trying to make these women and kids sick," Jim Bob Hardwick said as he dismounted, "they aren't paling. Not after all they've been through. And I'm not an idiot. I'm a guard. That's all I am." He grabbed the canteen from the horn, and the duster that had been strapped behind the cantle.

"When's my relief?" he asked.

"Morning." Brice turned his horse around, tipped his hat with a sarcastic smile at Cynthia and Ramona, then put his horse into a lope. Mal Martínez followed.

Jim Bob saw a piñon and a flat rock that looked like it offered the best position and the most shade. "Ma'am," he said, apologetically. "If y'all need anything, just come see me." With a sigh, he grabbed the reins to his horse and walked the animal to the shade.

Cynthia watched him till he got there, then she turned and smiled at the boys. "How's your mother?"

They broke into tears.

The number of women surprised her. There had to be at least a dozen—before the arrival of Cullen Brice's additions. Maybe more. Cynthia expected to find just those taken near Fort Savage. She found Mexican women, even two that she were told were Navajos, four Negresses, and a handful of white women, ranging in age from their early teens, maybe just older than the twin boys, to around the age of Mrs. O'Leary.

An Apache village, to most white observers, is primitive. But this . . . this . . . this prison where the women and young male captives were kept was wretched. There wasn't even a privy, just a ditch that reeked of foulness. A lean-to was considered a mansion. Some women slept three to a patch of dead grass underneath a ripped canvas tarp propped up with sticks, the canvas held down at the bottom with rocks. More had carved out a hole into the side of the wall, not deep enough to be called a cave. More lived wherever they could, wandering about like homeless—which they were— finding a shady spot the way Jim Bob Hardwick had.

Apparently, they ate together. She saw a firepit and a ring, with a coffeepot hanging over the blackened, lifeless—

for the time being—coals. There were two kegs of water, but no dipper. No tin cups except one by the coffee pot.

One of the prostitutes taken at Fort Savage rose from underneath a bedroll. Apparently, that was her home, and she stood, and walked over.

"I thought they might be killin' both of you," she said in a hoarse voice, and she acknowledged Ramona.

"Not yet," Cynthia said. "How's your . . . friend?"

The woman shrugged. "Alive. That's about it."

"I'm sorry."

She shook her head. "Don't be. She's alive. She'd be dead if not for you." She laughed without humor. "I got the bedroll. They made us fight over it." He pointed to a black eye. "Like animals." And she spit, then broke down into tears. "I . . . am . . . not . . . an . . . animal!"

Ramona rushed to her and let her bury her head against her shoulder. "I . . . wish . . ." the prostitute wailed between heartbreaking sobs, "that . . . they . . . killed . . . us . . . all!"

"Well, they didn't."

Cynthia turned to the young woman who spoke. She had dark hair to her waist, and she was wearing what had once been a bright red dress, but the sun and the elements had faded it to pink. It was also threadbare. She wore sandals that had to have been made here. She came up to Cynthia. The woman's eyes were blacker than any Cynthia had ever seen, and she had lived for years with the Chiricahua Apaches. She was taller than Cynthia, but not by much, Hispanic, of course, and might have been Cynthia's age. Or even much younger. Cynthia did not want to ask her how long she had been imprisoned here.

"You are Paulita," Cynthia said.

The woman laughed. "Yeah. *Reina de la Nueva España.* Come on, ladies. Let me show you around."

* * *

In one of the dry gullies, Cynthia knelt beside Mrs. O'Leary. The boys had managed to find a saddle blanket, and that kept their mother out of the sand. There was enough firewood stacked to provide shade—as long as the stack didn't fall over on her.

Paulita knelt on the other side, and pulled around the gourd she carried on a string of rawhide. She poured water into a cupped hand and brought it to the woman's lips, whispering in Spanish and smiling when she saw Mrs. O'Leary swallowing.

"Muy bien," she said, then began singing a pretty song in her native tongue. Afterward, she rubbed the moisture onto the widow's forehead.

"Gracias," Darnell told the woman. He shot a different look at Cynthia. "She's teaching us Spanish!"

"You boys tend to your mother. Don't let her drink all of this." The gourd came off her shoulder and she held it out.

"Come on," she told Cynthia.

The faces of both lads paled.

"Don't worry, *hermanos*. I'll bring this lovely creature back."

The next stop was where the other prostitutes taken at Fort Savage had found shelter. No roof, not even a saddle blanket. It was a hole in the side of the canyon wall, and Cynthia could tell it had been dug out by small hands. A woman's hands. Possibly even Paulita's.

A dress covered the broken legs of the seriously injured prostitute. When Cynthia reached to pull the calico away, Paulita's right hand shot down and held it firm. Her head shook. *"Por favor,"* she whispered, and Cynthia understood.

"She's burning up," a prostitute said between sobs.

"Infection," Paulita said.

Cynthia's shoulders sagged. Ramona whispered a prayer.

"She'd be dead," Paulita reminded them. "From what these two boys told me, she'd be dead. She's alive." Her head rose, and Cynthia turned to see a handful of other wretched women, most of them almost in shock, some of them looking like little more than skeletons.

"As long as we live," Paulita said, "we have a chance. As long as we don't give up, we have a chance. This woman is alive." She gestured at Cynthia and Ramona. "Because of these women. We are strong. That is why we are alive. We are strong. And with these two women, we are now stronger."

When they walked away, toward a lean-to, Paulita said, "The left leg will have to come off just below the knee."

"Oh, my God," Ramona cried.

"God's not here," Paulita said, "so don't go crying to Him. And I've seen many a man and even a few women with wooden legs. They don't cry about it. They get on with their lives."

"How do we amputate?" Cynthia heard herself ask.

"We get a saw. We get a keg of whiskey. It'll have to be tomorrow at the latest. That devil Linden might give us whiskey and a saw. Maybe even some bandages. I'll tell him that a Kiowa will pay twice the going rate for a one-legged woman. He'll find her special. Big medicine. Trust me, Boss Linden will figure that a keg of whiskey, some cloth, and the loaning of a saw is worth more than one dead woman tossed into a shallow pit and covered up. He's a businessman."

"He's a devil," Ramona spat.

Paulita laughed. "I like you, Dark Hair."

Then she stopped and stared at Cynthia.

"Your friend," Paulita said, nodding at Ramona, "is a town girl. I like her, but I don't know how tough she is. And you? Who'd you live with?"

"Apaches," she answered. "In Mexico. Three Dogs' band." Cynthia nodded at Ramona. "And the town my friend lives in is Purgatory City. It's about as hard as you'll find this side of hell."

Paulita nodded. "Good enough."

Cynthia studied the woman. "I was told you're the boss of this place. The Comancheros made it seem like I'd have to fight you."

"You'd lose that fight, girl," Paulita said. "Trust me. But we're not fighting. I've been here eight months. I was on my way to go to a finishing school in Boston. Well, I'm ready to finish this school." Her smile seemed insane. "I've just been waiting for some help that won't stop fighting till we've killed every single Comanchero in this hellhole."

CHAPTER 34

Once his hand found the bottle, Matt McCulloch pulled it out of the saddlebag by the neck. He left the tethered horses and walked toward his two companions and the prisoner who was about to become their reluctant partner. He pulled the cork out with his teeth, stopped beside Keegan, and held it out.

Keegan took only a small sip, nodded his thanks, and went back to cleaning his Springfield, resting his back against the cottonwood. When McCulloch held the bottle of rye out toward Breen, the bounty hunter started to shake his head, but thought better, and accepted the invitation. But his swallow hardly matched that of the Irishman. Then McCulloch moved to the bank of the creek, and he squatted beside Green Clayton. The man's cracked, split, battered lips moved, and he tentatively raised his right hand.

McCulloch let the man take two long pulls, but when Clayton started coughing, the horseman grabbed the bottle, returned the cork, and made himself a bit more comfortable, as Clayton bent over, cupped a handful of creek water, chased the rye with half of it, then splashed his face.

Their eyes met. Keegan pushed himself up, and moved closer, checking the action of the Springfield. Breen moved over behind the Comanchero, keeping an eye on ridgelines as the moon began to rise.

"Tell me," Green Clayton said in a hoarse, worn-down voice, "what you were thinkin'."

"I told the Comanchero I spared at Pale Canyon that I'd be riding down the main trail. Told him to have Boss Linden meet me and we could have ourselves a parley."

The old man let out a laugh that came out more as a cough.

"And how did you expect to find the blasted trail?"

"I would have. I will. With or without you."

"I suspect you might have done just that. But if you rode into Comanchero trading country alone, if the redskins didn't kill you before you knew you were dead, Linden's sentries would have."

"I never planned on riding into that country alone."

Clayton laughed again and shook his head. "Them two?" He gestured toward Keegan and Breen. "They would have dropped dead right beside you."

McCulloch's head shook.

Now, with the moon and stars brightening the evening, the Comanchero stared at him for a long while. McCulloch did not say a word, and barely breathed. It did not take long before Green Clayton understood.

"You planned on bringing me all along? Hell, mister, how did you even know I was at that plantation hellhole?"

"I didn't know you were there. Never heard of you. But I figured there likely would be one of that bunch picking that cotton. Peering needs workers who know how to live in this country, how to work, how to keep from dying of heat stroke or getting beaten up by the wind."

He shifted the Winchester repeater's barrel from right shoulder to left. "Or, if no one there could help me, I figured I'd just find a Comanchero and cut a deal with him."

"Finding a Comanchero can be easy enough. Living after you met him is another story."

McCulloch's smile was hardly friendly. "Tell that to the dead men I left at Pale Canyon."

Silence followed. Clayton eyed the bottle of whiskey, but McCulloch shook his head.

"Well," Clayton said after a moment, "I might be able to get you in. But you'd have to do some fast talking. And there's a mighty good chance some lookout won't recognize me and will just kill us both before we're anywhere near the trail into the Canyon of Weeping Women. But if four men come in, even bringing two pack mules, even outfitted like Comancheros, and they ain't expected, we'll be cut to pieces."

"Not four men. Just two."

Both Keegan and Breen straightened and gave him hard, questioning looks. And the Comanchero looked stunned, and even more shocked when McCulloch added: "And we'll be expected."

"If," Clayton whispered after a long moment to think, "that rider you sent out of Pale Canyon ain't already dead, killed by some redskin, or a hide hunter, or throwed headfirst by his hoss into a juniper."

"That's," McCulloch said with a nod, "a possibility, for sure."

The Comanchero looked over at McCulloch's fellow jackals. "You cuttin' these boys loose?"

McCulloch knelt now, putting the Winchester over his thighs, and extending the bottle, which Clayton accepted with all the gratitude a killer like him could show. He thumbed out the cork, and took a long pull. This time, he didn't cough, even when the whiskey exploded in his near-empty belly.

"Keegan and Breen will be our surprise," McCulloch said. "You and I ride in. With the pack mules. You signal the lookouts. We explain—you explain—to them what I'm bringing. Ammunition for those guns he stole from the army. With luck, and with your brains, we ride into the canyon and I start dickering with Boss Linden."

"He ain't no easy feller to bargain with. And once he has those mules—"

"I'll tell him I have four other mules. Lots of ammunition. But I'm only selling them two mules at a time."

The Comanchero's eyes turned greedy.

"Do you?"

McCulloch's face showed nothing.

Clayton took a shorter snort, returned the cork, and handed the rye back to McCulloch, who kept his right hand in the lever and trigger guard of his rifle, but took the bottle with his left, and laid it near his boot.

"Of course there ain't," Clayton guessed. "If they were, they'd be too far away for you to fetch in time."

McCulloch breathed in and out. "In time . . . for what?"

Clayton eyed the bottle, which McCulloch found and rolled toward him. After the man took one sip and wiped his lips with his sleeve, he held the bottle up toward Keegan. This time, the Irishman accepted.

"This has been in the works for years," the Comanchero said. "Boss Linden is a man of ambition. And murder."

The plan, as the Comanchero revealed it, was to rob a shipment of army guns. While waiting for the perfect job for that, they would be collecting as many goods—goods that could be drunk, worn, ridden, or shot, or goods of the living, breathing variety—as payment.

"The Indians pay mostly in horses, cattle, or other merchandise—gold, women, kids, just like they've been doing for years. Linden sells what he can, except for the gold, to merchants who aren't particular. Butchers and cattlemen in New Mexico Territory, sometimes up in Colorado. Or Mexicans. You Texans don't got no monopoly on shady dealings and corruption. Mexicans can use slaves for their mines, or wherever. Bawdy houses ain't too particular on what kind of females they get, and some mine owners like to have a white woman to show off as their kept woman. If she's pretty enough."

Most of that McCulloch had guessed or knew.

"This is to be Linden's biggest deal," Clayton said. "Selling as many guns as possible to injuns. But not just any injuns. Not just the Comanch'. He's to meet with Mexican miners, New Mexican businessmen and ranchers. It's like the store is closin' and ever'thing's for sale. I think Boss started thinkin' about retirement after you caught up with Brice and sent him to Huntsville. We was gonna make off with a fortune, Linden and me. But I got caught. Put in prison. And then when Brice got transferred to Peering's place, ever'thing kicked into full speed. Till those owlhoots and lyin', double-crossin' scum left me in that cotton hell. Busted out Brice. Left me behind. I figure they got greedy. Bigger split without me. Sons of—"

Jed Breen cleared his throat and asked: "How were they to know when the deal was going down?"

"Easy enough to figure that out," Clayton said. "Once newspapers started reporting about that army weapons heist, once they all figured Boss Linden was back in action and out of Mexico, they'd meet at the Canyon of Weeping Women." He looked at each man. "Understand, when Linden lit a shuck for Mexico, he didn't take every Comanchero with him. The way we figured, if he was out of the country, the Rangers, the sheriffs, and the United States Army would figure the Comanchero trade was dyin' down. And it was, somewhat, with most of the Comanches and Kiowas turnin' themselves in at the reservations in Indian Territory.

"But some of the boys stayed behind. You know that. Pale Canyon. And a war party might make a raid, steal some cattle, horses, maybe even a woman or two. They'd bring them to the canyon. The Canyon of Weeping Women. Mal Martínez and Wild Kent Montgomery was left in charge. Cullen Brice woulda been, till you up and put him out of commission—for a while."

McCulloch started to ask another question, but Breen had one first: "How did Brice manage to get transferred from Huntsville, where it's harder than hell to escape from, to Peering Farm?"

The Comanchero shrugged. "That, I don't know. I guess some money could have exchanged hands, as the newspaper scribes like to suggest. Or it could have just come down to plain ol' Texas pencil pushers' incompetence. Maybe they thought Brice had reformed himself. You'd have to ask Boss Linden that, and I don't reckon he'll ever be taken alive. Especially not if I see the lyin' piece of dung first."

McCulloch felt cold, though no chill had reached the Eroded Plains of Texas. "You said something about selling to not just Comanches, or any Indians. Do you mean selling to the white traders, the Mexican slave owners, the Colorado ranchers who don't—"

"You know exactly what I mean, McCulloch." Green Clayton laughed. "Those guns are gonna go to the worst redskin army you ever seen. You think you Texas boys got a whuppin' at Antietam and Gettysburg. Hell, those were just Yankee city slickers and Ohio farm boys who turned y'all back. Boss Linden put out the word that he'll be sellin' to the highest bidder, but that ain't his plan at all. He's gonna have a council with some parties interested in gettin' even for stealin' their country, killin' their buffalo, degradin' their women. Blood Moon was gonna be the Apache he wanted, but I read that he's dead. So my guess is Dog Heart will take up the cause for the Warm Springs 'Paches. The Comanches led by Black Forehead, what's left of them. Maybe Crazy Prairie Dog Eyes of the Kiowas."

"He's dead, too," Keegan said.

"Well then . . ." The Comanchero shrugged.

"Pony Soldier Killer," McCulloch whispered.

"Might be." Green Clayton's head bobbed, and his eyes shined with delight.

"Those three tribes . . . combined?" Sean Keegan practically gasped.

"Not three." Clayton laughed. "We was bringin' in Bad Buffalo of that Southern Cheyenne bunch. If he ain't dead."

"He's not," Keegan said. "Unless it was real recent."

The Comanchero eyed the bottle of rye, but this time McCulloch shook his head.

"The way we figured things," Clayton said, "is that with hundreds of guns given to those four bands, Texas and the United States—and Mexican—soldier boys would have their hands full for a year or two, and possibly three. So long, and so bloody, nobody would have time to think about comin' after the dirty-dealin' white men that sold those red devils all 'em guns."

A long silence followed. Clayton's laugh sounded gleeful. "So, you know this. You sure you want to ride toward the Canyon of Weepin' Women? Maybe you'd rather go to Mexico where it might be a hell of a lot safer. I gotta think that Bad Buffalo or especially Black Forehead would love to cut down any white traders he happened upon that wasn't already in that canyon."

No one spoke, so Clayton added, "What are you thinkin', Matthew McCulloch."

The grin held no humor. The eyes showed nothing but grit. And McCulloch's answer was not debatable.

"If Linden's selling to those four bands, and those four leaders, he never needs to have some ammunition to go with the guns."

One of the mules picked that moment to bray.

CHAPTER 35

Jim Bob Hardwick swung off his horse and wrapped the reins around a post near the log cabin. The mute Mexican girl stood on the porch, dark eyes burning into Jim Bob's belly. He looked around, saw no sign of Boss Linden, and turned back to the girl.

"I know you can't talk," he said, "but can you hear, Alyvia?" The eyes did not blink. She showed no sign of understanding. He tried one of the Spanish words he knew. "Do you *comprende*?" He dragged out the last word, but the woman's eyes did not even blink, and her lips remained flat.

He sighed, looked into the windows, the cracked door, and finally turned and looked toward the wall. That's when he saw Boss Linden, or at least a man who looked and dressed like Boss Linden—hell, that had to be the Comanchero chieftain. Nobody else wore those kinds of duds.

So he tipped his hat at the girl, saying, "That's all right, ma'am, I see him. *Adios*." He walked toward the big stone building. Two horses were grazing near the structure, and Linden was holding the door open. The stone appeared to be quarried locally, and the building was too big for an outhouse, but too small for a residence. Maybe four feet wide and six feet deep. Flat roofed, piled high with wood, dirt, and thatch. Not a window in the whole place, unless in the back wall. Those stones had to be at least two feet thick.

Smokehouse? Well, it didn't matter. It was none of Jim Bob's concern. His concern was finding Boss Linden. But now he stopped, still about fifty yards away, as a tall man wearing a massive feathered headdress stepped out of the stone building. Indian. Or a Comanchero who dressed like one. Jim Bob started walking again, staring at the horses. As he got closer, he saw that the bay had a Mexican-styled saddle rig and a bridle lined with silver conchos, but the brown-and-white pinto had a raw, ugly, plain saddle. Wooden, it appeared, with rawhide laid over the top, secured with brass nails. The horn and cantle rose high, curving fore and aft. No, that was an Indian all right.

The Indian stared directly at Jim Bob. Seeing no weapon, Jim Bob walked on. Boss Linden appeared unconcerned as he struggled with the door latch. No, the rattling of metal told Jim Bob that Linden was having trouble getting the door secured with a padlock.

Billy Ray had taught his baby brother to never sneak up on anybody, unless you aimed to do him harm, so Jim Bob walked harder than he had to, so that the jingle bobs on his spurs would chime louder. He kept coughing now and then. The Indian shook his head, but his lips never moved.

But Boss Linden heard Jim Bob's approach, and he came to his feet quickly, bringing his cane up and gripping the curved handle as though he intended to break the wood in half. The Indian stepped away, and Jim Bob raised his hand in greeting.

"Boss . . ."

That's all he got out of his mouth before Boss Linden stormed away from the stone building, cussing Jim Bob with every foul word he had ever heard. He started to raise his cane, and Jim Bob began to think he was about to be clubbed to death. Would the Indian take his scalp afterward?

"Are you daft, boy? I told you to guard those petticoats till you were relieved! Men are shot for abandoning their posts. I've executed men for stupidity. And you, sir, are certainly guilty of that."

"Wild Kent relieved me, Boss!" Jim Bob blurted out. "Honest to goodness, he sent me here."

The man stopped, the words reaching him and reasoning with him. He huffed and puffed, but gradually lowered the cane and leaned on it. Behind him, the Indian with the great headdress walked slowly, leading his pinto and Boss Linden's horse.

The Comanchero leader wet his lips. His head bobbed at last. "Wild Kent. I should have guessed." He looked behind him and said something in a language Jim Bob had never heard. The Indian laughed.

When Linden looked back at Jim Bob, the leader of the outlaws frowned. "Wild Kent Montgomery has an eye for women. If he sent you here, it means he is up to his wicked, wicked ways."

Jim Bob tensed. The first thought that flashed through his mind was: *If he lays a hand on Miss Cynthia or any of those poor girls, I'll throttle him.*

"I'll have to kill Wild Kent one of these days, if some hussy doesn't cut his throat first."

Boss Linden shrugged. He put his weight on the cane as he leaned forward. "Well, why are you here? Speak up, boy, things are about to get real busy in our lovely hellhole."

Slowly, Jim Bob reached into his vest pocket. He found the paper and handed it to Linden.

"That fallen woman, the one with the real bad leg injuries, well, that girl, that woman, I mean, Miss . . . Miss . . . Paulita. Well, she says she's got to get that leg off. One of 'em. Take it off, I mean. Cut. With a saw. What she writ down on that paper, that's what she needs."

Linden did not accept the note. Instead, he stared at Jim Bob and asked, "Can't you read the list to me, boy?"

"Well." Jim Bob felt his face flush. "Well, sir, you see. . . . My . . . schoolin' . . . it . . . it weren't . . ." He could read right well, but figured Boss Linden would like him better if he played the green, ignorant cowhand.

"I see, son. I see." He shoved the paper into a pocket, heard a horse snort, and his face changed from weariness to humor.

"Ah, Jim Bob." He turned, found footing on his good leg, and pointed the cane at the Indian. "You should be introduced to the first of our many guests. This is Bad Buffalo, came with thirty-two Southern Cheyenne warriors all the way from Low Water Creek near the border of Kansas and Colorado Territory." He then tilted his head back toward Jim Bob and spoke to the Indian in a language that was more grunts and snorts, except for Jim Bob's name, moving his hands and fingers in time to the foreign words he spoke.

The Indian raised his hand and said something equally unintelligible to Jim Bob, who awkwardly raised his right hand and said, "How." And felt like a kid when both the Indian and the Comanchero laughed.

They walked to the cabin, where Linden whistled and the mute girl stepped out and stared.

Linden limped up onto the porch and handed the woman-child the paper Wild Kent Montgomery and Miss Cynthia had written out, following Miss Paulita's dictation.

"Fetch those, Sweet Alyvia," Linden told her. "Deliver them to the women. Help Paulita if needed. Then be back here in time to cook my dinner." He moved his hands while speaking, the same way he had done when speaking in that harsh language to that Cheyenne chief, Bad Buffalo. He then turned to Jim Bob and said, "Get to it, boy. And tell Wild Kent to visit me before sundown."

Jim Bob started to make a beeline for the stone shed.

"Boy!" Linden barked, and Jim Bob stopped and spun back.

"Not that shed, boy. You stay away from that shed." He gestured in the opposite direction. "The girl will show you. And go easy on the keg of sour mash. We will be overflowing with thirsty guests in the next few days."

This storage shed was more of a dugout than heavy stone. It had a combination lock, but the mute girl's fingers worked the dial as though she had done it a hundred times. The lock opened, she hooked it on the latch and pulled the door open.

When Jim Bob started for the door, she held out her arm, stopping him and shaking her head. He figured he wasn't to be trusted inside the dark quarters, or maybe she knew he would spend an eternity in there just looking for what was needed.

He didn't see anything that looked like guns. Mostly sacks of grain and things like that, but the scent of bad whiskey was overwhelming. She pointed toward Jim Bob's horse, so he walked back to the animal.

Jim Bob didn't like it, but he just stood in the sun. And waited till the woman came out with a jug of foul-smelling whiskey.

The woman who did not speak would go inside the dusty room and come out with items. Two kegs were strung over Jim Bob Hardwick's saddle horn. He took the saw and slid it inside a saddlebag. She carried out bolts of white cloth, and when Jim Bob tried to take them, she shook her head with much vigor and stuck them under her left arm.

Then she nodded at the door, which Jim Bob closed. He shut the lock, tested the door, and walked to his horse.

He looked at the woman, sighed, and said, "I ain't got the ability to do them injun signs and talk that way. Wish I could. I'd thank you kindly. I'd . . . well . . . I'd . . . I'd. I'd."

"Do not say anything," she said.

He almost fell back against his horse.

"I am to help you. I am to help the woman who is hurt. I am to help Paulita."

"You can . . . talk!"

Her eyes blazed with fury. "Be quiet. You are the only one who knows my secret. You and Paulita. Now I am coming with you."

"You're gonna . . ." Jim Bob could not believe that this young, beautiful, dark-eyed girl could help saw off a woman's leg. Could help keep her alive. He couldn't even believe she could talk.

She fell silent again. Her head nodded in the direction of the camp of women and children prisoners.

He walked the horse, pulling it by the reins. The woman who could speak but chose not to walked beside him.

They passed an outer perimeter of guards, who nodded and leered, but mostly smoked their pipes. When they turned off on the trail to the women's camp, the woman cleared her throat. Jim Bob glanced at her. He whispered, "Miss Alyvia . . . ?"

"My name," she whispered, "is Maria." Her accent was unmistakably Spanish. Proud Spanish. "Maria Del Valle. I was stolen from Puerto Inocencio two years, three months, and fifteen days ago. Do not call me Alyvia. That is the name that stinking pig gave me."

CHAPTER 36

They made coffee that morning, quickly, just long enough to get the water boiling the grounds McCulloch had knotted in a handkerchief. Green Clayton got the first cup as Breen kicked out the fire. Then McCulloch handed the fancy pencils he had taken from Clayton's prison bunk, and the paper the warden had gifted him.

Sean Keegan rode up onto the bluff for a look-see, and Breen and McCulloch sipped silently and watched the old man draw. "All right," the old Comanchero said, and slid one paper toward McCulloch. "That's the bottom of the Canyon of Weeping Women." He pointed a long black pencil. "You see that. That's the box canyon where they keep all the stolen horses."

He had sketched a pony's head, a good likeness, McCulloch thought, given how little time he had taken to draw the whole map.

"This is the castle of Boss Linden."

McCulloch asked, "Stone, wood or—?"

"Cottonwood."

"What's that?"

The man shrugged. "Storage shed."

He pointed. "They got corrals, too. Plenty of 'em."
Kept pointing. "This is the place where they'll hold the big
fandangos. Ever been to a slave auction—I mean . . . before
the war?"

"No," McCulloch said flatly.

"Well, it's a lot like that. But you can't understand what
the savages are sayin' unless you get the lingo. Most often,
they talk sign language. I reckon you can do some of that."

No one answered, but all of them had some experience
in that.

"How does that work?" McCulloch set his coffee cup
down. "The auction."

The little man pointed, and McCulloch nodded at Breen.
"This is where you'll play a big part in the plan."

Breen moved closer. The old man waited to continue,
and before he resumed, Breen smiled at McCulloch. "That's
good to know." He looked at the map and whispered, "Good
to know that there is a plan."

Once Breen and McCulloch were satisfied, McCulloch
nodded at the paper, which now included other markings
made by the artist per suggestions by the bounty hunter
and the ex-Ranger. "Now, make two copies of this, just like
it is," McCulloch told Green Clayton. "So we'll each have
a copy."

"All right." The killer asked for Breen's pocket knife,
which he used to sharpen his pencils, then started drawing
again. "One thing you ought to know, though," he said as
he sketched mostly from memory, even the figures—horse's
head, corral rails, coffee pots, a Negro slave in chains, even
petticoats and teardrops. He talked as he continued to
draw. "Some things might have changed. I been out of the

Comanchero business for a spell. And Boss Linden is a careful man."

When the copies were made, Breen took two, one for himself and one for Keegan. McCulloch folded the third and shoved it into the pocket on his hip. He pointed at the papers and told Clayton: "All right, now Breen and Keegan need a map of how to get into that place. Without getting killed. Without getting spotted. Without getting caught."

Clayton shook his head. "There is one entrance, amigo. From the northern edge of the—"

The backhand knocked the man down. "Don't play us for fools, mister," McCulloch said. "I warned you about lying to me, too. Remember that. There's no way in hell Boss Linden is putting himself in a canyon with only one way in and out. You know as well as I do that he has to have a dozen, probably more, ways out of that canyon. So you're showing us the best ways."

After he pushed himself up and wiped his mouth, he tested his jaw, and the malevolence in his eyes told McCulloch that this man would kill him the second he got the chance. But Matt McCulloch had known that for a long time.

"Here's something else you need to remember," McCulloch said, and his eyes showed no fear. "You want to get out of the Canyon of Weeping Women as much as we do. And the thing is this: You die and I die if we don't have Keegan and Breen exactly where they need to be. Savvy?"

He waited. He had not played poker in a long time, but he remembered how to keep that poker face, not reveal his hopes, or his bluffs. There was another thought running through McCulloch's mind, and it almost made him puke up the coffee in his belly.

Ramona Bonderhoff and Cynthia Jane McCulloch would not get out of that canyon alive, either. Or if they did, and none of the Jackals made it, the two girls would wish they were dead.

"All right." Clayton stuck the pencil over an ear and slid the paper toward Breen and McCulloch. He pointed a stained finger and said, "This is—" but McCulloch cut him off.

"Hold it. Sean Keegan needs to hear this." McCulloch stood, removed his hat, and waved it over his head. Once the old horse trooper saw the signal, McCulloch motioned him to ride down.

Keegan was a wonder on that horse, dust rising, gravel and chunks of red and white rocks rolling down in front of the horse like an avalanche, the cavalryman leaning back in the saddle like he did this all the time. For a while, McCulloch remembered, that had been Sean Keegan's life.

After crossing the stream, he reined up, swung down, still carrying the Springfield, and hurried toward the three men.

When Green Clayton had finished, McCulloch waited for the two men to look him in the eye.

"You don't have to do this," he said. "You can ride off right now. I wouldn't blame you. No hard—"

"Shut the hell up, Matt," Jed Breen said.

"Laddie," Keegan said, and slapped Breen's back. "I couldn't have said it better meself."

Matt McCulloch's face tightened. Then his eyes jerked, and he was on his feet. Breen and Keegan turned around and looked up the ridge.

Green Clayton whined, "Let me handle this. I can—"

"Stay where you are," McCulloch said. "Just sit there."

Six Indians rode down the hill. Every face was painted, including the one on the black horse who wore nothing but a breechcloth and black paint across his entire forehead.

* * *

The warrior on the bay colt nudged toward the horses ground-reined on this side of the creek.

"Black Forehead," McCulloch called out, and raised his Winchester to his shoulder. "Tell your boy to stop. His pony takes one more step toward those horses, and I send him to hell."

The Comanche barked something, then moved his horse across the stream, stopping it a few feet in front of the four men. His eyes stopped on the sitting Comanchero.

The warrior spoke in his own language. Green Clayton rose, shrugged and responded, but used his hands to help speak the words.

"He speaks English," McCulloch said, never taking his eyes off the Comanche. "You speak English. We all speak English. Let's keep it simple."

"We was just saying howdy," the Comanchero said.

"*Paapi*," Sean Keegan said, "is not Comanche for *howdy,* you dumb peckerwood. *Paapi* means hair. These bucks aim to take our scalps."

Black Forehead laughed. "You speak Comanche?"

"Just enough to know what's in the speaker's heart—if he had a bloody heart."

Green Clayton coughed. Now he stood, and pointed to the mules. "We travel to the Canyon of Weeping Women," he said, using his hands and fingers to make sure the Co-manche war chief knew exactly what he was saying, and then spoke the same sentence in the Comanche dialect. "We bring gifts, much good, for Comanches."

The warrior looked at the packsaddles, the boxes, the satchels and sacks.

"Guns?" Black Forehead said in English.

"No guns," McCulloch said. "But you know the Coman-cheros under Boss Linden already have the guns."

Clayton translated that in Comanche and sign language, too.

"Not many of you boys left," McCulloch said. "I hear even Quanah turned himself into the bluecoats at Fort Sill."

The Indian slashed his left hand out to stop Clayton from translating. "It is enough."

McCulloch grinned. "Six warriors? You boys are good, but—"

"We will not be alone!"

Clayton started talking, the tone placating, the fear on his face obvious, but McCulloch again told him to shut up. When Black Forehead stared at him, the former Texas Ranger chuckled, and said: "You're not telling us anything we don't already know, Black Forehead." This time McCulloch handed the Winchester to the Comanchero, who seemed startled and stared at the weapon as if he had never seen one before.

McCulloch signed what he had just told the Comanche. Now he signed and spoke simultaneously. "You are riding to the Canyon of Weeping Women to meet with Comancheros who promise you guns and bullets. You are planning to unite with your red brothers from other tribes. Dog Heart of the Warm Springs Apaches. Pony Soldier Killer and his Kiowas. Bad Buffalo of the Southern Cheyennes."

The Indian glared at the Comanchero. "How did they learn this—*if not from you*?"

McCulloch kept talking. "I figure the Cheyennes will have the most. Smallpox wasn't as bad on them as it was on you boys, and you boys had smallpox plus a whole lot of hard-rock Texans. The Apaches have been putting up a hard fight, too. Dog Heart is brave. We know that. He might have as many as Bad Buffalo's bunch. Close to it, though, maybe more if he brings his women. I hear an Apache woman can outfight the best Comanche buck any day of the week. And Pony Soldier Killer?" He nodded. "Yeah, he'll probably have a dozen or so Kiowas. Maybe." He shook his head and chuckled. "But six Comanches. What a shame. Ten years ago I thought y'all just might be fierce enough to drive every white man, woman, and child out of the state."

He took a step back. "You boys should have followed Quanah."

He drew his Colt and put a hole in the middle of the black paint on the Comanche leader's forehead.

The boy who had been moving toward the horses charged, raising his lance. Green Clayton spun, levered a round into McCulloch's repeating rifle—though an unfired bullet was already chambered—and shot the youth out of the saddle.

Breen's Sharps brought down a pinto just as an arrow took off the bounty hunter's hat. He ducked, palmed the Lightning and killed the warrior as he rose in front of his dead horse.

Keegan shot a whooping warrior waving a war axe as his horse carried him across the stream. He fell into the water as his tomahawk slammed into the dirt while the horse kept galloping in the general direction of Peering Farm. The Irishman dropped the Remington and shouldered the Springfield he had shifted into his left hand. He aimed at the warrior charging back up the hill. His rifle boomed at the same time as the Winchester held by Green Clayton. One round tore off the top of the warrior's head. The other killed the horse. Neither Keegan nor the Comanchero would check to see who killed what, and neither would ever concede that their round had not struck the man. There was no way either would own up to killing a horse.

McCulloch dropped to a knee and let a lance sail over his head. He brought up the Colt, but Breen's double-action fired several rounds, and the last Comanche fell into the stream and his horse galloped off into the distance.

Now as gunfire echoed, horses galloped, Breen ran off to make sure none of their mounts ran. So did Keegan. McCulloch turned his aim on the wild-eyed Comanchero, who still held the smoking Winchester.

Their eyes met.

"Are you out of your mind?" Green Clayton roared. "You could have gotten us all killed. What the hell was that about? What the hell were you thinking? Is that how you plan on getting your girl out of the canyon."

Keeping the revolver aimed at the little man's chest, McCulloch took three steps, then jerked his Winchester from Clayton's tiny hands. Only then did he lower the hammer on the revolver and let the Colt slide back into the holster.

"Mister," he said in a low voice, "I wasn't about to let Black Forehead's bunch make it to the Canyon of Weeping Women. I was making sure he never got to see my daughter or Bondy's girl. And I was bettering our odds of pulling this mission off."

CHAPTER 37

"What is *she* doing here?"

Paulita spit into the dirt. Her black eyes burned.

Maria answered in quiet but proud Spanish. Cynthia had lived with the Apaches south of the border long enough to know basic Spanish. The woman had answered that she was here to help. But Paulita's fingers balled into fists, and she stepped forward. While that was happening, Cynthia made a quick study of Jim Bob Hardwick, who appeared ready to fight Paulita to protect the woman who, if Cynthia was to believe everything she had heard from the women captives who had been held in this purgatory the longest, was Boss Linden's kept woman.

Purgatory? She corrected her thinking. This was the deepest, ugliest, hottest pit in Hell.

Cynthia made her decision.

"We need all the help we can get," she said.

Paulita stopped, turned, and stared. Cynthia nodded at the woman's leg. "For this." She looked back at the woman Jim Bob Hardwick had brought, or maybe it was the other way around. "And everything else we'll have to do to get out of this place alive."

Paulita's eyes narrowed into slits, and Cynthia wondered how this fight would turn out. Cynthia had learned how to take a beating from Apache women, and her Apache husband, but then she had learned how to fight back. Paulita had been here a long time. It would be an even match. Touch and go. But Cynthia figured she had one big advantage. She was the daughter of a jackal.

Suddenly, Paulita stopped and smiled. Her face brightened. She turned to the dark woman and nodded. "Very well, Alyvia. You will help." She pointed at the hacksaw. "You will saw off the leg. And if this woman dies. I will cut off your head."

"My name is Maria," the Mexican girl said. "And if you call me the name that *pendejo* gave me again, it is your head that will be cut off."

"Bring that torch!" Cynthia yelled. "Now!"

Maria straightened, her hair matted to her forehead with sweat, and tossed the bloody tool to her side. She looked at Jim Bob Hardwick. "Go," she said. "Go. Be quick."

Jim Bob Hardwick looked like he was about to throw up on the poor prostitute's face. He had been holding her shoulders the entire time, staring at the work Maria had been doing, and it was hard, bloody work. A saw cutting through human bone. At least the woman had screamed once before passing out. Her lungs filled, released, filled, released. She was sucking in breath through the open mouth. And the blood that was seeping from the raw stump below her knee was bleeding cleanly. The rot had been removed.

Jim Bob released his tight hold. The woman would likely have bruise marks there for some time. He turned, fell, climbed to his feet, and staggered to the bucket of

boiling water. Below, he pulled out the torch, and zigzagged—
he might pass out, too, Cynthia feared—but found his way,
and started to hand the torch to Cynthia.

"No," she said.

"You must do it!" Paulita roared.

This was how it was planned. Cynthia held the tourni-
quet—nothing more than a weathered bridle rein—on the
lower thigh, releasing it every now and then to let the blood
flow. Ramona Bonderhoff held the poor girl's other leg.
She had taken a beating herself until a merciful God let the
prostitute slip into deep, deep unconsciousness. Paulita
held the leg above the cutting with one arm and pressed
down against the patient's wrist with her other hand. Jim
Bob was in charge of the woman's shoulders and head. A
prostitute named Dame Mae, or as she called herself,
"Damn Mae," kept the other arm pinned down.

Being closest to the fire, Jim Bob had to get the torch.

"Now!" Maria said as she pulled away, dragging the
lower leg that had been removed with her.

The flame touched the bloody stump.

It would take months, Cynthia thought, before that smell
ever left her nostrils. And longer, she knew, before she
could ever fry a steak again.

The jug went from Maria to Paulita to Dame Mae to Jim
Bob to Ramona, who dabbed a little bit on the sleeping—
thankfully—prostitute's lips. Her tongue wet the lips, and
Ramona let her have some more.

"Careful," Dame Mae said in a deep Southern accent.
"Greta ain't used to such fine refreshments."

Greta. Cynthia smiled. It sounded like a beautiful name
when spoken with a Southern accent. She glanced at the
woman, who must have been quite pretty before the years

of prostitution aged her. She wondered how old the woman was. Twenty? Thirty? She looked fifty.

Ramona drank, made a face, and handed the jug to Cynthia, who took a pull. The taste surprised her. She brought the mouth of the pottery to her nose, sniffed, and handed the container back to Maria.

"Tiswin," she whispered.

Maria nodded.

"The Apaches." Fear raced up Cynthia's spine. "Is Dog Heart and his band here?"

"No," Maria said. She did not drink more but let Paulita take another slug of the weak beer-like drink favored by Apaches. "They have been brewing this for a long time. For the fandango." She spit onto the ground as though trying to rid her mouth of the taste—but not the taste of tiswin. "But Pony Soldier Killer is here by now, or will be soon. A Kiowa rode in this morning, early, with word that Pony Soldier Killer is coming." Her head tilted to the jug that was going to Dame Mae. "He will not get tiswin. He prefers the rotgut traders' whiskey."

"How many men does Pony Soldier Killer bring?" Cynthia asked.

"The brave did not say. We will find out soon enough."

The jug had made its way back to Cynthia, who handed it to Maria, who passed it back to Paulita, who looked at the others, saw their faces, and set the jug behind her. Then she nodded at the sleeping, breathing, pale Greta.

"Will she live?" Paulita asked, and turned toward Maria.

"She won't die of blood poisoning," Maria said. She looked at Jim Bob. "Get her some water, Jim Bob. Tiswin won't do the job. She needs water to keep her hydrated. She'll need whiskey for the pain."

"How about laudanum?" Dame Mae asked.

Everyone looked at the prostitute with the Southern accent.

She shrugged and gave a shy look that probably excited many a young man in Mobile, Alabama. "Girl in my line of work," she said, "sometimes needs a little help getting to sleep. Let me find my handbag." She rose, knees creaking, and almost stumbled from exhaustion. "Dumb pecker-woods didn't think to search the handbag when they took us all prisoners."

Jim Bob let out a mirthless laugh. "You wouldn't happen to have a Remington over-and-under derringer in that hand-bag, ma'am. Would you?"

"No." She started away. "Just an Allen & Wheelock pepperbox. Thought about shooting myself in the head, but, hell, with my luck, that relic would just blow off a couple of fingers and my thumb."

Dame Mae handed Jim Bob Hardwick the small pistol. His hand almost swallowed the gun, and he looked up and asked, "You ever fired it?"

The prostitute shook her head. "I cleaned it before this trip. But I doubt if it's been shot since Daddy brought it home after he didn't find no gold in California."

Ramona reached over and took the hideaway piece. She had worked in her father's shop long enough, heard her father talk to customers enough, and had seen just about every kind of gun that found its way into Texas. "Twenty-eight caliber, five-shot, cap and ball, two-and-a-half-inch barrel. It's a bar hammer." She sighed and handed the tiny gun back, butt forward. "I'm not sure I'd have gumption enough to fire it. You're right. It could very well go off in your hand. Or shoot all five chambers at once. You ever fire it?"

"Like I said, no such luck." She slipped the tiny pistol into her worn-out handbag.

All of the women had gathered here, at the back of the canyon wall. They had brought Greta, who still slept. Paulita studied the group, then rose, "All right. The Kiowas are coming. The Cheyennes are here. Those sons of dogs who live like honest men in Santa Fe, Taos, Lincoln are here. The biggest of the thieves who call themselves Colorado ranchers is here. And the Comanches and Apaches are on their way. Now we fight. Or we die. Likely we fight and we die."

"How?" cried a wild-eyed blond girl who couldn't have been out of her teens.

"Yeah," said a woman whose face revealed a hard, hard life. "With one five-shot pepperbox."

"With our fingers," Paulita hissed. "With our knees. With our shoes. We claw out their eyes. We fight till they kill us, because, trust me, death is a whole lot more favorable than what they're planning for us."

Cynthia looked at the twins, who huddled beside their mother, who just looked the same.

"No," Cynthia said.

"What?" Paulita swung around and glared.

"We don't fight that way." She held up her hand to cut off any protest from both Paulita and Maria. "We fight. We fight hard. Maybe we die. But . . . but first . . . we have to have a plan." She looked at the closest two Hispanic women. "This is something my father taught me, my white father. Always, always have a plan. So I need to know every single detail about what's going to happen. You two know. So you're going to tell us all. Then we'll know exactly what we have to do."

* * *

"Maria." Cynthia smiled at the young woman. "You need to get back to Boss Linden. Don't give him any reason to suspect anything's going on."

"Yo sé." She rose.

"We'll go over the plan again tomorrow. And the next day." Cynthia made eye contact with every woman, even poor Mrs. O'Leary. She even looked at the sleeping Greta. "And every day till we start our war. Our war for freedom."

Jim Bob's mouth opened, but she held out her hand toward him, and he sighed and waited.

"There is one thing you must know." She paused. "No plan ever goes as expected. That is something my father taught me. Both of my fathers. My white father. My Apache father. But we are not fighting for glory and we are not fighting for land and we are not fighting for some flag. We fight for the lives of our young ones. Our old ones. We fight for our own lives. Our dignity. And we fight for the reason most men fight. Revenge." She smiled. "Revenge is good."

"But . . ." Darnell's voice cracked, and she turned quickly to see him brush away tears. "But we ain't got nothing to do."

"Yeah," Jim Bob Hardwick said. "Miss Cynthia, you've given instructions to all these women—young and old, practically. And you haven't told me what I'm supposed to do. If you think I'm gonna just stand here and let a bunch of helpless women—"

"Helpless!" Paulita spit between his boots.

"Well, not helpless, but . . . well . . . you're women. I'm a man. I'm fighting with y'all."

"Silencio," Maria said. She spoke softly, but everyone heard. When the voices died down, the dark-haired beauty smiled at Jim Bob, then looked at Cynthia.

"Jim Bob." Cynthia smiled. "Darnell. Danny." She felt the tears now, but would not let them break free. The memory almost made her shake. She could hear the voice. She could feel hearts breaking. "These are words I once heard . . . many years ago."

CHAPTER 38

"Matthew McCulloch Junior!"

"It's all right," Matthew McCulloch Senior says, and holds out a hand in a peaceful gesture to calm his hot-headed wife. "Let me handle this."

He drops the reins to his horse and the lead rope to the pack animal, turns away from his wife, puts an arm around his oldest boy's shoulders, and walks, steering him to the barn. The boy starts to struggle, but quickly knows he's not up to the challenge, and lets himself be taken out of the sun into the shadow. They stand in the open doorway. McCulloch smells odors he thinks finer than roses or that hair tonic the Purgatory City barber loves to splash on customers. Horse apples. Fresh hay. The smell of good horseflesh. And wood that had been pegged and nailed and split by himself and a few solid neighbors. He also smells the lather on his oldest boy.

Matt Junior had tried to shave this morning. His cheeks were marked with little red lines—which remind the older McCulloch of his own first attempts with his old man's straight razor.

"I can go with you, Pa," the boy says, trying to sound a whole lot older than he is. "I'm a man, now. You can't go after those Indians alone."

"*I don't intend to, Matt,*" McCulloch says. *He lets go of his son's shoulders.* "*Those Indians didn't just steal from me. I'll have Jim Ketchum. I'll have the Lazy K crowd with me. Maybe some Rangers and sheriff's deputies. And the bluecoats from Fort Spalding already got patrols out.*"

"*I wanna go with you, Pa.*" *He can see the tears starting to form.*

"*I want you to go with me, too, son.*" *The boy's face brightens, but McCulloch speaks quickly before the kid gets his hopes up only to feel them crushed again.* "*But! But . . . I got a bigger chore for you. An important one.*"

He pauses. He has seen something out of the corner of his eye. In the first stall. He has to kill that grin quickly. He looks tough. Concerned.

"*Riding in a posse, Matt,*" *he says,* "*is not for the bravest men. The bravest men are those left behind. That's not just true for us Texians. It's true for the Comanches, too. Kiowas. Apaches. They know that it's easy to go chasing after horse thieves, cattle thieves. It was easy to go running after Yankees during the late war. The hard task, the most important task, that's staying behind. You have the biggest job of all, son. You're in charge of protecting your mama, your little brother, and that wildcat of a sister. And . . . making sure those Indians don't turn back and steal any more of those mustangs.*"

He turns the boy around, and nods at his horse.

"*Now, I want you to do something else for me. Run over to my horse. Pull that Yellow Boy out of the scabbard and take it back to the house. Bring out that old Henry of mine, and a sackful of cartridges. You'll need that Winchester. It's a better model. Just keep it loaded and remember what I always told you to do. Take your time. Aim low. Don't waste lead.*"

He wonders if he ran as a gangly little clown when he was that age. Hears the boy say something to his stern-looking mother as he slowly pulls the carbine out of the scabbard and takes off for the house.

Matt McCulloch lets out a breath. He takes a step away from the barn, stops, turns back and stares inside the barn.

"Eavesdropping is not ladylike, Cynthia Jane."

"Don't wanna be a lady, Papa," he hears her say.

He laughs as he heads for his horse and mule.

Matt McCulloch shot up. His heart pounded hard against his ribs, and he felt himself sniffling. His eyes were wet.

Memories. They could kill a man.

"Want some coffee, Matt?"

It was Jed Breen's voice. He turned, grabbed his bandanna, and quickly wiped his face. His breathing returned to normal, and he smelled the last of the coffee. Facing Breen again, he saw the steaming mug, and he reached for it.

"Thanks, Jed."

The sip revived him. "Where's . . . ?" He looked around.

"Keegan and the puny Comanchero are going over the map," Breen said, pointing. "You know soldiers, Matt. They love looking at maps."

"You might want to look at yours."

He frowned. Set the cup down. Looked at the white-haired sharpshooter. "Didn't mean that, Jed."

"Sure you did, Matt." The man smiled. "I've studied it, though. And every chance I get, I'll look at it some more. And then, you know as well as I do, that we'll all have to improvise."

Matt took another sip. "Because plans never go according to plans."

"Yeah."

"Jed." McCulloch downed the rest of the coffee, figuring, lukewarm as it was, more on the cold side, it wouldn't damage his throat. He shook his head. "I don't feel . . . like . . . myself."

"More human." Breen sipped his own coffee. "Less jackal."

"I don't know. It's—"

"It's Cynthia, Matt." Breen smiled again. "She's your daughter."

He nodded. "Yeah, but, I didn't feel this . . . this way . . . when we were in Mexico last time. Going after . . . hell . . . chasing a rumor . . . that she might be . . ."

"Matt." Breen drew in a deep breath. "You were half out of your mind when we went into Mexico. And, yeah, you're right. You didn't know if she were truly alive. Now you do. And you're a father. You got a lot at stake in this one. And our odds aren't that good."

He sighed.

"You've been a good friend, Jed." He gestured toward the cottonwood where the old Irishman and the ancient Comanchero sat pointing at the map on the ground. "So has Keegan. Men to ride the river with, sure enough."

"Yeah." Breen tossed out the rest of his coffee. "Well, here's something you ought to know, too, ol' pard. I got a lot at stake in this, too."

McCulloch made himself stand. "I know, Jed. I've known it longer than anyone, maybe even you. Anyone but old Bondy. And Ramona, of course." He made himself smile. "But I always figured you just wanted to get your guns cleaned and sighted for free."

Breen actually laughed. Then he stood.

"Let's get them back, Matt."

"We will." He cleared his throat. "But I need to show you one more thing. Something that, once we're inside the Canyon of Weeping Women, is gonna give us a little better odds of getting out of this deal alive."

They laid the crates gently on the path that led out of the creek. Matt fetched a long screwdriver from a satchel and began prying off the lid. Breen helped him pull the top off and lay it on the ground near the three other long crates.

Then all four men stared inside at the boxes crudely marked .45 CALIBER. FOR COLT'S REVOLVING ARMS.

Green Clayton reached down and pulled out a box, but quickly frowned, cursed, shook it and threw it so that the box bounced off Matt McCulloch's chest.

"That's empty! It's an empty box!"

"Yes," McCulloch said. "It is." He dusted off the box, handed it across the crate to Breen, who took it, understanding.

"This one isn't." Keegan rattled another box, and opened it. He nodded. "It's full. He pulled out a brass cartridge, sniffed it, and slid it back into the box. He held it out for Clayton's inspection, but the old runt just shook his head, spit onto the ground, and turned back to McCulloch.

"So what the hell do you think you're tryin' to pull, Ranger?" The little man's dander was up, certain sure. "You think you can double-cross a cagey old jackass like Boss Linden? Do you—"

McCulloch's curse silenced the old man. "Do you think that even I would bring four boxes of ammunition to a band of the most miserable scum of the earth so they can sell bullets to Comanche raiders? You think I'm that low?

Well, think again. The only thing I'm dealing with these men is death."

Breen reached over and pulled out another box. He tossed it up, caught it, smiled, and looked across the wooden crate.

"But you said . . ." The Comanchero could not find any words.

"I bought every round I could find, Clayton," McCulloch told him. "In .45 caliber and .45-70 for the Springfields. Purgatory City, being the town it is, has a big business for firearms—but it ain't the armory at Harpers Ferry or Fort Union. I got everything I could get my hands on."

Breen reached down and pulled out another box below the top row. He laughed, and withdrew a longer box, which he tossed to Keegan. The Irishman laughed.

"What's it say?" Green Clayton asked. "What kind of ammunition is that supposed to be?"

"Doctor Eisenhower's Fast Cure for Dyspepsia and Indigestion." Keegan flipped the box back to Breen, who pulled out another box and held it up. "Branson's Cathartic Pills," Keegan read. "New, sugar coated!"

"You blasted fools." The Comanchero was flushed like a young woman whose buttocks had been pinched by a drummer. "We'll never get out of there alive. You can't play Boss Linden for a fool. You can't—"

"Holy mother of God," Breen whispered, staring at the bottom of the box. He looked up at McCulloch.

"Dynamite," McCulloch said. "Courtesy of the late Jim Ketchum, who never got around to blasting a deeper well for Mary."

Keegan crossed himself, for Mary and Jim Ketchum's sake maybe, or perhaps because he started to realize that Green Clayton had raised a mighty good point.

* * *

They opened the other lids, found more of the same, although some boxes held loose rounds in various calibers. And others held boxes of nails, from six penny to sixteen penny. Or loose carriage bolts, cut tacks, washers, sewing needles, more nails. Keegan looked at one, three and a half inches long. That would be sixteen penny. McCulloch had learned that from a carpenter who walked part of the way home with him after the surrender.

"This will go off like grapeshot," Breen said.

"Yeah." McCulloch's face hardened. "That's the plan."

Keegan reached down and withdrew a stick of dynamite. He said, "How do we get it to blow up? You just don't shoot it, laddie. I'm no artillery man, I know, but all the battles I fought . . ."

"Fuse," McCulloch asked. "I'll open one box, stick a lighted cigar."

Breen stiffened. "How in the hell do you get out of there alive, Matt, before those boxes all turn that trading camp into blood and bones?"

"You leave that to me," McCulloch said.

Keegan pulled out more empty boxes, reached in for another one of Jim Ketchum's old dynamite. He froze suddenly, paled, and swallowed hard.

"Matt . . ." His voice became the faintest of whispers. He raised his left hand slowly, almost like a snail's pace, and the sunlight reflected sweat on the fingers. "Sweating, laddie. Sweating."

McCulloch thought the old soldier meant he was sweating. Until he turned ever so gently and flicked his fingers toward the creek crossing.

Five savage pops followed, causing the horses to pull at their hobbles, the Comanchero to topple over, and Breen to stare at his hands which had dipped for a dynamite stick in the box closest to him. He became a statue. The stench was unmistakable as smoke and dust rose from where the droplets hand landed.

Sean Keegan hadn't been sweating.

The dynamite had.

"Nitroglycerin," McCulloch said.

"Nitro!" The Comanchero cut loose with every curse word he had ever learned, in multiple languages, as he slid away from the boxes until his back landed against the cottonwood. "Nitroglycerin. We all could have been blown to kingdom come."

Keegan laughed. "Aye, indeed, we could have, laddies." He stared at his fingers, and then at the wooden box in front of him. "But as we like to say: The good Lord looks after fools, children, and Jackals."

"Matt?" Breen's voice was hoarse. He still had not moved his hands out of the crate. "What do we do now?"

McCulloch just smiled. "A slight change in plans, boys. Just a slight change in plans."

CHAPTER 39

"This is the place," the Comanchero said in a hoarse whisper.

All four riders reined up, but no one dismounted—neither of the men even breathed—till the two mules slowed, stopped, snorted. One urinated. One found a clump of grass to chew.

"Laddies," Keegan said softly, "while I cannot say I have enjoyed the company, parting here shan't be too sorrowful." He slid out of the saddle, which he began taking off his horse. Jed Breen dismounted, and began unsaddling his horse, too. They used the bridles to take the horses back down the trail a few yards, then removed the leather, and slapped the animals' behinds. Both trotted south.

"I feel naked," Keegan said. "Cavalryman without a horse."

They were turning the horses free, so they might have a chance to live—in case the Jackals did not survive.

"You'll find plenty of horses in the Canyon of Weeping Women," Green Clayton said.

"Aye. I'd better."

Breen had pulled the map the Comanchero had drawn from his pocket. He unfolded it, looked at it, and then at the red-rocked hill. He nodded at a natural cut into the steep path.

"That the trail?" he asked.

"It's not much of one," Green Clayton said, "but if you can make it to the top . . ." He laughed and raised his head. The sky reappeared maybe four hundred feet higher. ". . . it's not too hard on the other side. And there's a coyote trail down for you, Yankee." He looked over at Breen. "You'll continue, just like the map says. Find a good place. And don't miss."

"I don't plan to," Breen said. He walked over to McCulloch and held out his hand. "Look after yourself, Matt."

"You, too." The shake was swift, firm, and meaningful.

McCulloch raised his head and nodded at the horse trooper. "See you when I see you."

"Aye. But, Matt . . . what if the plan does not work?"

The former Texas Ranger grinned a humorless grin. "We fall back on the next plan. Get the girls. Get out of there alive."

Keegan laughed. "I sure hope those Comancheros have more than just trader's whiskey on the other side of this hill." He shifted the Springfield and started for the cut. "A little Irish would sure wet me whistle."

Jim Bob Hardwick stepped out of the saddle, and wrapped the reins around the post. Maria, that beautiful but strange woman, scrubbed laundry in a bucket in front of the cabin. On the porch, Boss Linden on an overturned nail keg, smoking a cigar, laughing and passing a bottle to newcomers to the Canyon of Weeping Women. Four men, well dressed in Prince Albert coats and city hats, two of them Mexican, two American, all smoking cigars and holding brandy snifters.

Hardwick took a few steps before stopping. He saw Maria staring at him, even fancied that he caught a quick smile. But the woman then bowed her head and scrubbed the Comanchero boss's laundry harder. Hardwick looked up and waited. He waited until Linden had topped the glasses with the amber liquid.

"Gentlemen," Linden said as he stood, finished his brandy, and threw the snifter against a cook fire about ten yards away. He missed the stone ring, but the glass shattered on the ground, causing three old women—an Indian, a Mexican and a Negress—to look from their pots and pans. Then they went back to their cooking.

"To our success." The men toasted, drank, and threw their glasses. They had better aim than the Comanchero. The women, though, did not acknowledge the fancy toasting or good arms.

Boss Linden limped down off the porch and trained his hard eyes on Jim Bob.

"Wild Kent said you sent for me, Boss," Jim Bob said.

"Wild Kent. I sent Mal Martínez to fetch you."

That flustered the young man. "I . . . I . . . I just know, sir, that it was Wild Kent that told me to come quick."

"The sneaking, lusting fool." The man shook his head, cussed again, then glanced at Maria. He studied her for a long while before looking back at Jim Bob.

"You need something, Boss Linden?" Jim Bob tried.

"Yes, boy, I need something." He sighed. "I've got thirty-some Cheyennes and twenty-two Kiowas. But Dog Heart isn't here with his Warm Springs bunch, and neither is Black Forehead with his Comanches. The Cheyennes and Kiowas are growing impatient. And drinking my whiskey stash dry."

He paused. Jim Bob did not know what he could ask.

"And these fine gents want to do business, too," Linden said.

"I see," Jim Bob said, but he did not know what there was to see. He tried looking at the men on the porch, but the only thing he could tell about them was that none of them had picked cotton, served time in prison, or cowboyed for a living.

"Oh, forgive me, Jim Bob. Gentlemen." He leaned on his cane as he turned and smiled at the visitors. "Allow me to present to you our newest young ruffian. Jim Bob Hardwick. Señor Hardwick, allow me to introduce you to Don Salbatore Gandullo, who runs the finest brothel in Santa Fe . . . Bear Mannix, a cattleman on the Purgatoire River in Colorado . . . Señor Dario Packmor of Taos . . . and Livingston Langley, judge down Mesilla way."

Jim Bob couldn't tell who was who, but he nodded, saying, "Pleasure."

Having broken the snifters, those four men returned to passing the bottle of brandy among themselves.

Jim Bob looked back at Linden. "You need something from me, sir?"

The man might not have heard. That's what Jim Bob thought for a few seconds, but the cane twisted, and Boss Linden looked back at Jim Bob. "Yes," he said. "Yes, I do. Bring me the blond Apache."

He swallowed. "Sir."

"The blond hard-ass, boy. I have to please my guests. The judge and Don Salbatore are here as buyers, and they've heard a great deal of my boasting of her . . ." He grinned wickedly. ". . . talents. Bring her."

He started to turn back to the porch, but stopped, and looked back at Jim Bob, who hoped the man had changed

308 William W. Johnstone and J.A. Johnstone

his mind. Maybe one of the prostitutes would be a better match.

"Send Wild Kent Montgomery . . . no, never mind. Tell Mal Martínez to ride out of the canyon and spell Enrique. That will show that worthless *vaquero* to do what I say and not send Wild Kent Montgomery near those women. Where is Martínez? What was his pressing engagement?"

"Wild Kent said he was playing three-card monte with the Kiowas," Jim Bob said.

"Perhaps they will kill and scalp him. Save me the trouble." He started up the steps, but stopped again, and turned. "What is keeping you, boy?"

Jim Bob swallowed. "Well, sir. It's . . . Paulita and . . . Miss . . . Cynthia. They asked for . . . more bandages, sir. And some alcohol."

The Comanchero boss sighed. "It's always something. Everyone always wants something." His head shook. "Do you mean to tell me that that whore whose leg was cut off is still alive?"

"Yes, sir. She was conscious for a few hours yesterday evening."

"What joy. Providence. We all love providence." He sighed and looked at the beautiful woman washing his stinking clothes. "Alyvia! Oh, hell. Jim Bob, get that witch's attention."

"Ma'am." Jim Bob realized his mistake immediately. Maria was deaf and mute to Boss Linden.

"She can't hear you, you ignorant son of a—"

But Jim Bob was already waving his hands, and Maria turned toward him, then looked at the man with the cane.

Boss Linden stuck the cane under an armpit and began speaking in Spanish and moving his hands and fingers. When he was finished, Maria nodded, bowed her head, and walked toward Jim Bob.

"Take her with you, Jim Bob. You both know the way. And if Wild Kent even looks at Alyvia, do me the pleasure of shooting him in his belly."

Jim Bob grabbed the reins to his horse and waited for Maria to join him. Then they walked toward that storage shed that wasn't the big stone one.

After twenty yards, Jim Bob dared a glance at the quiet woman. She smiled at him, but kept looking straight ahead. A wide grin stretched across Jim Bob's face. Today was getting better already.

"How far?" McCulloch asked the murderous runt.

Green Clayton turned and stared up at the hard rock in the saddle. "We would have been there three days ago," he said, "if you hadn't decided to bring nitro along."

"I asked you a question."

"Yeah, but I didn't bargain for nitro. We could've been blown to kingdom come before we even knew that stuff was leaking out of them ancient sticks. We could all be—"

"You could still be at Peering Farm," McCulloch said. "Picking cotton."

"We still got to get that volatile stuff down into the Canyon of Weeping Women."

"It's wrapped up as best as we could do. And remember, only one box of that was seeping. And only a few sticks. Now I've called this tune. And this is the tune we're playing. How far?"

"Two hours to the sentry. And that's going slow. Which we'll have to be. Three hours down."

McCulloch looked at the sun, then at the hill Breen and Keegan were climbing, out of sight now, and for all McCulloch knew, dead. They could have fallen off. They could have run into Comancheros who were waiting for them.

He did not like having to trust a man like Green Clayton, but he had to get into that canyon someway.

McCulloch took one of the lead ropes and held it out. The Comanchero just stared.

"Take it." He smiled. "Keegan's gone. You want me to try to keep two mules from stumbling. Remember, two of those crates are packed with enough nitroglycerin to flatten this country like the rest of the Panhandle."

The man spit. "We're about to climb up to that wasteland." He sighed and wiped his mouth. "But it's an easier climb than what those pards of yours have."

McCulloch held out the rope, but Green Clayton made no move to take it.

"You trust me with that?" the Comanchero asked after a long pause.

"I trust you not to make a break for it. I trust you not to try to double-cross me. And I trust you to pick a right safe path for me to follow. Otherwise, they'll be picking up pieces of both of us from Cheyenne to Veracruz."

Green Clayton took the rope, and slowly, gingerly, turned his horse around.

Chapter 40

"Why?" Sean Keegan sat down for a moment to cut the dust in his throat with tepid canteen water and rub his feet through the thin leather of his army boots. "Why did that puny cuss give us two maps?"

Jed Breen laid his map across a boulder, pushed up his hat brim, and compared what Green Clayton had sketched with what he saw below and in front of him.

"In case one of us got killed," the bounty hunter whispered. He frowned.

"The swine's plan," Keegan said, "might have been for both of us to get killed."

Breen did not reply. He looked at the map again.

"Are we on the right trail?" Keegan asked.

Breen swore softly. "How in hell would I know? This whole country is like nothing I've ever seen."

"Aye. But no one has seen this, excepting Comancheros and Comanches."

The map was folded and stuffed into Breen's hip pocket. The bounty hunter picked up the Sharps he had leaned against a tan boulder, and nodded at a cut carved by thousands of years of rain. "This is the one," Breen said. "I think."

Sean Keegan tried to tell himself that he had survived many senseless and bloody battles following orders given with even less assurance than what Jed Breen had said. Then he yelled, "Down Jed!"

Breen dropped flat behind the rock. The knife came out of the sheath and Keegan let it flip. Then he was bringing up the Springfield, pulling back the hammer as he brought the heavy rifle to his shoulder. He aimed. But the man was down. Keegan curved around the boulder, shifting the .45-70 to his left hand and drawing the Remington .44 from his holster.

He eased to the top of the path, then looked down the trail, aiming his revolver at the unmoving man in buckskin with a big knife buried almost to the hilt just beneath his ribs.

Jed Breen stepped up beside him. "Thanks, pard," the bounty hunter whispered, and he eased down the path, ripped the knife out of the man's gut, and when the dying Comanchero groaned, Breen dragged the blade deep, and mercifully, across the bandit's throat. He wiped the blade on the buckskin trousers of the dead man, and raised it up the hill, toward Keegan.

The cavalryman accepted it, and slid it into the leather sheath.

"Well," Breen said, and he removed his hat, wiped his brow, and waited for his nerves to settle. "Now we know."

"Know what?" Keegan asked.

"Clayton didn't lie to us. "We're on the right trail."

"Amigo."

McCulloch reined up, but let the mule behind him stop at its own, casual, safer pace. Twisting in the saddle, he turned, putting his hand on the .44-40 Colt on his hip. Behind him, Green Clayton pulled back on his reins, and made an extra dally with his lead rope around the saddle horn. The small Comanchero turned, and looked down the trail.

A Mexican emerged from where the flat prairie ended, and the canyon country dropped off. McCulloch did not know where the man had been hiding, but he had found a good place. That hombre could have killed McCulloch and Clayton before they knew they were dead.

The man rode a buckskin, and he carried a Winchester Yellow Boy that had been studded with brass tacks on the forestock and stock, and the barrel had been sawed off to something like twelve inches. He put the carbine in his left hand, and held out his right toward Clayton Green.

"Martínez," the little killer said without any trace of friendship, or even humanity. But he did accept the hand.

"I thought I would kill you, but then I remembered that some tall, mean hombre is to be bringing bullets for the guns we stole."

"Yeah." Green Clayton shot McCulloch a glance. "He's tall. He's mean. And." He slowly, carefully, raised the lead rope just a bit. "We got enough bullets to mow down an entire army."

"That is good." The Mexican laughed. *"Muy bien."* He even grinned at McCulloch. "You do business, señor?"

"If the price is right?" McCulloch said.

Martínez laughed. "I like your partner, amigo. Come. We shall ride into the Canyon of Weeping Women. I will send Pedro up when we meet him at the entrance. It is good to see you, amigo. It has been a long time. Too long. Boss Linden. He will be happy to see you."

"I'd like to see him," Green Clayton said with no feeling.

McCulloch cleared his throat. "Word is," he said carefully, "you're having a big powwow. Lots of tribes." He nodded at the crates and satchels, kegs and boxes, strapped to the mule he had been leading.

"Sí." The man named Martínez nodded. "But so far our only Indian customers are Kiowas and Cheyennes. The Apaches? They no show. The Comanches? We have no word from them, either. But we have gringo and fine, wealthy businessmen from New Mexico and Colorado territories. You will make out like . . ." He wailed like a coyote on an autumn night. *"Bandidos."*

"Any sign of Black Forehead's bunch?" Boss Linden screamed. "Or those yellow-livered 'Paches?"

"No," Cullen Brice snarled.

One of the drunkards on the porch said, "Start the biddin', Linden, or we take our money back to New Mexico and wait to deal with Tafoya's boys."

Cynthia McCulloch stared at the Comanchero leader, who had to be drunker than any man she had ever seen. And she had grown up near Purgatory City.

She had lost track of the hours she had been standing in front of the cabin.

Boss Linden raised a bottle to his lips.

Cullen Brice turned, spit, and cursed.

One of the Indians—likely Cheyenne from the looks of him—barked something that made the Apache language sound as romantic as French.

"¿Cuánto más debemos esperar?" one of the New Mexican merchants bellowed. The brandy was gone. So was a healthy portion of tequila.

Again, Boss Linden sighed. He looked at the tub of hot water where Cynthia had replaced Maria to finish the evil man's laundry. She glanced at Jim Bob Hardwick, who was staring off toward where the women prisoners remained. Likely, she guessed, wondering about Maria. Cynthia's mind kept picturing the frightened twins—and their mother.

Finally, Boss Linden made his head move up and down. He found Cullen Brice and spoke softly, "All right. Go fetch the other petticoats. Bring Wild Kent with you. Miguel, get the Kiowas. Two Hatchets, go bring in Bad Buffalo and his dog soldiers. I'll get my ledger, and that sack of bank notes. The last sale starts in fifteen minutes. Get ever'body over . . ." Boss Linden's wave was ambiguous. ". . . yonder. I'll meet y'all directly."

He took a detour, however, toward the privy behind the canyon.

Jed Breen slid behind the rock. He leaned the Sharps on the branch of a pathetic juniper and pulled out the map.

"We found it." Sean Keegan began thanking mothers, and sons, and all the saints. Breen just glanced at the map and brought up Sharps. He stared through the scope for a minute, moving the rifle slowly from northwest to southeast.

Then he pulled his head away from the telescopic sight and swore vehemently.

"Nobody's there! Nobody's there!"

"Bloody hell!" Sean Keegan looked, too, but even with the naked eye he saw . . . "Horses. It's a boxed canyon of . . . horses!"

Keegan picked up the map. He looked at it, then at the terrain below.

"That puny cuss. I'll tear his bloody head off. He's tricked us. The sorry—"

"Maybe not." Jed Breen had to slow down everything, especially his heartbeat and his racing mind. "Remember . . .

Clayton said that Boss Linden might have switched things around. He has been in prison a spell."

"Aye. And he could also have been playing us for fools."

Breen nodded. That, most definitely, was a possibility.

"And ye won't be able to shoot that crate of nitro when Matt gives ye the signal. When we don't even know . . ."

Breen had already looked back at the map. He raised his hand, silencing the Irish trooper. "Let me think."

He studied the fingers of canyons that fed off the main one. He looked to his right. "All right, Sean," he said. "That canyon we saw over there." He pointed.

"Aye. As sorry a city as Liverpool. Huts and shanties and—"

"That has to be where the prisoners are. Where Ramona is. Most likely. And Cynthia. And who the hell knows how many other poor women and kids."

Keegan blinked, straightened, and waited, like any good horse soldier noncommissioned officer, for his orders.

"Find that trail down. Get down there. Get Ramona. Get Cynthia. And get as many women and prisoners as you can out of there."

He was already running.

"And where in bloody hell are you off to, laddie?" Keegan called after him.

"To find Matt," Breen yelled, and disappeared over the ridge. "Before it's too late!"

Everyone was moving away from the cabin of cotton-wood logs, except some of the big merchants, who were still on the porch, drinking Boss Linden's whiskey. Jim Bob Hardwick studied the open fields near the stone storage . . . vault. That was the best word he could come up with to describe the big, solid structure. He looked toward the privy, and then at the cabin, and then looked for Maria before he remembered she was back in the other side canyon. He frowned. Where Boss Linden had sent Cullen Brice. And where Wild Kent Montgomery, the treacherous wretch, was with those poor women, and the two twins, and . . . sweet, gentle, beautiful Maria.

Men, red-skinned, brown-skinned, and white, began leaving the area in front of the big log cabin toward the open field between Boss Linden's home and that strange big stone building. Jim Bob looked at the privy, and then he heard a familiar sound. He turned to his left and saw the horses. His stomach twisted, uncertain of what it meant, to see Mal Martínez leading two white men who pulled two scrawny, overloaded mules behind them.

"Hombre!" Mal sang out. "The bullets are here! The bullets are here!" He repeated his announcement in Mexican, and then in some language that had to be either Kiowa or Cheyenne. His eyes turned toward Miss Cynthia. Maria? Well, he had to concede that Maria was on her own. But she could take care of herself. He would have to protect poor Miss Cynthia. With his life if it came down to it.

"This way," called the Comanchero named Diego. He didn't sound confident of his orders, but Boss Linden had not emerged. And the white traders and the Kiowas and the Southern Cheyennes were already walking toward the clearing between the cabin and the stone building.

By then, Mal Martínez trotted his horse past. He barely glanced at the squirming, sweating, ugly little dude who pulled the first mule, and then his eyes took in the other man, ramrod straight, eyes looking one way, straight ahead, focused on his purpose until his entire body trembled, and he stared directly at . . .

Miss Cynthia. And that pretty but tough lady looked directly at him. Her mouth moved. Jim Bob Hardwick could read her lips.

Oh . . . my . . . god.

She followed him. So did all the others.

"Boss Linden!" a Comanchero called. "It's time, hombre." He swore, spit and cursed. "He wants to sell everything and he spends all his time in the privy."

Jim Bob Hardwick looked once more at the outhouse and then the big cabin. Seeing no sign of Boss Hardwick, he fell into what seemed to be a silent funeral procession.

CHAPTER 41

When Matt McCulloch swung out of the saddle, he pulled the Winchester from the scabbard and swatted the gelding's backside with the barrel.

Go on, boy, he thought, hoping to send his orders telepathically to the horse. *Keep going. Get as far away from here as you can.*

Then he stared across the open field at his daughter. And tried to send the same message to her. He sighed. That one, unlike the one delivered to the still trotting horse, had not worked.

He couldn't stop now. The cards had all been dealt. This was the hand he had to play. So he walked to the mule he had been leading, and ground-reined the lead rope. He moved closer to the mule, whispered a bunch of nothing into the animal's ears. Scratched its neck, told him he was a good mule, and walked toward Green Clayton.

The little man dismounted, and showed some sign of humanity when he swatted his horse's backside with a hard slap, all the while keeping a firm hand on the lead rope to his mule. McCulloch reached him and the two men stared at each other.

"Now what?" McCulloch asked.

"This is your plan, Ranger. You tell me."

"My plan," McCulloch said, "has gone to hell. Where is that Comanchero boss of yours?"

"For all I know," Clayton Green said. "He's dead."

The Mexican kept calling Linden's name. He wasn't dead.

McCulloch swallowed. He saw feathered headdresses he recognized as belonging to Southern Cheyennes. And he recognized the hard, ugly face of Pony Soldier Killer, the brutal, merciless Kiowa leader. And then he saw Cynthia, standing next to an armed young cowboy. McCulloch vowed to kill that lowlife if he laid a hand on that blond-haired beauty.

Reason returned.

He was alive. Cynthia was alive. Ramona? Well, he prayed for her, and her soul. His eyes briefly shot out toward the surrounding ridges. Maybe, God willing, Jed Breen was sighting down on this place with his Sharps. Maybe Sean Keegan was somewhere, yeah, maybe that grand old Irish blowhard had found Ramona and was leading her to safety.

He breathed in, breathed out, and saw the sweat running down Green Clayton's savage face.

The Kiowa chieftain barked something. More voices in various languages followed.

McCulloch wiped his hands on his chaps.

"Clayton," he whispered, "it's time to unload the merchandise."

CHAPTER 42

They tightly ground-reined the mule before moving to one side of the packsaddle.

Green Clayton's cold eyes met Matt McCulloch's. The men said nothing. They scarcely breathed. Both men's hands reached up toward the thick rope, and after a quick bob of the head from each man, they went to work.

Gently, almost as if they were holding a baby in their hands, they moved the long crate away from the mule.

McCulloch looked at the box's lid and the side nearest Green Clayton. McCulloch whispered, "This one is safe."

He thought about that after he had taken a few steps. Matthew McCulloch thought about a great number of things.

Where is my daughter?

What if the dynamite in this wooden box has begun to sweat out nitroglycerin.

What if the mule decides to sneeze?

They gently set the box on the ground, eyed each other, and moved back to the mule. This time they found the long crate at the bottom of the pack on the other side.

The Kiowas began singing.

One man shouted something in Spanish.

McCulloch tried to block out everything except the knots. He prayed Green Clayton was doing the same. When the knots fell free and the ropes dropped to the red earth, they stepped away from the mule, and looked down at the crate.

On the end closest to Green Clayton, McCulloch saw the red cross painted on the top of the lid. And on both sides. There was another one, with the cross in the middle of a circle. All painted red. Like a haphazard bull's eye. A target . . . for Jed Breen.

McCulloch glanced up the hill, but saw only red earth, blue sky, and the pale white light of a sun sinking toward the horizon.

An eternity later, they laid that crate on the ground.

Two more crates followed. Then satchels, And kegs. And then they had the pleasure of doing the same thing again. Four more crates, one with a shot of nitroglycerin. Enough to blow everyone nearby to Kingdom Come.

The last crate was laid near the others. They could breathe easier now. Hell, breathing at all was something positive. They came back to the pack mule and unloaded the keg of beer from St. Louis, which had to be flatter than the plains above the canyon's rim. They unloaded the satchels and the saddlebags and the sacks, and laid them atop the crates. They just made sure not to even sneeze or kick up a pebble toward those painted with the red crosses and the red circles around the red crosses.

"Where is Boss Linden?" one of the businessmen called out.

Matt McCulloch tried to clear his throat, but he could not have struck a well with the biggest drill in Texas. He wiped his palms on his chaps. Green Clayton walked on the other side of the merchandise for sale.

Merchandise of death.

Then, McCulloch turned and found the bright, if hard, face of his daughter. For just a second, maybe two, no more than three, Matt McCulloch thought he was looking at his wife. Then he thought he was staring at his baby girl. Now he saw a woman, full grown.

Cynthia smiled.

Matt tilted his head.

A voice ended the utopian illusion.

"What the bloody hell is this? This is my *fandango, mis amigos*. I call the tune here."

Matt turned away from his daughter, and saw Boss Linden slap one of the long crates. Matt flinched. Nothing happened. The leathery man stopped, next to another wooden crate. His face brightened. He shouted something in Spanish that Matt could not catch.

Then Matt McCulloch saw Clayton Green heading straight for the Comanchero boss.

"Mi amigo!" Forgetting his bad leg or the cane he held, Boss Linden held out both hands as if to hug his long-lost friend, and McCulloch understood that Linden had not sold out Green Clayton. It was probably just like McCulloch had said. The Comanchero wasn't freed at Peering Farm because none of the raiders expected Sean Keegan and Jed Breen to have been there to offer a stiff resistance. Green Clayton, McCulloch realized, saw none of that. He saw only revenge.

Green Clayton drew his bowie knife and rammed it into Boss Linden's belly.

CHAPTER 43

He was running now, across the field, half expecting to be riddled with bullets. McCulloch reached the far side, grabbed Cynthia's arm, and thought he must have pulled the limb from its socket. He was heading for the big cabin, but Cynthia freed herself from his grip. She stopped, turned, looked the opposite way, and then found her father's eyes.

"This way, Papa!"

It sounded like three words from a six-year-old girl.

She was running, then looking to her left, screaming, "Jim Bob! Follow us!"

McCulloch paused only for a brief moment, then pushed his legs to start heading the other way. Toward the big stone shed.

The Kiowas yelled, pointing at the running men.

Don Salbatore Gandullo, who had left the porch to see what these two new Comancheros had brought, stepped back and fell to his knees. His mouth widened, but no words came out.

Bad Buffalo had heard his medicine man tell him that no white man, not even a Comanchero, could be trusted. He had not believed that old Cheyenne, but now he understood the truth. There was something bad going on. This was not the way to sell guns and bullets to warriors. This was treachery.

He nocked an arrow, but did not release it to kill one of the two running white men or the blond woman who ran faster than both white-eyes. He stopped when his brothers pointed at the man with the cane and the tiny white-eye who had brought ammo for the guns they were to buy.

Colorado cattle baron Bear Mannix palmed his new Schofield and aimed it at the big man who was running after the blond girl. "Something's wrong. This ain't right." He pulled back the hammer.

"Holy Mother of God!" Judge Langley said.

Mannix turned toward the judge. Bad Buffalo did the same. Only he saw Bear Mannix with a drawn pistol, so he let his arrow fly.

Boss Linden staggered back, and Green Clayton pulled the knife out of the man's belly. Glancing at the blood staining his shirtfront, Linden called, "Alyvia," but he heard only a whisper. Alyvia did not come. Linden looked at Clayton, saw the hatred in his friend's eyes.

"Why?" Linden whispered.

Green Clayton started to slice Linden's throat, when he heard the gunshot. He spun around, dropping the knife and drawing a revolver. He spotted McCulloch running toward a pale-colored structure. So it wasn't McCulloch who fired. Then he saw a cattleman, lying in front of the porch of the big cottonwood cabin, a smoking gun in his right hand and an arrow quivering in the center of his chest.

He saw the Southern Cheyenne chief, Bad Buffalo, turn and fall to his knees, clutching his throat with both hands, unable to stop the blood that flowed as though his throat had been sliced with a bowie knife. He saw the Indian fall dead.

And he heard the Cheyenne warriors. How many had he been told were here? More than thirty? Several of them were charging toward the traders who had been drinking Boss Linden's brandy.

He turned back to finish Boss Linden.

"Don't!" Dario Packmor screamed. "Don't!"

The Cheyenne with the war axe did not listen. He brought the weapon down on the Taos merchant's head.

Green Clayton turned. His eyes met Boss Linden's. He saw part of the cane in Linden's left hand. He saw the handle in Boss Linden's right. He saw the shining silver dagger that was attached to the curved handle. And he felt that dagger ram him between his ribs.

Linden released the handle as Green Clayton staggered back, palming his gun. He thought he saw Alyvia running. He saw Cheyennes and Kiowas rushing his men, rushing the merchants he had invited. He saw the revolver in Green Clayton's hand. And his last thought before he fell back toward the boxes of guns and ammunition was that he would never get to feel the ocean breeze at Veracruz.

Judge Livingston Langley ran. He felt an arrow whistle past his neck. He saw Boss Linden, his shirtfront stained crimson, fall back, and land faceup. He saw the other Comanchero, Green Clayton, drop to his knees, and squeeze the trigger.

The crooked jurist did not hear the report of the pistol. He did not see smoke from the barrel. He did not even see the next arrow that flew past him disintegrate in flame. Nor did he even hear the explosion after the bullet from Green Clayton's revolver hit a long wooden crate. One second he was running for his life. The next second his life was over. And no one would ever find his body.

Cynthia reached the door first. Thank God, the place was unlocked. She did not question why, though she guessed that tequila and time and nerves and bowel ailments had befogged Boss Linden's mind. If it had been locked, they could have taken shelter behind it. . . . Maybe. . . . She pushed open the door, and fell down. She heard footsteps and grunts and heavy panting behind her.

Then—the whole room shuddered, sending dust, pebbles, maybe half of the Texas Panhandle, raining down on their bodies like an avalanche. Cynthia McCulloch covered her eyes with her right arm and let her left hand prevent the endless, hot particles from clogging her nose and mouth. Even through those thick stone walls, she felt heat that matched the hottest singes of hell. The entire building rattled, the mortar vanishing, she managed to glimpse, in one instance. But she heard nothing, as though her eardrums had been obliterated.

This was the way she had always imagined The End Of The World would begin.

CHAPTER 44

Jed Breen ran. He had spotted smoke from small fires—cook fires, likely—one where he thought the prisoners were being held. The other . . . ? Well, maybe he'd find Matt there.

The next thing he knew, he was lying on his back, stars of myriad colors flashing before him, his head hurt, he didn't know where his rifle was, and the bells pealing inside his eardrums almost made him scream. He also felt the sandstone rattling all around him.

He had read newspaper accounts about earthquakes, just never had been in one. He forced his eyes open. Gently brought his hand to the back of his head and felt a lump already forming, and real tender, but no blood. The ground still shook, and his ears would not stop ringing, but he was alive. He pushed his left hand blindly on the ground, and felt the warmth and smoothness of brass.

The telescopic sight on his Sharps.

He turned his head ever so gently, and finally got his eyelids to move up. It took a moment to focus. It took even longer for him to hold down the vomit. At last, he saw the .50-caliber rifle. It looked no worse for the wear, so he dragged it over and set it across his lap.

Now, all I have to do is remember how to stand up.

His mind cleared again.

He found the blue sky, a white cloud, the red rocks, and then he saw the billowing black smoke, like the funnel of a tornado, twisting, spinning, even sparks showering down from five hundred feet in the air.

It had not been an earthquake. He knew that now.

"Matt," he whispered.

He bit back the pain in his head, his back, his thighs, his heart. He used the heavy rifle to push himself to his feet. And began picking a path off the ridge and down into the Canyon of Weeping Women.

"We fall back on the next plan. Get the girls. Get out of there alive."

Matt McCulloch's voice echoed in Sean Keegan's head as he looked at the thick, violent cloud of ugly black smoke.

The explosion had knocked him off his feet. He pushed himself up, staggered, found his hat, and looked for his Springfield. It had to be here somewhere. He had been carrying it when the ground went from under him. Keegan then peered down from the edge of the cliff.

"So much for the luck of the Irish," he said.

The Springfield was a hundred feet below. The stock was busted off. He'd have to climb down and get it, and while Sean Keegan could ride a horse anywhere, climbing was not his best skill, other than climbing to his feet after getting knocked down in a fistfight or getting staggering drunk.

He drew the revolver from the holster, started walking, wiping the .44 with the kerchief he unknotted from his neck. Walking he did not care for, either, but he was going downhill, and the path here seemed easier.

Keegan shoved the yellow scarf into his trousers pocket.

He cocked the Remington.

He did not look at the black smoke. Could not stand to do that. That would remind him of Matt. Matt McCulloch, who had paid the ultimate price. He stared at the smoke from what had to be cook fires, in a feeder canyon that had to be where the Comancheros kept prisoners. That's where he was going. That's what his orders had been. Matt McCulloch had given Sergeant Sean Keegan orders. And Keegan was a man who obeyed his orders.

"Get the girls. Get out of there alive."

It seemed lighter inside the shed. When Matt McCulloch rolled over, sunlight baked his face and hands, he smelled smoke, and ash rained upon him.

His eyes opened, blinking several times, then he rolled over, looked at the stone floor of the shed, and jerked his head. He caught his breath. Cynthia lay there, faceup, blinking, breathing heavily.

McCulloch rose to his knees and saw the boy, young man actually, his back against the wall, bleeding from a scratch on his neck and forehead, and covered with white dust. He might have been in shock. But he was alive.

He looked up and saw black smoke, ash, dust, and a blue sky.

The roof of the shed . . . it was . . . gone.

"Stay here."

After rising to his feet, Matt McCulloch checked the rounds in the cylinder of his .44-40 revolver, pulled the hammer to full cock, and pushed open the door. The air felt heavy with dust, and the smoke made him cough.

"Stay here," he repeated, and stepped outside, aiming the Colt in the general direction before he quickly lowered it.

The door was pelted with stones, bent nails, bolts. The rugged walls were pockmarked from the canister he had loaded in the crates and bags.

Breen's voice echoed in his head: *This will go off like grapeshot.*

And then he remembered his own, callous reply. *Yeah. That's the plan.*

Slowly, he stepped toward the trading ground and Boss Linden's cabin.

Even twenty yards past the shed, cacti and junipers had been cut in half, or torn asunder. If Cynthia had not led them to this shed, they all would have been ripped to pieces.

He looked at the log cabin, engulfed in fire. Briefly, he heard someone scream. Mercifully, the scream went silent. Black smoke rose, twisting, turning, ugly, menacing. That log cabin had been Matt's destination.

Footsteps sounded behind him.

Matt growled. "I said . . ."

"We heard you." Cynthia stepped beside him. The boy with the gun took a few steps ahead of them, but stopped. He looked one way, then the other.

"What happened?" he asked. "Where is everybody?"

He could see a few bodies on the ground, near the burning cabin, scattered about. Where the crates of rifles and bullets—and, obviously, the nitroglycerin and dynamite—had been, a giant crater, smoking black and gray, grimly replaced them. There was no sign of Green Clayton. No sign of Boss Linden. He didn't think Jed Breen had done this with that Sharps rifle of his. He didn't know what had happened. But it had happened.

McCulloch looked at his daughter.

"You all right?"

She nodded. But she did not look away from the ugliness, blackness.

"Horses," McCulloch said, and realized he spoke in a hushed whisper. "Where are the horses?"

"Corrals." Cynthia pointed.

The kid pointed off farther south. "There's a box canyon yonder. Keep the stolen . . ."

They didn't hear the sound, but saw the dust, and several galloping horses near that far wall. Running toward the trail that McCulloch and Clayton had been led down.

"They look so pretty when they run like that," McCulloch whispered.

It was the only thing pretty about this canyon.

"They won't go far," the boy said. "And that ain't even a quarter of 'em."

The pistol shot echoed, but this one came from nowhere near the crater. Every head turned.

"Maria," the boy whispered. And he drew his revolver and started walking toward the sound.

"This isn't over," McCulloch said. He looked at his daughter. "Stay here."

"No," she said, and started after the boy.

Right then, Sean Keegan longed to have that Springfield instead of just a short gun.

A hundred yards ahead, on the flats, near the smoking campfire, a leathery man waved two pistols over the heads of several women. He appeared to be plumb out of his mind, shouting curses, then prayers, then calling out names, then aiming his guns at some of the women.

"Mal! Mal!" a young female voice said. "Don't hurt us. Please, don't hurt us."

Finally, the Comanchero with the women hostages said something Keegan could understand. "I don't know what the hell's happening." The accent was Mexican. "I don't know what the hell's happening. I don't know what the hell's happening."

Yeah, his mind was gone.

"But I will kill you all before I get myself butchered. Blown to bits. I do not know what the hell's happening. I do not know what the hell's happening. . . ." He began praying in Spanish.

Keegan couldn't see the women. They were likely sitting, lying down, huddled together, praying for mercy. He didn't recognize the woman's voice he had heard. But that madman with two guns a hundred yards away could be aiming one of those pistols at Cynthia McCulloch. Or Ramona Bonderhoff. Hell, he realized, it didn't matter if Cynthia or Ramona were there. He remembered his orders.

"Get the girls. Get out of there alive."

He pushed himself to his feet. And started running.

Another gunshot echoed off the canyon walls. The boy started off like a young colt trying to gallop for the first time.

McCulloch cupped a hand over his mouth, but stopped himself from calling out.

"What's his name?" he asked his daughter.

"Jim Bob Hardwick."

Hardwick. One of those scoundrels Breen and Keegan had gone after. Returned to the Peering Farm. He didn't know the Hardwicks had been Comancheros.

He started to shout, but stopped.

"Jim Bob!" Cynthia yelled. She drew a breath to yell for him to stop.

"No!" McCulloch's whisper was sharp. "Let him go. They hear us coming, we get killed." He looked gravely at her daughter, but saw in her eyes that she understood. He knelt, and motioned for her to do the same.

"You know this land better than I do," he said. "Where's he going? And how do we get there without getting spotted— or killed?"

The woman ran out of an arroyo, stumbled, turned, screamed, and scrambled to her feet. Jed Breen saw the dark hair, thought he recognized Ramona, and he broke into a sprint. He was still running when the other figure, a bearded man in buckskins, climbed out of the arroyo and came to his feet.

A gun barked. The woman screamed, fell, and then both the Comanchero and Breen stopped running. They saw each other. The bandit started to raise his pistol, but Breen had his Sharps coming to his shoulder, knowing he was out of pistol range. But the handgun stopped coming up, and the barrel pointed down.

Breen paused. He could see the woman. The revolver was aimed at her, and it sure looked like Ramona Bonderhoff.

"I kill her, hombre," the man called out. "Drop that fancy gun. Drop it or she dies."

"Hurt her," Breen said, knowing his threat would ring hollow, "and you die."

The man laughed. "We all die, hombre. But she dies first."

From the ground came a cry, "Jed . . ."

Breen's heart shattered, and all these years he had been telling himself that he was a bounty hunter, and thus had no heart. Besides, jackals were cold, heartless.

"I will not say it again, hombre. I will just put a bullet in her brain and then take my chances with you."

He pitched the rifle into the sand, and spread his hands away from the holstered Colt. The gunbelt had moved around while he ran, the holster behind him now, and the duster might have hid any sign that he was armed.

"Come closer, hombre," the man said, beckoning him with the hand that did not hold the gun. "I would like to see your face before you die."

Breen swallowed. He started walking. The Comanchero approached him, his grin widened. He kept walking, tried to focus on the man, and not the woman. Ramona Bonderhoff rose to her knees. She seemed to stare at Jed Breen. Maybe wondering if he were a ghost. Hell, Breen told himself, she could be a dance-hall girl who didn't even look like Ramona.

Then her voice reached him, "Jed."

"*Silencio,*" the Comanchero barked. He stopped walking. His grin widened. The pistol waved slightly.

"*Amigo. Por favor.*" He laughed. "Unfasten the gunbelt, hombre. With your left hand. *Muy pronto.*"

Breen pushed the tail of the duster away, sighed, and reached for the buckle. He felt himself shaking as Ramona stood. His heart pounded. He saw her raise the rock over her head.

The Comanchero turned. Breen grabbed for his Lightning. But even when the gun was in his hand he knew he could not risk a shot. He might hit Ramona. He might.

He heard the crunch. He saw the man stagger, turn sideways, and collapse.

Now Jed Breen ran. He ran until he reached Ramona, and swept her into his arms. He only glanced at the Comanchero. He picked up the gunsmith's daughter as she fainted dead away. And he carried her away from the man with the crushed skull. He carried her toward the smoking fire. He was so out of his mind, for the first time in his adult life, he even forgot about the .50-caliber Sharps rifle he had left on the canyon floor.

He didn't even hear the popping of gunfire nearby.

Sean Keegan had never been much of a hand when it came to running. That's why the cavalry used horses. And he had never been quite the shootist that Matt McCulloch was with a short gun. A Springfield? Now that was fine. And he had been fair with a saber back during the day. But running? And shooting? At the same time? That required an exceptional gunman.

The Mexican bandit saw Keegan, popped a shot, realized the range, and started charging. Keegan aimed, but remembered to hold his fire.

Get in range. Get in range. Get in range and pray to all the saints in Ireland that you get really lucky.

The Comanchero stopped, shoved one gun into his sash, and raised the other. He used both hands to steady his Colt. Smoke and flame belched. Keegan felt a bullet off to his left, and, instinctively, he squeezed the trigger.

The Remington roared. He heard the Comanchero laugh. Angry, he cocked and fired, cocked and fired.

He cursed himself. He had only three shots left.

The Comanchero's Colt barked, and Keegan felt a sharp pain in his side. Blood flowed. A scratch. But a bullet scratch hurt like hell.

He cocked his revolver, and quickly pulled the barrel up as he squeezed the trigger. The bullet punched a hole in the air, and nothing else, and then Keegan slowed.

He had to be hallucinating. Maybe the bullet had actually killed him and he was already dead.

The Comanchero turned around. He screamed as the women tackled him. Keegan blinked, pressed his left hand against his side, felt the blood, the pain. He started to stagger. He saw the women on their knees, pounding, pounding, pounding. The man's hat was flung aside.

One woman raised her hand. "Back away!" she said. "Back away!"

She aimed the Comanchero's Colt and fired at the figure in the grass. She kept firing until she looked up at Keegan.

Sergeant Sean Keegan stared at his gun as if it were foreign to him. He let it slide into the holster. He reached up as if to tip his hat.

He saw the ladies. They rose. Blood splattered two faces.

"Ladies," Keegan said. "Sean Keegan, ladies, at your service."

One of the women rose, used her torn sleeve to wipe the blood from her face. "They call me Paulita," she said. She looked at the knife in her hand, then used it to slice the bullet-riddled Comanchero's throat.

And Sean Keegan fainted.

CHAPTER 45

Maria screamed.

Jim Bob Hardwick would have known that voice any-where. He ran toward the smoke, jumped the ditch, rounded the bend, and slid to a stop. Maria knelt a few yards away, her nose gushing blood, and Cullen Brice held a revolver, cocked, and pointed right at Jim Bob's chest.

"Boy," Brice said. "You're a boil on my arse."

He pulled the trigger.

But just before Jim Bob heard the blast, he felt some-thing ram into his side. He hit the ground hard, rolled over, reached for a pistol he didn't have, came up, saw Cullen Brice running toward him, then stop and turn the gun toward the canyon wall. The Comanchero dropped to his knee. He glared at Jim Bob, aimed the gun, then laughed.

"I ain't got bullets to waste on a gutless wonder like you. Or that petticoat."

That's when Jim Bob saw Maria. Saw the blood pouring out of her shoulder, and realized she had leaped up, knocked him out of death's path. Her eyes were wide with shock.

"Maria." He crawled over to her. Tears half-blinded him. He pressed his hands against the bloody shoulder. "What . . . why . . . why'd you do that for?"

She smiled. Her breaths came quickly. *"Mi amor,"* she whispered.

Jim Bob saw one of the prostitutes—the one named Dame Mae—rise.

"Let me help." She paid no attention to Cullen Brice. She waved him off when he said, "Sit down, you stupid whore."

But then he rose quickly and swung the gun barrel. It caught the prostitute's head and drove her back toward the crippled woman, the crazy mother, and her twin boys. Dame Mae groaned. Her forehead was cut savagely. One of the twins crawled over to her and screamed, "Mama. She's hurt, Mama. She's hurt."

That crazy woman just blinked.

Cullen Brice turned around, stared again at the canyon.

"Whoever that is out there! You best come in. Come in now. Come in now with your hands up or I'll start killing every single man, woman, and child with me." He looked at Jim Bob and laughed. "Men? I mean three stupid boys and every worthless petticoat I see!" He cocked the gun and aimed it at Maria's chest. "I ain't foolin'!"

"No!" Jim Bob stuttered. "Please!"

Cynthia thought she would throw up.

No. Please.

She was almost there. She could have come up, and showed her father the man called Cullen Brice, and it would have been over.

"Easy," her father whispered behind her. "We'll get him."

And then she heard Darnell's voice again. "Mama. Please help. This lady. She's bad hurt." No response. Then the boy screamed, "Cynthia! Cynthia! Please help us. Please help us!"

* * *

Matt McCulloch cursed underneath his breath when his daughter stood up. She raised her hands over her head, and started walking.

"Cyn—" He cut himself off. She walked ramrod straight, no hesitation. She walked like he had so often walked. Proudly. Knowing she was in the right.

And then when the boy's voice cried out again, he knew that she was right.

Matt McCulloch stared at the Colt, shoved it into the holster, and pushed himself to his feet. He walked slowly, hands spread apart, and followed his daughter into the camp.

"Well, well, well, well." Cullen Brice kept the revolver aimed at the big man.

"Unbuckle it, mister, or you get it in the belly now."

The rig fell to the man's feet. Cullen Brice smiled. "That's better." He eyed the blond woman. "I shoulda figured it was you. You got sand. Who's your friend?"

When she did not answer, he pointed the gun at one of the twins.

"My father," she said. "Matt—"

"Oh, I know him by name, missy. Just wanted to know y'all's relationship."

Keeping the gun aimed at the kid, Brice turned to look at the big man.

"Like father like daughter, eh?" He smiled. "Matthew McCulloch. It has been a long time. I've been thinking about how I'd get around to killing you, and you just made it all so easy. You and your little girl."

He pointed vaguely at the smoke.

"What the hell was that about?"

"Just breaking up a little confab."

Brice laughed.

"You always had style, McCulloch. Gotta give you that. Boss Linden?"

McCulloch's head shook.

"Anybody left alive?"

"Probably. Hightailing it for parts unknown."

"And Linden's vault?"

McCulloch's head twisted.

"The stone shed. Don't tell me it got blowed up."

"It's there." McCulloch turned to spit.

"Mister," one of the women said. "Why don't you just take that money in that vault and leave us be?"

"That'll I'll do, missy," he said, never looking away from McCulloch. "After I send this star-packing jackass to hell."

He saw a flash of movement, and stepped back. It was that crazy mother of the twin boys, the one who hadn't spoken or hardly even made a sound. She was kneeling over the prostitute whose head Brice had cracked.

"Hey!" Brice said, and turned back toward McCulloch, aiming the revolver at the former Ranger's belly. "Leave that worthless biddy alone. Leave her alone. Get back to your boys before I make you the mother of two corpses."

Someone gasped. He saw the blond woman and her hard-rock father looking away from Cullen Brice, and he always hated it when he was not the center of attention.

He turned his head, then turned his full body. The woman, the silent brain-addled mother of those stupid twin boys, had stepped away from the unconscious prostitute. She aimed a little pepperbox at his chest.

"What the hell do you think you're doing, you crazy old sow?"

The gun did not fall away.

"I'm protecting my two sons," she said.

He sucked in a deep breath. The silent woman could talk. He wet his lips, nodded at Maria, and laughed. "Seems like everybody's talking all of a sudden."

He frowned, and let his eyes narrow. "I said put that gun down, lady. That little pepperbox looks like it'll blow up in your hand."

But it didn't.

It put one round neatly in Cullen Brice's heart.

Chapter 46

Matt McCulloch accepted the cup of coffee one of the women brought him. He leaned against the canyon wall, drained. He didn't think he could even lift the cup to his mouth, but somehow he did.

Sean Keegan limped in, helped by two women. The faces of the women reminded McCulloch of soldiers he had served with during the late war. They were the faces of people who had been put to the test, who had survived, and who had learned that war is a horrible thing, and that living is a gift to be cherished.

"You all right?" McCulloch asked.

"Aye." Keegan pulled his hand away from the bandaged side. "You?"

McCulloch took a sip of the brew, then passed the cup to Breen. His eyes landed on his daughter, who was helping Jim Bob Hardwick patch up Maria's shoulder. "Yeah," he said after a minute. "I think so."

"Breen?" Keegan sipped coffee and returned the cup.

"I don't know. I . . ."

Then he saw that white hair. A weight lifted off his heart as Ramona Bonderhoff and Jed Breen limped into the camp together, leaning on each other.

Breen's face lightened when he saw his two partners, and he nodded. Ramona seemed intent on taking him to the fire, where wounds were being patched, where a prostitute with one amputated leg, a prostitute with a thick white bandage around her head, and a dark-haired beauty with a bullet just pulled out of her shoulder lay, all being tended to by a woman who had helped Sean Keegan to this shady spot, several other women, and a mother and her two twin boys.

"I'm all right," Breen told Ramona. "How about you?"

Ramona nodded. "I'm fine, Jed." She smiled at McCulloch, then at Keegan, but her face had changed. She looked older. And a whole lot tougher. "Let me see what I can do to help." But she did not let go of Jed Breen's right hand until the last possible minute.

"Jed," Keegan said. He held up the cup of coffee, and Breen squatted to take it. "Where be ye Sharps, laddie?"

Breen blinked, looked around, then focused on the cup. He drank a sip, and said, "Hell if I know."

They looked at each other in silence.

The woman named Paulita stood. "Listen to me, women. And you two boys. And you—" She pointed at Jim Bob Hardwick. "I haven't seen you do a lick of work, mister. Well, you're gonna do some now." She pointed. "We need to get horses saddled. Those of you who haven't ridden anything but sidesaddle, well, that's going to change. We've got horses in that canyon. So half of us will be walking to bring those back. You two. Take that Winchester. Get to the trail that leads out of here. I don't reckon anyone's left alive that wants to do us harm, but there are supposed to be a hundred Apache Indians coming to get those guns that have been blown asunder. We're getting out of this canyon. You, you, you, you. You stay here. Make sure these boys don't die. And look after our wounded heroines. The rest of you.

We need grub. We need canteens filled with water. I don't know where the hell we've been since we got here, but it's a long way to civilization. It's a long way home. We're going home, ladies. We're going home. And I'd like to get there as fast I can."

"Amen!"

Cynthia stared at her father.

"Amen," she whispered, before joining the crowd of women to round up the horses.

Jed Breen lifted his head toward the black smoke. Then he looked at McCulloch.

"Nice plan, Matt," he said, lifting the cup in salute.

Matt McCulloch couldn't remember the last time he laughed, but it exploded so hard, some of the women turned to stare at him.

Sean Keegan took the cup from Breen.

"Well," the Irishman said. "It bloody well worked."

This time, all three jackals laughed.

EPILOGUE

From *The Emigrant City Weekly Clarion & Light*

STATE NEWS

The Austin Sympathizer reports in last Wednesday's edition that R. Aberbach, new Superintendent of Prisons, is closing the Peering Farm, located at the southeastern edge of the Eroded Plains. Budget cuts are cited as the reason, plus the extreme location of Peter Peering's cotton operation, and difficulty in finding guards willing to work in such a remote region. The price of telegraphs, sending, receiving, and repairing, was also mentioned.

Mr. Aberbach replaces the previous superintendent who was relieved of his duties for "personal matters," the governor has said. The *Sympathizer*'s diligent editor is trying to learn the details of those "personal matters."

From the *El Paso Independent,* we learn that the notorious band of Warm Springs Apaches led by Chief Dog Heart was turned back in a skirmish at Rattlesnake Ridge. An army patrol led by a Lieutenant Grimsley is said to have come across the Apaches and engaged them in a running battle that lasted over 36 hours. Two Apaches were killed, according to the report, and Dog Heart himself was injured. The cavalry suffered two minor injuries. Cheers all around to the brave boys at Fort Spalding near Purgatory City. Residents of Waco had the honor and privilege of taking in a three-day engagement at the Brazos River Opera House of a show featuring the latest "sharpshooter" of the Lone Star State. Yes, the *Citizen Banner* sends word that Mrs. Aoife O'Leary, who claimed the $1,500 reward for bringing in fiendish brigand Cullen Brice to the Mobeetie Texas Rangers with a clean bullet wound to his heart. (That led to our governor shaming that Rangers regiment and removing its captain, who never came close to capturing that villain and his associates.)

The plainspoken widow won the crowd over with her straightforward manner, with song and dance numbers by her precocious twin sons, Darnell and Danny. The act also including a sobering lecture from two former ladies of ill repute, one Dame Mae Nilsson and Pegleg Greta, titled "The Evils of the Flesh and What Life Has Taught Us."

We have hopes that we will be able to land this "hot" ticket after they have finished touring the dime museums in Chicago, New York, and Boston.

Speaking of outlaws, Boss Linden has disappeared, according to the Mobeetie *Register*. In fact, there has been no sign of Comanchero activity in months. Rumor has it, the *Register* opines, that Boss has retired to Veracruz.

That scoundrel Linden is not the only person to have vanished in the Southwest. The *Santa Fe Journal* notes that Don Salbatore Gandullo of the territorial capital, Judge Livingston Langley of Mesilla, and Dario Packmor from Taos have fled the territory, most likely jumping ahead of indictments expected to be handed out by a special investigator from Washington City. They were said to have been traveling to Texas on business, but there have been no sightings of them in Dallas, Fort Worth, Brownsville or Jefferson. Perhaps they decided to take in the waters at Veracruz, as the *Journal* points out that they were often linked to Boss Linden.

Perhaps Colorado cattleman Bob "Bear" Mannix went with them. The *Denver Crier* says he has "vamoosed," too.

Pity, say several Texas cattlemen, according to the *Fort Worth Times & Standard*. Many Lone Star ranchers have for years blamed the Purgatoire River rancher of showing questionable bills of sale for most longhorns wearing his brand. "Where is Black Forehead?" the *Shackleford County Weekly Herald* asks. The Comanche leader has not been heard of in some time, having left the reservation with evil in his mind and heart a few months ago. With Quanah's surrender at Fort Sill in Indian Territory, Black Forehead is the last of the true warriors. But where is he? Well, our sincerest hope is that he is dead and burning in Hell.

There is much news these days in Purgatory City, and not just regarding Lt. Grimsley's heroics in turning the Apaches back across the Rio Grande.

From the *Perdition County Weekly Reader* we learn that the highly regarded gunsmith Mr. Bonderhoff has announced the engagement of his daughter, Ramona, to Jed Breen. Breen, of course, is a notorious bounty killer and one of Purgatory City's fiercest Jackals. Word is that Breen has decided to give up his previous and nefarious trade to work on guns instead of firing them at human targets. Mr. Bonderhoff's choice of an in-law is deplorable, but we wish them all well.

More news in Purgatory City and Fort Stanton comes from the *Mostly Daily Texan* out of San Antonio. Gen. Blair, commanding the District of Texas, has confirmed the appointment of Sean Keegan as Chief of Scouts at Fort Spalding. A telegraph to Fort Sam Houston to confirm the veracity of this report shocked us with a blunt affirmation. Keegan, as readers might well remember, was driven out of the Cavalry for his hardheaded ways, dereliction of duty, and for disregard for human life. But, Gen. Blair says, according to the San Antonio newspaper account, "Keegan gets things done." Also from Purgatory City, this from the raucous city's *New Weekly Herald Leader,* Texas Ranger Captain J.K.K Hollister has appointed a new Ranger in his company, a young soul, previously unheard of, named James Roberts, who goes by the handle "Jim Bob." Ranger Roberts's new wife, we learn, is a beauty named Maria, who is helping Clarabelle cook Mexican dishes to go with her reportedly to-die-for hash browns. We might be tempted to travel to Purgatory City just to sample the Alamo Café's fare.

But the *New Weekly Herald Leader* also reported that Capt. Hollister's appointment came upon the recommendation of Matthew McCulloch, the third of Purgatory City's and West Texas's blight of Jackals. Even bigger was the fact that, the P.C. newspaper reports, James Roberts got the appointment only because the Jackal McCulloch turned down the position of lieutenant!

McCulloch, typically a taciturn man, said he is not interested in being a lawman anymore. He wants to spend his years catching, breaking and selling wild mustangs as long as he can "fork" a saddle. He is living now with his newfound daughter—a pretty woman, we have heard, with a reputation as that of "The Fourth Jackal." In fact, Purgatory City is being called now The City of Jackals, Men & Women.

We don't know how true that is.

Still, we wish Purgatory City and Miss McCulloch well. Mr. McCulloch was also quoted as saying that he looks forward to spending as much time as he can with his daughter. "She's a fair hand with horses," McCulloch is quoted as saying. "But I have a hankering to spoil grandbabies. So I'm looking for a good man. Who can handle her. I sure can't."

We, and most of CIVILIZED Texas, are not convinced that three notorious Jackals can follow the straight and narrow path. But here's hoping that they can and shall. West Texas will be a whole lot safer without their scandals, corruption, violent tendencies, and pure evil.

TURN THE PAGE FOR AN EXCITING PREVIEW!

**The baddest men in the West battle for their lives
against a relentless band of bloodthirsty prairie rats
in *Fort Misery*—first in an electrifying
new Western series from national bestselling authors
William W. Johnstone and J.A. Johnstone.**

Captain Peter Joseph Kellerman was once a promising
career soldier who'd proven his mettle in battle time and
again. Now he's fighting a battle with a whiskey bottle.
He's also in charge of Fort Benjamin Grierson, located
west of Hell, deep in Arizona Territory's Mohawk Valley
on the arid edge of the Yuma desert. The men under his
command aren't fit to wear the uniform: killers, thieves,
and ravagers, who are condemned to death but who've
chosen to serve, holding down the hated Fort Misery.

Santiago Lozado, the most wanted bandit on both sides
of the border, has set his sights on Fort Misery. He wants
vengeance against Kellerman for killing his son. Lozado
has raised an army of brutal Apaches and Comancheros
to slaughter every man wearing Union blue—only to
encounter a wild bunch of desperate men unafraid of
shedding blood and fighting to the death. . . .

**WILLIAM W. JOHNSTONE
and J.A. JOHNSTONE**

FORT MISERY

First in a New Series!

Look for* FORT MISERY *on sale now!

CHAPTER 1

West of the Arizona Territory's Tinajas Altas Mountains, west of Vopoki Ridge, west of anywhere, Fort Benjamin Grierson, better known to its sweating, suffering garrison as Fort Misery, sprawled like a suppurating sore on the arid edge of the Yuma Desert, a barren, scorching wilderness of sandy plains and dunes relieved here and there by out-croppings of creosote bush, bur oak, and sage . . . and white skeletons of the dead, both animal and human.

The dawning sun came up like a flaming Catherine wheel adding its heat to the furnace of the morning and to the airless prison cell that masqueraded as Captain Peter Joseph Kellerman's office. Already half drunk, he glanced at the clock on the wall. Twenty minutes until seven.

Twenty minutes before he'd mount the scaffold and hang a man.

A *rap-rap-rap* on the door.

"Come in," Kellerman said.

Sergeant Major Saul Olinger slammed to attention and snapped off the palm forward salute of the old Union cavalry. "The prisoner is ready, Captain."

Kellerman nodded and said, "Stand easy, Saul, for God's sake. There's nobody here but us, and you know where it is."

Olinger, a burly man with muttonchop whiskers and the florid, broken-veined cheeks of a heavy drinker, opened the top drawer of the captain's desk and fished out a bottle of whiskey and two glasses. He poured generous shots for himself and his commanding officer.

"How is he taking it?" Kellerman asked.

"Not well. He knows he's dying."

Kellerman, tall, wide-shouldered, handsome in a rugged way, his features enhanced by a large dragoon mustache, nodded and said, "Dying. I guess he started to die the moment we found him guilty three days ago."

Olinger downed his drink, poured another. He looked around as though making sure there was no one within earshot and said, "Joe, you don't have to do this. I can see it done."

"I'm his commanding officer. It's my duty to be there."

The sergeant major's gaze moved to the window, and he briefly looked through dusty panes into the sunbaked parade ground. His eyes returned to Kellerman. "Private Patrick McCarthy did the crime and now he's paying for it. That's how it goes."

The captain drank his whiskey. "He's eighteen years old, for God's sake. Just a boy."

"When we were with the First Maryland, how many eighteen-year-old boys did we kill at Brandy Station and Gettysburg, Joe? At least they died honorably."

"Hanging is a dishonorable death."

"Rape and murder is a dishonorable crime. The Lipan girl was only sixteen."

Kellerman sighed. "How are the men?"

"Angry. Most of them say murdering an Apache girl is not a hanging offense."

"That doesn't surprise me. How many rapists and murderers do we have?"

Olinger's smile was bitter. "Maybe half the troop."

"And the rest are deserters, thieves, malingerers, and mutineers, commanded by a drunk." Kellerman shook his head. "Why don't you ask for a transfer out of this hellhole, Saul? You have the Medal of Honor. Hell, man, you can choose your posting."

"Joe, we've been together since Bull Run. I'm not quitting you now." The sergeant major glanced at the clock and slammed to attention. "Almost time, sir."

"Go ahead. I'll be right there."

Olinger saluted and left.

Captain Kellerman donned his campaign hat, buckled on his saber, a weapon useless against Apaches but effective enough in a close fight with Comancheros, and returned the whiskey bottle to his desk. His old, forgotten rosary caught his eye. He picked up the beads and stared at them for a long moment, then tossed them back in the drawer. God had stopped listening to his prayers long ago . . . and right now he had a soldier to hang.

CHAPTER 2

No other frontier army post had gallows, but in Fort Misery they were a permanent fixture, lovingly cared for by Tobias Zimmermann, the civilian carpenter, a severe man of high intelligence who also acted as hangman. So far, in the fort's year of existence, he'd pulled the lever on two soldiers and at night he slept like a baby.

Zimmermann, Sergeant Major Olinger, and a Slavic Catholic priest with a name nobody could pronounce, stood on the platform along with the condemned man, a thin, young towhead with vicious green eyes. Fort Misery's only other officer, Lieutenant James Hall, was thirty years old, and some questionable bookkeeping of regimental funds had earned him a one-way ticket from Fort Grant to the wastelands. A beautiful officer with shoulder-length black hair and a full beard that hung halfway down his chest, Hill stood, saber drawn, in front of the dismounted troop, thirty-seven hard-bitten, shabby men standing more or less to attention. The troop had no designation, was not part of a regiment, and did not appear in army rolls. Wages and supplies were the responsibility of a corporal and a civilian clerk in Yuma, and deliveries of both were hit-and-miss. As one old soldier told a reporter in 1923,

"The army sent us to hell for our sins and our only chance of redemption was to lay low and die under the guidon like heroes."

A murmur buzzed like a crazed bee through the troop as Captain Kellerman mounted the steps to the gallows platform. Private McCarthy's arms and legs were bound with rope, and Sergeant Major Olinger had to lift him onto the trapdoor. Zimmermann slipped a black hood over the young man's head, then the hemp noose. He then returned to the lever that would drop the door and plunge the young soldier into eternity.

The army considered their castoffs less than human, and McCarthy lived up to that opinion. He died like a dog, screaming for mercy, his cries muffled by the hood. Despite the efforts of Lieutenant Hall, the flat of his saber wielded with force, the soldiers broke ranks and crowded around the scaffold. Horrified, upturned faces revealed the strain of the execution, soldiers pushed to the limit of their endurance.

"Let him go!" a man yelled, and the rest took it up as a chant. . . .

"Let him go! Let him go!"

A few soldiers tried to climb onto the gallows, but Sergeant Major Olinger drew his revolver and stepped forward. "I'll kill any man who sets foot on these gallows!" he roared. "Get back, or you'll join McCarthy in the grave."

That morning Saul Olinger was a fearsome figure and there wasn't a man present who doubted he'd shoot to kill. One by one they stepped away, muttering as the condemned man's spiking shrieks shattered their already shredded nerves.

The priest's prayer for the dead rose above the din. Sent by his superiors to convert the heathen Comanche, he'd attended six firing squads, but this was his first hanging, and it showed on him, his face the color of wood ash.

Captain Joe Kellerman—he used his middle name because Peter had been the handle of his abusive father—said, loud enough that all could hear, "This man had a fair court martial, was found guilty of rape and murder and sentenced to hang. There's nothing more to be said."

He turned his head. "Mr. Zimmermann, carry out the sentence."

The carpenter nodded and yanked on the lever. The trap opened and Private Patrick McCarthy plunged to his death. His neck broke clean and his screeches stopped abruptly like water from a shut-off faucet.

But the ensuing silence was clamorous, as though a thousand phantom alarm bells rang in the still, thick air.

And then Private Dewey Bullard took things a step further.

As Lieutenant Hall ushered the men toward the mess for breakfast, Bullard, thirty years old and a known thief and mutineer, turned and yelled, "Kellerman, you're a murderer!"

"Mister Hall, arrest that man," the captain said, pointing. "I'll deal with him later."

Sergeant Major Olinger stepped closer to Kellerman and said, "His name is Bullard. A troublemaker."

"I know who he is. He won't trouble us for much longer."

"Insubordination, plain and simple," Olinger said.

"Yes, it was, and I won't allow him to infect the rest of the men with it," Captain Kellerman said, his mouth set in a grim line.

CHAPTER 3

After breakfast, the troop was assembled on the western edge of the post that looked out over the harsh wasteland of the Yuma Desert. A few blanket Apaches, mostly Lipan, camped nearby, close to a boarded-up sutler's store that had never opened and a few storage shacks. The parade ground, headquarters building, enlisted men's barracks, latrines, and stables lay behind Captain Joe Kellerman as he walked in front of his ranked men. Dewey Bullard, under guard, stood a distance away, facing a stark sea of sand and distant dunes ranked among the most brutal deserts on earth.

"You men know why we're here," the captain said. "Under any circumstances I will not have insubordination at Fort Benjamin Grierson. I will not tolerate it. You men know why you're here. Deserters, thieves, malingerers, murderers, and rapists some of you, you're the soldiers no one wants. You're all condemned men, but the army is stretched thin on the frontier, and you were given a choice, death by firing squad or hanging, or the joys of Fort Misery. Well, you chose this hell on earth, and now you're stuck with it."

Kellerman needed a drink, the effect of his morning bourbons wearing thin.

"Look around you," he said. "There were eighty of you when this post opened and now there's thirty-six since Private Bullard will not be rejoining us. Forty-four dead. Nine of them were deserters and their bones are no doubt out there bleaching in the desert. I executed three of you by firing squad and two by hanging as you just witnessed. The other twenty-nine were killed by bronco Comanche and Comancheros. I know because I saw most of them die. And why did they die? I'll tell you why, it's because they were poor soldiers, coming to us half-trained and barely able to ride a horse. The result was the Comanche gunned them down like ducks in a shooting gallery. That will now change. By God, I'll make fighting men of you or kill you all in the process. In the meantime, I will not have an insubordinate piece of dirt like Dewey Bullard undermining my authority, especially now when this post is under siege." Kellerman paused for effect and then said, "In an alliance from hell, the Comanche and the Mexican slaver Santiago Lozado and his Comancheros vow to wipe us off the map by executing every man in the garrison. Well, I say let them try!"

To the captain's surprise, that last drew a ragged cheer, and Lieutenant Hall whispered, "There's hope for them yet, Captain."

"Yes, be hopeful, Lieutenant, just don't bet the farm on it," Kellerman said. Then, "Canteen!"

Sergeant Major Olinger formally presented a filled canteen to Kellerman, who hung it around Bullard's neck and then said, "Youngest soldier, step forward!"